Acclaim for
Grif Stockley and Gideon Page!

PROBABLE CAUSE
"Build[s] to a dramatic courtroom finish . . .
Mr. Stockley is a talented writer."
—JOHN GRISHAM
The New York Times Book Review

EXPERT TESTIMONY
"Stockley has produced a delightful and in-
triguing human story. It is to be hoped he will
use his newly found talent to dig into his past
experiences as background for more such capti-
vating tales."

—The Associated Press

RELIGIOUS CONVICTION
"Keeps us guessing until the last courtroom
scene. . . . A unique look at legal maneuvering
and suspenseful drama."
—*San Francisco Chronicle*

By Grif Stockley
Published by The Ballantine Publishing Group:

RELIGIOUS CONVICTION
PROBABLE CAUSE
EXPERT TESTIMONY
ILLEGAL MOTION

Books published by The Ballantine Publishing
Group are available at quantity discounts on
bulk purchases for premium, educational, fund-
raising, and special sales use. For details, please
call 1-800-733-3000.

ILLEGAL MOTION

Grif Stockley

FAWCETT GOLD MEDAL • NEW YORK

Sale of this book without a front cover may be unauthorized. If this book is coverless, it may have been reported to the publisher as "unsold or destroyed" and neither the author nor the publisher may have received payment for it.

Ivy Books
Published by Ballantine Books
Copyright © 1995 by Grif Stockley

All rights reserved under International and Pan-American Copyright Conventions. Published in the United States by Ballantine Books, a division of Random House, Inc., New York, and distributed in Canada by Random House of Canada Limited, Toronto.

This book is a work of fiction. Names, characters, places, and incidents either are products of the author's imagination or are used fictitiously. Any resemblance to actual events or locales or persons, living or dead, is entirely coincidental.

Library of Congress Catalog Card Number: 95-95316

ISBN 0-449-18332-7

This edition published by arrangement with Simon & Schuster, Inc.

Manufactured in the United States of America

First Ballantine Books Edition: April 1997

10 9 8 7 6 5 4 3 2 1

To my friend Charlie Glover, whose struggle against the HIV virus has been characterized by his compassion and service to others.

1

"PAGE!"

I look up at a black man who has appeared from behind his house which is halfway between mine and Pinewood Elementary on the corner. He shakes his head as if he has had about all of me he can tolerate. I think I know why.

"Woogie! Come on, damn it!" I yell. Like a marble statue, my dog is frozen in the classic posture of an animal doing his business in a neighbor's yard. Emerging at the east end of this castrated mixture of beagle and melting pot is a soft quarter pounder that would make a St. Bernard bark with pride. "We were trying to make the schoolyard," I explain. As persistent violators of the leash law at all times, Woogie and I escape detection at this time of day only in the dead of winter. On this gloriously mild mid-October afternoon at six o'clock in the evening there is still plenty of light.

"Over the years your dog has dumped enough fertilizer in my yard," my neighbor says mildly, "to start a nursery. Actually, I was about to call you."

"I'm sorry," I lie, racking my brain for his name. If my

memory is like this at forty-eight, I can't wait for fifty. Connery? No, Cunningham. Rosa, my late wife, would have known. A native of South America and dark herself, she knew everybody, black or white, on our street. The longer I live in this neighborhood, the fewer "pleas- antries" there are to exchange. Crime, drugs, racial ten- sions in the schools, etc., were supposed to have been solved by now; instead, the problems are worse. Twenty years later, Blackwell County, located in the center of the state, hosts the "Crips" and the "Bloods" and other gangs, almost all black. On our street, mostly a mixture of white retirees and middle-class blacks, it seems as if all we can safely talk about is the latest addition to our medical records, which, as the years pass, are becoming the size of the Dallas phone book. "I just had anal fissure repair surgery," Payne Littlefield, my next-door neighbor, recently confided to me. "I've never experienced such pain in my life! . . ." After a few minutes of this, I'd just as soon watch in silence as Woogie hoses down his rose- bush. I was more outgoing and neighborly when my wife was alive, but I realize I've become pessimistic about the possibility of lions and lambs even co-existing on the same planet, much less taking a snooze together. When Rosa and I moved to Blackwell County a quarter of a century ago I never dreamed I'd become so wary, but now fear is an emotion I carry around in my back pocket like a wallet. "It won't happen again," I say hastily to Cunningham.

My neighbor, a tall man in his forties who has the gut of an ex-jock, hooks his thumbs in his jeans. He works, I think, at the post office downtown. "I wanted to find out if you'd be interested in talking about the case of the Razorback football player charged with rape in Fayetteville yesterday. Dade Cunningham is my nephew. His father is inside."

Dade Cunningham. Now that's a name I know! Three years ago he was the most sought-after prospect from Arkansas since Keith Jackson signed with Oklahoma back in the early eighties. Lou Holtz had come within an inch of luring Cunningham to Notre Dame, but the pressure on the kid to stay in-state was tremendous. It would be like Rush Limbaugh announcing he was about to defect to China. Until yesterday, Cunningham, a junior wide receiver with 4.4 speed in the forty-yard dash, was a cinch to be a top draft choice whenever he decided to turn pro. He was on several preseason first team all-American lists and has already had a season most players only dream about. With that kind of future I can't help feeling a little sorry for him. This morning's front-page article in the *Democrat-Gazette* about Cunningham's reported rape of a University of Arkansas coed (her name was not given) has to be worth four or five points on the betting line out of Las Vegas for the Hogs' Southeastern Conference game against Georgia this week. On Saturday, Cunningham caught eight passes for over two hundred yards and two touchdowns against South Carolina in the Razorbacks' 24 to 17 win. "Sure, I'll talk to him," I say. "Let me get my dog home and put on some pants and a shirt." I have just been home from work long enough to get out of my suit, and I am wearing a pair of ragged shorts, a wrinkled yellow T-shirt that advertises "Lobotomy Beer" (a gag gift from my daughter on my birthday) and Adidas running shoes, which are badly in need of washing. Not exactly a business recruiting outfit.

"Don't take the time to change clothes," my neighbor says. "Just come on back. My brother's got to drive back to eastern Arkansas as soon as he can. He's got a sick child at home, and his wife needs him."

I nod and clap my hands at Woogie, who now that he has relieved himself, is markedly more frisky. "Let's go home, boy!" Usually, we walk around at the school while he sniffs the empty candy wrappers and waters the playground equipment. As I walk south to the house, followed by my reluctant dog, I try to remember the article in the *Democrat-Gazette.*

With the paper withholding the alleged victim's name and the university claiming privacy under a federal law, the story was mostly about Dade Cunningham's stats. All I remember off the top of my head is that the victim was a twenty-year-old white cheerleader and the rape was supposed to have taken place off campus. According to the paper, Cunningham claimed the girl consented. Of course, there's probably never been a rapist who hasn't argued the act was voluntary. Alleged rapist, I remind myself. There's a double standard at work here. The media withholds the alleged victim's name but not the alleged perpetrator's. What's sauce for the gander ought to be sauce for the goose, my criminal defense lawyer's mind tells me. But it doesn't work that way, and with Cunningham being black, if this case goes to trial he's got an uphill battle. Unless there's been a racial migration I don't know about, Washington County, in the northwest corner of the state, is overwhelmingly white, and I don't know of a single case in Arkansas where a black male was acquitted of raping a white woman. Maybe there are some, but they didn't teach them in law school.

"Sorry, boy," I say inside the house to my dog, who looks at me with the tragic eyes of one who is perpetually wronged. "We'll go later." Sure we will. He slinks into the kitchen to point out to me his empty food dish. A terribly neglectful master. He misses my daughter. So do I. But if I get this case, it will be a chance to see Sarah more often this year. Actually that still may be hard to do, as busy as she is. Sarah, a sophomore who has aspirations to be a varsity Razorback cheerleader, is cheerleading for the junior varsity (a necessary step, she tells me), and is working part-time for a professor in the sociology department. What a great kid. She has every reason to be royally screwed up, with her mother dying from breast cancer when she was thirteen and me half nuts during that time. Instead, she's got her head on a lot straighter than most kids her age I know. They would be crazy not to make her a cheerleader. Part Hispanic, Indian, and black as a result of her Colombian mother's ancestry, Sarah would not only help solve some cultural diversity problems but she is also a knockout. Voted a campus beauty her freshman year, she is the picture of her mother, who, even at the end of an eight-hour shift at St. Thomas Hospital, where she worked as a nurse, could look stunningly lovely. My only real complaint is that occasionally Sarah does get on a soapbox. Her senior year in high school she was on a fundamentalist religious kick. Now she seems normal again. If I handle her the

right way, she might be able to help get me some information providing this conversation with the father
works out. She surely knows the girl. Like Woogie looking for a corncob, I rummage through the garbage, but
the *Democrat-Gazette* article is drenched with stains
from last night's pizza and is unreadable. I grab a legal
pad and head out the door.

As my neighbor lets me in his house, a rangy black
man in his early forties stands up in front of a couch and
waits for me to come over to him. "This is the lawyer,"
my neighbor says to him, "I was telling you about. He
represented Andrew Chapman."

"Gideon Page," I introduce myself, and offer my hand,
thinking most people forget that Andy Chapman, a black
psychologist accused of murdering a retarded child, actually was found guilty of negligent homicide. Still, he
only got probation and didn't go to jail, so I'll take the
credit.

"Roy Cunningham," the man says, and engulfs my
palm in his. No wonder his son is a wide receiver. His
hand is practically the width of my notebook. Cunningham studies me with an intense expression. I doubt if
there is going to be a lot of small talk.

I retreat to a chair opposite the couch. My neighbor's
living room is small and decorated with family pictures.
A snapshot of the Cunningham brothers sits on the table
beside my chair. In the picture, which seems recent, they
are smiling. Today they are not. "Have you talked to any
other attorneys?" I ask, checking to see if I have any
competition. If he has already retained someone, in theory I'm not even supposed to be talking to him. Rules

governing professional conduct among lawyers have somewhat unrealistic expectations if you are trying to earn a living in solo practice.

Roy parks himself beside his brother, who is an older, softer version of himself. "A couple," he says brusquely, "but I don't know nothing about criminal lawyers. My wife and I own a grocery store near Hughes in St. Francis County. We've got four other kids to feed."

I guess he is telling me he couldn't afford them. Yet, it occurs to me that there are plenty of lawyers who would be willing to take this case for nothing on the hope that if Dade is acquitted, the attorney would soon have a great shot at the opportunity to negotiate his pro contract. With the kind of money these top players at the skill positions are getting, ten percent would be in the millions. Damn, I wish I had taken two seconds and changed clothes. I look like a beach bum. I cluck sympathetically, "These athletes are sitting ducks for women. Your son probably can't walk down the street without being harassed by them."

Cunningham sighs and looks at his knees. "My wife and I told him a million times to stay away from white girls. They're guaranteed trouble. I saw him in the jail for a little while yesterday afternoon. He said this girl practically attacked him."

"Had he been friends with her before this took place?" I ask. With grainy pouches underneath his eyes blacker than the rest of his visible skin, Cunningham looks as if he hasn't gotten much sleep in the last twenty-four hours. He probably hasn't. St. Francis County, only thirty miles west of Memphis, is over a five-hour drive from

Fayetteville, which is close to the Oklahoma border in the northwest corner of the state.

"He knew her a little just because she was a cheerleader," he says, smoothing out a wrinkle in his khaki pants, "but he'd had a speech class with her the previous spring, and he said they had worked together some. But that was all until this semester. They have another class together this fall, but he hadn't talked to her much until the last couple of weeks."

"Are you sure he hadn't had sex with her before this incident?" I ask bluntly, guessing their relationship may have more of a history than the father knows. It sounds like date rape to me. If Dade had been warned to stay away from white girls, he might have a hard time admitting he ignored his father's advice.

Roy Cunningham stifles a yawn. "I as't him. He says he didn't. He says they were studying together at a friend's house off campus. He said she was all over him from the time she got over there."

I jot down what he says, knowing there is a lot more to this situation than I'm hearing. If I want this case, I've got to give the Cunningham brothers a reason to hire me. "Has his bond been set?" I ask, wondering what James Cunningham thinks of me. We've lived on the same street for years and have barely nodded since Rosa's death. When she was alive, we went to a few parties in the neighborhood, but I never felt comfortable around the black males. Too much history and not enough future. I always had the feeling I was on their turf and never felt quite welcome. Still, one on one he seems like a nice guy, and Rosa liked his wife.

James answers, "It's fifty thousand. I've told Roy I'd help him take care of the bond once we got a lawyer for Dade."

I wonder if James is calling the shots on this job. I wish I had been more friendly over the years. "Good," I say. "The sooner he's out of jail, the better." I ask Roy, "Do you know anything about the girl?"

Anger comes into Roy's voice. "All Dade had time to tell me was that her name is Robin Perry and she's from Texarkana. She didn't even go to the cops until the next morning."

"It sounds like a classic case of a woman changing her mind after the fact," I suggest, knowing that this is what the father wants to believe; in this instance it is plausible. The girl may have decided to scratch an itch and later realized Dade wouldn't be able to keep his mouth shut. Not the end of the world in most cases, but this particular guy is black, which her parents would probably object to and would give credence to the questionable things that happen in the Razorback athletic program. In '91 there was a major incident in the athletic dorm involving a white woman and four black Razorback scholarship basketball players that is still talked about. No charges were filed because the woman was admittedly drunk and couldn't get her details straight, but it sent shock waves through the entire state. Who knows? Perhaps Robin Perry had mixed emotions at the time and convinced herself that she had tried to resist. Maybe we can put some pressure on the girl to drop the charge or at least reduce it. What if it had been Sarah? Would she pull a stunt like that? I can't imagine it.

"That's what it sounds like to me," Roy says, as his brother nods in agreement.

"Do you know if alcohol was involved?" I ask Roy. It is obvious that he thinks of his son as a victim.

"Dade said he hadn't had nothing to drink," he says defensively.

"I was thinking the girl might have possibly been drinking before she got there," I respond quickly, noting this is a touchy area with the father. His problem or his son's? Alcohol and women don't make for the greatest combination in the world. I've had a few problems in that area myself.

"She could have," James Cunningham says, his voice sounding like his brother's. Eastern Arkansas is like Mississippi. The Delta clings to your speech like rich soil.

"Even if he did," Roy says, his voice low and sullen, "my boy never raped nobody. I didn't raise my son to be a fool! He knows he doesn't need to force a woman. Just like you said, he's always had 'em runnin' after him."

I glance at my neighbor, who appears slightly uncomfortable at these remarks. Less sophisticated, or perhaps just more honest, Roy Cunningham isn't worried about how he is coming across to me. His son doesn't rape, because women line up to go to bed with him. Yet, in truth, he may be right. If women stopped wanting sex, we'd take it anyway. On the Discovery channel last week there was a program on apes in Saudi Arabia. The females seemed so loving and protective, so human. The dominant males were insanely jealous, forming harems of up to twelve females and demanding and getting sex at will. "You know this is different," James says to his brother.

"If the girl had been black, it would have been next to the funnies."

I look up to see a black woman standing in the doorway. "Hello, Gideon," she greets me warmly. "How're you doin'?" James's wife smiles as if I were their best friend.

Glad for the interruption, I stand up and speak, relieved I can call her name. "Gloria, how are you?" My neighbor's wife is an attractive woman. Her almond-colored eyes are always smiling, and ever since I've lived in the neighborhood she has maintained a willowy, svelte figure. She is a conscientious gardener, and her long, magnificent legs have piqued my interest every spring while she tends the roses, azaleas, pansies, and violets that bloom in the front yard. Today, her legs are hidden by baggy blue slacks. Rosa had always commented on her flowers and if she knew Woogie had shit on them, she'd be livid at me. She only allowed him to defecate in our backyard and handled his turds as casually as if they were leftover breakfast sausages. I gag if they are the least bit soft, but as a registered nurse, she dealt with far worse on a daily basis.

"I'm doing fine," Gloria says, putting her hands in her pockets. "How's Sarah? She's a sophomore, isn't she?"

I marvel at how much she knows. I can't even come close to remembering the names of their children. I used to try harder at this sort of thing. We had deliberately chosen to live in a mixed neighborhood that the blockbusters hadn't finished off. As a former Peace Corps volunteer in Colombia back in Arkansas with a wife of mixed blood, I was going to make the old sixties dream of racial harmony come true in Blackwell County, the so-called "civilized center" of Arkansas. Had I been that naive? Obviously so. "She's staying busy. In addition to cheerleading for the jayvees, she lucked into a good job at the university this summer working for a sociology professor who's got a big grant, and she's still working part-time for him some this fall." I wonder at this arrangement. Sarah is gorgeous and friendly and utterly unqualified to do more than run a copy machine. Dr. Birdseed, or whatever his name is, probably hasn't employed a male in years.

James clears his throat. His wife has interrupted for long enough. "How much longer are you going to be?" she says to him, her voice now businesslike, even cold.

Husbands and wives. He mumbles something I don't pick up. She nods and smiles at me. "Tell Sarah hello for me."

"Sure," I say, sitting down as she leaves the room. Whatever transpired, I'm apparently not being invited for dinner. I've forgotten that couples develop their own code. Rosa could give an entire lecture on almost empty leftover food containers by raising her eyebrow and sighing in her dramatic Latin way. I'm surprised that Gloria is not included in this conversation. She works in the federal district clerk's office and knows more lawyers than I do. Yet, she didn't even acknowledge her brother-in-law. Maybe they don't get along. The message I got was that she's spent years civilizing James; Roy and his family are a lost cause, and she's not real crazy about her husband putting up the bond. But that's reading a lot into it. Family dynamics are usually unresolved mysteries. I think of my only sister, Marty, who lives less than an hour north of here: we haven't seen each other but one time in the last year. History alone ought to bind us, but somehow it always ends up getting in the way.

I continue to ask questions, but I don't get much more information about the incident. Roy got up there too late to have a normal visit. He mostly tells me about Dade and can't keep the pride from his voice as he describes his son's athletic ability. "A recruiter from Michigan told me when Dade was in high school there were wide receivers in the pros who didn't have his speed and hands. I should have sent him up there, goddamn it. There would have been enough women there to keep him happy."

Black women, he means, I realize. The Ozarks are good for chickens but not cotton, with the result that historically few blacks have resided in the northwest corner of the state, a fact that rival recruiters probably don't overlook in their pitch to young men in their sexual prime. At six feet two and two hundred pounds, Dade has always gotten his share of attention from white girls, his father assures me. "I told him to leave 'em alone," he repeats, shaking his head. "With the shit that's happened up there, that's just looking for trouble."

I know what he means. Every few years there seems to be a major incident involving Razorback athletics. Yet Roy must know that as important as the Razorbacks are in the scheme of things in this state, you can't expect them just to stay cooped up in their rooms all year and only be let out on game days. "Was he home this past summer, or did he stay in Fayetteville?" I ask, wondering again how well Dade might have known the girl. Despite his father's injunction, this might have been a lovers' quarrel that got out of hand.

"I had him home working in the store," Roy says, edging forward on the couch. "He didn't want to be there though."

I can understand why a twenty year old spoiled rotten by the special life of the big-time college athlete wouldn't want to go home to share a room for the summer with his siblings in one of the poorest counties in the Delta. Sarah didn't want to come home either. My feelings were a little hurt, but I tell myself I understand. She's got her own life to lead, and it doesn't include pretending she's fourteen again, which is the age she claims I treat her as if she's home longer than a weekend. "He sounds like a real good kid," I say, meaning it. What did the other lawyers promise him? I don't know enough about this case to talk about it. I would brag about my success in rape trials, but I don't have but a couple of outright acquittals in this area. Most of these cases plead out without going to court.

"He's a hell of a good boy," Roy says, his voice flat, as he looks down at his watch. He has at least a two-hour drive ahead of him. Outside, he has a Ford pickup that looks ten years old.

"Is he doing okay in school?"

"Right on schedule," his father informs me in a monotone. He seems about to stand up. "He's not just up there to play football. We want him to graduate."

I've got to say something quick or I'm going to lose him. "I can see the possibility of getting this worked out," I say, more decisively than I feel. "The plain truth is that the Razorbacks need Dade more than he needs them. This is our best start since Ken Hatfield took them to back-to-back Cotton Bowls when they were still in the Southwest Conference. Dade is too important to the offense simply to kiss off the rest of the year without a very good reason, and the football program has been down too long to pretend this year isn't crucial. My recollection is that when the incident occurred in ninety-one involving the basketball team, it was right before the NCAA tournament, and none of the players got punished until after it was over. That was a year we thought we had an excellent chance to go to the 'Final Four.' He hasn't been kicked off the team yet, has he?" I ask, recalling that the article in the paper said neither the university nor Coach Carter had any comment, but the matter was being investigated. "If Carter has the discretion to keep him on the team, maybe he can finish the season. If we can talk the girl into dropping the charge or, in the worst-case scenario, get the prosecutor to allow us to plead to a reduced charge and get probation, all he'd have to worry about is any disciplinary action by the university. And then he could threaten to turn pro and skip his senior year. That ought to keep any punishment by the school to something reasonable. All that really happened the next year to the players in the ninety-one incident was that they had to sit out a few games at the start of the next season."

Roy Cunningham looks at me respectfully for the first time. "The school hasn't said nothin' about him being off the team, as far as I know."

"Well, we need to get busy as soon as possible," I say,

trying to apply a little pressure. "How much can you afford to pay?"

Roy steals a look at his brother. "Five thousand dollars," he answers quietly. "If my wife and I hired you,
when can you start?"

Five thousand dollars for a case involving as much
work as this one will is chickenfeed, but the publicity
alone will be worth it. "Immediately," I say, deciding on
the spot not to tie my representation on the rape charge to
a deal to represent him on a pro contract as his agent.
Something tells me that this may have already been tried
and failed.

Without looking again at his brother, Roy nods. "That
sounds good to me. Let me go call my wife, and I'll be
right back."

He goes out of the room, followed by his brother, and I
am left to think about this case. I am probably in over my
head. If the university decides tomorrow that Dade will
be kicked off the team and even out of school, what can I
do that will be worth a pitcher of warm spit? I am just remembering that in 1978 Lou Holtz, when he coached the
Razorbacks, applied the so-called do-right rule, and
kicked three black starters off the team who had been accused of some kind of sexual misconduct involving a
white coed in the athletic dorm. The university was
promptly taken to federal court by two of the state's most
famous civil rights lawyers to get the players back on the
team in time for the Orange Bowl against Oklahoma. I
can't remember the details, but they didn't succeed, and
yet the Razorbacks went on to crush Oklahoma 31 to 6,
which was poetic justice in the eyes of many white

Arkansans. It seems to me the players weren't even charged. The story was, as usual, the Razorbacks. Why did James suggest me? There are plenty of lawyers who have bigger names and more resources. As a solo practitioner, I'm going to have my hands full. Yet, why look a gift horse in the mouth? This case could lead to a whole new career.

While I am pondering these questions, Roy returns and tells me that I am now representing his son. Ten minutes later I am escorted to the door, having promised to drive to Fayetteville in the morning after I see a client. In return I have commitments from the Cunningham brothers for my fee and bond money. I need to think, and I drive north twenty-five blocks across town to a junior high school track that attracts dozens of joggers and walkers, most of them upscale whites from the neighborhood. I've fantasized for years that I would meet one of the women who come here, but it never happens. Some are very attractive, but I never quite manage to start a conversation that gets beyond the weather. Many of them are twenty years younger, and I look like a cardiac victim after ten minutes on the track, which may have something to do with it.

There is a good crowd tonight, and I stretch my muscles out on the grass of the football field inside the track while gawking at a blonde in pink spandex who is circling the track at a six-minute clip. Although I was a distance runner over thirty years ago at Subiaco Academy, a small Catholic boarding school in western Arkansas, I would be hard-pressed to stay even with her tonight. At five feet eleven, I am carrying saddlebags that could take

a packhorse across the Rockies. If I were able to knock
off fifteen pounds around my middle, I'd be in a position
to work out seriously.

As I begin to run, I replay the conversation with the
Cunningham brothers and wonder whether I'd be any different if I had a son. How can a man believe his child has
committed the crime of rape? Yet, Roy is obviously more
comfortable with his son's sexuality than I am with
Sarah's. Dade Cunningham has to beat women off with a
stick. I'd be livid if I found out Sarah was involved with
her professor. It happens. Lawyers with clients, doctors
with patients, teachers with students. Dominance. Control. We love to call the shots. A form of rape, I guess. I
think of those Saudi apes. The females bent over and sub-
missive. The penises were startling in their resemblance
to ours and brutal as jackhammers.

I build up some speed, but I can't catch up with the
blonde tonight. Twenty-five yards ahead of me, she is
running easily, her hair swinging behind her in a ponytail. I pass an old man who must be in his seventies. Not
an ounce of body fat on him, but he is running in slow
motion. He winces at me as if to say it doesn't matter
how much care you take of yourself: the genetic clock inside your body is ticking away like a time bomb. If aliens
are looking down on the track, they must be scratching
their heads. Why would any sane species chase each
other around and around until they nearly pass out?

I glance at my Timex. If I step it up a bit, maybe I can
catch up with the blonde. As she rounds the curve by the
goalposts on the east end, her long legs scissor the air.
Sweat streams off my face like water cascading over a

spillway. I am gaining on her, but my breathing is becoming ragged, and I can barely see. I pull to within ten yards of her. From the rear she looks great. Fantastic legs and ass. There is something about women who run. It is as if she senses someone is chasing her and she picks up the pace. As I come to the curve at the west end, a sharp pain grabs my side and suddenly I feel weak. Only five yards separate us. My eyes seem about to swim out of my head, but I squint to see the outline of her left breast on the curve. Packaged by the spandex, it looks magnificent. She could be a model working out. I accelerate and am within two yards of her when my stomach turns over. I feel about to throw up. Immediately, I pull up and step off the track into the football field. Have I given myself a stroke? I put my hands on my hips and slowly make my way across the grass toward the bleachers on the north side. You idiot, I think to myself. What was I going to do if I caught up to her? I wipe my eyes with my shirt and realize I could have killed myself. My stomach feels better, but my legs are wobbly.

As I cross the track to ascend the bleachers to the only exit, the blonde passes in front of me and is every bit as lovely in full profile as she appeared from behind. Fully focused on maintaining her long stride, she doesn't even glance in my direction. She doesn't know I'm alive.

"Hey, Gideon! You look terrible!"

Still half blinded by the sweat pouring off my head into my eyes, I look up toward the stands and see grinning at me my old friend and fellow lawyer Amy Gilchrist. We keep bumping into each other. First, classes in night law school, then she was in the prosecutor's office while I was at the public defender's, and we had some cases against each other. Now she's in private practice, a grunt just like myself, hustling for cases and hoping the bills don't come in all at once. I stagger across the surface of the track toward her. Her right leg is stretched across the metal railing that separates the bleachers from the track. She bends at the waist, making her torso parallel to her leg. Amy is short, compact, and cute as a button. If I weren't almost twenty years older, I would have hit on her somewhere along the line in the last four years. "If you were any more subtle, Gilchrist," I say, wiping my face with my arm, "you'd be mistaken for a blowtorch."

Amy touches the toes of her Nikes, a feat I haven't managed in years. Dressed in short shorts, a T-shirt that advertises a 10K race in Hot Springs, and spotless shoes, she looks damn good. "You looked like you were chasing that blonde," she says, nodding with her chin toward the east end of the track. "But she was too fast for you."

I climb the concrete steps and collapse on the first row beside her. "Everybody's too fast for me," I say, too tired to lie.

"You need some water," she says handing me the plastic container beside her. "And your hair looks like it's been electrocuted."

Instinctively, I feel my head. My hair is mashed up on the sides and I smooth it down. My bald spot feels like the size of a crater on the moon. I must look like a jogger from hell. No wonder the blonde speeded up. "Gilchrist, how have I been coping without you?" I say, taking a swig of water from the blue jug. If she is worried about germs, she shouldn't have offered.

"Obviously not very well," she says humorously, her eyes on the runners passing in front of us. "I've been waiting for years for the opportunity to straighten you out, but you've never called me."

I cut my eyes at her to see if she is serious. Amy is the kind of woman who is so likable and friendly she seems as if she is flirting with every man within ten yards of her. Reluctant to invest too much in this conversation, I banter, "I've always been afraid I'd have a heart attack and you wouldn't try to revive me."

Her blue eyes, round as two dimes, twinkle mischievously. "It would depend on how you did. You're not that old."

I take another pull at the water. We are having quite a randy chat for friends. "Aren't you still a Holy Roller or whatever?" I ask rudely, but wanting to know. Over a year ago through an odd combination of circumstances I saw Amy at a service of the largest fundamentalist church in Blackwell County. I was in attendance as part of my preparation for defending a murder case; Amy was there apparently because she wanted to be. My girlfriend at the time had astounded me by joining the church, causing irreparable harm to our relationship.

"Nope," she says, apparently not offended. She smiles. "I'm still searching though."

"Aren't we all?" I respond tritely, but relieved. My own search is a little closer to home. For the most part I gave up on religion after Rosa died of breast cancer. "So, your place or mine?" I kid, forcing her to be serious.

She giggles deliciously. "Aren't you still seeing Rainey McCorkle?"

Some women love to flirt if they think you're safe. "Rainey and I could never work things out," I say truthfully. "We haven't gone out in months." Occasionally, she phones to ask about Sarah. Sometimes, I hear a wistfulness in her voice, but basically, she has decided she needs to find a man with fewer warts. For my part, I want someone who needs fewer certainties.

Amy removes her leg from the rail and gives me a dazzling smile as she heads down the steps to the track. "Well, give me a ring sometime."

"I will," I call after her, deciding to break my self-imposed vow not to go out with women as young as Amy. Since they haven't exactly been lining up outside the house, it has been an easy pledge to keep. I decide to go home, though I've hardly worked out. If she compares me with some of the guys circling the track, she could easily change her mind.

After a shower I put on a pair of pants and a T-shirt and call a much younger classmate who graduated law school with me from the University of Arkansas at Little Rock. Barton Sanders is the only lawyer I know in Fayetteville. Most graduates migrate to the center of the state, but Barton moved to Fayetteville to take advantage of a real estate operation that was already thriving under his father-in-law. Rich and well connected, Barton is a dyed-in-the-wool Hog fan and may be able to help me jump start this case if he is willing. Though we are not close, we were friends in law school and I have been by to see him a couple of times since Sarah has been in school at

Fayetteville. His wife calls him to the phone, and I tell him I am representing Dade Cunningham.

"No shit?" Barton exclaims, his voice high and reedy as usual. "That's incredible!"

I ask him to fill me in on what he has heard. Although he is excited to be in the loop, it turns out he doesn't know much more than Roy Cunningham. "It's like there's a news blackout at the university—while they stew about this thing. The girl's father is a big Baptist," he says, supplying me with one fact I didn't have. "Lots of money. The girl is a looker, too. Have you seen any games this year?"

"Only the one in Little Rock," I answer, delighted there have been no announcements that Dade has been suspended. The fact is things have been so slow lately that I haven't really been able to afford the trips this year to Fayetteville, but I don't let Barton know it. "Do you have any idea how well Coach Carter would react to a phone call from me? I want to slow this down before they make any decisions that would be hard to reverse."

"Let me make some calls, and I'll find out," Barton volunteers. "I know a couple of guys who know him pretty well. Carter's the type of guy who might be willing to talk about this, but I bet he's getting a lot of pressure from the higher-ups to drop him from the team. The old do-right rule. With all the crap in the past, this is a real PR problem for the school."

"I know," I concede, "but Cunningham's the difference between the Sugar Bowl and another .500 season. All I want to do is talk to Carter. I've read that he sticks up for the players." Years earlier Dale Carter had brought Houston a couple of almost undefeated seasons but had a problem with the bottle and got run off. He dried out and had been coaching quarterbacks with a number of teams when Jack Burke, the Razorbacks' athletic director, tapped him in the spring to revive the team after a number of bad seasons.

"He does," Barton agrees. "In his interviews, he always says he knows what it's like to be down. I'll see if I can get his number. It's probably unlisted."

"Thanks, Barton," I say. "I appreciate it."

"I'm always glad to help a real lawyer," Barton says slavishly.

"Barton, you make more in a day than I make in a month," I remind him. Barton (who was advised by our trial advocacy professor not even to try cross-examining a dead dog because he got so flustered in class), has the kind of mind that can trace a chain of title practically without pencil and paper. I could have five computers working night and day and never get a parcel of land back further than three owners without becoming hopelessly confused. The last time I saw him he had on a Rolex and a gold ring that ought to be locked up in Fort Knox. The metal on my body couldn't even buy me lunch.

"Don't kid me, Gideon," he says. "I read about you in the papers. You're the real thing."

Why discourage him? If he wants to believe what he sees on the tube, that's his problem. "Whatever you can find out," I say, "I'll be in your debt."

"No problem," he says, his voice rushing on to another topic. "Here's something that might help. Did you notice this case was actually filed by the assistant prosecuting attorney, a kid by the name of Mike Cash? Our prosecutor is on vacation for three weeks in the wilds of Canada. There's a feeling that Mike should have waited until Binkie Cross got back in town to bring this kind of charge. There's a rumor going around he has a sister who was raped and he's got an itchy trigger finger when he comes to that kind of crime."

This is welcome news. There is nothing to say that a charge can't be dismissed. I thank him and hang up so he can get on the phone. While I'm waiting, I call Sarah to let her know I'll be coming up tomorrow. She answers on the fifth ring and sounds sleepy. It is only seven-thirty. She shouldn't be tired this early on a Tuesday. "What's wrong, babe?" I ask. "You sound exhausted." I try to imagine her room. Unless she has improved her housekeeping, there are more clothes on the floor than in her closet. At least she is living in a dorm. Apartments are nothing but trouble. The year I lived in one at Fayetteville my grades dropped a full letter.

"I'm fine, Daddy," she says, yawning audibly. "I had a math test yesterday and stayed up late. I was just taking a nap so I won't be sleepy later on."

Damn, what is going to happen that she has to take a nap for? I know I shouldn't ask. If she doesn't want me to know, I couldn't dynamite it out of her. "You have a party to go to in the middle of the week?" I yelp, knowing I sound stupid and old.

There is silence on the other end. "It's not a big deal," she says finally. "I was just leaving."

So make it quick, Dad. I look down at Woogie, who is

curled up on the cool linoleum. He isn't giving me the bum's rush. "How was your test?"

"It was hard," she admits.

College algebra. I made a "D" in it almost thirty years ago at Fayetteville. An excellent student otherwise, Sarah has unfortunately inherited my math brains. "Hang in there," I advise. "And don't get behind." The pearls of wisdom are really dropping tonight. I get to the point of why I called. "I'm coming to Fayetteville tomorrow to interview a client. Do you know Dade Cunningham?"

"Dad!" Sarah shrieks into the phone. "You're representing him?"

"His uncle is James Cunningham, who lives down the street," I explain. "I just talked to Dade's father about an hour ago. Do you know Dade?"

"This is so weird!" Sarah wails. "You're really going to be his lawyer?"

"Is it going to cause you any problems?" I ask. My daughter has never reconciled herself to the way I pay her bills. She concedes that in the abstract criminal defense work is a necessary evil, but like most people, she believes that once someone is actually charged with a crime, the only worthwhile thing left to do in the case is to figure out the length of the prison term. I should have realized Sarah wouldn't be too thrilled about my taking this case. A kid goes off to school to get away from her parents, and here I am popping up again.

"I guess not," she says, her voice sounding even more tired than when we began the conversation. "I've seen him at pep rallies and stuff like that. He was in my western civ class last year. I know him well enough to say 'Hi,' but that's all."

Not bosom buddies then. When I took WC, they might as well have taught it in Razorback Stadium. "People won't even know," I tell her, "that we're related."

"Of course they will," Sarah contradicts me. "This is like the stock market dropping three hundred points in one day up here. All anybody talks about is the Razorbacks."

An exaggeration, but I know what she means. Bill Clinton is the number one fan. "Have you heard anything about the incident?" I can't help but ask, though I know she is anxious to leave.

"Dad, please don't try to get me involved," she says impatiently. "I know how you've used Rainey."

Sarah is always accusing me of using people in my life to get information in my big cases. My off-and-on girlfriend Rainey, a social worker at the state hospital, seemed like a member of my staff she was so helpful. Sarah would become incensed when I asked Rainey to hide a client or witness for a night or two at her house as I had to do a couple of times. Rainey never complained. Other things about me upset her. But not my work. Invariably, she would get sucked in once a case got going. "Have you heard anything about what Robin is like?" I ask.

"Dad!" Sarah pleads.

I back off. "Be careful tonight," I advise, unable not to have the last word. I let her go after telling her I will call her for dinner tomorrow evening. I assume I will be spending the night. It is too long a trip to make often. My fees will be eaten up in transportation and lodging costs. Yet, if I end up negotiating Dade's pro contract, it will be the best time I ever spent. "I love you, Sarah," I say, finally.

"I love you, too," she says, her voice full of exasperation, before she hangs up.

After taking a Lean Cuisine out of the freezer and popping it in the microwave, I open a Miller Lite and sit at the kitchen table and wait for Barton's call. I try to read the part of the paper I missed this morning but give up because I'm thinking about the case and Sarah's comments about the Razorbacks. Why are they so damn important? Not just to me, but to hundreds of thousands in the state. Including the President of the United States. And it is winning that is crucial. Not merely competing, not good sportsmanship, not the sheer athleticism of our players, imported or not. Winning, in our brains, equates with respect. And this is what we crave. Why wouldn't we feel as good about ourselves if we were to achieve the lowest infant-mortality rate in the country? Frankly, we'd rather beat Alabama in football or Kentucky in basketball.

At ten Barton calls back and gives me Coach Carter's home and office number. "He still may be in his office," he says. "The coaches stay up there late during the season. The two men I talked to said to call him immediately. It can't hurt. Of course they are the type who would want Dade to play even if he had murdered the chancellor."

I laugh. Razorback football and basketball. The meaning of life. I thank Barton and tell him I will come by his office in the next couple of days. Then I dial Carter's home number.

"Coach Carter," he says, answering on the first ring as if he were expecting my call. His voice, familiar through radio and TV, is raspy and tough like a drill sergeant's. Carter has none of the slickness of the younger breed of coaches, who look and sound as if they were in constant rehearsal for later careers as sport announcers.

I explain quickly who I am and why I'm calling. "From what I've heard, I think there's a real strong likelihood that Dade didn't rape this girl, Coach Carter. I'd very much like for you to talk to him yourself before you take any disciplinary action. I should have him bonded out of jail tomorrow afternoon and can have him in your office anytime you say."

"How do you know he didn't rape her?" he demands, his voice hard as graphite.

"His father's talked to him," I say. "Dade swears it was consensual. For whatever reason, it sounds to me like she was trying to set him up." I tell him also that the rape charge may have been filed prematurely and why. He clears his throat a couple of times but hears me out. "This isn't a cut-and-dried kind of case where you have a girl who's been beaten up and raped. She waited until the next day to say anything and didn't have a scratch on her. Everything I hear about Dade is that he's a good kid. In my opinion, he deserves at least a conversation with you before anything else happens to him."

Carter clears his throat again and grunts, "Where can I reach you tomorrow afternoon about five?"

My mind goes blank. I can't even think of a single motel in Fayetteville. "I'll call and leave a message for you."

I think I have my foot in the door, but I have no real idea. If Carter doesn't want to talk to Dade, I sure as hell can't make him. I thank him and hang up. As I begin to pack, I worry that I may be jeopardizing Dade's criminal case by having him talk to Carter. He may say something to implicate himself. By trying to save his football career, I may end up helping to convict my own client. Human greed. I can feel it working in me like a virus. After I talk to Dade, I can always change my mind. I'll cross that bridge when I get to it.

It is hard to get to sleep. When I try to quit thinking about Dade's case, my mind automatically defaults to Amy. Damn, she looked good. I'll call her when I get back or maybe sooner. Woogie, at my feet, moans in his sleep. Do dogs dream? I will. My life hasn't had so many possibilities in quite some time. Better not seem too eager or I'll scare her off.

2

"IS HE GIVING you a plane, too?" Julia, the receptionist/secretary for the lawyers on the sixteenth floor of the Layman Building, asks sarcastically when I hand her Roy Cunningham's check to deposit for me. "If you're looking for an excuse to learn some bankruptcy law, this case is it."

Julia, a relative of the owner, retains more job security than a U.S. Supreme Court Justice. If she has ever managed to repress a hostile thought in her life, none of the lawyers on our floor has witnessed the blessed event. "This is just the first installment," I whisper cryptically, looking across the waiting room at my new client, a young woman who looks, as most women do these days to me, young enough to be my daughter.

Julia tugs at the imitation black leather skirt that barely covers her crotch. Not a woman to let the weather dictate her wardrobe, she seems to outdo herself each day. Her hips should sweat off a couple of pounds before lunch, and she won't even have to stand up. "Oh sure!" she says. "And the Tooth Fairy's gonna place it under your pillow."

I resist the temptation to tell her why I took this case. If

31

it doesn't pan out, I'll never hear the end of it. "What's my new client's name again?" I ask, bending my head so the woman won't read my lips. From a distance of twenty feet, she looks as fresh and wholesome as the proverbial farmer's daughter. With thick brown hair framing a face as round as a globe, her greatest asset is her youth.

"Jeez!" Julia huffs. "When are you getting tested for Alzheimer's?" She prints a name on her pad. I try to focus without my reading glasses. Gina Whitehall, I make out, squinting at Julia's grandiose but nearly illegible handwriting. "Before long you're gonna need a map just to get to work."

"You'll be old one day, too," I mutter, about to pass out from Julia's overly sweet cologne. For the better part of every morning she will give off an odor that suggests she has spent the previous night swimming in a vat of artificially flavored fruit juices whose bottom is pure Nutra-Sweet.

"You're not trying to look down my blouse, are you?" she asks suspiciously, as I straighten up.

"Not for all the tea in China," I assure her, dutifully smiling at my new client. About once every couple of months Julia wears a see-through blouse with a purple bra underneath and then threatens to sue for sexual harassment if any of the lawyers lose eye contact with her for even an instant.

As I escort Gina Whitehall back to my office, Julia, apparently through for the day, frowns at me as she picks up one of the innumerable women's fashion magazines she brings to the office. My friend Dan Bailey, whose office is around the corner from mine, has remarked that as Julia's skirts get shorter and her blouses sheerer, the reception area is taking on the atmosphere of a cheap escort service. As little money as Dan and I make from practicing law, maybe we should consider starting one.

"Mr. Page," Gina Whitehall says in a shy voice as she sits down across from me, "I can't pay you very much."

What else is new? I stare at this slightly plump, buxom girl, who looks as if she ought to be studying for a geometry quiz instead of sitting in a lawyer's office. She is wearing the uniform of the young: jeans, a T-shirt, and tennis shoes without socks. She is fair-skinned and has bright Kewpie-doll blue eyes that will forever make her appear younger than her chronological age. "Well, don't worry," I lie boldly, making a virtue out of necessity, "you can't be old enough to be in too much trouble."

Red splotches of color appear on both cheeks like warning lights on a dashboard; and as quickly as the most tormented of my female divorce clients, she bursts into tears. I push the box of tissue toward her, wishing I had canceled her appointment.

"They want to take my baby!" she gasps between sobs.

There is no mascara or makeup to smear, and the tissue comes away clean from her face. Though I am reconciled to the firestorm of raw sensations my female clients often bring to my office, I continually marvel at the differences between the sexes. Popular culture now teaches men we should be crying, too—"getting in touch with our feelings"—as if they were physical objects that could be aroused as easily as an adolescent penis. Yet, somehow, I doubt if women (despite what they say) would be quite as attracted to us if we, too, went around sobbing. "Your parents?" I guess. Though she seems on first glance more intelligent than this, she has probably dropped out of school and married a boy whose idea of success is fixing flats the rest of his life. Not so discreetly, I look at my watch. I'd like to be on the road by ten. Maybe one of my friends on the floor (Dan?) would like this melodrama. It will probably be the kind of case that requires a mediator rather than a litigator.

"No!" she wails. "The Department of Human Services."

I try not to wince, realizing how wrong I am. This is guaranteed to be a mess. "Neglect or abuse?" I ask as gently as I can. My prospects of getting paid even fifty dollars seem dimmer than ever. It is always the poor who end up losing their kids.

Gina grits her teeth and then forces out the words: "They're saying I deliberately burned Glenetta in a tub of hot water, but it's not true!"

Struck by the ferocity of her denial, I wait for additional tears, but there are none. Yet, almost no one, in my experience, unless confronted with indisputable evidence, would admit to such a horrible act. Surely she does not know I was once a caseworker for the same agency that is after her child. The burn cases were so nauseating I came to prefer investigating sex abuse. "How bad," I ask, fearing the worst, "is she burned?"

"Real bad," the girl gasps. "They say she might die."

My stomach turns at the thought of the pain that has been inflicted on this child. If she does die, Gina will be facing a murder charge. And why not? No frustration, no matter how great, can justify an adult's torturing a child.

Even if it were an accident (and doctors can form an opinion by the pattern of the burns), the guilt she is surely feeling must be overwhelming. Even sixteen years later I remember the night I pinched Sarah's leg because I could not get her to stop crying. I lied to Rosa when she came in from work, telling her Sarah had run into the edge of the living room coffee table. "Were you alone?" I ask, hoping she wasn't. Sometimes, it is a boyfriend or babysitter who does these things.

"Yes," she says, her voice trembling. "I was giving her a bath and went downstairs to get a towel. I heard her scream. By the time I got back up to her, she was already burned. I pulled her out right away, but it was too late."

She seems believable. The stress in her voice gives it the tinny quality of an old woman's; however, her anxiety could be the result of fear and guilt, a combination guaranteed to add years to even the most baby-faced suspect. Creasing my tie, I fold my arms across my chest, not willing to make this explanation any easier for her. This case, if I take it, will be a lot simpler if she admits to hurting the child deliberately. She adds, her voice seemingly puzzled, when I do not reply, "She must of turned on the hot water. There was only a couple of inches of barely warm water in the tub when I went downstairs."

In silent rage I squeeze my arms, wanting to rail at her. If she isn't a criminal, she is criminally stupid. Still, I could easily have burned Sarah when she was a baby. The phone rings; someone knocks at the door; lapses of attention occur with even the best parent. Yet, somebody hasn't believed her, and despite the incompetence of many of the caseworkers, the medical support the state agency receives from St. Thomas is first-rate. "When you got her out of the tub, what's the first thing you did?"

Without a moment's hesitation, she says, "I called nine-one-one."

About to nod, I check myself. This is the right answer. If there is any evidence of delay, she won't have a prayer. My mind travels back seven years to my days as an investigator for the state and retrieves terms such as "stocking and glove burns" which are descriptive of the injury to the flesh at the water line. Too, if a child has been held down in scalding water, the buttocks will be less burned, because the porcelain won't be as hot as the temperature of the water. A "doughnut burn" is the delightful phrase I recall. "How old is Glenetta," I ask, "and why didn't she climb out of the tub when the water began to cook her?"

Her eyes blinking rapidly, Gina hugs herself as if she is cold and begins to rock slightly as she anticipates my reaction. "Two and a half—maybe the water hurt her too bad to stand."

It is this response that makes me think she is lying. Any normal two and a half year old is fully capable of climbing over the edge of a tub. I stare at this sad example of motherhood, wondering how I can get her to admit that perhaps in a moment of the never-ending stress of raising a child by oneself she might have been trying to teach Glenetta a lesson. "When a child touches a hot stove," I say, "he pulls his hand away. I think the way a judge will look at this is that Glenetta would have reacted the same way."

Unable to meet my gaze, she lowers her eyes. "I don't

know why she didn't get out." There is defeat in her voice as if she knows what the outcome will be as well as I do.

"How old are you, Gina?" I ask, wondering if she has some relatives who can take the child if it lives. Unless she is willing to admit what she has done and gets into intensive therapy and parenting classes, she doesn't stand a prayer of ever getting her child back. This is a tricky situation. If she confesses, the criminal justice system will be hanging on her every word. She still could be charged with attempted murder.

"Nineteen," is her sullen reply. Clients of all ages expect their lawyers to believe them regardless of how improbable their story. One of my main tasks as an attorney is to administer a dose of reality without insulting the person sitting across from me—assuming I want to keep the individual as a client. I would be more than happy if this girl flounced out of here in a huff; yet, she is Sarah's age, and I can't help feeling sorry for her.

I flip through my Rolodex, looking for Legal Aid's number. "Have you got a job? You might qualify for Legal Services. If you do, they don't charge anything."

There is a certain dignity in the posture and voice of this girl as she replies stiffly, "They turned me down. They say they don't take every case even if you're eligible financially."

Super. Legal Aid won't even take it. A tab marking the beginning of the "L's" snaps off in my hand. Cheap crap, formerly county property. I took the Rolodex with me when I left the Public Defender's Office, rationalizing my theft with the thought that few persons would want the telephone numbers of some of the women I dated right after Rosa's death. "Are you on AFDC?" I ask, picking up a confetti-size piece of plastic and dropping it in my wastepaper basket as if I want to impress this girl that I am some kind of neatness freak. Accident or not, the public will pay a fortune for the care of this child. Medicaid, I suppose. What did the state of Arkansas do before Lyndon Johnson was President?

"I get a little," she admits, "but my caseworker said it'll be stopped. And I've been waitressing off and on at D.Y.'s since I was sixteen."

"The place on the interstate to Memphis?" I ask, surprised. Could this plain, almost country-looking girl be a hooker? D.Y.'s makes it into the news from time to time for general rowdiness and an occasional drug bust. Dan told me just a couple of weeks ago he used to eat free at D.Y.'s for a period of time during which he represented some prostitutes who operated out of there. Maybe Gina has us confused. If so, I need some serious work. Dan is obese and his thinning hair in the last couple of years has gone squirrel gray.

"It's not as wild as people think," Gina says loyally. "And the food's great. You can ask Mr. Bailey."

Shit! I should have known. I was going to dump her on Dan and he beat me to it. No wonder Julia set this up. Now is the time I ought to run her off. Yet, I remember from my many years as a caseworker, few lawyers in Blackwell County know anything about juvenile court (Dan included) or have the desire to learn, since there is no money in it. I pull a legal pad from the right-hand desk drawer and realize to my dismay that Julia has gotten white tablets again. They're cheaper, she says. Probably better for the environment, too, but after yellow, a white tablet is like trying to write on a neon sign. "How many times have you been convicted of prostitution?" I ask bluntly, sore that Dan is punting this one without even asking me.

"Never!" she says emphatically. "Mr. Bailey has got me off twice. He would have helped me, but he says you're the real expert in this area."

Child abuse defense attorney—a charming specialty, one I'm sure that will lead its practitioner to the upper echelons of Blackwell County's legal elite. I begin to make some notes. "He means I used to work for the Division of Children and Family Services. Actually," I say, hoping this girl will take the hint, "I've never tried a case as a lawyer in juvenile court."

"That's okay," Gina assures me, crossing her long legs, her best feature. "I'm sure you'll do fine."

Thanks for the vote of confidence, I think. Dan, you owe me one. "How much money do you have?"

"Two hundred dollars in cash," she says, and begins to reach into her purse, a scarred black piece of plastic junk that wouldn't find a buyer at the lowliest garage sale.

Feeling the beginning of a dull headache, I massage my forehead. Will private practice always be this pathetic? After two years I ought to be attracting a better clientele. Every time I think I'm about to break through to another level, I endure a dry spell or wallow around with cases like Gina Whitehall's. Just say no, I think, but she looks so vulnerable and young I can't bring myself to turn her down. Knowing I could get stuck out at juvenile court for most of a day, I say gruffly, "I'll need at least a thousand."

Knowing she's hooked me, she reaches into her wallet and peels off four fifty-dollar bills and lays them on my desk. Her business is strictly cash and carry. "I'll pay the rest before trial."

I grab up the bills and slip them into my wallet. Now at least I won't have to stop at the bank before I leave for Fayetteville. "I'm just signing on for the juvenile court case," I say pointedly. "If you get charged with anything in criminal court, you're on your own."

She nods, and as I watch her read through my standard retainer agreement, I realize I am being paid with the earnings she receives as a prostitute. I wonder who her customers are. Mostly truckers probably, but who knows? As innocent and natural as she looks, she might attract a diverse group of customers.

For the next forty-five minutes I get as much information as I can. At least she has brought the petition and the affidavit of the caseworker, a woman by the name of Sheila Younger. Based on the allegations of the department, it is clear that the case will turn on the opinion of a burn expert. The documents recite in water at a temperature of 140 degrees from the faucet the child would need to have been exposed only about five seconds to receive full and partial thickness burns over forty percent of her body. The mother's story that the child was left briefly in the tub is considered inconsistent with the evidence, obviously a reference to the medical opinion of a doctor at St. Thomas, where the child was taken by ambulance. As an artfully drawn complaint, the petition leaves a lot to be desired, but since a probable cause hearing has already been held, there is little to do now but go forward. "Were you having some problems toilet training Glenetta?" I ask at the end of the interview, still hoping this girl will level with me. She wouldn't be the first parent in Blackwell County to have decided to teach her child a lesson for soiling her pants.

"She's real good about that," Gina says, as if the child were playing quietly in the next room. If the judge will listen to her, Gina, with a little work, should do reasonably well on the witness stand. Many parents in abuse or neglect cases are their own worst enemies, floundering hopelessly as witnesses in a system that seems to entrap them even as it promises to help rehabilitate their families. Wise beyond her years to the game that is being played, this girl knows she is being watched and has visited the child in the hospital at every opportunity. I would prefer to believe she is motivated by her concern and love for her child, but all the same it is nice to have a client who knows the clock is still running.

"What about Glenetta's father?" I ask, suspecting this will be futile.

A sardonic smile coming to her unpainted, pouty-shaped lips, Gina looks at me as if I had asked whether her wedding announcement will be in the society pages. "I don't think a convicted car thief with a cocaine problem is going to be the answer to my prayers."

I grunt noncommittally, putting my pen down and pushing my chair back from my desk. Most of the time, the practice of law is about as exciting as looking a name up in the phone book. I have fired blank after blank with

questions about her parents (estranged since she announced she was pregnant, they sent Glenetta a card on
her birthday) and friends (off-and-on prostitutes who
supplement their income with tips waitressing at D.Y.'s
or vice versa). One normal witness testifying with a
straight face that she would nominate Gina as the Mother
of the Year would be nice, but, as is typical with most of
my criminal defendants, I expect there will not be a long
line of dignitaries waiting outside the courtroom to testify that a model citizen is being hounded by the American judicial system. This case is a long shot at best.
"Nothing is more stressful," I say, "than trying to raise a
child by yourself with no help and very little money. If
you were maxed out that day and held your baby down in
the water out of frustration, it's understandable." She
opens her mouth to speak, and I raise my hand to keep
her from interrupting. "If you go into court and admit
how strung out you were that day and agree to attend parenting classes and get counseling, I think there's a decent
shot you might get her back some day. The intent of the
law is to rehabilitate families, not split them up."

Gina clutches the tissue in her hand. "But it was an accident!" she exclaims. "They can't take her from me if it
wasn't my fault, can they?"

Almost everyone will lie under stress. The more pressure, the more lies. Yet, for some reason I change my
mind and believe this girl is telling the truth. She has
looked me straight in the eye and has stuck to her story.
So why didn't the child climb out of the tub? What about
the pattern of the burns? I don't know how to explain
these questions any better than my client right now. "Not

if it wasn't your fault," I respond carefully. If her kid dies, she won't have to worry about a juvenile court proceeding. "Keep visiting her every day," I advise, "and try not to piss off the nurses and social workers at the hospital. Just remember they're writing down everything you're doing and not doing and will continue to do so until you go to court."

Her blue eyes darkening, Gina gives me a fierce look. "I don't want you to be my lawyer," she says stubbornly, "if you think I meant to hurt Glenetta deliberately. I can find somebody else if I have to."

What a bluffer! I've always been a sucker for this line. Though it seldom happens, lawyers want to believe they are representing an innocent person. As I look at her, I realize that if she had a more oval face, she would be almost pretty. "I do believe you," I say. Though she is surely a novice in her profession, she is quite an actress. She knows two hundred dollars won't buy her much of a lawyer for a trial that will determine custody of her child and avoid a possible criminal charge. Perhaps she is telling the truth. I look at my watch again and stand up. "I've got to drive to Fayetteville this morning, so I need to get on the road. Did you get a trial date?"

"November seventh," Gina says as she pushes herself out of the chair. She is tall, perhaps five feet eight. If she owns a decent dress, she will look better than the average parent who comes into juvenile court.

"That's not far off," I say, having forgotten how quickly adjudicatory hearings are set in juvenile court. I walk her out to the reception area. "I'll call early next week. I'm going to want to see the tub and for you to show me how it happened."

She gives me a wan smile. "Just give me a call."

I watch her exit through the glass double doors to the elevators and remember I didn't give her a receipt. "How much is this client paying you?" Julia sneers. "A couple hundred?"

My face burns with embarrassment at the accuracy of her guess. "Why didn't you tell me she had been Dan's client?" I bluster, long having subscribed to the belief that offense is more fun than defense.

Seated, Julia cocks her head at me. "Go bellyache to him if you got a beef. I'm not paid to gossip with you guys."

"I think I will," I say, eager to escape. Gina doesn't seem the type to worry about receipts anyway.

Dan's door is rarely shut, and today is no exception. I enter to find him happily eating a bag of peanuts, his latest diet food. "I know what you're going to say," he says grinning, offering me a handful of goobers. "So let me explain."

I look at Dan and shake my head. Incorrigible is too kind a description. Instead of diplomas on the walls, Dan has tacked up cartoons. But rather than caricatures of national figures or Arkansas politicians, bizarrely displayed around him are blown-up strips of hoary, unfunny soap operas like *Rex Morgan, M.D.*, *Mary Worth*, and *Apartment 3-G*. Handling mainly minor criminal offenses and a steady diet of domestic relations cases, my closest friend justifies his choice of artwork as offering cautionary tales to the dozens of tormented women who frequent his office. If his clients think they have been unlucky in love, Margo, a bitchy, but glamorous executive secretary in New York's *Apartment 3-G*, has been regularly duped by the opposite sex for many years. Long-suffering and underappreciated nurse June Gale will never get that lunkhead of a doctor Rex Morgan to the altar; Mary Worth, a widow obviously celibate now for decades, fills her time by incessantly interfering in the problem-filled lives of her friends and acquaintances. The message is clear to the female visitor: if things are still this bad for women in the funny pages after all this time, they shouldn't expect too much out of real life. "If I had just told you about Gina's case," Dan says, cracking open a peanut with his left thumb, "you would have turned it down on the spot."

I reach across the desk and take a peanut. "You're damn right I would have," I complain. "Even Legal Services turned her down on the basis of merit."

Dan expertly skins the reddish, papery husk from the meat with his thumbnail and pops the nut into his mouth. "Who would be better than an expert like yourself to represent her?" he says glibly. "She's a good kid, and I kind of believe she didn't do it."

One of the goobers inside the shell falls to the floor before I can extract it. I look down at the carpet and see peanuts everywhere. This must be how the diet works. It takes forever to shell the damn things, and then you lose half of what you try to eat. "Mother of the Year material, no doubt about it," I crack, eating the remaining nut before it disappears. "She's a whore dog, Dan. Not a lifestyle guaranteed to warm a juvenile judge's heart."

"Never convicted," Dan says modestly. "The Department of Human Services won't know a thing."

I study the cartoons behind Dan's head. Unlike Dan and myself, the characters, despite their problems, never age. "Two hundred dollars," I bitch, "is all she gave me."

Dan smiles benignly as his right hand catches in the almost empty bag. "See, she's just like us—just a little whore."

Before I walk out the door to get on the road to Fayetteville, I call Amy. "Gilchrist," I say when she comes on the line, "I was gonna try to play it cool, but I couldn't wait." I don't tell her that I've just interviewed a prostitute and started thinking of her.

"Men are so stupid," Amy says cheerfully. "I practically invite you to move in with me, and you have to think about it."

I laugh, trying to picture her in her office. She is in the Kincaid Building two blocks west of the courthouse. Mostly a domestic law practice. Women attorneys seem to settle into it, though she knows as much, if not more, criminal law than I do. "Can we eat first?" I ask. "Are you busy Saturday?"

"I have to warn you that I'm on a ten-thousand-calorie a day diet," she says. "You might want to check the limits on your Visa card."

I think of her trim, compact body. Maybe she's really fat, and it's all being held in by a giant safety pin. I don't think so. She didn't have that much on last night, and what I saw looked firm. "Where do you put it?" I ask admiringly. If I eat a single cookie, I can see the outline of it in my stomach for days.

"In my mouth," she says. "I'm busy right now. Call me Saturday, okay?"

"Sure," I say and hang up, a little disappointed. I had wanted to brag that I was going to Fayetteville to represent Dade Cunningham, but maybe it will impress her more when she reads it in the papers. I stand up and retrieve my briefcase from the top of the filing cabinet, realizing I am abnormally pleased. It's time to quit thinking Rainey and I will get back together. A part of me is still in love with her, but some things aren't meant to be. Amy sounds like she'll be fun. Why have I avoided younger women so religiously since Rosa died? Fear of looking stupid, I guess. Am I worried what Sarah will think? Act your age, Dad. She would like for me to be neutered, I'm sure. Poor baby. In my parents' day, when nobody got divorced, we didn't have to worry about our parents humiliating us quite so much. Now we act as crazy as our children. No wonder the country is on the verge of anarchy.

3

AS DADE CUNNINGHAM and I come out of the Washington County courthouse into clear, dazzling October sunlight, I look around for the media, but apparently the word of his release hasn't gotten around.

"What happens now?" Dade Cunningham whispers respectfully beside me. He is quite a specimen. Under his T-shirt his shoulders look like slabs of frozen beef. For a wide receiver he is more muscled-up than I would have imagined. His father is much darker, his features more Negroid than his son's. Dade, I realize, looks remarkably like Jason Kidd, the incredible point guard recruited hard by the Hogs who ended up at California and turned pro after just two years. I wonder about his mother. I can't imagine she is white, but she can't be far from it.

"We're going to my motel to talk." I have checked into the Ozark Inn, a dump on College Avenue that actually looks okay on the outside. Inside, it's better not to look too close. If cleanliness is next to godliness, the Ozark is not exactly on the highway to heaven. But for twenty-five bucks I didn't expect the Taj Mahal, nor did I get it.

Dade nods gloomily, but based on our conversation so

far, I realize he doesn't have the slightest idea of the obstacles ahead. He will be arraigned tomorrow afternoon. Now all we have to do is get out of here without saying anything to the media that will piss anybody off. "If anybody asks you a question," I instruct him, "just say your lawyer has told you not to comment."

Dade slows his long stride to match mine. He is a good three inches taller, and makes me feel as if I'm hobbling along on a walker. "Even to my friends?" he asks naively.

"Nothing about what happened between you and Robin Perry," I say, realizing I may be advising him to spill his guts to his coach later on today. Yet, he can't tell his story too often, or he will trip himself up for sure.

In my room at the Ozark just down the street from the courthouse, I call Coach Carter's office to leave my number and then Sarah to suggest we tentatively agree to meet for dinner at seven in the restaurant at the Fayetteville Hilton. I wouldn't mind going by to see her room—after all, I'm paying for it—but she dismisses the suggestion.

"You don't want to come up here," she humors me. "It looks like I'm doing the laundry for the whole dorm." Deftly, she changes the subject. "Did you get Dade out of jail?"

"I'll tell you all about it at seven," I say. "We're going to talk right now."

My daughter groans. "It'll be on the news, won't it?"

"Probably," I say, feeling guilty. This is supposed to be her turf now. Yet, why doesn't she feel pride that her old man is in the news with a hot client? I guess I understand. If love and hate are emotional kinfolks, pride and embarrassment share a common ancestor as well. It always surprises me that I want her praise and approval as much as she wants mine.

"Dade won't be coming to dinner, will he?" she asks, her tone clearly indicating her preference.

I look over at Dade, who is pretending not to be listening. I haven't given any thought as to how he will be seen by other students. Given her own bloodlines, Sarah is hardly a racist, but she wouldn't be wild about going to dinner with somebody who has been charged with raping a classmate. She knows all too well that the overwhelming number of the people I represent are guilty of something. "No, and I may have to cancel. I'll call if I do."

"Okay," Sarah says with obvious relief. "I'll see you at seven. You think you can find the Hilton?"

"Even I can find some things," I say. Neither of us is noted for having a sense of direction. I hang up, thinking that Sarah has rarely displayed any subtlety in my presence. What she is like with others I can only imagine. Perhaps because of her mother's early death, no third party has buffered our relationship. There has been no mutual interpreter. Sometimes in the past, her senior year in high school especially, emotions passed between us unfiltered by thought, creating situations that were often turbulent.

I hang up and suggest Dade call home from my room. Collect, I tell him. I'm not getting enough to pay his phone bills, too.

Now it is my turn to eavesdrop. I am referred to as the "lawyer." He looks over at me from the one chair in the room and says into the phone that "we're going to talk." I am reminded of my conversations with Sarah when she's not in a mood to talk. Dade, I notice, is more respectful than my daughter, limiting his infrequent responses to "Yes, ma'am," and "No, ma'am." After a few moments, with a pained expression, he hands me the phone. "She wants to say something to you."

Expecting the accent of a poorly educated eastern Arkansas black woman, I am surprised to hear a rich contralto voice that rings with authority, though it still retains the drawl of the Delta. "Mr. Page, what happens now? Is he out of school?"

"We'll have to see about that," I say. "I wanted to talk to him first." I haven't even considered the possibility that the university would not want him to come back to school. I've only worried whether he will be kicked off the team. "The incident happened off campus," I continue, "so ordinarily I would imagine it would be handled like any criminal matter. This might be different. I'll just have to find out and let you know."

"I've told Dade to do exactly what you say," she informs me, "but we expect you to consult with us. When will you be in your office again? I want to meet with you face-to-face."

There is no give in this woman's voice. No wonder Dade didn't want to come home during the summer. "Friday," I tell her. Why are black women so much stronger than black men? If Roy Cunningham is in the house, he must be in the bathroom. I haven't heard a peep out of him. "Do you and your husband want to come over then?"

"One of us has to be in our store," she says. "I'll see you Friday at ten. Roy has your card, doesn't he?"

I find myself saying, "Yes, ma'am," and grin at her son. After I hang up, I tell him, "Your mother doesn't mince words, does she?"

Dade arches his muscular frame and yawns, showing strong white teeth. I doubt if he got any sleep last night. "I'm surprised she let you off the phone so soon. She wanted me to go to Memphis so I'd be closer to home."

"I'm from eastern Arkansas, too," I tell him to let him know we have something in common. If you're from the Delta, Memphis means more to you than Blackwell County.

Dade ignores my attempt at camaraderie. "Did she sound mad?"

"A little," I tell him. "A rape charge is serious business."

"Robin didn't do nothin' she didn't want to do!" Dade shoots back, now rigid in the chair.

He must be scared to death. With the image of Rodney King's beating by the LA cops forever embedded in the national consciousness, the literature of white justice is getting richer all the time. Why should he trust the system when he has up-to-the-minute documentation that it is still brutal beyond his worst nightmare? At this point I am just another white face who will be telling him what to do. I need to humanize myself to this kid if he is going to trust me. Probably he thinks of me as another coach. If he wants playing time, he'd better make me happy, and in this situation that means telling me what he thinks I want to hear. Convincing him that all I want to hear is the truth

might not be so easy. I pull out a yellow legal pad from
my briefcase and begin to make some notes, first estab-
lishing that he refused to give a formal statement to the
police without a lawyer being present. Thank God for
TV. He sounds so vehement that I find that I tend to believe he is innocent. I want to. Rape is too ugly a crime to
pretend criminal defense work is just another way to
make a living. "Why don't you start from the beginning
and tell me when you first met Robin?" I suggest.

Instead of immediately answering, Dade bends down
to tie a shoelace on his Nikes. "How come," he asks, obviously not yet comfortable with me, "they hired you?
Are you famous or something?"

"I've won some cases," I allow, "but I'm a neighbor of
your Uncle James. He introduced me to your father."

Dade looks skeptical. "You live on the same street?"
He knows as well as I do that there are few integrated
neighborhoods anywhere in Arkansas.

"I was married to a woman darker than you are," I explain, and give him a mini-version of my marriage to
Rosa. I conclude by saying, "My daughter Sarah is a
cheerleader for the junior varsity."

"Sarah Page is your daughter?" Dade asks in amazement. "I know who she is. Man, she's a . . ." His voice
trails off.

"A beautiful young woman," I help him. What would
he have said? A fox. A cunt? I know how guys talk about
women. Or at least think, since some of us, anyway, have
been forced to become so politically correct in our
speech. As my friend Dan says, it's still okay to want
pussy, you just can't say the word.

"Yeah," says Dade, a smile coming to his face for the first time. "She's real nice."

Her body, he must mean, since they hardly know each other. I realize I'm glad he isn't coming to dinner with us. Why? Racism? Or is it that I don't want him sizing her up like a piece of meat? Yet, I've done the same a thousand times when I've thought I wasn't being observed. There's a difference though. I've never raped anybody. Dade Cunningham may have. I understand now why Sarah would be uncomfortable. "She's a super kid."

"Yeah," Dade mutters, not at all expecting a dinner invitation, nor perhaps even remotely desiring one unless I am going to pick up the check. What was I thinking when I mentioned it to Sarah? Most of my clients I wouldn't trust to take out my garbage. Is it because this kid is a Razorback? Or have I gotten to be too impressed with the notoriety of defending high-visibility clients?

"What happened?" I prompt him.

He sets his jaw, and as he talks I can now hear his mother's voice. "Robin was in my communications class last spring. We sat next to each other and got to be friends in that class. She was okay. I'd be nervous right before I had to make a speech, and she'd talk to me, kind of calm me down. After the pros, I want to be a sports announcer like Greg Gumbel. Anyway, I started coming to class early, so Robin and I could go over stuff if I had a speech or something. It was easy for her. She talked all the time anyway. Some white girls you know are laughing at you as soon as they're out of sight. She wasn't like that."

He pauses, and I ask, "Anybody in the class know y'all

were working together?" I remember my own anxiety in a speech class taught by a retired Army colonel from Illinois. My small-town eastern Arkansas accent sounded to me stupid and hicky. Try as I might, I couldn't pronounce a single vowel to suit him. "Mr. Page," he said the last week of school, "you turn single letters into whole words." I can imagine Dade's embarrassment and consternation if he got an asshole like Colonel Davis. No matter how intelligent he may be, Dade has already given himself away by saying "wid" for "with," "chew" for "you." Perhaps, when he really concentrates, he can sound the "s" on all his verbs, but I know from my own experience it is difficult to worry about form and substance at the same time.

"I don't know," he says. "We'd just meet in the classroom early, since it was empty. It wasn't an everyday thing. She'd practice on me, too, when it was her turn."

I try to form an image in my mind of the scene he has described. With his strong chin and firm mouth Dade is undeniably handsome. Throw in his coffee-with-cream six-foot-two-inch frame, his earnest manner, and status as a Razorback, and it is easy to see why even the whitest coed in the state would be interested. "Did she flirt with you?"

"You mean, did she come on to me?" Dade asks, slinging his leg over the chair, which seems built for endurance rather than comfort. "We kidded around some. I know it's hard to believe, but I thought it was just a friendship thing. She was good in that class and could watch and tell you exactly what you were doin' wrong and how to fix it."

I put my pen down. This kid is growing on me. He doesn't put out the arrogant, in-your-face trash I'm accustomed to seeing on TV from some black athletes. Yet, I know I'm seeing the side he shows to his coaches. "Did you see her outside of class last spring?"

The chair groans as Dade shifts his weight. "I invited her to a party off campus over at a friend's place. She and a roommate came. Jus' a couple guys from the team and two girls. Nothing happened."

"Tell me about it," I encourage him. "Did you have sex with her that night? I hear she's pretty good-looking."

"I didn't even touch her, man!" Dade says vehemently. "It was jus' a party. I invited her, kind of to thank her for her help."

"What were the names of the people there?" I ask, noting his aggrieved tone. Maybe he can't admit he was attracted to her because of his father's admonition to stay away from white girls. "I'm going to need to talk to as many people as possible. The more I know about this the better off you'll be."

Dade rubs his right hand over his face. This isn't his idea of fun, obviously. "It was jus' Harris and Tyrone and Tawanna and Doris. I don't even remember her roommate's name."

I try to get comfortable on the bed. This is going to be like pulling teeth. "Who are Harris and Tyrone and what are their last names?"

"Harris Warford and Tyrone Jones. They're on the team, but they don't play much. Tawanna Lindsey was with Harris that night. Doris Macy wasn't with anybody. She just kind of hangs around Tawanna. We cooked some ribs and drank a couple of beers. That's all I remember. We ate and listened to some music, talked some. Robin's roommate, I remember, knew a lot about sports. She asked a million questions about different team members, stuff like that."

"Whose place was it?" I ask, writing furiously.

"Eddie Stiles. He's a student," Dade says. "He actually wasn't there for the party. He jus' lets us use it sometimes—to get away from the dorm."

"Did you want to have sex with her in the spring?" I ask. "She must have liked you, or she wouldn't have come."

"I don't know!" Dade answers irritably. "Nothin' happened. It was just kind of a social thing."

Denial. I've never seen anybody operate without it. "Dade, it's okay if you liked her sexually even the first moment you saw her. It's human nature. We are attracted to certain people. We can't help it. All the lectures in the world can't change that. A jury would understand that. In fact, I doubt if they would believe you if you didn't admit you were attracted to her."

Dade leans forward and rests his forearms on his thighs, staring straight ahead. "We were jus' friends— that's all."

I see I have a lot of work to do, but it can't be done all in one day. "Did you see her again outside of class in the spring?"

He shakes his head vehemently. "Jus' that one time. School was about out, and we had exams. I went home."

"Did you call her or ask her to do something before summer came and she couldn't?"

"I might of called her once, but outside of class I didn't see her."

This kid has been brainwashed more than he realizes, but so far he is so sincere I feel good about him. Even if he is lying about his feelings, a jury in a normal case could get beyond that. The trouble is that he is black. They'll have to get beyond that first. "So how did you begin to have contact this fall?"

Dade folds his arms across his broad chest. "She's a cheerleader, so I'd see her at pep rallies, and I was in this course called public speaking with her. She didn't get friendly like she was last semester until a couple of weeks ago, and then we started working together like we did before."

"So it was her idea," I conclude, watching his face carefully. This kid seems incapable of guile, but I remind myself I've had plenty of clients who had no difficulty believing their own lies.

"Now it seems that way," he says thoughtfully. "She'd talk at the first of the semester, but it was like she was too busy."

"Had you asked her to work together, and she hadn't wanted to, or what?" So far it seems that Robin called the shots.

"Not really," Dade replies casually. "You can jus' tell."

This kid is more sensitive than a lot of guys his age. His light color may have something to do with that. Thus far, he seems about as far from a rapist as I can imagine. "So you just started working together again?"

"Yeah," he says blankly. "We had a big speech coming

up, and we agreed to get together and work on it a little bit the night before."

"Whose idea was that?" I ask.

"Well, this fall we didn't have a chance to practice before class. She had something before ten. I guess I did."

"So did you suggest a place or she?" Robin could have easily manipulated this conversation. Dade seems as naive as most boys about girls. Yet, even if he is not, he gives the appearance of having been reluctant to push too hard.

"I remember talking about our rooms," Dade says, "but you can't study there with all the shit that goes on. I guess I suggested Eddie's house if he wasn't going to be there."

Robin could have easily made this idea inevitable without saying a word about it. If this case goes to trial, one mother on the jury with a son the right age could hang up the case. Mothers know what idiots their male children can be. "Who's this Eddie again? What's his last name and where's his apartment?"

"House," Dade answers. "It's a rented house on Happy Hollow Road. I don't even know if it's in the city limits. Eddie Stiles. He's just a student that kind of hangs around the players a lot. He's okay. He lets guys use it pretty much whenever they want."

"Is he rich?" I guess, wondering how common this arrangement is. With all the wannabes and hangers-on surrounding the Razorbacks, it can't be terribly unusual. I wonder if any NCAA rules are being violated.

"I heard his family owns a big funeral home in Tulsa," Dade admits. "He drives a new Cutlass."

I wonder if he is black, but at this stage it seems rude
to ask. I don't want to turn Dade off. A lot of white kids
have too much money; why shouldn't one or two blacks?
"I take it that he wasn't around that night?"

"I didn't see him the whole day," Dade says.

I assume the cops have talked to Eddie. He could help
or hurt. Either way, I need to talk to him. "Did you drive
over together?"

"She said she'd meet me there," Dade says.

I wonder about Robin's motive. It sounds as if she
wanted to be able to leave if Dade got out of hand. I am
writing with my legal pad on my knees, and the bed
creaks every time I shift my weight. Too bad the Ozark's
decorating budget didn't allow for a table. "Why don't
you just tell me from the moment she showed up what
happened?"

Dade grabs the sides of his chair. "It wasn't ten minutes before she had forgot about the speech. You can tell
when a girl wants to be fucked, jus' the way she looks
and acts."

I interrupt, "How was she dressed?" I need to see a picture of Robin, so I can get an image in my mind of what
happened.

"Skirt and sweater," he says. "She always dressed up,
even for class."

I remember seeing Robin, but it was from Row 42 in
War Memorial Stadium at Little Rock during the Memphis game two weeks ago. As bad as my eyes are getting,
I could have been standing next to her and not have recognized her. "Did you have anything to drink," I ask, "or
could you tell if she had been drinking?" A good answer

would be helpful here. If she had been juicing herself up beforehand, it would at least be arguable she had more than studying on her mind.

"I smelled wine on her breath, but we didn't have anything at Eddie's. It happened pretty fast."

"Did Eddie just leave his place unlocked?" I ask, glad I didn't have a friend like Eddie in college. I got in enough trouble.

"He gave me a key," Dade says. "A couple of guys had them."

I think I'm getting the picture. "So it wasn't uncommon to take girls over there." Robin shouldn't have been there. No woman asks for rape, a logical impossibility if there ever was one, but perhaps someone on the jury will want to punish her for being in the wrong place at the wrong time. If they had really wanted to find a place on campus to study, it would have been easy enough.

"Not really," Dade says. "You got to get off campus sometimes."

"So you've slept with girls over there before?" I say bluntly.

Dade makes an angry face for the first time. "I didn't rape nobody though. If you're an athlete on this campus, you can get girls. That's no shit."

"Were you attracted to her?" I ask again, knowing this is a sore point with him, given the lectures he must have received from his parents.

I hear Dade's stomach growl. Jail is a great place to begin a diet. Patting his stomach through his wrinkled shirt, he says, "She wasn't my type. A little thin, you know

what I mean? No titties, no butt. I like girls with meat on
'em."

I scribble as fast as I can. "So what did she do?" I ask,
knowing there are a hundred details to fill in. But Dade
seems in no mood at this first meeting to write a book on
the subject.

He looks at a spot on the ceiling and says emphatically,
"She wanted it. She came over to the sofa and took this
paper out of my hand and sat down by me. She started
writing on it, and talking, kind of bumping against me on
the sofa. Hell, I knew what she wanted and I kissed her.
And before I knew it we were in the shower and damn
she was hot! Shit! What else could I do? I only fucked
her once, and then she got out of bed and took off like
a bat out of hell. It was like she got what she came for,
and that was all she wanted. While we were doin' it, she
didn't complain or tell me to stop or nothin'."

I look at Dade carefully, knowing he has had almost
forty-eight hours to come up with this story. It could have
easily been a form of "study rape." "When you say she
was 'hot,'" I ask, neutrally, "try to remember exactly
what she did or said."

He shrugs, "She was all over me. Kissing me, rubbing
my dick, hugging me. She even washed me. All the time
talking 'bout how she liked me and what a good body I
got."

I wish I had remembered to bring a tape recorder. Obviously, her statement, which I should get tomorrow, is
going to be quite a bit different. "Is she going to be able
to testify you hurt her in any way?"

Dade scratches his left armpit. He hasn't had access to

a shower in over forty-eight hours. I've had clients who contracted lice in jail. "She didn't holler or anything."

"Did you use a rubber or any kind of birth control device?"

Dade admits candidly, "I never even thought about it. It wudn't like we stopped to talk about it."

I write, "no rubber," relieved at least his story seems consistent. I can see developing an argument that Robin was simply curious and decided to scratch an itch and felt overwhelming guilt afterward. Why shouldn't she be attracted to him? They were friends; he's a hunk. As routine a part of the culture as casual sex has remained, despite the threat of AIDS, it is not out of the realm of possibility that though Robin felt extremely ambivalent about what she was doing, curiosity and youthful desire got the better of her. Hormones and alcohol have been used to explain the behavior of young males since somebody first slipped on a fermenting grape. If women expect to be treated like men, why doesn't the same rationalization apply to them? A decent argument may be that it now does, but the difference is that they haven't learned to stop feeling bad about behavior men take for granted. In concrete terms, ladies and gentlemen, my brain preaches, Robin Perry had a few glasses of wine beforehand, and wanted to see what it was like to sleep with an African-American who was a star football player. He accommodated her, but by the next day she was feeling so terrible about it she claimed it was rape.

I go over his story again and realize I am convinced he didn't rape her. There is something I find myself responding to in this boy. I might change a few things about him, but I would change a few things about myself as well. "Assuming Coach Carter is willing to talk to you," I say, putting down my notebook, "we need to decide if you should talk to him and tell him your story. It's possible that he may let you stay on the team if you can convince him you're innocent. Whatever you say can be used against you. The cops will talk to him, and if you contradict yourself, it'll be used against you."

"I want to keep playing!" he says, his voice anguished.

"That's what I want for you," I say. "But there's a risk involved each time you talk." I do not say that if he plays out the season and continues to do as well as he has done thus far, he will be worth a lot more money (assuming he is found innocent) to whoever negotiates his pro contract.

"What do you think I should do?" he asks, his brown-green eyes searching mine as if I had been representing him all his life instead of just the last couple of hours.

Damn. Lawyers have too much power over other people. "I think," I say slowly, hoping I am not acting too much from greed, "that if you get the chance you should talk to your coach and tell him the same things you've told me."

He nods affirmatively. I've told him what he wanted to hear, and I know it, too. In a year or two, I hope I can look back on this and not come to the conclusion that I exploited him. Shit, I may be so rich that I won't even think about it. "What is Coach Carter like?"

Dade grins. "He's pretty damn tough. I'm in shape though. I was dogging it in two-a-days in the beginning, and he chewed my ass out good till I got with the program. I didn't think I was, but he was right. If you give it a hundred percent, he doesn't get mad if you screw up. He just comes over and shows you what you did wrong. My grandmother died on Monday the week of the South Carolina game. He told me to go home and not worry about it—that I'd start and have a good game. I did. If he doesn't like you though, you might as well quit. He'll run you off if he thinks you're bullshitting him."

Coaches. They are the closest things to dictators the United States has. Nazis, most of them. Probably the worse they are, the better their records. Frustrated drill sergeants and about the same level of intelligence. I hated my track coach at Subiaco. Hell, he wasn't the one running 880 yards in ninety-degree heat. Still, I was the Class A state champion my senior year, the only thing I ever won in my life, outside a racquetball game at the Y.

While we are talking, the phone rings. It is Carter, who tells me to bring Dade to his office at seven tonight. Hoarse, as if he has been shouting, he asks me not to talk to the media. They will know soon enough. I call Sarah back and leave a message on her answering machine to meet me a five-thirty at the Hilton.

Dade understandably is anxious to get back to his room and take a shower, and I drop him off at Darby Hall, agreeing to meet him outside Carter's office promptly at seven. "Don't talk to anybody about this," I say, knowing it will be difficult for him to keep his mouth shut.

Sarah, who is not usually punctual, is waiting for me. Though I saw her two weeks ago (for only a few minutes) after the Memphis game, my blood quickens just seeing her face. She has been off at college for over a year, but still I haven't completely adjusted to her absence from the house. During the few weeks she was home before and after the summer term I saw how much she had matured; with too much time on my hands, probably I have regressed. "Hi, Daddy," she says, in a restrained voice that signals her lack of enthusiasm for the object of my visit.

Despite her misgivings, she returns my hug. She needs me more than she thinks. "You look thin," I criticize. "It's obvious you're not eating right. I want you to order a steak tonight."

Actually, she looks great. In her striped tank top and white slacks and with her usual exotic earrings (tonight metal in the shape of musical notes), Sarah will ensure that we get excellent service from the male employees at the Hilton.

"Oh, all right," she says, in mock protest. When we sit down, she says, "You probably eat worse than I do, judging from what was in the refrigerator when I was home the last time."

A waiter, obviously a student, comes over to check out Sarah. "Would you like something to drink?" he says to me, unable to resist staring at my daughter.

With Dade's interview with his coach looming ahead of me, I resist ordering a beer, though I would love one. A sign of my less than successful coping skills now is that I drink more. Easy to recognize, but hard to do much about. The house has been too quiet with just me and Woogie. Several nights in the past year I have waked up on the couch in the den in the middle of the night after having an extra shot of bourbon I didn't need or even want. "Iced tea," I say reluctantly.

"No beer?" Sarah asks, surprised. She orders a Coke.

Each of us imagines the other wants alcohol. I explain that I have more work to do, but she steers the conversation away from the case and tells me about the project she's working on for the professor who gave her a job this summer. "He's writing up the results of this massive interdisciplinary study on the Arkansas Delta," she says. "It's a spin-off of the Delta Commission. You've heard of that, haven't you?"

I fiddle with my silverware, trying to concentrate. Some kind of economic development scheme to beef up that portion of the southern states the Mississippi runs through. No dice. The country is broke. Congress didn't want to pay for it, and neither did the states who would supposedly benefit. "It didn't really get off the ground, did it?" I ask, watching our waiter nudge another boy who looks our way.

"It's spawned enormous academic interest in the region," Sarah says self-importantly, oblivious to the attention she is attracting. "It's almost as if the portions of the South where slavery was the most concentrated have been punished. Parts of Arkansas, Mississippi, and Louisiana are like Third World countries. They're desperately poor!"

The boy brings our drinks and practically sits down at the table with us. I've never heard Sarah display the slightest intellectual interest in her courses. All she has cared about was the grade, not the subject matter. "Is the poverty a big surprise?" I comment. "We kidnapped people from a totally different culture and virtually turned

them into farm animals until machines made them obso-
lete."

Sarah nods as if I'd said that two plus two equals four.
"But that doesn't explain why the Delta's still statisti-
cally behind the rest of the country after the invention of
tractors and cotton pickers and other laborsaving de-
vices," she lectures me. "Why hasn't the Delta prospered
like the rest of the country? It's intellectually dishonest to
say that the South got behind after the Civil War and was
raped during Reconstruction and never caught up. That's
a Southern myth. Besides, when one observes countries
such as Germany and Japan after World War Two and
Taiwan and South Korea today, it's a radically different
picture. Those countries are booming economically. But
the Delta is virtually a wasteland. Why?"

I think I'm supposed to ask. Every time I've mentioned
Bear Creek in the last couple of years her eyes have
glazed over. Small wonder: she's heard all my boyhood
stories a dozen times. Somebody, Professor Birdbath, or
whatever his name is, has found a switch I didn't know
existed. I'm not sure I like it. She sounds ridiculous.
"Observe" Germany. Can't she and Birdbreath simply
look at it? I powder my tea with two packets of Equal and
say, "I give up. What's wrong with us?"

Sarah hasn't even looked at the menu. She says, "The
theory, being developed by Professor Beekman and others, and it's only provisional, is that in places like the
Delta, the need to control social relationships is more of a
motivating factor than economic self-interest. In other
words, in other geographic regions of the country, indigent blacks are effectively ghettoized and isolated in a

social sense, but in the small towns of the South there is no way to do that. You can't move to the suburbs in Bear Creek."

Amazed by the transformation of my daughter into a pretentious junior graduate student, I stir my tea until I've almost created a whirlpool. If Sarah ever read the front page of the *Arkansas Democrat-Gazette* at home, she has kept it a well-guarded secret. Not that I care. Surely she has more interesting things to do at this stage of her life than worry about the unsolvable problems of humanity, or so I thought. Since she doesn't want to be pumped about Robin, I wouldn't mind simply visiting with her, but she seems too serious. Professor Beekman has seen to that. "I assume you're talking about political power," I say lamely, never having given a moment's thought to the Delta's economic problems since I left there for good a quarter of a century ago. "Is this Professor Beekman you work for black or white?"

Sarah cocks her chin at me, a sure sign I have annoyed her. "What conceivable difference does that make?" she says. "These people are highly regarded in their fields. Dr. Beekman is white, but the multidisciplinary team he heads has at least two African-Americans on it."

"It sounds like awfully soft research."

"It doesn't have to be a mathematical formula to be true," Sarah shoots back. "I wanted to ask you something about Bear Creek, and I want you to think about this. Did you ever notice how light-skinned the leaders of the African-American community were before the civil rights movement caught on there?"

"Are you ready?" our waiter says, demanding attention

from my daughter. This is the kind of place I could walk in naked and nobody would notice me.

I smile at the boy, who is hopelessly smitten. "We better order," I say, thinking I'm going to need my strength if I'm to get through this meal. A little more grimly than I would like, Sarah nods and studies the menu while I order fried chicken, the cheapest meat dish on the menu. Unaware of my shoestring budget for this case, she takes me at my word and tells the boy to bring her the club steak—not the top of the line but no bargain either.

As soon as he is gone, Sarah looks at me expectantly. "It never occurred to me to pay attention," I confess, remembering the question.

"What researchers have observed is that the white power structure habitually handpicked the whitest-looking African-Americans they could find for so-called leadership positions. These blacks were imitation whites. The civil rights movement, of course, changed all that."

"It sounds like," I point out, "blacks discriminate on the basis of color, too."

"As a reaction," Sarah says stubbornly, "against whites choosing lighter-skinned Negroes to be their leaders."

Tax dollars are being paid to study the skin color of small-town Negroes? No wonder there's a deficit. Before I can respond, we are interrupted by a classmate of Sarah's who visits until our food comes, and fortunately our conversation about her job never regains the level of intensity it had when we first sat down. This version of my daughter will take some getting used to. I bring the conversation around to the condition of her Volkswagen, and whether it will make it home for Thanksgiving. It better. I've put nearly a thousand dollars into the damn thing in the last two months.

Finally, as we get up to leave, she asks, "Now that you've talked to Dade Cunningham, do you think he's guilty?"

Poor Sarah. What an uncomfortable position I've put her in. "Well, I haven't heard the girl's side," I say, picking up the check, "but after talking to Dade, I honestly don't think he raped her."

She bites her lip. I know she doesn't want me doing this case, but if it works out, she could benefit in ways neither of us dreamed possible. I wonder what she has heard. She probably knows more than I do at this stage of the case. I decide I'd like to meet this Beekman and tell Sarah I might drop by her office tomorrow. It won't hurt the man to know Sarah has a father who will be checking up on her. Some of these profs, as far as women go, are probably major-league hitters. Sarah is showing all the signs. I've never heard her talk like this before. If Beekman is interested, it is easy to understand why. Half the crew of the Hilton practically follows us to the door.

"Thanks, Daddy," Sarah says, giving me a hug in the parking lot. "That was good."

Expensive, too, I don't add. I still feel guilty about not being able to send her out of state, so it would be too cheap to complain about a meal. I watch her pull out ahead of me and marvel at how well she has turned out. I must have done something right, even if at the moment she sounds like one of those Southerners who finds out how good it feels to beat up on our benighted past. She is young and so self-righteous it makes me want to gag. Experience will knock some of that out of her, I hope.

I look at my watch. Quarter to seven. Time to go see Carter. I turn left onto Dickson and head for the campus. Carter's supposed to have as great a football mind as Lou Holtz or Jimmy Johnson. It doesn't matter. He could have an IQ of 7. There's only one bottom line, and that's your won-lost record. A 5 and 0 record says it all for the time being. I just hope he isn't as politically correct as my daughter, or we are in trouble.

4

DALE CARTER LOOKS older than sixty. His face is lined like an ex-smoker's, and his unruly hair, more gray than brown, is sparse. His gray sweats don't hide his gut. This is a man who didn't get his job on his looks. "Dade," he says, without shaking his hand, "come on back to my office. Are you Page?" he asks me warily, as if he had taken a course on lawyers in school and flunked.

"Yes, sir," I say, offering my hand. "How are you, Coach?"

He gives me the quickest handshake I've ever had, and I feel contempt radiating from all directions. It looks as if we will be going through the motions. Hell, why not? The state of Arkansas, even if it's through the auspices of a pissant assistant prosecutor who's had a bad family experience, has put its credibility on the line by charging Dade Cunningham with rape. How can it help the football program in the long run if he lets Dade play out the season? As we follow Carter like two schoolboys about to get a whipping, I think again how easily I am able to deceive myself into believing anything I want. The old saying, "If wishes were horses, beggars would ride," fi-

73

nally makes sense. For the last twenty-four hours I've
been acting as if I were king of the rodeo, when the truth
is I'm one of those clowns that tries to distract the bull
when the king gets bucked off. I've got to figure out a
way to get on this man's good side, and it better be quick.

I glance over at Dade, who looks scared. I don't blame
him. Carter opens the door to his office, and I recognize
Jack Burke, the athletic director. Burke is relatively new
to the program, and has stayed in the background since
he got the job a couple of years ago. Older than his football coach, but not by much, he actually shakes my hand
instead of jerking it away as if I had shocked him. He is
dressed in a drab gray three-piece suit, as befits his status
as an administrator. A former head coach himself at Mississippi State who was a star halfback at Fayetteville in
the fifties, he had indifferent success and made his way
back to Arkansas, where his only visible decision in the
two years he has had the job was to hire Carter. Considered relatively weak after some of the former power bro-
kers who have occupied his position, Burke doesn't
figure to be my problem. He put all his eggs in Carter's
basket, and now he's got to live with his decision, rotten
or not.

Carter's office has got to be unusual for a football
coach. Instead of pictures of star athletes, he has photographs of urban landscapes that look as if they were
taken from some fancy book on architecture. I recognize
San Francisco, Chicago, New York, and Dallas. What is it
supposed to mean? Perhaps in keeping with his cerebral
image, he is trying to make the point that the real world is
not the four or five years spent as a Razorback athlete. On

his desk is a picture of a plain-looking woman his age—
his wife, I assume. She is no better-looking than her
mate. More of the real world, I guess. Though there is a
couch in Carter's office, he indicates that we should sit
across the desk from him, and Burke, now out of my line
of sight, takes the couch. This will obviously be Carter's
show. Leaning back in his chair with his hands clasped
behind his head, he ignores me and says wearily, "Dade,
I don't think I have much choice but to take you off the
team at least until your trial is over."

Dade looks over at me in shock. I say to Carter,
"Coach, he hasn't done anything to be punished for. I'm
convinced this wasn't rape. Dade didn't force her to have
sex. She wanted to. He shouldn't be punished for that." I
tell him what I have heard about the assistant prosecutor.
"This charge may end up getting dropped when the man
who was elected to do the job gets back from his vacation."

Carter stares at me as if I had suggested that he resign
as head coach. "You don't know that. What is your interest in this anyway? Dade's family doesn't have any
money. Is your representation tied to his future pro contract or what?"

Dade shoots me a look of total confusion, and I say
hastily, "Absolutely not. I happen to live down the street
from his uncle, who's a friend of mine, and he asked me
to help out." Carter is as shrewd as his reputation makes
him out to be. I have stretched the facts a little, but basically what I have said is correct. I see no point in admitting that I hope to represent Dade on down the line.

Indifferent to whether he is insulting me, Carter asks Dade, "Is this right?"

Dade nods. "My mama said Uncle James and he are neighbors. He's got a daughter who's a cheerleader for the jayvees—Sarah Page."

Carter shrugs. "People, including coaches, try to exploit these kids all the time," he says. "It makes me sick."

I try to seize the tiny opening he has given me. "That's what I think this is all about. It's not just greedy lawyers who use athletes. This girl, who pretended to be a friend of Dade's, knows how vulnerable athletes up here are to the charge of sexual misconduct. What I figure is that she got interested in him because he was a star and a real attractive young man. They were in class together and she got to know and like him. One thing led to another, and she went to bed with him. Later she got scared people would find out about it, and knowing how her parents would feel, she claimed she was raped. I don't need to tell you there's a lot of racial prejudice in this state, and I'd be willing to bet her parents, who I hear are very prominent in southern Arkansas, would have yanked her out of school if they found out their daughter was going to bed with a black male, even if it was Dade Cunningham. Dade, tell Coach Carter what you've told me," I say, looking at my client. I can't read Carter. For all I know, he may think I'm a total opportunist and Dade is guilty as hell. Without more time, I can't prove him wrong on either count.

"I didn't force her, Coach," Dade begins, his voice full of emotion. He suddenly tears up, surprising me. I don't know about the coaches, but I am not used to seeing men the size of Dade Cunningham cry. "I didn't even know she wanted to do it until she got over to Eddie's house."

"Who's Eddie, son?" Carter asks gently. For the first time since we've been in the room he is completely focused on his player. I look back over my shoulder and see Burke leaning forward, straining to hear.

"Eddie Stiles—he's a student," Dade explains, wiping his eyes.

Damn. I wish I had this on tape and could show it to Dade if he goes to trial. No jury, even an all-white redneck one, could fail to be moved by the genuine emotion in Dade's face and voice. He has to be telling the truth. As I listen to him again, I fear that by the time he goes to trial he will have told the story so many times the details will be too stale for him to summon the raw emotion he is displaying today.

Carter is unable to restrain himself from interrupting with questions. "Dade, you know you wanted in her pants," he responds after Dade says they decided to meet at Eddie's to study together, "or you wouldn't have gone off campus."

Instead of denying it, Dade stares at the floor. Carter doesn't know how many lectures Dade has had on this subject from his parents. "I didn't force her, Coach," Dade says finally.

Lust is not a crime, I want to yell at Carter, but he won't appreciate my interrupting him. If he thinks I'm trying to manage this interview, it'll make him more suspicious than he is already. Men and women can't really be friends, the smirk on his face means, and everybody over the age of twelve knows it. No matter how liberated or sophisticated we pretend to be, sex is always lurking right beneath the surface, and you'd have to be an idiot or liar to pretend otherwise.

Twenty minutes later Carter seems satisfied he has asked every question he has on his mind. He shifts his gaze to me. "If I were to leave Dade on the team," he says, rubbing his forehead wearily, "I'm gonna get my ass fried. You know how reporters are. They'll say I'm doing it just because I need Dade. The sons of bitches will have a field day. They're so hypocritical they make me want to puke. They'll lie, cheat, and steal to get a story—all in the name of the so-called truth—when all they're doing ninety-nine percent of the time is repeating gossip and rumors and other people's opinions. They can cheat on their taxes, their wives, their expense accounts, because they're not public figures, but we live in a fish-bowl up here. I can't take a crap without some columnist saying something stinks in the athletic department. Regardless of what I do about Dade, my advice to you is be damn careful of what you say or do, because you'll be reading some half-assed version of it for breakfast the next day."

Abruptly, Carter stands up, ending his brief tirade and our conversation. Jack Burke, his boss, hasn't said a word. "I don't know what I'm going to do," Carter mumbles. "I haven't heard the girl's story. I've just heard gossip and read the crap in the papers."

Now on my feet, I say, "I should be getting a copy of her statement from the prosecutor tomorrow. I'll be glad to let you take a look at it after I get it."

"You better get it here fast," Carter warns. "I get a lot

of unsolicited advice and most of it is to do something quick to keep the heat off. There're a lot of cover-your-ass kind of people associated with a university."

"I'll have it before noon," I promise, praying I can deliver. "Dade's arraignment is at nine tomorrow morning. Afterward, I should be able to talk to the assistant prosecutor who brought the charges and get a copy of the file."

"I suspect I'll be right here," Carter says wryly. He doesn't offer his hand, which I take as a bad sign.

Before we head for the door, I ask, "Have you heard anything about Dade's status as a student? That's not a problem, is it?"

For the first time Jack Burke speaks. "That's another part of the university's business, not ours," he explains. "Since the incident occurred off campus and the Fayetteville police are involved, the administration may choose not to deal with the arrest as a disciplinary matter; but it has the authority. I haven't heard what's happening about that."

I don't believe him. He must mean that no decision has been made. "Let's go, Dade," I say, pretending not to be concerned; yet, I have the feeling Dade may have more to worry about than a criminal rape charge and Coach Carter's decision.

Dade nods but turns to Carter. "Coach, I want to keep playing!"

Carter's head bobs in a dismissive gesture. "I know, son."

I touch Dade's arm and lead him out the door. Poor kid—he doesn't have a clue as to how this all fits together. Hell, I don't either. He may need three or four

lawyers before this case is over. Unfortunately, he has
just one, and I'll be damned if I'm prepared to take on an
entire university bureaucracy.

Twenty minutes later I am alone in my room at the
Ozark, sipping on a well-earned bourbon and Coke and
trying to make sense of all that has gone on in the last
twenty-four hours. Carter remains a mystery. He hates
the media, but what coach or politician who has been
around for a while doesn't? I've been burned by them,
too, remembering the day when a TV camera was shoved
in my face after an attorney had committed suicide in my
front yard. I nearly lost it. Hell, the rumor went on for
weeks that I had killed him. The best thing I have going
for me in this case is my client. I truly believe he is innocent. I haven't been able to say that about many of the
criminal defendants I have represented.

I watch the ten o'clock news on Channel 5 and hear
my name mentioned. The local news anchor, a stunning-
looking young woman with long ebony hair and green
eyes that are gorgeous even on my TV screen, says the
university is investigating the matter and has "no comment" at this time. Ditto for Coach Carter. There is no
mention of my visit with Dade. The news anchor says,
"At least for tonight Dade Cunningham is back on campus." I go to sleep, wondering if it will be his only night.

The Washington County courthouse, built in 1904, is
the color of gingerbread and bristles with steeples and
multiple arches. Upon entering, I notice again the mural
that bears the legend: OUR HOPE LIES IN HEROIC MEN. No
mention of women. After a bad night's sleep (I kept get-

ting up to go to the bathroom: the chilly October weather
up here in the mountains has that effect on my bladder), I
don't feel particularly heroic, but Dade's formal entry of
a plea goes smoothly enough, and I get my first glimpse
of Don Franklin, the circuit court judge, and Mike Cash,
the assistant prosecutor who started all this mess.

Franklin seems low key, a low-voltage kind of judge
who prefers that lawyers keep the theatrics to a mini-
mum. In his late sixties, he treats Mike Cash with a kind
of avuncular condescension, giving me some hope that at
some later date when "Binkie" Cross, the prosecutor, returns, this case can be made to go away. Seated almost
too quietly beside me, Dade, dressed in a dark sports coat
a size too small and slightly wrinkled khaki pants, looks
terrified. "Nothing of importance will happen this morning," I reassure him for the third time. Like a deer caught
in the headlights of a car, he sits motionless with a wide-
eyed stare on his face. This is no street-smart kid beside
me. I'd rather have him like this than the kind who comes
off cocky and arrogant, sneering all the way to the elec-
tric chair.

After the court enters Dade's not-guilty plea, we get a
January 7 trial date and are excused from the courtroom.
I ask Cash when he'll have time to talk, and he tells me to
come to his office in half an hour. Cash is young and he
dresses well. His gray suit is a worsted wool herringbone
that fits him like a glove. It doesn't hurt that he is my
height minus about twenty pounds. He can't be more
than twenty-six or twenty-seven. Probably a real eager
beaver.

A gaggle of reporters and TV camera persons are on us

immediately when we exit the courtroom, but I give them virtually the same brief comment that I did going in, "My client is not guilty of any crime. Any sexual contact between him and the complaining party was completely consensual. We are not going to try this case in the media, and we don't expect the prosecutor to do so either. That's all we'll have to say until after the trial." I look around for the green-eyed reporter from the ten o'clock news, but she may not be out of bed yet.

"Dade, are you still a Razorback?" a woman hollers at him as we push our way out the door.

I have directed him not to answer, but I notice he shrugs his shoulders, indicating he has no idea.

"Dade, is it true that you met with Coach Carter last night?" the same reporter persists, preceding us down the steps onto College Avenue. Young, with her long hair pulled back, and wearing a blue suit, she may be a reporter for the *Traveler*, the university newspaper, or for the *New York Times*. These days everybody looks high school age to me.

Afraid that Dade will talk, I say quickly, "We are not taking any more questions. Let's go, Dade."

Damn if she doesn't follow us to my car around the corner on Center. "Dade, are you still in school?" she asks twice.

I almost lose my cool. In the past I've had a weakness for women TV reporters. Fortunately, this girl is not my type. Too young, even for me. Still, I admire her persistence. Dade looks at me as if he wants to respond, but I shake my head. I don't want him to say anything that will piss off Carter or the university. If we appear to put pressure on them publicly, it will surely backfire. Carter may need Dade, but not if he starts shooting off his mouth.

For reasons of space, I presume, the prosecutor's office is a block away in a four-story redbrick building with arches but no steeples. Cash comes sooner rather than later, and we are ushered into his office, which, if not a cubbyhole, is surely not the prosecutor's. "I'd like to see Dade's file," I say immediately.

"I can't give it to you today," he says, avoiding my eyes, his voice sounding mechanical.

"I just want to see the girl's statement," I reply, feeling myself already getting angry.

"I can't do it," he answers, sounding no different from a million bureaucrats I have encountered in my lifetime.

Suddenly, I get it. Somebody has contacted his boss, who has put him on a leash so short his feet don't even touch the ground. I'd go to the judge, but there's nothing in the rules of criminal procedure that says I'm entitled to see the file five minutes after the arraignment. "What if Dade agreed to give you a statement this morning? Can't I at least read what the girl said?"

Cash, his face stiff as poker, says, "Mr. Cross will be back in forty-eight hours. You'll have to talk to him."

I look at a picture of his wife or girlfriend on his desk. Young and pretty, like him. Ordinarily, I could work up a little sympathy for him but not today. His rashness has caused all kinds of trouble. "I thought he was going to be gone another week," I say, not bothering to hide the contempt for this kid I'm beginning to feel in my panic. Coach Carter can't wait two more days. He probably is feeling too much pressure already.

I stand up. "Let's go, Dade," I say, trying to get out of here before my tongue gets the better of me. Cash is humiliated enough already. Anything I say will get back to Cross, and I don't want to alienate him before I've had a chance to talk to him. Cash shrugs, knowing he can't very well protest my lack of cooperation.

I find a phone and call Carter in his office and explain what has happened. He doesn't seem as upset as I thought he would—a sign, I'm afraid, that he has already made up his mind, or that somebody has already made it up for him. "I'll have a statement out about Dade's status before practice this afternoon," he says curtly.

My fears are confirmed. "It still doesn't change the facts. Dade's innocent until proven guilty, and that's the way the system ought to work on campus as well."

Carter pauses as if this statement is so naive that he won't dignify it by responding. "I've got to get off," he says abruptly and hangs up.

In the Blazer, driving back to the campus, I try to put the best gloss on things I can. "I don't think he'll take away your scholarship until the case is tried. The worst he'll probably do is suspend you from the team."

Dade looks out the window on Dickson Street at the D-Lux. Best cheeseburgers in Fayetteville. I spent many pleasant hours drinking beer there my senior year. He says glumly, "I might as well transfer."

He still hasn't got it in his head that he may be transferring to the Arkansas State Penitentiary next semester. Yet, it's better that he not get depressed. He won't be any help, and I will need all I can get before this case is over with. "Don't start getting your head down, Dade," I warn him. "If you start acting like you're guilty, that's what people will believe. I can't have you acting all down-in-the-mouth in public. Even if things don't go our way at first, we've got to keep fighting. I think eventually you're going to be cleared. If it takes a trial, so be it. Next year this time will just be a bad dream."

His attractive face still somber, he asks, "Do you really believe that?"

I stop at the light at the intersection of Arkansas and Dickson at the edge of the campus. Hell no, I don't. If he weren't black, I might. How many blacks in Arkansas have ever won a rape trial involving a white woman? None that I know of. The best thing we can do is to keep this case from going to trial. And while that's possible, it seems like a long shot. "Sure I do," I lie glibly. "It doesn't really matter what Coach Carter does today. You and I are in this for the long haul." If by some stroke of luck this case has a happy ending, I hope he remembers that. I let him out at the jock dorm after getting his promise to keep his mouth shut and to call me as soon as he hears from Carter.

I head back downtown to Barton Sanders's office. This is the kind of case where insiders have a distinct advantage. I know there are attorneys up here who have represented athletes, and I need to pick their brains. I suspect, however, they have more to do today than spoon-feed me on how to help my client.

Barton can be counted on to be behind his desk on Mountain Street, just a block from the courthouse, and I am received without a wait. Extending his small, pudgy, ink-stained hand to me, he asks immediately, "Did you get hold of Carter?"

I sit down across from him, my eyes already glazing over at all the abstracts that surround him. How does he read this stuff day after day? "We met last night," I say, and bring him up to date. Barton listens wide-eyed as a child. Clearly, this is what he would like to be doing instead of getting filthy rich. At my request, he makes phone calls to three attorneys who have represented jocks in either disciplinary proceedings with the university or criminal cases. Typically, nobody is in his office. You can never find a lawyer when you need one, I think glumly. I should have gotten Barton to call one of these guys night before last, but my ego told me I didn't need any help. I ought to call Roy Cunningham and punt this case. I don't know what I am doing. Worse, I don't know where to start.

Over lunch at a café two doors down from his office, I ask Barton, "Are there some more buttons I should be pushing?"

Our waitress is an elderly woman who takes our order and kids with Barton, an obvious regular. After she leaves, he says, "I think you're stuck for the moment. I wouldn't want to be Carter right now for love or money. He's got to dump his best player on the eve of the Tennessee game. What I've heard in the last twenty-four hours is that if he leaves Dade on the team, he'll be crucified. Five years ago maybe he could have gotten away with it; now, it's a different ball game. The talk is that the university got such a black eye after the ninety-one incident that it can't afford to do nothing. And since Dade's already been charged, that makes it ten times worse."

I am eager to talk, but a client of Barton's comes over, and invites himself to sit down and proceeds to discuss some land transaction near Beaver Lake for an entire hour. Barton looks at me apologetically, but he must be on this guy's clock, because he pays his client the same rapt attention he gave me in his office. Finally we escape, with me somehow stuck with the check. I catch up with Barton on the street, thinking I am out of my league up here.

"I'm really sorry," Barton says sincerely, his warm puppy eyes moist in the bright noontime glare. "There's a few million dollars involved on this deal, and I couldn't blow him off."

A few million. Is that all? "He wasn't worried about confidentiality," I mutter, although I couldn't understand a thing they were talking about. I'd still be trying to pass the real property course if Barton hadn't tutored me. Of course, I helped get him through trial advocacy. Hardly tit for tat, given our incomes now; but if he thinks he owes me, I won't discourage him.

"He probably thought you were an associate and were charging the firm," Barton says, laughing, as we return to his office. While he picks up his messages, I marvel at all the wasted space. He is by himself, and yet he has a small office building all to himself. On the walls are photographs of the area including Beaver Lake, the President's retreat for a couple of days his first summer in office, and numerous aerial shots of the Ozarks. Knowing Barton, I suspect he is trying to figure out a way to buy northwest Arkansas for himself and his clients and lease it to the rest of the state.

One of the pink slips is from a lawyer Barton called to help me, and from his desk he gets him on the speaker-phone, explaining who I am and what is happening in Dade's case. I have never heard of Bliss Young, but then, I doubt if he has heard of me.

After a few inane pleasantries, I blurt, "Is there any-body I should be calling? What should I be doing now?"

Bliss Young snorts, "Helping Dade pack his bags prob-ably. If he hadn't been charged, his chances of playing might have been even, but his luck ran out when Mike Cash got hold of him. All you can do now is to prepare for trial. If Carter doesn't throw him off the team, the uni-versity will." I listen impatiently while Young in great de-tail tells me a story about his representation of a student athlete before the university judiciary board. "Now that's a three-ring circus," he says.

I draw my finger across my neck. Barton nods, but he can't shut this guy up. He drones on for ten minutes non-stop about the lack of due process. God, lawyers like to hear themselves talk. Finally, when he pauses to take a breath, I tell him I'll take a rain check, but that I have an-other appointment.

Pissed at being interrupted, he hangs up abruptly, and I apologize to Barton. "I wasn't trying to hack the guy off, but I'm looking for some way to deal with Carter."

Barton nods sympathetically. "I know you're frus-trated," he says, "but I think there's not much you can do now except wait for him to make a decision." We are like housewives in a TV soap opera who can do nothing but wring their hands until the next commercial. He offers me a cup of coffee.

"What's the prosecutor's name? Cross?" I ask, deciding to move on to a more promising subject. "Tell me about him."

"Yeah, Binkie Cross. He must give a lot of money to the Razorback Club," Barton says, his tone slightly aggrieved. "He always gets better seats than I do."

I stir my coffee, envying the paneling in Barton's office. He has enough wood in here for me to build a new house. Money and influence. Where you sit at Razorback games depends on the generosity of your contributions to a private organization whose books haven't been open to the public and your friendships with Jack Burke and others who control it. "Somehow, I'm not terribly surprised."

"Even if I could put two words together in public without sounding like I had an IQ of 4, I wouldn't be the prosecutor for love or money," Barton needlessly confesses. "You've got all these groups up here—gays and lesbians, environmentalists, foreign students. They've always got a beef about something, and the media loves to stir 'em up. Binkie always looks stressed out at bar meetings. Lot of toes to avoid. I hear he may not run again."

That's the trouble with power. You exercise it, and people get pissed off. "So, he's not real crazy about his job, huh?" I say, encouraging him.

"Ol' Binkie," Barton hoots from behind his desk, "thought he was gonna be a hero and just prosecute drug cases and regular crime stuff. Bullshit! Last month at the Washington County Bar Association luncheon he said half the people in Fayetteville want the other half in jail. One group wants to impeach him for not prosecuting gays under the sodomy law; gays want him to arrest that same group for harassment. The pro-choice people want injunctions against the right-to-lifers, who want them charged with murder. By the time you get through trying to pacify all the special-interest groups, it's already five o'clock. I thought he was gonna cry."

Sounds like ol' Binkie might like to avoid a trial. Barton, I decide, likes gossip more than I remember. "What else have you heard about the girl?" I ask, not worried I'm taking up his time. He obviously can afford it.

Barton fingers his tie, a plain brown number that looks like a long dirt stain against his starched white shirt. "Not much about the girl, but her father is rumored to be a big contributor to the Razorbacks. They say he gives so much that if he wanted, he could sit in Nolan's lap during basketball season. Big Baptist, too. One of the leaders in driving the moderates out of the seminaries. They tell me a liberal Baptist these days is one who thinks Jesus might have sported a beard."

I try to grin at this feeble attempt at humor. Barton wasn't known as a stand-up comedian and hasn't improved much. Still, this information is useful. The old man may have mixed emotions about what a trial will do not only to his daughter but to the Razorbacks as well.

"Back in the old days, everybody would have wanted to keep the lid on," Barton says. "The girl would have dropped out of school, and it never would have gotten beyond the gossip stage."

The old days. Barton must be all of thirty. As we are

talking, Lila, one of his two secretaries, a girl who must be a student at the university, bursts into his office, and says excitedly, "Dade Cunningham's still on the team! Coach Carter's just announcing it. Turn on your radio!"

Barton reaches behind him to his stereo and we hear the leathery voice of Dale Carter. ". . . I realize I take this action against the advice of Chancellor Henry, who has strongly recommended a different course of action. But I am convinced it would be unfair to discipline Dade until he has had a trial. After reviewing this matter, I have to say that I have heard no evidence that leads me to believe that a crime has been committed. It would be improper for me to say more at this time. The young woman has made serious charges against Dade in the criminal courts of this state, but it's my view that due process of law requires that Dade be presumed innocent until proven guilty. For this reason I'm not, at this time, suspending him for a violation of team rules. This is not to say that I consider the matter closed, nor am I making any judgment about whether a violation of the law occurred. If information is made available that persuades me that Dade is a threat to her safety or anyone's safety, I will change my decision in a heartbeat. That's all I'm going to say on this matter. Athletic Director Burke has authorized me to say that he supports my decision at this time."

"Hot damn!" I exclaim excitedly. "Carter is one tough son of a gun!"

Barton snaps off the radio. "God bless him!" Barton laughs. "He just bought himself a load of trouble. They're gonna come after him with everything but the kitchen sink."

I look at Lila, who has remained in the room. "Why?"
I say. "Why shouldn't he be presumed innocent? All
Carter did was maintain the status quo until the trial.
What's wrong with that?"

The girl looks at me coldly, as if I had suggested that
this were a case about as significant as a traffic accident.
In her expensive ash-colored cashmere sweater and heels,
she could be Barton's mistress. She turns and flounces out
of the room.

Barton closes the door. "There's your problem, right
there," he says, frowning. "Some women will go apeshit
over what Carter's done. There're a bunch more on the
faculty and in administration than there used to be."

"There's also a bunch of people," I remind Barton,
"who want to see the Hogs play for the national championship on New Year's Day in New Orleans. Without
Dade, we won't even make it to the Weedeaters Bowl.
Can I use your phone? I want to call his parents. They
can stand some good news. I'll charge it to my phone."

Barton graciously exits his own office, and I get
Dade's mother on the second ring. Over background
noise in the Cunninghams' store, I give her the news. "I
arranged for Dade to see Coach Carter last night," I say
self-importantly. "I think we persuaded him that Dade
was innocent and that he should wait until the trial to see
if he should take any action against him." Actually, I am
exaggerating my own role, but perhaps not. All I know is
that if I get Dade off, I want her and her husband to know
that won't be the only thing I have accomplished.

"Thank you, Mr. Page," she replies formally. "But the

main thing we're concerned about is what happens to him in January."

"I am too," I add hastily, "but this was an important step. If Dade continues to play and does well, it can't help but improve his credibility at the time of the trial. If the season is successful, every juror in Washington County will know it. I'm not saying that things should work that way, but it's a fact just like it's a fact that we'll have to overcome the color of Dade's skin when the girl testifies at the trial. I don't have any reason to believe there's any less racism in the northwest corner of the state than there is in eastern Arkansas."

I hear the sound of a cash register while she says something to a customer. "Do you still plan on being in your office tomorrow?" she asks finally. "I can't talk right now."

"I'll be there," I say, already having forgotten she is driving over to Blackwell County to visit me. "I have a hearing at nine, but it should be over before ten." I'm pleading out a drug dealer who is managing to avoid serving time by turning over a thirty-thousand-dollar pimpmobile to the Blackwell County Drug Taskforce. What they will do with it I wouldn't want to speculate.

Five minutes later, I get hold of Dade in his room. It sounds as if he is having a party. I hope not. He has practice, and he damn well better have a good one. I congratulate him and tell him to keep his mouth shut. We have dodged one bullet. The next one won't be so easy. I say that I have called his parents and for him to call me at my office if he hears from the university. I explain that Coach Carter will be taking a lot of heat and to make sure he thanks him. "What he's done is controversial. Don't let him down, and keep your cool when you read or hear something negative. It's going to happen. Don't say anything to reporters. This isn't over yet."

"I know," Dade says.

You don't have a clue, I think, but it will be no good to harp on it. Better that he have a good practice and concentrate on Tennessee. "It's my job to worry about what happens next and your job to play football and keep your grades up, okay? I'll be back up next week, but I'll be in touch with you before then."

"Okay," he says, a little sullenly. I know I am being condescending, but I have trouble doing one thing well at a time much less two. I doubt if Dade is any different.

"Dr. Beekman," Sarah says shyly, "this is my dad."

Beekman, a medium-height, sandy-haired guy in his early thirties, smiles easily, as if he has nothing to hide. "Charlie Beekman," he says, rising from behind his desk and extending his hand. "Sarah speaks of you so often that I feel as if I already know you."

My dad the Neanderthal, probably. "I was on my way out of town and wanted to come by and see Sarah," I explain, getting a good grip and squeezing hard. If he's hitting on my daughter, I want him to remember this handshake. "I understand you're interested in the sociology of the Delta."

He waves his hand for me to have a seat. I look at Sarah, whose expression is rapturous. She smiles at me as if God Himself had invited me to drop by for a chat. I sit down beside Sarah in a straight-backed chair with no arms like some dumb student about to get chewed out for failing his course. "The Mississippi Delta has so much potential," Beekman says eagerly. "But it's been terribly neglected academically in the last fifty years. Both communities, African-American and white, contain some very talented people, as I'm sure you're aware."

I shrug, looking around the room for clues to this guy's testosterone count. Mounted on the wall behind him are familiar photographs of small-town life in the Delta, also rice fields, a cotton gin, the old bridge over the Mississippi connecting Arkansas to Memphis. The pictures don't hold a clue to the poverty and racial tension. "We all seemed pretty ordinary at the time I lived over there," I say, not wanting to give anything to this guy. "Of course, it was a different world back when I was growing up."

He nods, and I swear I think he winks at Sarah as if to say that, yeah, your old man is the real thing. A Southern cracker still fresh out of the box after all these years. "The Delta Commission's goal was to find ways to keep people like you at home to build it up."

"I don't think one more lawyer would have made much difference," I say, trying to keep this conversation from becoming too serious. I haven't got time to hear him lecture me on the revitalization of the Delta. "Is Sarah doing a good job for you?" I ask, more interested in Beekman's present relationships than his academic pursuits. I want to ask the guy if he is married and how many kids he has, but Sarah would go through the roof.

"She's wonderful!" Beekman says enthusiastically. "Best student I've ever had work for me." He smiles at her as if she had just agreed to go for a weekend in Cancun.

I turn to Sarah, who is blushing. "I guess being a clerk in a video store during high school," I say sardonically, "was more training than I realized."

"I do a lot of proofreading," Sarah mumbles, obviously wishing her employer's delight wasn't so obvious. "I check citations, stuff like that."

"She's great on computers, too," Beekman gushes, "a really bright kid."

I hope he remembers the "kid" part. Beekman, I have to admit, with his warm brown eyes is a decent-looking guy. Not a hunk, but probably the type who knows how to talk to women. The sensitive kind, who gets half their clothes off before they know what they're doing. "She was a good student in high school," I say, hoping he's getting the point. Beekman's not wearing a wedding ring. Of course, it could be on a shelf in his closet. It would be tempting for a visiting professor not to bring a lot of baggage. I stand up, knowing Sarah would have been more than happy for me to have confined this visit to a handshake. "I've gotta get on the road," I say. "Nice to have met you, Dr. Beekman. Hope to see you again. I'll be back up several times this fall, I'm sure."

"Looking forward to it," Beekman says, smiling easily.

Sarah precedes me into the hall. "You didn't have to come by," she says, blushing again.

"I couldn't leave town without seeing one of the Seven Wonders of the World."

Sarah rolls her eyes. "You sound jealous!"

"That's ridiculous! It's just that I've never liked professors much," I say. "They've got too much time to think." It is time to change the subject. "You heard about Dade, I guess."

"It's all anybody's talking about, except Dr. Beekman. He doesn't care about anything but his research."

Sure, sure. My poor, naive daughter. "What are they saying?"

She pleads, "Daddy, don't try to use me, please!"

"I'm not," I say, a little disappointed in her unwillingness to help me out. I should understand, but I don't. I tell her that I will be back up early next week. She gives me a quick hug, glad to be rid of me. Parents, like children, should be seen but not heard. "Do you think Coach Carter was wrong to leave Dade on the team?" I ask. "He's innocent until proven guilty, isn't he?" If she won't serve as an informer, she can at least act as a sounding board.

"I don't know how I feel," she answers stubbornly. "I've already heard there's going to be a meeting of some women tonight to discuss it. I may go."

"That's fine," I say neutrally. She may eventually give me some details of campus gossip if I can resist pumping her so much.

Driving home through the glorious fall foliage I wonder if I am guilty of projecting my feelings onto guys like Beekman. What do young women see in us old guys? It sure isn't looks or staying power. And, in my case, it isn't money either. Maybe women really are looking for their fathers. God help Sarah if that's true.

5

ON RETURNING TO my office from my plea hearing in circuit court I spot through the glass doors a woman I assume is Lucy Cunningham standing at Julia's desk. Dade has her identical copper coloring, her handsome face. I see Julia's lips move, and the woman turns to look at me as I push open the glass. She nods, unsmiling, before I can call her name. Not exactly pretty (though she may have been as a girl), she is a tall, striking woman with a full, sorrowful face. Whom does she remind me of? Coretta Scott King, the widow of the slain civil rights leader, whom, I realize, I've never observed to smile in all the years of seeing her on television.

"Mr. Page," she says quietly, with more dignity than usually heard in our waiting room, "I'm Mrs. Cunningham, Dade's mother."

She offers her hand. My immediate impression is that this sophisticated woman is not a likely candidate for wife of a black store owner in the rural Delta. She's wearing a red-and-white-striped knit tunic over a matching red skirt and four-inch heels. She is my height and looks to be about my age. Her hand, soft to the touch, offsets

98

some of her severity, and yet, such is her presence, that even Julia, unoccupied behind her desk, falls silent as I greet my client's mother and escort her back to my office.

"Would you like some coffee?" I ask as she sits down across from me.

"No, thank you," she says, studying my diplomas behind my head. "What else have you learned about Dade's case?"

So much for small talk. I pull out my notes and for a solid hour we discuss her son. She questions me closely about what I have learned about Robin Perry. Women, if Lucy Cunningham is any guide, are ruthlessly cynical about each other. We men only think that we pursue women. Judging by her manner and questions, Mrs. Cunningham knows better, or perhaps she simply knows how the female sex reacts to her son. Are black women, I wonder, more suspicious than their white counterparts? Rosa, I remember now, thought so. Black women were "in the bottom of the barrel," my wife uttered once in that quaint way she had of translating English into Spanish and then rendering it back into the American idiom.

"I wonder if Dade sat down by her in that communications class," she muses, in a soft bottom-land accent that is rich as the silt from the Mississippi River, "or whether she picked him out."

I make some notes of my own. "I'll ask him," I say, more impressed with her than her husband. Roy, in the few minutes I spent with him, seemed angry and bitter. Lucy Cunningham is far more subtle and determined.

"He probably didn't notice," she says dryly. "Until this happened, he was pretty full of himself."

I nod, glad that she has a more realistic view of her son than her husband. "It's easy to see why he would have been," I say, wondering what it would be like to be the object of all that attention. "He's movie-star handsome and a Razorback, to boot. Heady stuff for anybody in this state."

Lucy Cunningham sighs and seems to look past me at the wall. "Except for the one or two who are good enough for the pros," she says, her voice soft and resigned, "it's mainly a waste. They don't go to Fayetteville to get a degree; they're there to win games for the greater glory of the people who run this state."

There is no bitterness in her voice. That's just the way things are, her tone implies. I disagree. Sports is the only unifying force in Arkansas, the only successful enterprise black and white males share. "Didn't your husband follow the Razorbacks before Dade went to Fayetteville?" I ask, smiling, to let her know I take issue with her but don't want a fight.

"As long as we win for you," she rebukes me. "We all get along together until something like this comes up. Roy knows that. Do you think Nolan Richardson has any illusions about why whites think he's become a good basketball coach in the last few years?"

"He's very successful now," I concede, hoping I haven't alienated her. A white man's naïveté is par for the course.

"After his first couple of seasons, they said he was a good recruiter, but a bad coach," she lectures me. "If he starts losing again, they'll say the same thing, meaning, he's dumb. We know what most white people think about us."

I blink at the bluntness of this woman, but I realize she must consider me different from the average white. Still, I am uncomfortable with the way this conversation is going and point to the front page of the *Democrat-Gazette*. "A lot of people are supporting what Coach Carter did yesterday." An informal survey by the paper showed more support than I anticipated. There was the expected grumbling by some women's groups and some others, but no official word by the university that anyone had filed a complaint with the All-University Judiciary Board, the school's internal mechanism for dealing with this kind of case, according to the paper. Predictably, some feminists were outraged, calling Carter "a Neanderthal" who should be fired. Carter's actions condoned violence against women, etc., etc.

Mrs. Cunningham has been making notes in a three-ring binder notebook and taps the blue plastic cover against her lap. "But a lot of people are upset by it, too. I hope it was a good idea to try to keep him on the team."

I reassure her that it was. "The best way to ensure Dade gets a fair shake at the trial is not to let anyone shift the burden of proof onto him beforehand. I know you don't know me, but I want you to trust me on this."

She says, unsmiling, "I know very well who you are, but you don't have the slightest idea who I am, do you?"

Puzzled, I squint at this woman as if her identity will become apparent if I continue to stare at her. There is nothing about her that is familiar, but my memory for faces is so bad I could have easily met her in the past. Yet, someone with her direct manner and striking appearance would be hard to forget. "I meet new people almost every day," I say, as if this fact were a decent excuse.

"I'm from Bear Creek," she says abruptly. "Believe it or not, you and I have the same grandfather."

"I beg your pardon?" I exclaim. Suddenly, ancient gossip, never substantiated, and fervently denied by my mother in a long forgotten conversation when I was sixteen, spews up in my brain like mud dredged from a canal. Bobby Don Hyslip had called me a nigger-lover one broiling summer night at the Dairy Delight, and I had made the mistake of listening to him. Bobby Don, whose alcoholic father was a fixture at the Bear Creek city jail, had never liked me because he claimed that my father, a schizophrenic and alcoholic, had always received special treatment from the powers than ran the town until he died when I was fourteen. Bobby Don was absolutely correct. His daddy, Barney, was a worthless river rat who fathered kids all over town and never worked two days straight at his job at the sawmill, while my father was a respectable druggist who owned his own business for twenty years until his illnesses got the best of him. "You're always actin' so superior. You know your granddaddy knocked up a nigger bitch!" he had yelled out of his beat-up Ford. "You got high-yeller cousins runnin' all over Bear Creek."

With that, he had peeled out in the gravel. That night when I got home I had confronted my mother who swore there wasn't a word of truth in the story. I didn't believe it then and don't believe it now.

Lucy Cunningham's face softens. "I've known who

you were since I was a little girl. Your daddy owned a drugstore on Main Street before he got sick and hung himself in the state hospital."

This casual account of my father's death, though correct, irritates me by its presumptuousness. Since he owned the only drugstore in Bear Creek, it does not surprise me she knows a little of my history. My paternal grandfather had been a small-town entrepreneur, owning a service station, the first car wash, a diner, and now that I remember it, according to my sister Marty, for a short while he owned a liquor store and the movie theater in the black section of Bear Creek. His proprietorship of the latter two enterprises was hardly proof he had a sexual relationship with a black woman. "Did you hear that growing up?" I ask. Granddaddy Page died from a heart attack when I was about ten.

Lucy Cunningham gives me a knowing smile, but her voice is less intense. "Many times."

When I was growing up in Bear Creek, gossip was its major form of recreation, and racial segregation was hardly a barrier to its transmittal. It sounds like the kind of crap Barney Hyslip would make up and repeat endlessly at his occasional job at the sawmill. I have no intention of dignifying that kind of talk. "How did you get my name?" I ask, my voice stiff.

Lucy leans back in her chair, apparently regarding me with satisfaction. "When you represented that black psychologist charged with murder, I saw your picture in the paper and realized who you were," she says, folding her arms across her breasts. "James told me you lived right down the street from him and had been married to a South American woman darker than me."

Is she insinuating that a predilection for black women runs in my family? Of my childhood in Bear Creek I recall only selected vignettes, few having to do with my grandparents. Everything was subservient to my father's growing paranoia that the Communists were taking over the country and his eventual hospitalization and suicide. "Rosa was truly a remarkable woman," I say, determined not to sound defensive. I don't feel comfortable with Lucy Cunningham. Why has she brought up the rumor about my grandfather?

"Gloria told me your wife was beautiful," Lucy Cunningham acknowledges. "She liked her a lot."

"Rosa never met a stranger," I say, forcing a smile. There is no hostility in her voice. Probably, she sees this wild story as a bond rather than as a barrier. I don't know. I am guilty only of ignorance and the arrogance that comes with being white. They knew us; they had to know us. As a child before the civil rights era, I had no need to know more than the first names of the men who cut our grass and the women who ironed my family's clothes.

"Gloria says you haven't been much of a neighbor since she died," Lucy observes. "How come you haven't moved out?"

"No need to." I shrug, embarrassed to admit the reason is financial. "Except for the sounds of gunfire coming from the housing development a few blocks away, it's a quiet neighborhood."

Abruptly she stands up. It is as if I had said that except

for stomach cancer, I feel pretty good. "I hope you can help my son," she says, extending her hand to me.

I take it and gently squeeze her dry palm against my sweaty one. For the last few minutes this woman has had me totally off-balance. I'm glad this interview is over. "I'll do everything I can."

As I step inside the waiting room after the elevator door shuts, Julia remarks, "Did your wife look like that?"

Never ceasing to be amazed by what comes out of her mouth, I gawk at her. There is no sarcasm in her voice. God only knows what Julia knows about me. Usually, she seems so self-absorbed that I'm surprised when she can remember my name. "She was darker and a lot prettier," I say, daring her to make a smartass remark.

Popping a pastel jelly bean into her mouth, Julia says, "You know who she reminded me of?"

"Coretta Scott King," I answer, again thinking of the bruised sadness in her eyes. Her past has probably left some scars. She wouldn't have made that crack about my grandfather if it hadn't.

"Yeah," Julia says, with what could almost be termed respect in her voice. A first. "Her husband was supposed to be so great," she says bitterly, "and he was off screwing all those white women and was so dumb he didn't even know the FBI was listening. But did she ever act in public like it bothered her? Hell, no. That's real class. I bet she gave him shit in private."

There are no other persons in the waiting room. I lean against the wooden counter that separates Julia from the public. Julia, in her twenties, can't have any personal memories of the civil rights movement. "I've never exactly thought of you as a liberal," I say, glancing at her skirt as it creeps up her legs. If it rides up much further, I'll be able to see her belly button.

Following my gaze, she tugs ineffectually at the fabric. "You guys don't know anything but what I want you to," she replies softly. "All you got is an idea based on what I look and sound like here between eight and five and that's all."

My face reddens at my own condescension. She is right, of course. We take her for granted. Her life is probably much richer than my own. I have assumed it was superficial, a soap opera unworthy of my attention except for idle speculation between me and Dan about her sex life. "That's true," I mumble, and return to my office to make a rare call to my sister Marty.

"Come out tonight and Herbert will cook some steaks. I'm real busy now," she says loudly into the phone when I ask her if she has time for some questions about Bear Creek. In the background I can hear the sound of women's voices. Marty owns a used-clothing store in Hutto, a town on the western edge of Blackwell County. "How's Herbert?" I ask, wondering what it must be like to have married four times. Marty has said she would keep on going down the aisle until she got it right.

"He's the kindest man I've ever known. If he leaves me, I'll kill him." She whispers, "On top of being such a real sweetheart, he's great in bed, too."

I feel myself blushing. Is this my unhappy sister Marty? Her life in the last few years has sounded like daytime TV: serial divorces, eating binges, and hot-check charges. "What time?" I ask, afraid to encourage her.

"About seven," she says. "Bring a bottle of red if you want."

I tell her I will, and before I can put the phone down, Julia appears in my doorway. "Can you see a walk-in? This guy looks like he's got some dough, but I don't think he's gonna come back if you don't see him now. He's kind of excited."

I try to schedule everyone for an appointment, but sometimes it doesn't work. "What's his problem?"

"I don't know," Julia replies, clearly uninterested, as she checks her inch-long nails. "Something about a landlord-tenant problem."

"Sure, I'll be right out," I say, hoping the man is the property manager for a corporation that owns half the real estate in Blackwell County. Barton has inspired me. As long as I don't have to try to read an abstract, I'll be okay.

When I get out to the waiting room two minutes later, my potential client is pacing the floor. A short, compact, balding man wearing a plaid sports coat and dark slacks, he looks up and says, "Mr. Page? I'm Gordon Dyson."

"Nice to meet you," I say as we shake hands. I escort him back to my office, thinking this guy looks familiar. Maybe I've seen him running at the track. He declines my offer of a cup of coffee and perches on the edge of the chair across from my desk. "What can I do for you?"

He sighs so heavily that I think he is going to confess he has been embezzling from a bank. Instead, he says in an anguished voice: "I can't get rid of my son. He won't leave."

Dyson looks about my age, maybe a year or two older. "What do you mean, he won't leave?"

"He's twenty-three," Dyson says, rubbing his head, which is a little too big for his body. "I paid for his college education, gave him a nice used car, but he came home after he graduated from Duke and now he won't move out."

Duke! That must have cost a bundle. At his height, I doubt if the son was on a basketball scholarship. I doodle on my legal pad. "Is he working?"

"He's a waiter," Dyson says, his voice resigned. "I've paid close to a hundred thousand dollars for his education, and he's a waiter at Brandy's."

Brandy's is a relatively new restaurant in Blackwell County. The night I went there with Dan they never quite got around to serving dinner. The waiters wear bow ties and white shirts. By the time the bill comes, you realize you've paid thirty bucks for hors d'oeuvres. It's hard to justify leaving a big tip when all you've eaten is snack food. "What does your wife say?"

Dyson looks down at the floor. "She says she knows it's time for him to leave, but every time I'm ready to go to the mat over this, he makes her cry and she backs down."

"What's wrong with kids today?" I say philosophically, wondering if Sarah will turn out this way. She seems independent now, but when she graduates I may have to scrape her off the wall to get her out of the house. Dyson, still looking down, is, I notice, slightly humpbacked. He looks as if it is from carrying the weight of the world on his shoulders.

Almost inaudibly, he says, "We've spoiled him so bad that he can't imagine life without a house, an automobile, TV, stereo, a computer, new clothes. The idea that my son might have to start his life without a new automobile paralyzes him. He couldn't get out of bed for a week after we had that discussion."

Suddenly, I know where I've seen that hump. Dyson's a cop! Or used to be. I haven't seen him around in a couple of years. "Can't you just pull a gun on him?" I say, only half-joking. "Surround the house and starve him out?"

Dyson gives me a sour smile, as if he has tried that already. "He doesn't take me seriously since I quit the force and started my own security business. The more money I make, the worse he gets. I should have waited until he got out of college."

"What's his name?" I ask, reaching for a law book on the shelf behind me.

Dyson gives an embarrassed laugh, then says, "His Christian name is Gordon Jr.; his friends call him 'Gucci.' "

I can't repress a chuckle as I flip through a volume of the index to the Arkansas statutes. "Does he pay any rent?"

"He was supposed to pay a hundred a month," Dyson says, "but that didn't last. He owes fifteen hundred if I wanted to count it."

I locate the Unlawful Detainer Statutes. "Does your wife ever go on any trips by herself?"

"Sometimes," he says. "The business won't let me get away."

I run my finger down the page until I find the language I'm looking for. "Why don't you surprise her with a trip to New Zealand next month? It should be spring down there. She'll love it. While she's gone, we'll evict him. We only have to give him three days' notice. We'll have him out before he knows what's hit him."

Dyson smiles for the first time. "Won't I need my wife's approval?" he asks. "Her name's on the deed."

I put a paper clip on the page so I won't have to look it up again. "I'll send you a power of attorney for her to sign before she goes," I tell him. "She won't suspect a thing if you play your cards right."

Dyson brings a finger to his lips and begins to chew on a nail. "What's your fee?"

If he can afford to send his wife to New Zealand, he can afford to pay me. "A thousand if he contests it, and I have to make two court appearances. Five hundred if he doesn't show up and moves out without any hassle."

He nods. Money is no object, his expression says. I get a few more details and walk him to the elevators. He will call me the moment his wife steps on the plane. As we shake hands, I ask, "Why don't you just hire your son?"

Dyson's face darkens. "I wouldn't pay that kid to take out the trash."

"I see." Confident he will call me, I wait politely until he gets on the elevator and the door closes in my face. There is nothing like faith in the younger generation.

At the appointed hour I arrive at my sister's house bearing a bottle of Cabernet Sauvignon and am greeted by Herbert, a short, thin, virtually hairless guy in his fifties. An electrician by training, Herbert now owns his own contracting business and builds homes all over Blackwell County.

"Movin' a lot of paper these days?" Herbert asks, inspecting the wine as he pumps my hand. He is dressed in cowboy boots, denim jeans the color of sawdust, and a sweatshirt with a picture of Ross Perot on the front of it.

"I wish I had invented the fax machine," I say, taking his question to heart. From my one other visit with him (city hall on their wedding day six months ago), I know he views lawyers as an unnecessary evil. Fixed overhead, he calls us.

"If your profession would agree to be deported," he says, leading me through the living room into the kitchen, "business activity would jump overnight by fifty percent in the United States, and we'd have the Japanese and Germans on their knees begging for mercy in five years."

I look around my sister's living room, which is as big as an airport terminal. Marty's passion for plants has been indulged to the limit. I feel as if I'm in a greenhouse. The water bill alone must be the size of my mortgage. In the kitchen Marty greets me with a rare hug. "What do you hear from Sarah?" she asks, pecking me on the cheek.

"I was just up there," I say gloomily, handing her the wine. "She isn't lacking for male attention."

"If I looked like her," Marty says, glancing at her husband, who has come in behind me, "I probably would have gotten married five more times before I met the right guy."

Herbert beams as if Michelle Pfeiffer had told him she wanted to run away with him. True love. It took her only fifty years to find it. "Sweetness, why don't you go put the meat on the grill while I visit with my brother for a few minutes? He looks too serious for this to be purely a social call."

With a beatific smile on his face, Herbert takes the plate of meat and disappears out the kitchen door to the backyard.

"Herbert must worship you," I say, amazed that a grown man would allow himself to be called "sweetness" in front of another living human being.

"He does," Marty says happily. "God knows why. When I met him I was a hundred pounds overweight, drank too much, and felt sorry for myself twenty-three out of every twenty-four hours. Now look at me!"

I do. Relaxed and calm, Marty hasn't looked this good since she was a senior in high school. I hope Amy will do for me what Sweetness has done for her. With her short dyed-blond hair cut in a pageboy, Marty, who is two years older than I am, looks almost pretty. Her blue eyes, not as deep-set as my own, along with a small nose and generous mouth are her best features. She is flat-chested, like our mother, and is wearing a man's blue workshirt (Herbert's, I presume) and a pair of Bermuda shorts that reveal a decent pair of legs. "Fantastic," I concede. "What's his secret?"

"Unconditional love," Marty says, opening her refrigerator. "I thought only dogs and newborn babies got it. I have no idea why he loves me so."

I lean against the kitchen counter and take the Miller

Lite she hands me. Determined to lay Lucy Cunningham's comment to rest, I blurt, "Speaking of love, do you remember any stories about our paternal grandfather having fathered a child with a black woman in Bear Creek?"

Marty takes her own beer and sits down at the kitchen table. A solid oak, it came from a tree off land owned by my more reputable maternal grandfather, who was a physician. "So that's what this visit is about, huh?"

I sit down across from her, taking a "tiddy," as Marty has long called the rubber container that fits over aluminum cans to keep them cold. I sum up for her the context of Lucy Cunningham's visit and our brief conversation on the subject. "Do you know what she's talking about?"

Marty, in the manner of older sisters, used to get an expression on her face that was half grimace, half sneer, whenever I said something particularly stupid. Forty years later it reappears. "What utter, pathetic crap!" she says, and pauses to sip at her beer. "She saw in the paper you represented that psychologist, remembered some old gossip, and thought to herself, have I got a white man by the tail! I bet you a dime to a doughnut they haven't paid you a fifth of what this case is worth. Am I right?"

I twist my own can in my hands. "That isn't all that unusual."

"Don't you see?" Marty shouts, though I am less than three feet away. "She's guilting you, Gideon! They want you to work for nothing, and that's how they're doing it. You owe us, whitey. Hell, that's all they've been saying for the last four decades! Do yourself a favor, okay? Don't get sucked back into all that shit that's going on over there. The best thing you and I ever did was to get the hell out of eastern Arkansas and never to go back. Your problem is that you've always let yourself get messed up with this race crap. Listen, our childhoods have taken us both thirty years to get over. That'll never change. You can go over there a million times and never straighten things out. Just be glad you're free, and stay out of there."

The anguish in my sister's voice is real. "Did you ever hear talk about Granddaddy Page?" I ask, wondering why I never asked her. Actually, now that I think about it, we weren't around each other much in those days. She worked at Silver Dollar City in Branson, Missouri, during the summers while she was in college, and since I spent the school year at a Catholic boarding school in western Arkansas, by the time I saw her at Thanksgiving I must already have buried it.

Her mouth dry after her speech, Marty swallows a mouthful of beer and wipes her lips with the back of her hand. "Among a hundred million other pieces of crap, yes, I heard it. When I told Mother, she said he owned some rent houses over in nigger town. One day he went over to collect the rent and stayed more than five minutes, and that was enough to get the talk started. All of a sudden he's some nigger's daddy. God, Gideon, for a lawyer, you're so naive!"

I remember why I do not get along with my sister: she has all the sensitivity of a tree frog. Most educated people in central Arkansas are civilized enough not to refer to African-Americans as "niggers." Marty prides herself on being politically incorrect at all times. "Mother always tried to keep things from me," I say, my voice suddenly bitter. I'm angry, but I don't know why. Perhaps I'm mad at my mother. She never told me Daddy wouldn't get well again. Marty always knew things I didn't.

Marty puts down her beer can. "She coped as best she could. Bear Creek wasn't exactly a picnic for her with Daddy the way he was and you acting like such a snot."

As my sister busies herself with making a salad, I ponder what she has said. In fact, she is mostly correct. I was on my way to becoming a small-town punk after my father's suicide at the state hospital. The monks and brothers at Subiaco Academy chewed at me night and day the first year until I began to straighten up, and I actually began to like the place by the time I was a senior. Marty, I conclude, is probably right on this, too, but I don't have to fall for it. Lucy Cunningham is trying to get something for nothing. Considering how poor eastern Arkansas is, it is understandable. Growing weary of my sister's name-calling, I say, "I take it you don't call the blacks who shop in your store 'niggers.' "

Marty points at me with her knife. "Don't start that phony liberal crap with me," she says, her voice immediately warming to the subject. "If they didn't act like niggers, I wouldn't use the term, but good God, why are they so self-destructive? How many of the men support their children? Where are their families? All these damn gangs and senseless shootings—they don't care whether they live or die anymore. Blackwell County has as high a murder rate as New York City, did you read that?"

"Things seem to be getting worse," I admit, draining the last of my beer. There was an article this week in the

Democrat-Gazette about school bus drivers and the anarchy that reigns before the kids even get to the classroom. The violence, intimidation, and profanity were shocking, and the article, without mentioning the ethnicity of the students, left no doubt about their race. One poor driver lost it fifteen minutes into her route and headed straight to a police station.

"Worse?" she chuckles bitterly, spearing an onion. "They're committing suicide. You know, desegregation was the worst thing that ever happened to them. Schools have been fully integrated for a quarter of a century, and they're still not catching up. Of course, they blame it on whites. They blame every problem they have on racism, and all whites want to do is to get their kids a halfway decent education and keep their children from being mugged. Even some of the blacks who have money send their kids to white private schools. They hate niggers, too."

Despite myself, I laugh, irritated that I am doing so. I say soberly, "A lot of the motivation by whites to get away is just plain discrimination, and you know it."

Marty again jabs the knife at me. "Why shouldn't we be able to discriminate against people who turn the schools into a battle zone? You know the schools weren't like this when it was only white kids. Below a certain economic level, it's a whole different culture. Jesus, Gideon, if two come in my store and start jibbering that nigger talk, I can't understand 'em."

I crush my beer can in frustration. It is hard to argue with the substance of what she is saying. At a bus stop I pass every day downtown I can't pick up half of what is said by the blacks. "I hope you don't talk this way around Sarah," I say, willing to score a point any way I can. "You seem to forget she is part black."

Marty finally puts down the knife and replaces it with a peeler and goes to work on a cucumber the size of a baseball bat. Her zest for her work makes me glad she isn't a urologist. "It's not race or color, damn it, and you know it. I'm talking about intelligence and character. Remember the Chinese families we had in Bear Creek. They were smart and they worked their butts off. Henry Quon was vice-president of my senior class and editor of the annual. Mary Yee was captain of the cheerleaders the year before I graduated. Tommy Ting was a year behind you and he was the smartest one of them all. They didn't ask for a damn thing. Their families worked night and day in those junky stores they owned selling to niggers. I guess they still are. The point is, slavery was the biggest mistake this country ever made. We should never have brought a damn one of them over here, and you know it."

I cannot resist smirking at this final leap of logic but realize it is pointless to respond. I don't understand either why blacks haven't made more progress in the last thirty years. Is everything the fault of whites? She is right about the Chinese families in Bear Creek. The adults kept to themselves, and their children starred in whatever activities were available. I don't remember that they dated, but, hell, maybe they were afraid they would bring their race down by mixing with us. I flip the empty can into the box Marty has marked for recycling. She doesn't seem the type. "So your solution," I say mockingly, "is to run away from them, huh?"

Marty makes a face that suggests I have been working too long around lead-based paint. "In this country that's all you can do anymore. Even the black teenagers carry guns in Blackwell County. If any white public official dared to suggest aloud in public that blacks might be the cause of their own problems, it'd start a race war. This state's become so damn 'PC,' you'd think we were living on a college campus on the East Coast. No white person can say what we think without being called a racist. Hell, it's easier just to move. Don't tell me you wouldn't get out of your neighborhood if you could afford it. Compared to that housing project just east of you Somalia looks like a vacation spa. I'm surprised you haven't been killed by a stray bullet."

"Needle Park," she means. "It's not so bad," I lie. Actually, it is. A person drives through the streets of the Blackwell County Housing Authority at his own peril. Gang warfare, arson, drugs, drive-by shootings, and theft are regular occurrences. A high percentage of the units are boarded up because of the rampant vandalism and pilfering. It is Marty's strongest argument that something is terribly wrong in the black community.

"Don't bullshit me," she snorts, opening her refrigerator and handing me another beer. "I read the papers. That place is a hellhole if there ever was one. The kids can't even play outside because of all the shit that's going on."

"It's poverty," I respond. "The blacks in my neighborhood don't act like that. They're just as middle class as they can be."

"I didn't say every black person is a nigger," Marty says, washing off a handful of raw carrots. "But tell me the truth. Ever since Rosa died, you don't have a thing in common with them, do you?"

"I don't really have the time to socialize much since being out in private practice," I say, once more puzzling over the reason why I don't interact more with my neighbors. When I returned from the Peace Corps, I had every intention in the world of living out my ideals. After all, I had spent two years in a nearly color-blind society on the northern coast of Columbia. Spanish, Indian, and African blood came together in that area of South America like tributaries forming one giant river.

"That's crap, too," my sister says benignly. "With Sarah off at school, you probably just sit in the house and drink."

Damn. Has she been peeking in the window? "Neither of us has led exactly model lives," I say, more than ready to shift the spotlight off myself.

"You can say that again," she says, with a big grin on her face. "But the difference is that I've finally got my shit together."

"And I'm happy for you," I say sincerely. "It looks like you've got a good fit."

As if on cue, Sweetness comes in with the meat, and as he passes in front of me, she pinches him on the butt. He laughs, delighted at the attention she gives him. Though Marty and I are not on the same wavelength and probably never will be, I am pleased for her. True love has been a rare animal in her life and is worth a celebration.

We get through the meal arguing politics. Sweetness can't stand the Clintons. Bill is an opportunistic career politician who can't keep his pants zipped; Hillary is a ballbusting feminist. Since Sweetness's construction company has benefited mightily by low interest rates and his wife runs a prosperous business, it is hard to take him too seriously. Perot, I point out, sounds like a Peeping Tom with all his investigations of employees and enemies. "I'd rather have a President who does it," I say loyally, "than one who pays people to dig up the dirt on the rest of us."

Marty laughs at me. Politics has never been my game. I figure we get the government we deserve and usually let it go at that. I drive home, not sorry I came. For all her harshness, Marty makes sense. If I'm smart, I'll forget Lucy Cunningham ever said a word about my grandfather.

Saturday the *Democrat-Gazette* is still carrying Coach Carter's decision and the reaction to it as page-one news. With Woogie at my feet beneath the kitchen table, I read the paper over a cup of coffee. I had hoped the furor would die down, but as one reporter noted, the women's groups on campus have found a cause to rally around this year. A new group, WAR (Women Against Rape), has sprung up overnight. Their leader, Paula Crawford, a law student from Rogers, is a long-haired, willowy blonde whose picture reminds me of Gloria Steinem. She claims that the university, by its inaction, "is sending a message to women on campus that they are third-class citizens." The article says over a hundred women attended. Other reactions on campus seemed divided. Though several faculty members who were willing to be interviewed professed to be outraged by Carter's decision, some students, typically males, thought Dade should be allowed to remain on the team until he was found guilty of a crime. The leader of the African-American group on campus was reported saying that if Robin Perry were black, no one would be paying any attention, a fact, he claimed, which showed that "racism is alive and well on the University of Arkansas campus." My eyes wander back to the picture of WAR's leader. She isn't bad looking. Years ago, you used to hear more about feminists. Rosa, I recall, had mixed emotions about them. She liked the part about equal pay, but being a devout Catholic made her uneasy about their stand on abortion. I remember that she went to a couple of meetings, but they got mad if you disagreed with them. Rosa liked men. A lot of them didn't, she said.

While I am reading the funnies, the phone rings. "Dad," Sarah says, when I answer the phone in the kitchen. "Did I wake you up?"

Instantly I think something is wrong. It is only nine o'clock. To my knowledge, Sarah hasn't been up this early on a Saturday since she was ten years old. "Are you okay, babe?" I say anxiously, wondering what she could want.

"I'm fine," she says. "I just haven't been able to sleep very well the last couple of days. I've been going to some meetings that have been held by a group of women who are upset that Dade is still allowed on the team. You may have read about it. They call themselves WAR—Women Against Rape."

I pick up the front section of the paper again. "What do you think of Paula Crawford?" I ask, squinting at her picture. "Do people like that still burn their bras?" I ask, hoping I can get her not to sound so serious. Her voice sounds like it did when she got on her fundamentalist kick a couple of years ago.

"Dad, they make a lot of sense," my daughter says, "if you take the trouble to listen to them. All she does is point out that this country has a history of violence against women that has become an epidemic. I've never paid much attention to women who identify themselves as feminists but she really isn't all that radical. Dad, I want you to be honest. Do you think Dade could be lying to you?"

I look out the kitchen window and see nothing but driving rain. The weather for the game in Knoxville this afternoon is supposed to be no better. Dade won't even be able to see the ball, much less catch it, if it doesn't clear up a little. "Sure, he could be. That's always a possibility. But after listening to him for two days, I'm convinced he's not."

"Do you realize how common date rape is?" Sarah asks. "It happens a lot."

"I don't doubt it. But the problem with statistics is they don't help you decide if a particular male at one moment in history did or didn't commit rape. It's like saying women don't do as well at math as men and then making a prediction about how you're going to do on a test."

"That's not the point," Sarah says. "A student has been accused of a violent crime, and it's business as usual. That's wrong. He should at least have been suspended from the team until this is over."

"Why?" I argue. "Why should one student have that

kind of power over another? Dade is no threat to her. All he wants to do is play football."

"He shouldn't be allowed to!" my daughter says emphatically. "She's quit the cheerleading squad; it should be the other way around."

This is interesting news. Maybe some of her colleagues will be more likely to talk to me about her if she's no longer around. "I think she's overreacting," I say unsympathetically. "I doubt if Dade would try to assault her in front of fifty thousand people."

"Don't you understand, Dad?" Sarah almost shrieks. "She feels ashamed. Everybody knows who she is. She's been degraded and humiliated by this. Her life is going to be affected forever, and everyone else is acting as if it's only the accused who has rights. What about her right as a student to be believed, to be taken seriously? The police believed her enough to file charges, at least."

"The assistant prosecutor," I correct her, and then explain he may have been influenced by personal considerations. I add, "She'll be taken seriously in court, and the likelihood is that because Dade is black and the jury will be white, he won't be. Women can complain all they want to about the difficulty of proving a rape charge, but when the accused is a black male, it's a different story." Despite trying to keep my voice under control, I know I am almost shouting at her. "Besides," I add trying to lighten things a bit, "Dade may be our kinfolk."

As soon as the words are out of my mouth, I wish I hadn't said anything. Sarah exclaims, "What are you talking about? How could he be?"

"He's not at all," I say hastily and then have to explain

about Lucy Cunningham's visit and her remark and then my mother's denial. "It's the rankest kind of gossip, but once it gets started, people will repeat it for the next fifty years. I know how the President feels. If you believe what you hear, he's gone to bed with every woman except Mother Teresa."

"But it was Dade's great-grandmother," Sarah says, refusing to laugh. "His mother ought to know whether it was true or not."

"No, she doesn't!" I say sharply. "She knows gossip. She knows what she's been told. Just because somebody repeats a story doesn't make it true. When are you going to learn that?"

Sarah's voice loses some of its certainty. "Is his great-grandmother still alive?"

"I don't think so," I say, though I have no idea. This is a closed subject as far as I'm concerned.

Knowing I don't want to pursue this subject, Sarah returns to the reason she called. "If people didn't care about winning so much, Dade would probably be off the team," she says stubbornly.

I start to tell Sarah about what I have heard about Coach Carter and his reputation for sticking up for players, but the truth of Sarah's remark is self-evident. The pressure to win must be factored in somewhere, whether it is acknowledged or not. "We blow it up all out of proportion," I concede. "You might be right." I do not want to alienate Sarah. Nobody is more important to me. I tell her that I will watch the game this afternoon on TV with Dan but omit telling her about my date with Amy tonight. I don't want to get her started on how young Amy is. We talk a few more minutes about nothing in particular, and I hang up, wishing I had warned her not to get too caught up with WAR. I don't have anything in particular against the women's movement, but I know women, just like men, can find reasons to feel they've been given a raw deal. Hell, she could have been born a Muslim woman in Bosnia. Now *those* women have something to complain about.

At two Dan comes over to watch the game, wearing a "Hog Hat," a red plastic contraption complete with snout that looks ridiculous but is in great demand. He is also carrying in a cooler of beer, which he seems already to have sampled. "Go, Hogs!" he screams as he sits the cooler down beside the couch in my den. "Kill the bastards! Cripple 'em! Tear their heads off! Rah! Rah! Rah!"

I laugh, knowing Dan doesn't really care about the game. In fact, he visibly flinches at a particularly vicious tackle. It's the beer and comradeship he enjoys. I take a Miller Lite and tell myself to go slow. The last thing I want to do tonight is nod off at nine o'clock. "I still can't believe I'm taking that dependency-neglect case you ought to be doing," I chide him as the Razorbacks kick off. "I'll get you back, don't think I won't."

Dan plows into the cheese dip I have provided, using a tortilla chip like a road grader. "You're a miracle worker," he says, grinning. "You'll get her off. You know as well as I do that Dade Cunningham ought to be here watching with us instead of getting his butt soaked in Knoxville. Did you bribe Carter or what?"

As the game progresses, I tell him what has occurred. Dan may not be much of a courtroom lawyer, but he usually displays some common sense as long as it is not related to his personal life. While we talk, the Hogs look tight as if all of them are feeling the pressure, not just Dade. Tennessee scores twice in the first quarter and would have scored again in the first half but fumbles inside the ten yard line. On offense Jay Madison, the Hogs' quarterback, overthrows Dade twice, once for what would have been an easy touchdown. Open underneath a deep zone coverage, Dade has caught five short passes but has dropped one in a critical third-down situation. Once he does catch it, he runs without authority, unlike the first five weeks of the season when he averaged twenty yards a reception.

As the teams come off the field at halftime, Dan mutters, "What's the fuss all about? They couldn't beat their way out of a paper bag."

I open only my third beer of the day and push the "mute" button. "They can't even blame the weather," I say gloomily. The rain has stopped, leaving the turf slick, which gives the offense an advantage, since it presumably knows where it is going.

"Carter might want to take advantage of the halftime and make some calls for a job in the Knoxville area," Dan cracks. "He bet on the wrong horse. I almost feel sorry for him. What's he really like? He looks like he's a hundred years old."

I watch Carter on the screen trotting with his head down to the visitors' dressing room. His eyes appear to be almost shut and his lips moving. "He's praying for a stroke," Dan hoots, "so he won't have to come back out on the field."

"That or a drink," I say, marveling at the pressure men put themselves under. No wonder we die sooner than women. "He's probably not a bad guy, just in over his head like the rest of us. He gave me the impression that he cares about Dade, but who knows? He's got a lot riding on him."

"Like you, huh?" Dan says softly. I have told him how much I would like to negotiate a pro contract for Dade.

"Like me," I admit.

In the second half the Razorbacks play like a different team. Dade catches six passes in the third quarter alone and runs like a wild man, scoring twice, and with the second extra point the score is tied at 14 to 14. In the fourth quarter Dade takes some sickening hits as the Vols' safety, gambling now that he isn't going long, time after time explodes against his back just as the ball reaches him. "He's going to need a bone surgeon just to scrape him off the field," Dan says, wincing after a particularly brutal tackle. Still, Dade holds onto the ball.

"What did Carter tell them at halftime?" I ask, delighted with the change in their play.

"He's a genius, all right," admits Dan. "*We* can't even get Julia to take her turn at making the coffee. Maybe Carter can come to the office and give a talk on motivation."

With Tennessee leading 17 to 14 with five minutes to go, the Hogs begin their final drive from their thirty. Double-teamed now, Dade is used as a decoy until in the final minute, he slants across the middle and catches the ball without breaking stride and reaches the three when he is crushed by two huge tacklers. After a timeout, with the entire crowd on its feet, according to the announcers, Jay Madison sends Dade, followed by three defenders, into the left corner of the end zone and then practically walks in untouched for the victory.

Dan and I yell and give each other high fives, startling Woogie, who watches from the end of the couch. "God, this was great," Dan says, "and I don't even care."

I am limp and almost hoarse from yelling at the TV screen. How odd that this should matter so much. I, and most of the rest of the state, will be happy the rest of the day. In large part, we have Dade Cunningham to thank for that. I hope people will remember it.

Totally out of character, Saturday night I bring Amy flowers.

"Why, Gideon, how nice!" she says, obviously flabbergasted but pleased as she opens the door. "You don't seem the type to buy a girl play pretties."

"It's pretty rare," I admit. "I'm basically cheap and unromantic but still very lovable." I hand her the flowers and wander around her living room. Amy lives in an apartment just off the freeway. It seems inevitable that I compare her to Rainey, whose living room was filled with books. I don't even see a bookcase, just pictures by artists I've never heard of. I liked Rainey's house better, with its hardwood floors and plants. But what did books ever do for our relationship? "I didn't know you were into art," I say, staring uncomprehendingly at an abstract poster.

"Still sorta, kinda, a little, I guess," Amy says, coming up beside me. "I got a degree in art history at college. Really dumb—a rich girl's major. My father was a retired factory worker in Jefferson County. He worked overtime at a paper mill in Pine Bluff so I could study in the East what Picasso was thinking about during his Cubist period. I'd come home from college every June, and Daddy would ask me what I'd learned. I think I gave him a little stroke every year. I didn't have the nerve to ask him to pay for law school."

"How'd we do it?" I say, remembering my own exhaustion during those years. Amy worked in the circuit clerk's office during the day, and walked across the street to go to school at night.

"I didn't do it very well," Amy admits. "My grades, you remember, were average."

"Better than mine," I point out. Amy is a good lawyer. In fact, she was a rising star in the prosecutor's office until she got pregnant a couple of years ago and had an abortion. Her boss, a right-to-lifer, disapproved, and Amy left shortly afterward.

At Amy's suggestion, we drive out Darnell Road to eat at the Greenhouse, a Mexican restaurant open only on the weekends. Dressed in jeans and an old Clinton-Gore T-shirt, Amy teases me as we get out of the car. "Who is celebrity lawyer Gideon Page escorting tonight to the fashionable Greenhouse restaurant? Why it's that cute, pixieish Amy Gilchrist! What a darling couple they make! A blend of ancient history and hot-off-the-press slut puppy. Page is taking her arm; no, he's leaning on her. She gently touches his face; no, she's wiping it. She murmurs sweetly into his right ear. He cups the leathery,

Perot-size orifice and shouts: 'What? What did you say?' "

Walking into the restaurant beside her, I laugh and nudge her with my elbow. "Do we look that ridiculous?" My voice is plaintive, my worst fears activated.

"If they bring a highchair for me"—she snickers—"try to take it in stride."

The Greenhouse is about as plain vanilla as restaurant decor gets. With its bare concrete walls, sturdy Formica-topped tables, and iron chairs, we won't, despite Amy's running commentary, make it into next week's society section of the paper, but the food, chicken enchiladas for both of us, is delicious and reasonably priced. "I was afraid you'd want to go out to a classy joint and spend my money," I say over bread pudding and a cup of decaf.

Amy, who is still nursing her first and only beer, shrugs. "I knew better than that. As cheap as you are, you'd pout the rest of the evening. If I were truly liber-ated, I'd offer to pay half, but I just talk a good game when it's to my advantage."

I laugh at this woman, putting me in mind of Rainey at the beginning of our relationship before she got so seri-ous. Or maybe I was the one who got too serious. Noth-ing is off-limits with Amy. In the fading moments of the late June twilight we drive further out Highway 10 to Lake Maumelle and park overlooking the water, where she asks me about Rainey. "What happened, Gideon? I thought she had you headed onto the kill floor for sure."

Marriage as slaughterhouse. I snicker at the image. As we get out of the Blazer, I wonder how to respond. "Every time we got close," I say, thinking I see a sailboat in the distance, "one of us would push the self-destruct button. It wasn't meant to be. We had our chances but wouldn't take them. She still calls occasionally to ask about Sarah."

Amy picks up a rock and throws it into the water. "She's probably still in love with you. If we start dating and I tell my friends," she says glumly, "I'll probably open up the paper and read you two have taken out a marriage license."

What an imagination this woman has! "Nope, that's over with. Actually, Rainey liked Sarah better than me. What she liked was to rescue me. It was easier than loving me."

Amy turns and says primly, "I'm not much of a rescuer."

"Well, I'm not drowning." I kiss her then. It seems as if we have been doing it for a long time. We stand in the darkness and nibble each other until the bugs get into the act, and then we drive back to her apartment where I accept her invitation to come in for a beer.

Amy seats me at her kitchen table and opens her refrigerator. "You're not going to believe this," she says. "I forgot I was out."

I come around behind her and look. The inside is as bare as my own. What do single people eat? She has three Diet Cokes on the bottom rack, and a jar of orange juice on the top with nothing in between. "I cleaned out the refrigerator today in case you tried to inspect it," she adds.

As with so many of her remarks, I don't know whether this one is serious or not. "I think the point is," I say with mock solemnity, "there is supposed to be food in here, but I'll give you an 'A' for effort. It's really clean."

"Whew!" she says, shutting the door and leaning back against me. "I was afraid I wasn't gonna pass."

"You passed," I concede. We resume kissing then, and after a few moments she leads me into her bedroom where we make love. Amy is as passionate as I thought she would be. She seems pleased with my efforts, too, afterward, lying back against her pillows and smiling contentedly in the soft glow of the lamp beside her bed. I think I'm going to like this woman.

At home, in my own bed, I wonder why Rainey and I never made love all those months. Too complicated for her own good, she spent a lot of time picking at life as if it were part of the DNA chain she had to unravel. Amy is more direct and so much less analytical. What did Amy and I talk about tonight? The game, the Razorbacks, her work, not much really. Rainey could get so damn moralistic. I'd like to keep things with Amy simple for a while if I can. It's a nice change.

SUNDAY AND MONDAY the news from Fayetteville is mixed. As I work to rearrange my schedule so I can get up there the last part of the week, it is obvious that the pressure on the university to discipline Dade is building. According to the *Democrat-Gazette,* WAR's Sunday night rally attracted a crowd of four hundred people, including faculty members. The administration was denounced as "totally and irreversibly sexist," and Paula Crawford, WAR's leader, demanded that Coach Carter and Jack Burke, the athletic director, resign. Yet, there is no doubt Dade's performance against Tennessee has helped him. In the letters-to-the-editor column two self-identified "fans" recite Carter's argument that if Dade is kicked off the team or disciplined now, he will be denied due process of law. University officials were quoted as saying they would have a statement later in the week.

Monday night I notice in the mailbox a letter from Fayetteville in Sarah's neat handwriting. I open the door and let Woogie out in the darkness by himself (he is hungry and will be back within fifteen minutes), and mystified, I sit down to read the letter at the kitchen table over

133

a beer. I never get a letter from her at school. On her word processor, which I am still paying off, she has written:

Dear Dad:

As you know, I've been going to some meetings sponsored by WAR, but I've also attended a couple of workshops they put on over the weekend. You could call them "consciousness-raising" sessions, I guess. As I've told you, I never identified with the term "feminist" before, and I'm still not sure I know what it means, but Paula and some of her group have made me think about some things that I hadn't realized before. Since it is hard for me to talk to you sometimes (you can be real intimidating!), I thought I'd try to write about them. Here goes:

Did you ever realize that I've spent half my life on a diet? Ever since I was ten, I've thrown away good food and then got hungry later and ate junk. Then, I'd have to diet some more. All my friends in high school were like that. Do you remember Amber Norworthy? She used to make herself throw up in the bathroom at high school after her mother caught her doing it at home. I can see now in retrospect that Betty Davenport was anorexic. Lots of other girls I knew were close to it.

Ever since I was little, I've spent my entire life worrying about how I look, how much I weigh, and how I measure up in comparison to other girls. I know Mom looked great all the time, but I don't think she liked all the emphasis on her appearance as much as you did. She was from a culture even more macho than the U.S.

In South America women are even more objects than we are here. You should know that.

The Women's Movement was supposed to make us free. Well, we aren't! We are slaves to cosmetics, body surgery, diets, pornography (look at the ads in magazines), and violence against women. I didn't understand any of this before I joined WAR. I thought women who joined groups like this were just bitter because they couldn't compete against women who were more attractive. That's not true! They just quit accepting all that garbage about how women are supposed to look and act in society.

Even before I went to school, Mom painted me up like a little doll. My fingernails, my toenails—I wore makeup even before junior high! You probably don't remember because you never really paid attention. You just assumed that was the way it was supposed to be. I don't blame Mom. She was just too brainwashed by her culture before she got over here.

Dad, I would really like for you to talk to Paula. She is so smart. I know you're a big supporter of individual rights and free speech, but I bet she could convince you that all pornography ought to be banned because it's harmful to women. She says it can be banned because it can be interpreted as a violation of the Equal Protection Clause of the 14th Amendment. I don't understand the legal arguments but you would.

I know some kids (guys, mainly) resent the new sexual harassment policy on campus, but all it means is that if you sexually harass somebody, you're denying them an equal opportunity at an education. I know I sound simplistic, but Paula and some of the others can explain these things really well.

I know what you're thinking—that I'm going off the deep end again—like the time I joined Christian Life. Please don't have a knee-jerk reaction like you usually do. You always overreact to everything!

I want you to do something for me: I want you to ask the judge to let you no longer be Dade's attorney if you become convinced that he is guilty. What if it had been me he raped? Would you want him to go free?

Please don't make any more cracks about women burning their bras! This group is not like that.

Love,

Sarah

P.S. I've quit jv cheerleading even though I think I had a good chance of being a Razorback cheerleader next year. It's really just kind of a sex show—women in skimpy, tight outfits performing for men. I want to have more control over what happens to me instead of just reacting to the prevailing culture, which, you'll have to admit, is pretty sick. I'll see you later this week.

I read the letter twice. I should have seen this coming, I think, as I swallow more beer. Sarah is always vulnerable to whatever comes along at the moment. If I hadn't been so nuts after Rosa died, none of this would be happening. What gets into her? How does she think I'm going to make a living if I defend only people I know are innocent? And what is wrong with being beautiful? Actually, it wouldn't bother me in the slightest if she didn't feel as if she had to spend as much money on clothes as she does. Unless she shaves her head, she's going to be gorgeous, no matter what. I scan the letter again. I never knew she worried about being fat. She never has been even close to being five pounds overweight. And if researchers have proved a direct casual link between pornography and physical violence against women, I've missed it. Up until now it's always been the right wing that wanted to ban porno shops and movies. This is ridiculous! My apolitical daughter becoming left wing and going so far around the bend she's meeting conservatives on the other side. I can't believe she's quit cheerleading. Regardless of the cost, I was all set to make every home game for the next two years just to see her. Damn these groups! They get their teeth in you and won't let go until you're a carbon copy of them.

Desperate to find out what this all means, I call Amy and launch into a feverish description of what Sarah has been doing. "It just sounds like they're trying to make her feel guilty about being who she is," I say, without letting Amy get a word in edgewise. "In one paragraph she goes from screaming about the cosmetics industry to pornography. I don't get it. It sounds like if you're beautiful, you should burn yourself at the stake to make these women happy. What the hell's going on up there?"

"Whoa, boy!" Amy commands, giggling at my hyperbole. "I suspect you're like a lot of people, including women, and are pretty confused by what's going on today in what passes for the women's movement. I'll grant you it's pretty weird. At one end you've got people like Catharine MacKinnon, a law professor, who truly believes there is a relationship between pornography and violence against women and would ban it; but, then there're women like Camille Paglia who say that women are buying into a victim psychology that wrongly defines us as weak and powerless. I can identify especially with the part about her physical appearance. I've spent my whole life trying to look, as my mother says, perky and cute, since I don't have a chance of looking like the Sarahs of this world. As a case in point I've barely eaten anything since I gorged myself Saturday night, so I know how Sarah feels."

"But she's never been fat a day in her life!" I say, remembering all the times when Sarah complained about her appearance although she looked perfect.

"Society has made us worry about it constantly," Amy responds. "You'd have to be a woman to really understand it."

I sip at my beer, which I have brought into the kitchen. "I don't see why she quit cheerleading," I gripe. "That seemed harmless enough to me. It's not like they got out there naked."

"I admire her for it," Amy claims. "It took guts to give it up. Most of us don't do anything but talk."

A lot of people are better off that way, too. "When this dies down," I predict, "she'll regret it."

Amy says, quietly, "It sounds to me like you don't take Sarah too seriously."

"I do, too," I reply hastily. "It's just that I don't want her to be overly influenced and do things she'll wish she hadn't."

"Gideon, you want her to make mistakes you approve of and not her own. Don't forget she's twenty years old."

That must sound old to Amy. "She's still a child," I respond. "I know her. She's like a lamb being led to the slaughter."

"How ridiculous!" she says affectionately. "I forget how melodramatic you are."

"When it comes to Sarah," I confess, "I don't have much perspective. I guess it's just that I've got her close to being grown up, and I don't want her to blow it."

"Are you crazy?" Amy says, sounding almost smug. "You know there's no magic age when humans stop screwing up. Look at us."

In the last couple of days Amy and I have talked on the phone, and I have probably confided in her more than I should. I find myself telling her about Rosa, Sarah, even discussing my relationship with Rainey. She seems wise beyond her years, but it comes as no surprise to me that most women have more insight into relationships than men. But, as she says, it doesn't keep them from messing up their lives. Her abortion was a case in point. Only last night she told me about an affair she'd had with one of the men in the prosecutor's office when she worked there. He was terrible, but she'd fallen head over heels in love with him. "I thought you'd be more sympathetic," I complain. Rainey, with a daughter older than Sarah, would have been reassuring.

"I am sympathetic to her," Amy says dryly. "You don't want her to grow as a woman because it threatens you. I think you should be proud that she's involved in something more than boys or cheerleading. She's trying to deal with things that are important to women, and she's willing to challenge you. Lots of girls her age would keep their mouths shut and their hands out."

"Sarah's never done that," I say. "She's always been on my case."

"Poor Gideon!" Amy teases. "What a hard life he has!"

"Wait'll you have children," I say irritably. "It's not as easy to raise them as you apparently think."

"Don't be such a baby!" Amy says uncharitably. "Sarah's doing great. If you have any sense, you'll support her in this."

I'm ready to end this conversation and am rescued by Woogie, who is scratching at the front door. I hang up after telling her that I will call her when I get back. We're supposed to go out again this weekend.

While I am giving Woogie his dinner (a good reason not to be a dog), the phone rings again. "Mr. Page," Dade says, his voice anxious, "I've been trying to get hold of you. I got something in my mailbox telling me there's gonna be a hearing on Friday at ten."

"Who's it from?" I ask, thinking how inevitable it was that the university would get involved. Despite the signs, like an idiot, I had harbored the hope that somebody would make the decision to let it be resolved in court. I should have started preparing for this last week.

"A woman named Clarise Dozier. It says she's the Co-ordinator of Judicial Affairs. It says to contact her for a prehearing conference where she'll explain my rights."

"I want you to call her tomorrow first thing and tell her you and I'll be in her office at ten. Find out where to go."

"Am I gonna be kicked out of school?" Dade asks. "Can they do that?"

He is scared. I can hear it in his voice. That damn group WAR. The university couldn't stand the heat. Yet, if I were the father of the girl, I'd be screaming they should have done this five minutes after criminal charges were filed. "No," I tell him, "you're not going to be kicked out of school. Let Coach Carter or one of the coaches know what's going on. I'll call you about nine-thirty tomorrow morning and find out where to meet you. By the way," I add, trying to relax him, "you had a great game against Tennessee. Think y'all can beat Georgia?"

"I don't know," Dade mumbles.

He sounds as if he is in shock. "Listen to me," I say sharply. "Until somebody in authority says otherwise, you're still on the team. So you have to make the most of it. How you did last Saturday is going to affect some of the people who will be sitting in judgment on you, no matter how much they'll pretend it doesn't. I'll try to get it delayed so that you can keep playing. Maybe we can drag it out until after the season is over. You've got to practice and stay focused like you're playing for the SEC title this weekend, you hear me?"

"Yes, sir," Dade answers. I can barely hear him.

After he hangs up, I realize I didn't even ask him what else the notice said. I try to call him back, but his line is busy. It doesn't matter what the paper says. We both know what can happen. The university can do whatever it wants if it takes the trouble to go through the motions. Yet, who is really the boss hog? The chancellor? Hell, the governor may be calling the shots for all I know. I fight

down a panicky feeling. If he does get kicked out of
school, the effort to keep him playing will have back-
fired. Maybe I should have advised Dade to request a sus-
pension from the team until after his trial. That might
have headed off this hearing. I call Barton's number to
find out the name of the lawyer I blew off last week. No
answer. Shit. Four days. This is a rush job if there ever
was one. I dial Sarah's number but get her answering machine. Relieved (I don't know what I would have said), I
leave a message that I will call her tomorrow.

I hang up and realize I was going to drop Woogie off at
his kennel on my way out of town. Now I won't have
time. I call Amy, who says she'll be glad to take him.
Would she be calling me to ask me to do the same thing
for her? Probably not. I hate to use Amy, but the truth is,
she is so damn user-friendly.

Clarise Dozier's office is on the second floor of the
Student Union across from the library. She is a tall, smiling woman of about my age, but her gray hair, pulled
back in a bun, and the vanilla-colored shawl she has
draped around her shoulders make her look distinctly
grandmotherly. She takes my hand and looks me in the
eye. "I'm glad you could come with Dade, Mr. Page. Unless you've done one of these cases before, the hearing
Friday will probably be quite a bit different from anything you've experienced. Please have a seat. Can I get
either of you some coffee?"

Dade shakes his head, but I say, "Thank you," taken
slightly off guard by her unexpected courtesy and friend-
liness. We could be here to dispute a parking ticket. If she

is uncomfortable at being in the presence of an alleged rapist, I can't tell it. I look around her office and notice mainly photographs of campus architectural projects under construction. I recognize Bud Walton Arena, the new home of the Razorback basketball team. Seating about twenty thousand people, it is a magnificent structure. A good omen, I tell myself.

After handing me my coffee, Ms. Dozier warns me, "Frankly, lawyers find our hearing procedures a little unsettling. Are you at all familiar with what we do?"

I do not say I received and mostly ignored a mini-lecture on the subject from a Fayetteville lawyer just last week and ask for a full explanation. Rubbing her hands together as if she knows she has her work cut out for her, she nods. "Well, we view the hearing process as a part of the educational mission of the university. Punishment is not our goal here, education is, and, if warranted by the facts, that can entail correction."

She makes this statement with a straight face. Doubtless, this message is appropriate when someone has been accused of playing his stereo too loud, but I suspect that if the board finds that Dade is guilty of what he's been charged with, it will entail more than writing one hundred times on the blackboard: I won't rape Robin anymore.

"What is the burden of proof?" I ask, looking down at the form that Dade handed me on the way over. It lists Robin as one of four witnesses. The other three are identified as Robin's roommate, a woman from the local Rape Crisis Center, and a nurse from Memorial Hospital. It has already occurred to me that this proceeding will be useful for discovery purposes. Arkansas does not require witnesses to talk to opposing counsel in criminal cases before trial. Depositions are not allowed, so I can't force a witness in a criminal case to say a single word. All I can do is get the statements they gave to the prosecutor.

"The same as in civil court cases," Ms. Dozier says. "Fifty-one percent. I'll just run through the procedure, if you don't mind, and then you can ask questions."

"Fine," I say, feeling like a schoolkid in front of this woman who surely was a teacher at one time.

Ms. Dozier refers to a sheet of paper on her desk and says: "Let me start with the individuals who will hear this case. The All-University Judiciary is made up of nine people—five faculty members, one of whom is the chairperson, and four students. Dade will have a right to have present two counselors who may advise him but who can't speak or ask questions. This isn't like a case in court where the judge acts like a referee for the lawyers. It is much more informal than that. We aren't bound by hearsay rules or rules of evidence, though, of course, the 'J' Board takes the source of information into account in assessing credibility. The hearing is closed to the public and confidential. The complaining party and respondent each have the opportunity to make an opening statement. The members of the board and the opposing parties can then ask questions of the witnesses and each other. Dade will be allowed to summarize his position at the end, a closing statement, if you will, and so will the complaining party. I've written down the names and positions of the witnesses who'll be called by the complaining party. They include her roommate, a woman from the Rape Crisis Center who met the complaining party at the hospital, and a nurse there."

As the woman drones on, I realize quickly why this procedure drives lawyers crazy: we don't get to do anything to help our clients except whisper in their ears. Dade could hang himself if we aren't careful. "What is the range of possible punishments?" I ask.

"Educative sanctions," Ms. Dozier insists on saying, "range from probation to expulsion. The board also could suspend the student from representation of the university in intercollegiate activities." She hands me some papers labeled, "Student Judicial System Procedural Code," and the list containing the names of the witnesses and adds, "This contains everything I'm saying and more. You'll notice that appeals go to the vice-chancellor and chancellor, but there is no rehearing of the facts by them. Finally, the chancellor reviews the decision of the vice-chancellor."

I flip through the papers. "How do I formally request that the hearing be postponed?" I ask. "Three days isn't much time to prepare when so much is at stake."

Ms. Dozier's smile disappears. "You could ask Dr. Ward, the faculty member who presides over the board, but I don't think you should expect it to be postponed. Actually, it is in the university's discretion to require immediate expulsion and have a hearing later."

Her tone leaves no doubt that had the decision been left up to her, Dade would have been living off campus by now. I may still ask for a postponement. "Are you a member of the board?" I ask.

"I'll be there," she assures me, "but only in my capacity as coordinator. I have no vote."

Good, I think but do not say. "Dade," I ask, "do you have any questions?"

Dade shrugs. "No." He seems intimidated by Ms. Dozier, whose voice has become increasingly stern. I have my doubts about his ability to ask any meaningful questions at the hearing. Of course, that is what lawyers are for.

I stand, followed by Dade. "I'll call you if I have any questions," I promise Ms. Dozier, whose smile has returned now that we are leaving.

"That will be fine," she says. "The hearing will be down the hall in room two-thirteen."

"We've got a lot of work to do between now and Friday," I tell Dade once we get outside. "I want you to get in touch with Eddie Stiles and the four people who you told me were at the party last spring with you and Robin. Tell them you need them to meet me at the Ozark Motel at ten tomorrow. Try to see if any of your friends know anything about Robin and her roommate. And let your mother know about the hearing. Tell her I'll be calling her, okay?"

"Yes, sir," Dade replies, his voice listless.

"Come on now!" I snap at him. "It's really going to be just your word against hers. This isn't going to be any picnic for her either. You can do this."

"She talks real good," Dade says, not quite looking me in the eye.

A pretty black girl, dressed in a beige sweater and tight jeans, yells in our direction: "Come here, Dade!"

This is not the time or place for a pep talk. Students, several of them black, look over at us from a huge bulletin board where they are gathered. This must be where the black students hang out. I see more here than I have on the rest of the campus combined except for Darby Hall, the athletic dorm. "Believe me," I whisper, "she'll be a lot more nervous than you will. I'll see you tonight. I'm going to the prosecutor's office and see if I can get the statements she and the others have given."

Dade nods again perfunctorily, and I head for my car, wishing I knew what I could say to him that would get his head off his chest. Yet, I have the same discouraged feeling that is registered on my client's face. If Dade were going to appear before a group of kids like himself, he would have more of a chance. Instead, I have no doubt the students on the "J" Board will resemble Robin (in more ways than just skin color) instead of him. Surely, there will be one black face, but all it will take to "discipline" him will be a majority vote. As I unlock the Blazer, I think of Marty's comments about blacks and nearly laugh out loud. I don't think she would choose to trade places with Dade right now.

Binkie Cross, the Washington County prosecuting attorney, has the bearing of a hillbilly—not the wormy, inbred sodomite who buggered poor Ned Beatty in *Deliverance*, but the rugged, lean, born individualist to whom the law is at best a painful necessity. At six-five he towers over me in an ugly brown suit that is too short in the sleeves and pants. Oblivious to his appearance, he sticks out his hand and swallows mine in his. "Sorry, I missed

you last week," he says. "I was on vacation. Call me
Binkie, by the way. Everybody else does."

"That's all right," I say, deciding not to mention that I
heard his vacation was being cut short. He may feel he
needs to protect his assistant, and I don't want to make
him defensive. "I'd just like to get a copy of the file, and I
was told only you could let me have it."

Binkie winces as if he had been reminded of an unpleasant conversation. He invites me to sit down, then
says candidly, "I would have preferred that my deputy
wait until I was back in town to file a charge that serious."

I nod, delighted to hear him say this. "I wish he had
too, because I don't think my client is guilty of anything
but some incredibly bad judgment."

"How do you mean?" Cross says casually, as if we
were colleagues instead of on opposing sides. He looks
about my age, and I wonder if he went to school up here.

"To hear him tell it," I respond, "sex was her idea,
more than his. If you've seen this kid, you realize in a
hurry he's not lacking for female companionship."

"How come he didn't talk to the police?" Binkie asks.
"If he had, I doubt if Mike would have been in such a
hurry to charge him."

"Kids have seen a million cop shows on TV where the
Miranda warnings are given," I say. "It probably wasn't
such a bad idea at the time. I'll bring him down to talk to
you anytime you want. I'd like to get this university hearing out of the way first though."

Binkie reaches into his desk and pulls out a manila
folder and hands it to me. "I had this made for you Mon-

day," he says. "I think it's up to date. The girl's statement is near the top."

"I appreciate it," I say, genuinely relieved I'm not getting another runaround. He knows that I don't want Dade talking to him until I've seen the evidence against him. "How was your trip?" I ask, deciding I like this guy. He doesn't seem as if he is going to make me jump through any unnecessary hoops. To impress the voters, some prosecutors will make you play games with them from start to finish. Maybe he's not going to run again. That would be fine with me.

A slow smile spreads to Binkie's sunburned face. "Damn, it was wonderful!" he says enthusiastically. "My wife and I were bushwacking through a provincial park outside of Vancouver and we walked right up on this big ol' brown bear. I guess the look on our faces scared him because he took off the other way. If he hadn't, we would have become permanent residents. God, it's pretty country up there," he adds wistfully.

"The closest I've come is a nature program on TV," I confess, "but I've heard it's wonderful." Poor guy. He sounds as if he had died and gone to heaven. I'm lucky he didn't come back mad. I would have if my vacation had been interrupted. "I'll be happy to produce Dade for some blood, hair, and saliva samples the first of next week," I say, trying to appear equally cooperative. "You don't need to file a motion."

"Why don't you bring him in next Wednesday at eleven?" Binkie says, looking down at his calendar. "I've got some time that day to take his statement."

I pull out my calendar. Hell, I might as well move up

here. "That's fine," I say, eager to leave so I can go over the file.

Binkie looks at me square in the face. "I knew Chet Bracken," he says. "You must have been pretty good if he wanted you to work with him."

Now I understand the reason for the respect I am getting. I don't say that if he knew the circumstances of my relationship with Chet he wouldn't be impressed. "Chet was the one who was pretty good," I say.

"He was the best damn trial lawyer I ever saw," Binkie says flatly.

I don't disagree, but at the time I knew him Chet was riddled with cancer and couldn't think straight for more than an hour at a time. I stick out my hand again. "Maybe in the next couple of weeks we can figure out what really happened. I know the last thing a prosecutor wants to do is to send an innocent kid to jail."

As I hoped, Binkie does not give me an automatic response. He clasps my hand and looks me in the eye. "If I'm not convinced this boy raped her," he says earnestly, "I'll dismiss the charge. You can take that to the bank."

"I'll hold you to it." Maybe I'm a fool, but I believe this man. He doesn't seem the type who needs any trophies on the wall. Indeed, he doesn't display even a single diploma. Behind him are pictures of him and presumably his family in the mountains. If he is as decent as he appears, we might not have to try this case.

In my room at the Ozark, I begin to have some real hope. Robin's statement, and that of her roommate, Shannon Kennsit, aren't as strong as I feared. Robin's explanation of why she waited a full nine hours to go to the hospital comes across, on the printed page, as vague and not particularly believable. According to her, she was afraid that she would get in trouble with her parents because they would think she had been dating someone black, when, in fact, they had only been friends. Too, she was afraid nobody would believe her because of the incidents involving athletes in the past. What incidents? She doesn't say. According to Shannon Kennsit, it was she who convinced Robin that she had to go to the hospital and report the rape. On this point, Robin seems to suggest that she had been planning to go to the police when the shock of what happened had worn off. She claimed to be in a daze when she had returned to the Chi Omega House that night and had gone straight to her room and had taken a shower, telling no one what had happened until four that morning when she had awakened Shannon with her crying. She didn't remember if anybody had seen her when she came in.

On some points, with the exception of the sexual encounter itself, her story resembles Dade's, but, of course, here it differs dramatically. He was the aggressor; he grabbed her arm and said, "Don't make me have to hurt you." He forced her to undress and get in the shower with him. The questioner, a Detective Farley, got her to state there had been penetration (as he had to for there to be a charge of rape), but she was vague on other details. All she had come over to do was to work on the speech with him. They had been friends since the spring. She'd had nothing to drink. It was obvious that Dade had a couple of beers at least, but she hadn't thought he was too drunk to work on the speech. He had let her go afterward with the warning that if she told anyone, no one would believe it was rape, and he would smear her name all over campus.

The statements of the Rape Crisis counselor and the hospital nurse are predictably supportive. They were already preprogrammed to believe Robin and accordingly interpreted her every act and emotion as consistent with someone who had been raped. It crosses my mind that by the time she went to the police she may have convinced herself that Dade had raped her. Consensual sex became an act of force. If people can convince themselves they've been kidnapped by aliens and then returned safely to earth, concocting a rape story and then believing it should be a simple enough task for a college girl who has all night to dream it up.

My stomach growls, letting me know it is already past noon. I walk across College Avenue to a Burger King and order a Whopper. I sit next to a window in relative peace, mulling over the possibilities of what actually happened. Robin could easily be telling the truth; yet, for all I know, this could be the tenth lie she's told this year. It would be nice to know what her credibility level is. How do I find out about her? Dade may or may not be much help. I doubt if he spends a lot of time at the Chi Omega House. Sarah must know a dozen kids who are at least aware of Robin's reputation if she doesn't already know it. I get up and call her from the pay phone and leave a message on her machine that I'm in town. It should be an interesting conversation if I ever get hold of her. I got your letter and think you've lost your mind.

Typically, a no-win situation with my daughter. She won't be satisfied with anything short of total surrender.

I pick up a copy of the *Democrat-Gazette* and see an article in the second section on Dade's hearing. So much for confidentiality. WAR will probably hold a rally outside the Union calling for Dade's castration, I think gloomily. Yet how could I expect that information to remain a secret? I myself told Dade to tell the coaches. Suddenly, it hits me that Coach Carter would make a perfect character witness for Dade at the hearing. Even if the faculty and student members of the "J" Board pretend that it's no big deal for the Razorback football coach to appear before them, it would be, and some of them will be influenced whether they admit it or not. If Carter had a losing record, it might be a different story, but the Hogs for the first time in years are now ranked in the top ten, thanks to the win over Tennessee. There can't be five people on the campus who don't know about the game this weekend with number one ranked Alabama.

Back at the Ozark, I call Carter's office and am told by his secretary that he is in a meeting. Undoubtedly he is with his assistant coaches drawing up a game plan for the Crimson Tide. The best time to get him, I realize, is late at night. I leave my name and number and say it is important.

Then I call the Cunninghams collect and report on the upcoming hearing. Roy, who takes the call in his store, asks the same question as his son: Is Dade going to be kicked out of school? I assure him, without the slightest evidence to back me up, that his son is in no danger of being separated from the campus. I know he and Lucy will be talking to Dade before Friday, and any lack of confidence I convey to them will get back to Dade. Acting in effect as his own lawyer at the hearing, Dade must not panic. I promise to let them know as soon as we get a decision and hang up, knowing how helpless they both must feel.

Resigned to a sickening long-distance bill, I call Dan and ask him for some names of kids at the university who might know something about Robin. "Doesn't Brenda have some friends who have kids up here who are sorority types?" I ask. Brenda, not Dan, had family money in the beginning of the marriage. She has always struck me as the kind of woman who still goes up for alumnae weekends and bores the girls to death. "I need to get the inside skinny on the girl and I can't get my own daughter to do any of my legwork for me."

"Brenda and I haven't spoken to each other for weeks," Dan laughs.

"What else is new?" I say half seriously. I never know how to take Dan on the subject of his marriage. He and Brenda appear to me to have a terrible relationship, but seem determined to outlast each other. He has me on the speakerphone. I hear a crackling sound. As usual, he must be eating something and needs both hands. If he doesn't die of heart disease, nobody should.

"Hell, I know a couple of kids who are up there," Dan says. "Want me to call 'em and see if they'll talk to you?"

Bless Dan's soul. Of course, he owes me for taking on his prostitute. "If you would," I say sincerely, "I'd be grateful. Dade's got a university administrative hearing Friday, and it'd be nice to find out that the victim was a known pathological liar. Apparently, they'll let in the worst gossip imaginable. You ought to be up here. This is your kind of law practice."

Dan snickers appreciatively. "What's your number? I'll call you back when I hear something."

I tell him and get off the phone. It's my dime. While I am working on some questions that Dade can ask of Robin and her witnesses, I get a call from Carter's secretary telling me to hold on for him. Normally, I can't stand people who are too self-important to make their own calls, but I make an exception for Carter. We need him too bad. "Carter," he barks. "Is this Page?"

"Coach," I plunge in, "we need your help at the hearing. I'd like for you to be a character witness for Dade. As you know, they could kick him out of school, not just off the team."

For an instant I think I've lost the connection, but Carter comes back on after a moment and says, "I'll have to think about it. They're scorching my butt over this."

I don't doubt it. "You're getting a lot of support, too, though," I guess, although my actual knowledge is limited to the two letters in the paper.

"Some," he admits. "But I haven't exactly made myself popular with the university bigwigs. A lot of 'em wanted me to suspend Dade the rest of the season. It's not just pressure. I've had some calls from administrators who sincerely believe he shouldn't be playing until he's had his trial. Hell, my own wife thinks I did the wrong thing."

This confession is alarming. If it gets out that Carter is having second thoughts, Dade won't have a chance. "I've finally gotten the statements of the witnesses if you want to see them," I tell him, trying not to sound as if I'm begging. "I'm even more convinced now that Dade didn't do anything the girl didn't want done. She corroborates everything Dade told you except for the alleged rape itself. It's just her word against his. Her roommate sure doesn't help her, and the nurse and the Rape Crisis woman just say what you'd expect. What you said at that press conference last week is truer today than when you said it. He shouldn't be punished until he's had his day in court."

"Bring the statements by in an envelope and drop 'em off with my secretary," Carter instructs. "I suspect we both want this kept confidential, so I'll burn 'em when I'm through."

"I'll get them to you in the next hour," I promise. I hang up, wondering how cynical Carter's decision to keep Dade on the team really was. Maybe, down deep, there's a little bleeding-heart lawyer trying to get out. Somehow, I doubt it. Coaches at this level know the public wants only one thing—and that's to win.

As I look through the Yellow Pages to find a copy place, the phone rings. It is Sarah. "I got your letter, babe," I say carefully. "It was interesting."

"Dad!" she yells into my ear. "I blew your mind! You can admit it. Have you thought about what I asked you to do?"

Anxious to drop off the statements, I plead a standard excuse. "You mean withdraw? I haven't had time, but I will."

"At least come to the rally tonight, okay?" Sarah says. "You've got to hear Paula. Even if you don't agree with her, I think you'll be impressed. It's at seven in front of the Student Union."

"I'm running around like a chicken with its head cut off getting ready for this hearing on Friday," I explain, trying not to sound irritated. "But if I can come, I'll drop by."

"It's the last one being permitted on campus this week," Sarah says. "There's a rumor that Robin is going to speak."

"Be identified publicly?" I ask, skeptical. "I thought she had quit cheerleading because of all the trauma."

"She probably felt ashamed," Sarah says, "until some-one explained that it was Dade who ought to feel too ashamed to show his face in public. That's what our soci-ety does to women."

Maybe I will come after all. "Are you sure you did the right thing in quitting?" I ask, unable to keep my mouth shut. "You really seemed to enjoy it."

"Absolutely," Sarah assures me. "I was willingly par-ticipating in my own exploitation."

For God's sake! "What do you mean?" I ask, knowing I don't want to hear this answer.

"For example," Sarah says earnestly, "women who act in pornography films are often physically and emotion-ally coerced into it. They don't have a choice. I have a choice in whether I should take part in a spectacle that glorifies violence, the passivity of women, and male dominance."

And all this time I thought it was just a game. Why did I think the University of Arkansas was a safe place for her? First, it's blacks in the Delta, now it's women—what next? But I am living proof a person can get into trouble up here. Except my trouble was more traditional. Too much Southern Comfort, too many girls, and not enough elbow grease. "We'll have plenty of time to talk about all this," I say, "when you come home Thanksgiving."

"Thanksgiving weekend," Sarah says promptly, "I want us to drive over to Bear Creek and talk to Dade's great-grandmother if she's still alive. I know you say it's gossip that your grandfather had a child by her, but I want us to check it out."

How did this conversation get so quickly out of control? What has gotten into her head? "That's fifty-year-old gutter talk," I say, knowing the hold on my temper is going. "The last thing that poor old woman needs is to be stirred up."

"Then I'll go myself."

"You will not!" I yell, horrified. I can just see Sarah running from house to house telling my old classmates she's looking for one of our relatives.

"Dad, I've got to go," she says. "I'm almost late for work. We'll talk about this later."

Great. I don't know who is worse—Professor Birdbath or Paula Crawford. "Okay," I say, suddenly feeling weary. "Maybe we can have dinner one night. I'll call you."

"I love you, Daddy."

"I love you, too, babe," I say, grateful for small favors.

7

BY THE TIME I pull onto the campus for the WAR rally (a little late, so Sarah, if I see her, won't be as likely to introduce me to anyone—my mind keeps playing a tape of me being called up to debate one of the speakers), I am feeling better. It has been a profitable afternoon. Besides getting the statements dropped off, I now have free office space. Barton has taken pity on me and graciously offered the free use of his library while I am working on the case in Fayetteville. I even have my own key. After an hour's wait at Memorial Hospital I found out that the nurse who examined Robin is on vacation this week and won't be at the hearing Friday. I've also learned that this board does not have the power to subpoena witnesses. Bliss Young, the lawyer who had tried to tell me how the "J" Board worked last week, was willing to cover much of the same ground for me again, and this time I actually listened. If for some reason Robin chooses not to appear, they can't make her. Additionally, Young told me to remember that I could advise Dade to challenge any of the board for bias. Members have recused themselves from hearing a case once they have been forced to admit they

159

have too many connections with one of the parties. Finally, Young told me that while the matter is being appealed, all action is stayed, which means Dade plays in the Alabama game, even if they issue a decision as soon as we finish the hearing. That should cheer him up considerably.

If I worried about being singled out, I shouldn't have. There must be close to six or seven hundred people gathered in front of the Student Union. I am amazed. Any other time on this campus you'd only find this kind of enthusiasm for a pep rally. Doesn't anyone remember the Hogs are playing Alabama this week? When we played Texas while I was in school, the campus was in a frenzy the whole week before the game. I do not see Sarah as I try to make myself inconspicuous at the edge of the crowd. To blend in a little better, I have taken off my tie and have worn a sports coat. The weather is cool and dry—perfect football weather. The women are mostly in jeans and sweatshirts (there don't seem to be many sorority types here), but the crowd seems to be about a quarter male, many of whom are professor types, though not many my age. Inevitably, there are a couple of TV cameras and several reporters.

The speaker, a blond woman with a short haircut, who is wearing jeans and tennis shoes (despite my best intentions, I can't help wondering if she's a lesbian—Sarah would drive a spike in my eye if I admitted this to her), is exhorting the crowd to write or call the university administration to expel Dade. ". . . He has been charged by the state of Arkansas with a crime of violence, and yet despite having full authority to remove him immediately if the safety of other individuals is at stake, the university allows him to remain on campus. Why? Because the University of Arkansas doesn't care about what happens to women if there's an important athletic contest at stake. This is the reality of where women are in this state, in the South, in this nation which gives only lip service to the notion of equality. . . ."

As she harangues the crowd (impressively, I concede—her delivery is appealing and well paced despite the scratchy sound system), I tell a male nearby that I just arrived and don't know who the speaker is. "Paula Crawford," he whispers. "She's a law student."

My mouth flies open. What happened to her hair? Is Sarah going to chop off her beautiful, thick, curly mane, too? Why do they do this? It's a form of mutilation, as far as I'm concerned. I turn back to Ms. Crawford, who hasn't paused for breath. "It is a question of our values as human beings. A woman cries that she has been raped, and no one at the school takes her seriously. But we take football seriously at this school and we take basketball seriously at this school, and if anything jeopardizes the well-being of those sports, another part of the administration acts very quickly, indeed. The first official response on this campus that was taken after Robin Perry said she was raped came from the athletics department, which says volumes about what we value at this university . . ."

As she talks, I look in vain for Sarah. She must be here, but it is too dark and crowded to see her. I wonder if she is going to speak. Surely not. On the other hand, who better than a recent convert? Suddenly, Robin Perry is being introduced, and the crowd, which had been standing in rapt attention, bursts into applause. ". . . enormous amount of courage for her to be here tonight and come forward publicly," Paula Crawford is saying. I can't see anyone on the stage, and then a tall, blond girl appears on the steps beside Paula. Thin, but obviously attractive even at this distance, she is wearing stone chino pants and one of those classy barn jackets I've seen on some of the wealthier-looking white students. Robin has the physical grace of a model. Though Dade has described her as a good speaker, tonight, not unsurprisingly, she seems almost too shy and nervous to do more than nod at the crowd. Finally, she manages to say, "I want to thank everybody for their support. I can't tell you how many other girls have told me that they have been a victim of date rape since this has occurred. It is a crime that most girls still do not talk about, but it happens much more frequently than we are aware. Thank you for being here."

As the crowd claps enthusiastically, Paula whispers into her ear. Robin shakes her head and disappears into the crowd off to the left. Paula resumes talking, and then introduces another girl who begins to talk about rape statistics, and with her droning, whining voice she immediately loses the crowd's interest. I am worried now that I will be spotted by a reporter I recognize and decide it is time for me to leave.

Back in my room, I leave a message for Dade on his answering machine that he should bring his friends to Barton's law office, and I read off his address. He picks up just as I am hanging up. He sounds anxious again, and tells me that he can't find Eddie Stiles and hasn't found anything out about Robin Perry that I don't already know.

I reassure him that Eddie Stiles is not an essential witness Friday and ask him to keep trying to find out anything about Robin. "How was practice?" I ask, trying to calm him a bit.

"It was hard to concentrate at first," he says, "but I got into it."

I tell him he will be playing in the Alabama game, which has the desired effect of pepping him up a bit. I wish I could tell him that all he had to worry about was playing football, but I can't. Somehow, I'm supposed to turn this boy into a lawyer between now and Friday morning. How ridiculous! I'm not even going to try. "I went to the WAR rally tonight," I tell him, "and saw Robin for the first time. She's pretty, all right."

"What'd she say?" Dade demands, excited again.

I wish I hadn't brought her up, but he will hear about it anyway. "Hardly anything," I say, and then summarize the rally for him.

"She doesn't seem the WAR type," Dade observes. "She dresses too good for them."

"That's for sure," I say, wondering whether there is a way to turn Robin's appearance against her. Maybe we will simply have to depend on the unconscious reactions of the members of the "J" Board. I can't imagine any of that group will identify themselves as ardent feminists. Then again, probably Robin herself would resist that label. Tonight, she didn't have any trouble convincing herself she was merely a victim, one of many.

After trying to reassure him, I hang up and attempt to

reconstruct exactly what Robin said. Something isn't jelling. I stare at the unadorned pale green blank wall across from the door. Robin identified with girls who had been "date raped." According to both her and Dade, it was more like "study rape." What if both are lying? Dade could be lying because he was warned repeatedly not to become involved with white girls, Robin because she knows what her parents and others would think. But then maybe Robin was merely trying to identify with the girls who had talked to her. I know I'm not going to be able to even scratch the surface of this case before the hearing Friday.

The phone rings again, and it is Dan, who tells me that after getting permission from their parents, he has contacted a couple of girls inside the Chi Omega House, although getting them to say even one negative word about Robin is impossible. "She's become the patron saint of female rectitude," Dan explains.

Thank goodness the trial isn't Friday. Robin is riding a wave of sympathy that seems unstoppable. I tell Dan about her appearance tonight. "The last time anyone clapped for me like that was the night I graduated from high school."

"She's pushing the envelope then," Dan says. "A lot of people don't like those women's groups."

"Maybe so," I agree, "but publicly this group isn't nearly as radical as its leader is in private, according to Sarah. How can anyone not be against rape?"

"Because they're picking on the Razorbacks," Dan points out. "That's a major faux pas in this state, and you know it."

"It might be in Little Rock and Pine Bluff," I concede, "but up here on campus the powers that be have to be more sensitive to the idea that the university is supposed to be more than a sports factory."

Dan says melodramatically, "I hate it when we try to put on airs in this state."

Since he's paying for it, I tell him what's been going on since I last talked to him. "Barton's still a nice guy," I say, "even if he is filthy rich. He's letting me use his library as an office when I come up here."

Dan moans, "Rich? In trial advocacy, he was terrible."

"The guys who make the real money practicing law," I lament, "wouldn't know a criminal defendant unless they caught them trying to steal their Rolexes."

Dan tells me he will keep trying to find some other girls who know some dirt on Robin but not to get my hopes up. "It's a tight group," he says. "But, of course, a middle-aged male lawyer isn't many coeds' idea of their typical confidante."

"I need a mole," I agree. "Somebody somewhere surely must dislike Robin even if it's out of simple jealousy. But thanks for trying. By the way, speaking of young women, have you heard from your friend Gina? I keep forgetting I've got her dependency-neglect trial the end of next week."

"She's very impressed with you," Dan coos. "She thinks you look like Nick Nolte."

She's impressed with my fee. No wonder I'm poor. I finally get Dan off the line by telling him I have to work. I still want to talk to the woman from the Rape Crisis Center who came to the hospital to go through the process with Robin, but she hasn't returned my call either. I dial her number but for the second time today talk to her husband, who must be a student. He is evasive about when she will be in but says he will give her my message. Sure he will. People don't like lawyers. I can understand that. I'm not that crazy about them myself. We're too much like public urinals: an unpleasant necessity sometimes but rarely an uplifting experience. I go to sleep waiting for Coach Carter to call. I'm not sure I want him to be at the hearing. Like everything else about this case I'm doing, it could backfire.

At eleven the next morning (an hour late, I point out) Dade brings into Barton's office Harris Warford and Tyrone Jones. Harris, especially, is enormous. He must weigh almost three hundred pounds and be six and a half feet tall. I wonder how come he isn't on the starting team. Dressed in black sweats with Razorback insignia all over them, he looks like a road grader with decals. Tyrone, a defensive back who isn't even on the second team, naturally isn't as bulked up, but he is plenty big. Wearing an Oakland Raiders cap over similar black sweats, he has a scowl on his face that looks as if it might be permanent. Even though they are obviously friends of Dade, I'd hate to meet these guys in a dark alley. "The girls didn't show up," Dade explains.

So much for black women supporting their men. "I'd like to talk to at least one of them," I tell Dade. The "J" Board will figure any team member will give favorable testimony to Dade. "Let's see if we can get them in the same time tomorrow, okay?"

Dade, who is dressed in jeans and a University of

Arkansas athletics department sweatshirt, says grimly, "I'll try." Poor kid. He's finding it isn't easy to rally the troops. I know the feeling.

We do not have a productive session, but I learn a few things. The main one is that I do not want Tyrone within two miles of the hearing or a jury. He has an attitude problem that couldn't be hidden even if he had been dead a year. Cocky, arrogant, he must be Carter's worst nightmare. He is from Houston and has the big-city kid's mentality that "baad" is beautiful, and life is one short beauty contest. Rightly or wrongly, if he were the one on trial, it would take a jury about two seconds to convict him. He has everything but a neon sign blinking the word "RAPIST" over his head.

Harris, on the other hand, turns out to be a big teddy bear, and it is he who gives me the most information about Robin. "She acted to me like she kind of liked Dade," he says, oblivious to my client's discomfort. "At Eddie's she was pretty quiet while her roommate did all the talking. I remember her smiling a lot."

Unfortunately, Harris cannot be more specific, though he is willing to talk at length about the evening they were all together. I wish the girls were here. Doubtless, they would be quite a bit more attuned to any signals Robin might have been generating. I see I should have interviewed Harris out of Dade's presence. He might remember more if Dade weren't glowering at him.

"I would have fucked her, too," Tyrone volunteers as I usher them out the door about noon. "She is one good-lookin' bitch."

Thank you for that poignant observation, Tyrone. This

case could definitely be worse. I could have Tyrone for a client. I tell Harris that I might want to use him as a rebuttal witness at the hearing and explain what that means. He nods soberly. I like him as much as I dislike Tyrone. I only wish he were normal size. Anybody this big and black has got to be a little scary to the average white juror in Arkansas.

After I go to lunch with Barton, I decide to pay a visit to the Chi Omega House. Probably neither Robin nor her roommate, Shannon Kennsit, will see me, but what do I have to lose? If this were a civil case, I could take their depositions, but this hearing doesn't qualify as either. I park in a visitor's slot near the Administration Building and walk east on Maple, passing the law school.

I am thankful I didn't want to be a lawyer right out of undergraduate school, for I would have squandered that money as badly as I wasted the money that my mother spent educating me. For the first time in years, I ask myself if it was as much fun as I have told myself I remembered it. Now it seems more frenzied than anything else. What I remember most is always being hungover and late to get somewhere—to a class, to a meeting, to some event, because I was too intent upon cramming it all in, including enough alcohol to float a battleship. Was the Peace Corps an escape from all that activity, or was it a refuge from the impoverished emotional existence I thought awaited me if I returned to live in eastern Arkansas?

As I look across the street at the coeds walking past the sorority houses on the other side of the street, I realize I still don't know the answer. The only conclusive fact I have in my head thirty years later is the knowledge that in a drunken stupor early one morning I lowered my pants and crapped on the steps of the Chi Omega House to protest being dumped by a girl I thought I cared about. I cross the street, deciding to wait another thirty years before making my confession.

I last a total of five minutes at the door before being told in no uncertain terms by the housemother, an attractive, blue-haired woman by the name of Ms. Fitzhugh, that neither Robin nor Shannon will be available to see me. Yet, maybe the word will get around to the other girls: if you hate Robin or Shannon, you can tell your story to Dade Cunningham's lawyer. The little flurry of activity my presence produced was almost comical. You would have thought Fidel Castro was at the door. I should have said that I was a recruiter from WAR and had come by to pack up Robin and take her on a national protest tour. That would have really upset them. These girls in their stockings and tailored clothes don't seem ready to storm any barricades. I remain impressed that Paula Crawford was able to persuade Robin to appear at the rally. Maybe she could give me lessons.

During the next day and a half of trying to prepare for the hearing I encounter several more dry holes: Despite going to her house, I never am able to talk to the girl who volunteers for Rape Crisis. Wednesday night Coach Carter calls back and hems and haws but finally tells me that he can not appear as a character witness for Dade because it would "compromise his future neutrality" in the matter. What neutrality, I want to scream at him but don't. His tone makes it clear he has made up his mind (or somebody has made it up for him) and I thank him again for all he has done. Dade, he says, is having some good practices this week and seems ready for the Alabama game. Not as sanguine about the hearing, I decline to reassure him that all is going well in my area.

Thursday morning only one of the girls from Dade's party back in the spring at Eddie Stiles's rented house shows up at Barton's office and is no help at all. Doris Macy would gladly say that Robin and Shannon raped Dade if I wanted her to, but witnesses as eager as this girl hurt the credibility of an entire case. I remember that she is the one who has been described as a "hanger-on," and I tell her I will call her if I decide she can help at the hearing.

Thursday afternoon before practice Dade shows me where the incident occurred. Even taking a shortcut, Happy Hollow Road is at least a couple of miles east of the campus. Out Highway 16 on the road to Elkins, Dade directs me to turn off to the left, and soon at the end of the blacktopped street we come upon an ugly yellow frame rectangle that can't contain more than a thousand square feet. There is no house around us for a hundred yards. To the north are fields and the slopes of Mount Sequoyah. As isolated as a place can be in this developing area, this is a perfect spot for an interracial tryst, but a lot of trouble to go to to find a place to study. "I can't find Eddie anywhere," Dade apologizes. "I've tried for two days straight."

"Don't worry about it," I say, stopping the Blazer in a wide space in a road. This place is so rural that the house even has a well. It is boarded up, but still, it's a nice touch. I say, "Dade, you need to level with me. Had you ever had sex with her before? It's okay if you did. In fact, it'll help our case if you did."

Stubbornly, Dade shakes his head. "This was the first time," he says. "She didn't fight me or anything."

Damn. There has to be more to it than this. "You think people are going to believe you each drove out in separate cars three miles to this place to study? Nobody is that dumb."

Dade looks off into the woods. "I tried to kiss her that evening in the spring, but she didn't want me to."

Ah, now we're getting somewhere. I ask, "What do you mean she didn't want you to kiss her? Why'd she come over if she wasn't interested?"

"That's what I said!" Dade responds hotly. "She and I was off by ourselves in the kitchen getting a beer while the rest of 'em were in the living room. It pissed me off. She said we were jus' friends, and if I was gonna do stuff like that she was gonna leave. She said she'd come because Shannon was such a big fan and wanted to meet me. We went back in the living room, and that was it. Both of us was kind of cool the rest of the semester, but like I told you, she started getting real friendly just a week or so before she claimed I raped her."

More than ever, I'm convinced Robin changed her mind. This year Dade was a bigger star than ever and still a nice guy. His body obviously hadn't deteriorated any over the summer, and she thought she would try it out, but started feeling guilty almost immediately. Or maybe it was date rape. People lie to themselves all the time about what they are doing and why they are doing it. I go back over his story, but I don't get much more out of him. I just hope I'm not the last person to know what happened that night.

Thursday night I finally get hold of Sarah and meet her for dinner at a café Barton has recommended only a block east of the Ozark. "Danny's" has pictures of Elvis and Marilyn on the walls and plays one after another "The Thrill Is Gone," "Dancin' in the Street," "The Great Pretender," and "Bridge over Troubled Waters," before it seriously nosedives with "Breaking Up Is Hard to Do." With the music, black-eyed peas and cornbread on the menu, and peach cobbler for dessert, this is my kind of place. Sarah, ever cautious of good food at a reasonable price, orders a Caesar salad and talks about the WAR rally after I explain I was there, too. "You should have stayed around to the end to say hello. I would have introduced you to Paula. She'd like to talk to you."

I bet she would. Women seem to love to try to straighten me out. "I would have liked to talk to Robin," I say, as I sugar my iced tea, "but she doesn't want to talk to me." I do not mention that I couldn't get my foot in the door at the Chi Omega House. It would embarrass her that I tried.

"Dad, it took a lot of guts for her to speak at the rally," Sarah says defensively. "I couldn't have done it."

"Yeah, how did Paula manage to bring that off?" I ask, noticing that Sarah is wearing no makeup. Great. Next, she'll be telling me she's joining a convent.

"I've told you," Sarah says, spooning ice from her water and putting it into an ashtray. "Paula is very persuasive. I think you're afraid to take her on."

A no-win situation if there ever was one. "You make her sound like a prize fighter," I say, over "Midnight Hour," the Wilson Pickett version, though I like the way it was done in the movie *The Commitments*. Maybe Sarah and I should just listen to the music.

We continue bantering throughout the meal. Sarah hits me with a few feminist jabs, but I don't have the heart to take the gloves off, or maybe I have too much sense. Maybe she's right and women are exploited night and day in this country. But if things are so bad for them, why do women outlive men so long? God help us if the statistics were reversed. Before she cranks her engine in the Volkswagen outside the restaurant, I tell her once again that I still think Dade is probably innocent.

"Why? Why can't you believe her?" Sarah demands, hugging her jacket against her in the cool mountain air.

"I can't go into the reasons," I say hiding behind legal ethics and feeling guilty because of it. "Mainly, I just think Dade is telling the truth."

"And I think Robin is telling the truth! Why would she lie about a thing as serious as rape?" Sarah says, her voice trembling now.

"I don't know," I admit. "I wish I did."

"I wish you did, too." Angry, Sarah roars off, grinding gears as she goes. I need to get her a new car. What she's driving now would crumble if she went over a curb at ten miles an hour.

Friday morning at ten the press is out in full force. I've told Dade to ignore the questions and the cameras again as best he can. The hearing itself is supposed to be confidential, but as I shove a microphone out of my face going up the stairs, I get the feeling the hearing is going to be televised to the entire country.

We are apparently the last to arrive. Inside room 213 the "J" Board is lined up on one side of a long conference table, and the witnesses, including Harris Warford, I'm relieved to see, are lined up on the other. The head of the board, a Professor Haglar from the history department, tells us to sit across from him and introduces the "J" Board members too fast for me to write all their names down. Robin is sitting in a chair off to the side, presumably with her attorney, and only looks up briefly. Up close she is even prettier than I had imagined and looks as if she had just come from a modeling assignment. Her face is made up to beat the band and she is wearing silver jewelry over a flax vest that covers a scoop-necked cotton T-shirt. Her outfit is completed by an expensive-looking long green print skirt.

Haglar seems nervous and keeps turning to look at Clarise Dozier, the Coordinator of Judicial Affairs, who is seated on his left, for reassurance. She smiles as if he is doing beautifully although he is visibly sweating, and we've barely begun. "I want to remind Mr. Page and Mr. Sanderson that under our rules you may not ask questions of witnesses or argue the case, but you can advise your client on any matters you wish. I also want to point out that Professor Haglar is sitting in for the regular 'J' Board chairperson, who is ill today," Ms. Dozier explains, reading my mind. "We'll probably go a little slower than usual."

That's okay with me. Dade seems lost already, which

is understandable under the circumstances. The board is right on top of him. In a courtroom the defendant has more personal space, but I remind myself this is "educational." Sure. I write Sanderson's name down and make a note to ask Barton about him. For all I know, he may be a family friend and not a lawyer. I'm surprised one of Robin's parents is not here. But perhaps she didn't want them. On the conference table in front of Ms. Dozier is a tape recorder which may come in handy later. While Haglar assures us that this proceeding will be very informal and goes over several items that I've already covered with Dade, I study the faces of the rest of the board. Though a couple of the male professors have opted for shirts open at the throat and sports jackets, the others, perhaps sensing this may be the high point of their semester, are wearing their Sunday best. The black female, a Ms. Osceola Glazer (whose name I did get), is actually wearing a dark jade polo dress identical to one owned by Sarah. Introduced as an assistant professor in the math department, she looks young enough to be a student. The university had few black teachers when I was here. I doubt if it is any different now. It occurs to me that no Arkansas jury will be as educated or as economically well off as this group. Unfortunately, what they may make up for in their presumed lack of racial prejudice may be overshadowed by their political correctness.

Dr. Haglar asks me if we have any more witnesses who will be showing up, and when I tell him that Harris is our only one, he has each witness formally identify him- or herself and then explains to them that they will now be excused so that they won't hear each other's testimony.

Ms. Dozier leads them out a door in the back of the room to another office where they will wait until they are called. It is my first glimpse of Shannon Kennsit and Mary Purvis, the Rape Crisis counselor, neither of whom would talk to me. Shannon is by far the more interesting looking of the two. A redhead with permed hair down to her shoulders, she is wearing a hot pink silk blouse and tight black pants. She looks nothing like a female sports junkie, but I overheard her ask Harris about the Alabama game as they walked out the door.

When Ms. Dozier is seated once again, I whisper to Dade that he should read aloud the first question on his pad. He raises his hand and is recognized by Haglar. Speaking in a stiff voice, Dade asks, "Are any of you members of WAR or any similar group, or have any of you attended one of their meetings or rallies?"

No one raises a hand or speaks, and he continues to read questions designed to get at whether any of them know Robin or her roommate. One studious-looking girl with big glasses whose name I have written down as Judith raises her hand and says she sits beside Robin in a psychology class but that they are only acquaintances. Dade looks at me uncertainly, but I shake my head. We can't very well ask her to recuse, nor would I want her to. Judging from her tone, she may think that Robin is an airhead beauty queen and not particularly credible. I point to a question on the legal pad, and Dade reads, "Have any of you formed an opinion about this matter as a result of talking to others or news coverage?"

Typically, no one speaks up, but it is a question that has to be asked and just might keep one of these people

honest. The truth is, all of them have some opinion even
if it is not a strong one, but human nature being what it is,
the answer is almost always in the negative. By letting
Dade conduct what in a courtroom would be voir dire, or
an examination of the jury's qualifications, my plan is for
him to get over his nervousness before he begins to testify. Sanderson, who has a young face but is prematurely
bald, asks the board if any of them knows Dade personally. Again, no one raises his or her hand. He then asks if
anyone will be influenced by Dade's status as a star football player. Again no one answers. I hope to hell someone
is lying.

Haglar calls on Robin, who has been completely silent,
to come sit at the table and give her opening statement.
Accompanied by Sanderson, she sits toward the end of
the table near the door where we entered, and Sanderson
sits between her and me, partially blocking my view of
her and certainly Dade's, who is sitting to my right. I start
to protest that she should change places with Sanderson,
but realize it will just irritate the board.

Robin, to my dismay, is disturbingly convincing. Without halting or even clearing her throat, she tells the board
her story, which uniformly tracks the statement she gave
Detective Farley. Though it is vague in spots, she leaves
no doubt that she was convinced she had no choice but to
submit to Dade. "I know some of you are probably thinking I was stupid to go over there, but I never really believed anything like this would ever happen, especially
not with Dade," she says, her head turning slowly back
and forth, making sure she has eye contact with each
board member. "Shannon and I had gone over to that

same little house in the spring, really so she could meet Dade—when you talk to her you'll see she's a real Razorback fan. We felt perfectly safe the whole time. Two other players were there and, I guess, their two girlfriends. They were as nice as they could be. One is here today, I think, as a witness for Dade. . . ."

As she talks, I go back and forth in my mind as to whether Dade should try to get her to admit that he had tried to kiss her in the spring, but it seems too damaging. If she isn't going to mention it, he might be better off not bringing it up because in some ways her story helps Dade. He comes off as a perfect gentleman. She has admitted as much. As she concludes, I whisper in his ear not to mention it to the board. He nods, relieved.

Though we have practiced it several times, Dade's opening statement doesn't come out of his mouth nearly as smoothly as Robin's. Halfway through it, he begins to ramble and says crudely, "Robin didn't get anything she didn't want."

Though it is clear what he means, this one simple statement might well make him sound far more brutal than he is, and I look at the faces of the females on the board to gauge their reaction. Perhaps I am imagining it, but Judith what's-her-name seems to turn even paler than she already is, and she shrinks back in her seat. Dade comes off in this exchange as a defensive, almost sullen young man with a chip on his shoulder, doubtlessly a victim in his own eyes, but one who doesn't inspire sympathy. Instantly, I regret not having him admit that he tried to kiss Robin. Without that admission, his actions seem purely motivated by lust.

The board members begin to ask questions. Predictably, they are most interested in why Robin waited so long to go to the hospital. Growing more comfortable by the minute, Robin speaks with a practiced earnestness that is impressive. "I think I was almost in shock from the time I left the house on Happy Hollow Road until I woke Shannon up with my crying. If it hadn't been for her, I don't think I would have gone to the hospital. I was too ashamed. Until I talked to Shannon, I was afraid nobody would believe me, just like Dade said. . . ."

The "J" Board doesn't roll over for her. One of the female professors asks why she took her car if she wasn't worried about anything happening. "I just wanted to be able to leave whenever I thought I needed to," she says carefully. "Maybe down deep I wasn't as sure of the situation as I thought I was."

"Why did you feel ashamed?" a male professor at the far end of the table asks.

"I don't know," Robin says, her voice hoarse with emotion for the first time. Her eyes redden and she begins to cry. "I guess because I knew it was my fault for going over there by myself. And I knew how much pain this was going to cause my parents. They're very conservative. It was stupid to go there by myself; I admit it."

We stop for a moment while she composes herself, and I have a chance to study her. Damned if I can tell whether this is all an act.

Throughout she is vague on the actual details of the rape, and understandably the "J" Board is reluctant to press her too closely. The student at these hearings, according to the papers Dozier gave me, is permitted not to answer a question if she or he chooses not to, and theo-retically, no inference of wrongdoing can be made. She isn't even under oath. If she chooses not to answer, she can simply refuse, which she couldn't do at a trial.

There are several other questions, but Robin, though shaky, handles them well enough, and at a bathroom break requested by the oldest professor there, I take Dade into a corner and try to persuade him that he should ask her if she admits that he tried to kiss her at the party in the spring. If she does, and she further contends she re-sisted him, then he can ask her why she so willingly came over alone a few months later.

Dade, sweating profusely in a dark wool suit that is too tight in the shoulders, flatly refuses. "I'm not doing it now. I should have told them when I first started talking. They'll think I'm lying now."

"No, they won't," I plead fervently. "Tell them the truth. Tell them your parents told you never to get in-volved with a white girl, but that you liked her. There's nothing wrong with that."

Dade shakes his head and leaves me standing by my-self. I follow him back to the table, feeling terrible. I should have figured this out better beforehand, but I just kept going back and forth in my own mind and had hoped I could resolve it before the hearing in a way that made sense. Shit, I hate this business of the lawyers not being able to ask questions. It isn't fair to the student.

The board members are not as gentle with Dade. Clearly, some of the faculty members think he forced her to have sex. Though their questions are not unexpected, it is the tone that bothers me. I whisper to him that he should continue to say that he never threatened Robin, nor did he ever say that she would not be believed. All I can do is sit here and listen to him repeat his answers and hope he doesn't trip himself up.

"Mr. Cunningham," a Dr. Darcy asks, after a flurry of questions by the males on the board, "did her coming out there give you the wrong idea, as Robin has suggested?"

I can't decide whether she is trying to trap him or not. Even if he agrees, that is still no justification to force her to have sex. I whisper to him that now is the time for him to say he had tried to kiss her in the spring and that he thought she had changed her mind about their relationship. Even if it sounds crude, it may be his best chance to convince them he didn't rape her.

Dade nods, but answers, "It was just how she acted when she got there," and describes how she had come over to him after a few minutes. "She wanted me to kiss her, and it was her idea to get in the shower, but when it was all over she just got up and left."

Frustrated, I force myself to sit poker-faced. There is nothing I can do. I don't want to give them the impression I am arguing with him. Judging by their frowns, this answer doesn't sit well with some members of the board, who obviously would find more plausible a case of classic date rape. A professor named Dow asks the same question for the second time, "Now, what did you tell her you would do if she told anyone?"

I can't remain, in the words of one of the "Irangate" lawyers, a potted plant, any longer. "Dr. Haglar, this has already been covered."

Professor Haglar, not unlike some judges I've ap-

peared before, mutters something unintelligible and
clears his throat and nods indecisively. I whisper to Dade
to say that he has already answered that question twice.
He does, and five minutes later there is finally silence in
the room.

Dr. Haglar looks down at his watch, and after consulta-
tion with Ms. Dozier, suggests that since we are moving
so quickly we work through lunch, since it appears we
could be through before two. Not a single board member
objects, and Ms. Dozier goes through the door in the
back of the room and brings back Shannon Kennsit. I notice for the first time Shannon is wearing a "Beat Alabama" button over her left breast. She is that not-so-rare
article, a genuine female Razorback nut.

If Dade's trial comes off, I fear she will be a devastat-
ing witness. In comparison to Robin's coolness, this girl
is friendly and open as a puppy and entirely believable.
She, too, in response to the questions, tracks the statement she gave to the police. She tells the board that she
was in the room with Robin the night of the rape and she
was sure she didn't have anything to drink that night before she left the sorority house. She describes the little
party she and Robin attended as "fun" because she got to
talk to a real star for the first time.

One of the male students whose name I didn't catch
asks if Robin had ever said that she liked Dade or thought
he was attractive. I listen carefully for Shannon's answer,
but she disappoints me by saying, "She never said she
liked him like he was some guy she had a thing for," her
tone matter-of-fact. "But she liked him as a person. She

thought he was a friend, I guess, not just somebody she was helping."

The black math professor, Dr. Glazer, picks up on this question. "Ms. Kennsit, if Robin had been attracted to Dade," she asks, her voice slightly ironical and detached, "given the fact that he is an African-American and she is white, and the fact that public interracial relationships are rare on this campus, is she the kind of person who would be sure to confide in you or her friends, or might she be more cautious and not say anything, especially at first?"

Shannon, whose most attractive characteristic as a witness thus far has been her lack of guile, hesitates for the briefest of instants before answering, "Robin is kind of private, but I think she would have told me if she had liked Dade, you know, that way."

"Ms. Kennsit," the same woman asks again, "who else might Robin have confided in?"

Bless this woman's soul. Whether she knows it or not, this woman is helping us out, if not today, then for the trial. I think she is trying to help us out. "Robin and I are best friends," Shannon says eagerly. "If she didn't tell me, I don't think she would tell anybody."

I don't think this girl is lying. But if Dade is telling the truth, there is more to this case than meets the eye. Robin could easily be hiding something but what is it? I don't have a clue. At least I will have plenty of time to work on Dade before the trial.

The hearing speeds up considerably after Shannon finishes. Mary Purvis, the counselor from the Rape Crisis Center, is the next witness, and I don't regret not having caught up with her. She is in her early twenties and she lacks the experience to make a useful witness. A student board member, a boy I thought was having trouble staying awake for the last hour, asks her exactly how many rape victims she has counseled after she says that "Robin's reaction was typical." Three, is her reply. No one asks her any more questions after this admission.

After she departs, Dr. Haglar says that the board will consider the hospital admission record which contains the nurse's comments and the physician's examination. Since this evidence is favorable (there is no indication whatsoever that Robin was hurt or suffered any sexual trauma), I have no problems with it.

The last witness is Harris Warford, who tells the board that he saw Dade about nine-thirty, less than an hour after the rape was supposed to have occurred. "Did he seem any different to you or say anything about what had happened?" Dr. Haglar asks.

Buddha-like in his calm passivity, Harris appears more relaxed than any witness so far. "Dade seemed puzzled more than anything," he says quietly. "He told me he'd gone to study at Eddie's house with Robin, but ended up doin' her. He said it was weird because she was all hot, and then when it was all over, she got out of there like she didn't even know him. I kidded him about how she must not have liked it, but he said she wasn't hurt or anything. She just got up and took off."

This answer prompts a number of questions, but the most persistent come from Dr. Glazer, who asks, "Did Dade ever tell you or anyone you know that he liked Robin more than just as a friend, or that he'd like to have sex with her?"

"After the time she and her roommate came to Eddie's house in the spring, we ragged him some about her," Harris says without changing his expression, "but he never said he liked her."

"Do you think he did?" Dr. Glazer presses him.

"Dade had plenty of girls," Harris says as if he were commenting on the weather, but not answering her question. "He didn't worry much about any particular one."

Dr. Glazer, judging from her expression, doesn't seem to think much of that answer, but lets it go, and ten minutes later Dr. Haglar, after consulting with Ms. Dozier, announces we are done. I had expected the hearing to last much longer. Dade is visibly relieved, but if he thinks this was bad, the trial will be ten times worse. Dr. Haglar says that a decision will be made as quickly as possible, and shows us a way out through the back door to avoid the reporters. I look at Dade, who nods gratefully at him. He has to be ready for practice at three. I take it as a good sign that a couple of the students wish him good luck against Alabama.

Taking the stairs two at a time, Dade asks, "What do you think they'll do?"

"I don't know," I say honestly as I try to keep up with him. "They weren't as hostile as I thought they'd be. But we can't forget that the burden of proof is not like it is in a criminal case. I think it will just come down to whether they want to believe her or you."

Amazingly, we have come out at the back of the Union, and there isn't a reporter in sight. I remind him not to make any comment regardless of the outcome. "Remember that you have a right to appeal, and nothing will happen until that process is over, and it could take weeks. Good luck tomorrow."

He nods. "You'll do more at the trial, won't you?" he asks. "I know you couldn't ask questions or say anything here."

I laugh for the first time today. "A hell of a lot more. I can guarantee you that."

Twenty minutes later, as I go to check out of the Ozark, I have a message to call Barton before I leave town: he has a ticket for me to the Alabama game. Good ol' Barton! I had resigned myself to watching it on TV with Dan tomorrow. I hope he has a place for me to stay, too. The Ozark and every other motel around here has been taken this weekend for weeks, probably months. The game is at two, so I can still get home tomorrow night in time for my date with Amy. I'll need to find a washing machine, too. I've run out of clothes.

"Hell, you deserve to go to this game," Barton says an hour later. He hands me a beer he has taken from a little bar he has in a small room off his office, which is now unofficially closed in honor of the Arkansas-Alabama battle to come tomorrow. "You're single-handedly responsible for us having a chance to win it."

I pop the top on a Tecate and marvel at the human animal's capacity for hero worship. "I haven't done much," I say modestly, knowing Barton won't believe me. "But at least he'll play tomorrow, whatever they decide."

Outside, we can see students driving the square, honking their horns, their "Beat 'Bama" signs plastered all over their cars. It is not even five o'clock in the afternoon, but Hogs football fans have waited years for a chance to play a game that means something. If we win, we'll surely be ranked in the top five and have a real shot at playing for the national championship on New Year's Day. "If the board's smart," Barton says, pouring bourbon for himself, "they won't announce their decision until Monday. Why take a chance on messing with Dade's head? That boy's gonna need to concentrate all he can."

"That's for sure," I say. There is no point in tormenting Barton with the information that a good many people within the university community would like nothing better than to skywrite over Razorback stadium tomorrow afternoon a message that the business of rape is more important than a football game.

Within an hour's time Barton and I are feeling no pain, which is fortunate, because he gets a call from his wife to turn on the five o'clock news. The "J" Board is reported to have made a decision. Barton snaps on his stereo, and we see the luscious female reporter, who is usually on later, reading into the camera, ". . . will no longer be permitted to take part in intercollegiate athletics the remainder of the year but will be permitted to attend classes. Clarise Dozier, the All-University Coordinator of Judicial Affairs, has just explained that any disciplinary action will not go into effect until the vice-chancellor and chancellor have ruled on any appeal and reviewed the actions taken by the board. This means that star wide receiver Dade Cunningham, unless head Razorback football coach Dale Carter says otherwise, will be in the starting line-up against the Crimson Tide tomorrow afternoon. . . ."

"Shit!" Barton whines at the screen. "Those assholes could have waited! If we lose, it'll be their fault."

I reach for the phone and dial Dade's room and get his answering machine. Hoping I don't sound drunk, I say that he shouldn't worry and that if he needs to call me, I can be reached at either Barton Sanders's home or his office tonight and tomorrow morning. Barton gives me the numbers, which I read into the phone, wondering how Dade will react.

I hang up, pissed at the "J" Board but knowing it could have been worse. While Barton continues to rant, I try to think what lesson there is to be gained from their decision. Obviously, they don't consider Dade presently a threat to Robin, but they believed her over him. Not a good sign, but I don't know what factor politics, campus or otherwise, played into their decision. A lot, probably, since Dozier told me they try to achieve a consensus. I'd love to know what part WAR's rallies played in this decision, but I know I never will.

"You got problems," Barton says, gloomily sipping at his drink. "If you can't convince students and professors Dade is innocent, think what a bunch of hillbillies on that jury will do to him."

"Thanks for reminding me," I say, glad Barton called about the ticket before we got the news. I don't seem like such a hero all of a sudden. I call Sarah to find out her reaction, but only get her answering machine as usual. She is probably out celebrating with Paula Crawford. On second thought, they are probably furious Dade wasn't kicked out of school. Nothing will ever satisfy them.

Unlike last week in Knoxville, the weather stays gorgeous all morning Saturday, and walking to the stadium it is easy to forget that football at this level is essentially a business. Hundreds of tailgate parties are going on simultaneously in a sea of Razorback red; multigeneration Arkansans gather together outside their RVs in lawn chairs and wolf down tons of barbecue, potato salad, cole slaw, and baked beans and drink beer, Diet Coke, and iced tea, trading friendly insults with the healthy contingent of Alabama fans who are, as usual, cocky but not obnoxious, at least not before the game. Truly, it is a cultural thing, right or wrong, the way we live. If the fans are right, the Hogs are back. The Alabama game will prove it.

During the warm-up I train my binoculars on Dade and am shaken as twenty yards downfield he drops a perfectly thrown ball. When he trots back in, Carter, who apparently has been watching too, says something to him, and Dade listens with his head bowed. He didn't call last night or this morning. I spoke with his mother briefly before I left for the game, and she hadn't heard from him either. If he is able to turn pro after this season, I wonder how much money this game alone will be worth to him. Alabama's preseason All-American safety, Ty Mosely, will be covering him all afternoon. If Mosely shuts him down, it will be hard for a pro owner to forget his statistics, since he will have seen the game. As the cheerleaders minus Robin Perry lead the crowd in calling the Hogs, it is impossible not to feel a shiver run down my spine. It is just a game, I tell myself. Of course, it's not.

The Hogs come out as fired up as the crowd and outquick the bigger Tide linemen as Carter keeps the ball on the ground even in obvious passing situations. By the second quarter with the Razorbacks on top 10 to 7, it is easy to forget Dade is even on the field. Jay Madison, the Hogs' quarterback, has thrown a total of three passes, all screens to his backs. Incredibly, with one minute left in the half Alabama fumbles inside its own five, and the Hogs recover and go up 17 to 7 at the half.

I realize my dominant emotion is one of relief. The game will put a crimp in some of Dade's total season statistics, but if Arkansas wins, it can't hurt him too badly. If Madison doesn't throw the ball to him, he can't drop it. Just at the kickoff I return to my seat from a trip to the bathroom. Predictably, someone was drunk and sick (it sounded like an animal giving birth to a too large offspring). The crowd around me is reasonably in control, but it won't be if we win. I don't look forward to the drive back to Blackwell County after the game, no matter what happens.

As I feared, Alabama's strength begins to tell by the fourth quarter, and their offense begins to look like Sherman marching through Georgia, and they go ahead 21 to 17 with five minutes left. Now, stuck on our twenty-yard line, we have to throw, and everybody in the stadium knows it.

Quickly, the battle between Ty Mosely and Dade becomes awesome to watch. Dade is a step faster, but Mosely has an uncanny gift of being able to react while the ball is in the air, and unless Jay Madison throws the ball almost perfectly, Mosely will just get a hand on it and knock it away from Dade at the last moment. Though there is now double coverage on Dade, the Hogs are still able to move downfield, thanks to Madison's success in finding secondary receivers. With the ball on the twenty with one minute left, Dade has caught four passes on this drive, three for first downs, so there is no doubt about his ability to perform under pressure. Forgotten is his dropped ball in warm-ups. Even if we don't win, he has performed creditably.

With second and ten, Dade accelerates faster than I've seen him all day and blows by Mosely and heads for the corner of the left end zone. The right safety comes over to cover him, but Dade suddenly plants his foot and cuts to the right at the instant the ball is thrown. The exact moment the ball reaches him, he is almost decapitated by the left safety who has come over to cover him. Somehow, Dade manages to hold onto the ball while being knocked into the end zone, and the stadium erupts as I've never seen it. In my excitement I trip over the seat in front of me and fall forward onto the back of a huge fat guy who is so deliriously happy he jumps up and down with me clinging to his shoulders. "We win! We win!" he screams as tears stream down his cheeks.

Twenty minutes later I am on my way out of town, heading back to Blackwell County, listening to the post-game comments on the radio. Coach Carter calls Dade's catch the greatest he has ever seen. His interviewer does not mention that if the All-University Judiciary Board's decision is upheld, it will be the last one he'll make as a Razorback this season. Caught hopelessly in traffic on Highway 23 (I'll have to call Amy and tell her I'll be late), I think that the reason men like sports is that if we try hard enough we can pretend for a couple of hours that the real world doesn't have anything to do with us.

8

AT TWO ON Monday I am picking up peanut shells from my carpet when Dan saunters into my office. He has converted our office into a peanut warehouse Jimmy Carter himself could be proud of. He has agreed to go with me to the apartment of Gina Whitehall, my dependency-neglect case, to see how difficult it might have been for the child to turn on the water. I have the trial later this week. The police have investigated the incident, and I don't want to cross-examine a cop without having seen the place for myself. "Are you still going out there with me, or are you coming to weasel out?"

"What a mess!" he exclaims, ignoring my question. "It looks like those bars where they throw the shells on the floor."

"Most of them are yours," I say irritably. "How much weight have you lost?"

Squeezing into one of my chairs, Dan snorts, his double chin wobbling like a helping of cranberry sauce, "Three pounds. You get sick of the damn things awfully fast."

I throw a handful of shells into the wastepaper basket

beside me and then, despite my best intentions, I take another peanut from my desk drawer.

Dan extracts a reddish substance from his teeth with a
straightened paper clip and wipes it on his pants. We
seem to be regressing into after-hours behavior without
much prompting. He reaches into his pocket and pulls
out another nut, shaking his head. "I hate these damn
things."

I grin at Dan. The son of a gun is irrepressible. His
marriage is terrible; his law practice is at a standstill; he
is a hundred pounds overweight; he has the emotional
maturity of a five year old; and I wouldn't trade his
friendship for anything. As we talk, the phone rings. It is
a psychologist friend I contacted at the university to see
if there was any research on the reaction of small children to burns. I push the speaker button to let Dan hear. It
is not as if he doesn't know the client.

"Gideon," Steve Huddleston says, his baritone voice
not quite as low over the phone, "I thought I better get in
touch with you. I can't find anything specifically on reactions of small children to the sort of situation you described."

Damn. I look at Dan and shake my head. I would have
figured that with as much useless research as is cranked
out in this country some academic psychologist would
have zeroed in on this area, given all the attention to child
abuse nowadays. "What do you suggest?" I say glumly.
Gina Whitehall had better start preparing for a criminal
trial. If her kid dies, she will be charged with murder.

I listen to Steve clear his throat and watch Dan draw a
finger across his own. He ought to be handling this case.

Steve says, "If you'd like, I'd be willing to testify generally about the problem-solving ability of a child this age. The fact is that a two and a half year old wouldn't necessarily be able to figure out that she could escape the pain of the hot water by climbing out of the tub. The literature shows by that age a child just doesn't have the reasoning ability, and I imagine the panic a child would feel wouldn't improve it any either."

Dan waggles his jowls at me in approval. "You realize the client can't afford to pay you an expert witness fee," I say, making sure I'm not going to be hit with a bill down the road.

"All I want is a subpoena," he says, "so I won't have to take a vacation day."

Spoken like a true state employee. "No problem." I smile, watching Dan pop another peanut into his mouth. I'll get him a subpoena, but I suspect I'll forget about the statutory fee of thirty dollars. After all, he'll still be receiving his salary from the state. "Can you be prepared to back that statement up with some research?"

"That'll be simple enough," Steve says, sounding pleased to be part of this. Some professors love to testify. "Do you want me to bring it?"

"Just know it," I say. The Department of Human Services won't be prepared to rebut it. There is no sense letting their attorney pick it apart. I give him the date and time and tell him I will be calling him back to go over it Thursday afternoon.

"Where do you find these guys?" Dan asks, genuine admiration in his voice.

"People like to help. You forget I worked for the state

for years as a child abuse investigator. You get to know all kinds of folks. Let's go," I say, feeling a little better. This doesn't mean we'll win, but at least I'll have something to argue to the judge.

Dan looks sheepish as he says, "I can't make it."

I had a feeling he would wimp out on me. I ask, "Why the hell not?"

"I guess I feel too weird," he says, looking down at the floor. "I slept with Gina once at her apartment."

I look at Dan in disbelief. "You're shitting me."

Dan's eyes dart around the room, landing everywhere but on my face. "That's a hell of a thing to do, isn't it?"

I try to conjure up the scene: a fat, middle-aged, balding lawyer dropping his trousers to bed down a farm-girl whore who paid his fee with a screw. Now I understand better why he dropped her on me. "Where was the kid?" I ask, wondering if my client's child could have been playing in the tub and was burned while Dan was busy with her mother. I feel disgust creeping over me like a dirty fog.

"Day care, I think," Dan says, his face red with embarrassment. "I only did it once, but I still feel like an asshole about it."

I think of the girl: except for her eyes, as uninteresting as a digital clock. I feel sorry for her, but Dan is my friend, and I feel worse for him. Brenda must be giving him hell to drive him to a whore, but he is possibly exposing her to AIDS. "Did you use a rubber?"

"Two," Dan says, breathing hard. "I couldn't feel a thing."

"I've heard that's more dangerous," I say coldly, "because they break that way."

Dan looks miserable. "You know, if she reported me to the ethics people, they'd probably jerk my license for this one."

I stand up, embarrassed for my friend. It hasn't been too many months since Dan pleaded guilty in municipal court to shoplifting fifty cents' worth of food. "Lawyers have done a lot worse than snitched a Twinkie or bartered their fee," I say loyally, putting the best spin I can on Dan's activities.

Dan stands and waddles over to the door. "That's what's pathetic about me. I'm so damn petty."

Awkwardly, I clap him on the shoulder as he goes out ahead of me. "No," I say, turning out the light and locking the door, "your problem is you're so damn human."

Walking toward his office with his head down, he mutters, "In my case, I don't see there's a difference."

I head down the hall for the elevators, thinking that at least Dan has the guts to admit it and the decency to be ashamed. The older we get, the crazier we become. At the front desk, Julia pops a bubble when I tell her I'm going to Gina's house.

"Don't do anything I wouldn't do," she says, checking her tiny lips in a compact mirror for remains of the explosion.

Don't tell me that, I think. Julia is wearing a conservative and even elegant dark green paisley dress, but the top two buttons of her blouse are undone, revealing the top of a black lacy bra underneath. "Maybe I'd be safer," I say, smiling at the outrageous pretense that we are civilized, "if I didn't do anything you would do."

Julia makes a face but doesn't respond. It is rare that I get the last word. As I stand before the elevators, smugly I glance back at her. She has made a circle with her right thumb and forefinger, and with her left index finger she moves it back and forth through the O she has formed, all the while shaking her head. A female client for one of the other attorneys on our floor is seated a few feet away from her desk and is watching Julia with a look of utter amazement. Is this really a law firm?

A light rain has begun to fall, further darkening my mood. I hope the weather clears before I return to Fayetteville on Wednesday for Dade to give Binkie a statement. The euphoria from the Alabama game has already begun to fade, and the question uppermost in my mind is how long it will take the university administration to review the "J" Board's decision. If I could get Binkie to drop the criminal charges against Dade, surely that would influence their decision. Dade is doing his part: the Hogs have jumped to fourth in the UPI Poll and fifth in the AP. We play Auburn, ranked third in both polls, Saturday, and a win, if both Florida and Notre Dame lose, should put us on top. Surely the vice-chancellor and the chancellor are feeling some heat to let Dade finish the season when he is so clearly central to our chances. There isn't a person in the state who didn't feel the excitement when the Razorbacks won their first NCAA basketball championship. With Clinton taking what seems to be a daily pounding by the media, it is about the only thing in the state to feel good about.

On I-640 heading east I pass a billboard and see beaming down at me a slutty but expensive-looking model advertising pantyhose and think again of Julia's parting gesture. No wonder women are cynical. They expect the worst from men and with good reason. We are the ones who commit the rapes, the murders, the never ending garden-variety domestic beatings that seldom get reported. So what else is new? If we ever admitted to ourselves how little men have changed since we dropped down out of the trees, we might just give up on the spot.

I find Gina's half of a duplex apartment easier than I thought I would. Just five minutes off I-40 east on the road to Memphis, she is within walking distance of a pancake restaurant, a motel, and a gas station. So much for the zoning laws. On the other hand, given what she does for a living, her place is probably zoned commercial.

Gina comes to the door of her duplex dressed in a thin white T-shirt and purple short shorts that showcase her long legs. With big shoulders and a high waist, she gives the impression today of having a large frame rather than being overweight, as I remembered her in my office. Dumbly, I realize she expects to have sex with me, too. Why else would I have come to her place? Lawyers don't usually make house calls. In my own mind, my motives are pure since I set this visit up before I knew Dan slept with her.

"Hi," she says demurely, her round eyes reminding me of two blue buttons. "Come on in."

As I enter the room, a small black mutt comes up to me. Gina scoops up the dog and speaks baby talk to it. In her own apartment as she coos to the animal, she seems about twelve years old. The only piece of furniture in the darkened living room is a tattered tan couch. It is cold in here. This bleak area won't qualify for *House Beautiful*, but since most people don't use their living rooms either, why bother at all? "I'd like to see the tub," I announce instantly, and presumably like her customers, follow her up a flight of stairs to my right. Ascending the steps, I observe that the couch is too short and narrow for a successful business transaction. Off to the left at the top of the stairs, I see what must be her bedroom. I have to check an impulse to enter it. I have never been in a prostitute's room unless I count my Peace Corps days in Colombia. My main memory is of pictures of JFK and the Pope side by side, a piece of pottery resembling a coffee urn where she squatted in front of me afterward to wash herself, and a health card showing regular visits to the doctor to inspect her for VD. Before AIDS, prostitution seemed a business like any other, the customers wanting to dawdle and the sellers wanting to hurry them along. Since the advent of the HIV virus, the oldest profession must be like working on the bomb squad. All I remember about the Colombian whore I saw occasionally is that the door to her room was off its hinges. She said that while drunk she had broken it. I had no reason to doubt her.

Gina's bathroom is cleaner than I expected, cleaner than my own, I'm sure. "Tell me again why you left the baby alone," I say, looking at the fixtures. Instead of a difficult knob a child would have to grasp to turn, there is only a single lever, perhaps the width of the blade of a kitchen knife, for hot and cold. Trying the lever, I find it moves easily and convince myself that a small child could turn it.

Gina sits down on the closed toilet seat and crosses her legs. We could be a couple debating who left the ring in the tub. She says, "All the towels were dirty. I remembered I had some clean ones in the dryer downstairs and I went down to get them."

Logical enough, but would someone financially strapped as this girl have a washer and dryer? I make a mental note to check when I go downstairs. "How long were you gone?"

"Just a minute or two," she says, hugging herself.

I turn on the hot water full blast and look down at my watch to time how long it will take to partially fill the tub. She has said there was only an inch or two of water. If that is true, it doesn't make sense that the child would have a burn line right below her nipples if she had been forced to sit down in the water with her hips flat against the bottom of the tub. I have not seen anything in the report from Social Services showing the depth of water at the time the child was burned. In four minutes the tub fills to about three inches of water. Perhaps she was gone longer than she is admitting. I turn off the water. "Has anyone from Social Services timed how long it takes to fill the tub?" I ask, my face now bathed in sticky steam.

She hands me a towel to wipe my face. "Not while I've been here," she says. If the child were sitting up, I estimate it would take eight inches of water to burn her as the DHS report suggests.

I plunge my right hand into the water up to the wrist

and jerk it out immediately. The flesh is stinging and red. The pain must have been excruciating for the child. How could she not have tried to climb out if at all possible? I stand and run cold water over my wrist and look at myself in the bathroom mirror. My forehead feels as if it is covered with thick lard and my hair is plastered against my head. In the heat of the bathroom I don't look any better than the typical middle-aged men who, drunk, and stinking with their exertions, must come in here to piss after having sweated out an orgasm in her. How do women stand to be prostitutes? Block it all out somehow. How does this woman, innocent or guilty, bear to think about her child's blistered flesh? The same way, I guess.

We go downstairs, and I ask for a glass of water. I follow her into the kitchen, and notice a utility room off to the right with a rusty washer and dryer. If she is lying, it isn't about her domestic appliances. "How is Glenetta doing?" I finally ask as I sit down in one of the two folding chairs at a card table by the refrigerator.

Like the bathroom, this small space has a used look and reflects something of the habits of the owner. Pinned against the door with magnets is a calendar whose motif is cats, a birthday card whose cover depicts two Chippendale-like (young with hairless chests) male models in minuscule but bulging briefs, and a picture of Glenetta. The photo shows the child digging mischievously at an unseen object in the garbage can here in the kitchen. Glenetta, sturdily built, in a red playsuit, has brown curly hair and her mother's round eyes.

Following my gaze, Gina hands me tap water in a bright green plastic cup and says, "She's a lot better. Just like you said, they watch every move I make when I go visit."

We talk about the case for a while as I go over the questions she is likely to be asked on cross-examination. Her credibility can make or break the case, and I emphasize this point more than once, thinking as I do that it is not unlike Dade's situation in this respect. All this heavy duty science around, and most cases come down to a matter of whom you believe. "You've got to convince the judge how much you care about Glenetta and that it was a single isolated act of negligence that could have happened to any parent," I say. "Nobody can do that except you." The problem is that since the first time I talked with her she has displayed little outward emotion. Perhaps, this is how she is normally (I should ask Dan), but on Friday I want some anguish.

"That's all it was," she says, scanning my face coolly as if she is figuring how much to charge a customer or how long it will take to slop the hogs. Gina, who is wearing no makeup and only a swipe of lipstick, is living proof that beauty is in the eye of the beholder. "I've got to go to D.Y.'s in a little bit. You want to go back upstairs?"

I give her a smile that is more embarrassed than real. "I don't know what Mr. Bailey told you about me," I say, "but I don't expect to be paid that way."

"Oh," she says, stroking the dog that has come into the room since we have been talking and has curled against her feet. "I just figured that's why you came out here."

I realize now that everyone who sees me in court with this woman who knows her past will assume that I slept with her. I can't do anything about that. I assure her, "I just wanted to get a visual picture of what happened. Do you have a camera?"

Startled perhaps by an involuntary reflex, the mutt jumps off and runs out of the room. Maybe I'm one of those weirdos who gets off on pictures instead of the real thing. "I've got one," she says cautiously, "but it doesn't have any film."

"Before the trial Friday," I explain, "I want you to take some pictures of the bathtub and be sure to get the lever that regulates hot and cold, okay? I want the judge to see how easy it would have been for Glenetta to have turned on the hot water."

Understanding finally that I'm not really a dirty old man, she nods. "I can do that."

At the door Gina gives me a genuine smile for the first time since I've met her. "You really seem interested in trying to help me," she says, smoothing a torn place in the mesh of the front door screen.

"I'll give it my best shot," I promise. I don't want to be seen as merely going through the motions to get a fee in this case. Besides the fear that somebody will think I'm sleeping with her, I find I am motivated by my new status as a star football player's attorney. Of course, if Dade is convicted, things will return to normal. You're only as good as your last case. If these aren't the most honorable of motives, I figure that since the road to hell is paved with good intentions, any psychological explanation for my accepting this financially unrewarding undertaking is so much window dressing.

I drive back to my office in a downpour, wondering

again if I would have turned Gina down if I hadn't slept with Amy Saturday night. People don't steal food if there is enough to eat, but given my own rationalizations for my behavior over the years, I don't figure I'm all that much different from Dan.

Dade and I are immediately ushered into Binkie Cross's office Wednesday morning at eleven. Cross smiles at Dade, who is dressed in coal-black sweats, property of the Razorback Athletic Department, and offers his hand. "That was a hell of a catch," he can't resist saying. "How'd you hold onto the ball?"

Dade, as I have prepped him, smiles at this man who holds his life in his hands and grasps his outstretched palm as firmly as if he were catching a football. If Binkie wants to dismiss this case for lack of evidence, there is not a soul on earth who can stop him. Though he has probably answered that question fifty times now, Dade says modestly, "Lucky, I guess."

"Hell, most receivers wouldn't have been open," Binkie says, pointing to a conference table on which rests a tape recorder. "There wasn't any luck to it."

Far be it from me to argue the point. As we sit, Mike Cash enters the room and shuts the door behind him. We speak, but I don't get up. If this kid hadn't been such an eager beaver, we probably wouldn't be here. Binkie says, "I'm gonna put him under oath and on tape, okay?"

This is a calculated risk, but I don't see that we have much choice. If Dade wants to avoid a trial, he is going to have to cooperate. We begin, and Binkie proves to be a thorough questioner. By this time I have asked myself or heard most of what he gets out of Dade, but there are some things neither I nor the "J" Board learned, the most important of which concerns the clear suggestion that Dade may have had something to drink that night, after all. "Are you familiar with Chuck's Grill on Dickson?" Binkie asks casually almost halfway through the interview.

Dade immediately becomes uncomfortable and begins to mumble, which he has not been doing. "I've been there a couple of times."

"Did you go there the night this incident allegedly took place?"

Oh shit, I think, wondering whether to pull the plug on this little chat. Dade says in a barely audible voice, "Yeah."

"Did you have anything to drink?"

"I don't remember," he says. "I might have had a couple of beers."

Son of a bitch! I yawn, as if this isn't any news to me. He can be impeached on this point if Binkie can get hold of the tape of the "J" Board hearing, which I suspect he can. Though the hearing was supposed to be confidential, not all those people can keep their mouths shut. Yet, this isn't fatal, I tell myself. By itself it isn't a case breaker. The problem is, credibility is everything in this case. I can hear in my head already Binkie's argument: Ladies and gentlemen, if the defendant is lying about one thing, what else is he lying about? Binkie establishes the time (about seven), and asks who was there, though Dade professes not to remember talking to anybody except Chuck.

Binkie asks Dade several questions about Eddie Stiles,

and again Dade evidences some nervousness. Binkie implies that the elusive Eddie, at the least, by letting Dade
and other team members use his apartment, is violating
NCAA rules by extending benefits to athletes that aren't
being extended to other students. Far worse, Binkie
leaves the impression that Eddie may be involved in
drugs. He asks Dade directly, "Do you have any knowledge that Eddie Stiles is either directly or indirectly involved in the sale of illegal substances?"

Dade replies in the negative, but by the time we are
through I am wondering how innocent my client really is.
He wouldn't be the first or last player to have a drug
problem. Yet, it is as if Binkie is merely warning Dade
officially that he better stay away from Eddie. He has
asked the questions on the record that he had to ask, but
Binkie, like everybody else in this state, is a Razorback
fan. Surely he doesn't want the football program penal-
ized. I hope that is all there is to it. He tells me he should
be getting in touch with me in a few days, and as we are
about to leave his office, he shakes Dade's hand again as
if he isn't too concerned about what he has learned. I nod
again at Mike Cash, who apparently has orders not even
to open his mouth.

After waiting not so patiently for Dade to give hair and
saliva samples (it seems a waste of time now that he has
given a formal statement admitting intercourse), I drive
him back to the campus and give him hell for not leveling
with me. "This is how a defendant gets convicted in these
kinds of cases!" I storm at him as I come to the light on
Arkansas and Dickson. "What else have you lied to me
about?"

"Nothing!" Dade insists, looking at the window. "I had forgotten about having a couple of beers. I drank them over an hour before I met Robin. It wasn't a big deal."

As the traffic thickens near the university, I wonder if this is merely the tip of the iceberg. Maybe this wasn't such a good idea after all. Still, I'd rather find out now than be clobbered with it in trial. "You can bet your last dollar the prosecutor will make every lie you tell a big deal if this case goes to trial."

Dade is silent, perhaps because every time he has opened his mouth I have yelled at him. Perhaps it is my imagination, but as we drive through the campus on our way to Darby Hall, it seems as if the students walking along the streets are livelier, more animated. A couple of male students spot Dade as we stop at the light at the law school and yell at him, "Great game, Dade!" The win over Alabama has put a spring in their steps they didn't have before. It is incredible that a game should matter so much, but it does. Too bad we couldn't have had the trial on Sunday.

Before I drop Dade off in the parking lot next to his dorm, I ask him about Eddie Stiles. "Level with me on this guy, okay? Did he ever give you drugs?"

"I didn't know he even sold!" Dade says vehemently. "He just let us use the place."

"For your sake," I say angrily, "I hope you're telling the truth. You know you've got to stay away from people like that—anybody who tries to give you a freebie of any kind. There're a million people out there trying to use athletes."

Chastened, he nods. I should know. By any honest definition I'm one of them. As Dade gets out, I make him promise to call me if he hears any information about Robin. "Until we hear different, we've still got a trial date in January."

"Do you think we'll hear this week about what the school will do?" he asks.

"I don't know what either the prosecutor or the university will do," I confess. Politics within a university bureaucracy is as mysterious to me as the inside of a computer. "But it seems to me that if you keep winning, it will be harder for them to want to punish you." As soon as I say this, I realize more victories could have the opposite effect on the university. The school administration may bend over backward to make it appear that it is not making a decision based on our chances of playing in a major bowl on New Year's Day.

Dade suddenly looks older than his twenty-one years. How much more pressure can he stand? I ought to be happy if he just tells the truth. I leave him on the sidewalk outside his dorm and drive over to Ole Main, thinking I remember that Sarah has told me that she works until one on Wednesdays. Maybe she can grab some lunch with me.

Sarah is walking out the door as I come in. She says she has class in ten minutes but tells me there is a WAR rally again tonight and that I should come. I explain that I have cases piling up on my desk back home and don't mention there is a possibility that Dade's case could be dismissed. I don't want to get her started. As students stream past us on their way to classes, I ask, "Did you hear about the polls? The Hogs are as high as fourth."

She reaches over to pull off a thread from my sports coat, which after five years of constant wear doesn't have many to give. I need to break down and buy some clothes. Maybe I could get Amy to go with me to keep me from buying stuff that looks like I'm getting buried in it. "Dad," Sarah says softly, "that's what's wrong with this place now. Sports is all anybody really cares about. It's absurd."

She's right. It is ridiculous, but according to Dan, so is having two eyes, two ears, two arms, two legs, and only one penis. "You're absolutely right," I say, trying to keep things light, "but it beats armed insurrection."

As I walk down the hall with her, she asks seriously, "Do you really think men are just so naturally aggressive they can't help being violent?"

Part of me is glad she's got class. "I do better when I don't think, babe," I say, trying to finesse this subject. "After about two seconds I get bogged down. If they haven't figured this stuff out by now, I sure as heck don't figure my two cents' worth will make a dime's worth of difference."

She smiles indulgently, confident that her generation, or maybe even Paula Crawford by herself, will find the answers. If they do, I just hope women don't line us up and shoot us. I give her a hug and tell her I will see her soon. She confides, "There's a rumor going around that the administration will decide this week about Dade."

Interested in this information, I ask the source, but am told it was just "some girls talking." I leave and, forgetting that I haven't eaten, drop by my "office" on Mountain Street and discuss with Barton the statement Dade gave this morning to Binkie.

Behind his desk, hands clasped behind his head, Barton rocks back in his swivel chair and stares at the ceiling. "If Dade is doing drugs," Barton says, "there's no way Binkie will cut him any slack. That's one subject he's tough as nails on."

"Dade swears he's not," I say, still irritated by the revelations of an hour ago. "I don't know whether to believe him or not."

Barton glances at his Rolex. "These kids aren't saints," he says primly. "They're treated like gods when they win, and it's easy for them to get used to it."

Barton is busy, and I should get out of here. I need to think about this case before I do any more about it. From the library I call Binkie back and get him in his office. "Are you getting ready to slap some new charges on Dade?" I ask bluntly as soon as he comes on the line. "Obviously, you know a lot more about this situation than I do."

"I wasn't trying to sandbag you," Binkie says, not quite apologetic. "It's just we've known for years the owner of Chuck's Grill gives big-time players like Dade free drinks. A player with his reputation can't go anywhere without somebody knowing who he is. And as far as drugs go, I can't prove for sure yet that Eddie Stiles is dealing, but whether he is or isn't, I'd make sure Dade stays as far away from him as humanly possible if I were you. Dade seems like a good kid. I'd hate to bust him for drugs, but I would. Real quick, too."

"Tell me about Eddie," I say, thinking I should pay him

a visit before I get out of town. He and I could benefit from a heart-to-heart talk.

Binkie responds, his voice becoming slightly sarcastic. "He's one of those part-time students who never graduate and seems to have more money than he should. His thing is hanging with jocks. He pleaded guilty to possession of marijuana on a reduced charge in Oklahoma City a couple of years ago, but that's his only record we know of. Maybe he's a wonderful guy and has a heart of gold, but I doubt it. I just hear his name a little too often to be convinced of it."

Before I hang up, Binkie tells me that Eddie can usually be found at a bar named Slade's, which is on the road to Springdale about five miles from campus. "We talked to him during the investigation, but he didn't give us anything. He admitted he owned the house on Happy Hollow Road and sometimes let athletes use it. We know he rents a couple of other houses in Fayetteville to students. That was it. That's why we didn't bother with a statement from him."

I thank Binkie for the information and hang up, thinking he is probably one of the most decent prosecutors I've ever run across. What good will it do to put one more black male in prison? A lot of crime comes simply from being around the wrong people.

Instead of heading south out of town, I point the Blazer north toward the Missouri border. On both sides of the road is wall-to-wall commercial activity. Unlike the area of the state where I grew up, northwest Arkansas is booming, thanks in no small part to the thriving poultry industry. Still, the Arkansas Roosters doesn't have quite the same ring. I find Slade's in a shopping center that is crawling with customers. It seems an unlikely place for athletes, but inside it has student-friendly prices and its walls are lined with framed 8 x 10 pictures of Razorback stars all the way back to the sixties. I take a seat at the bar and order a beer from a pretty brunette in a football jersey and wait for my eyes to become accustomed to the gloom. With a mix of mainly guys ranging from obvious students to construction worker types, Slade's is doing a healthy business for a weekday afternoon. Maybe everybody drinks free here. I wonder where Slade is. There's not a male behind the bar, and I don't see any blacks either and ask the barkeep if she has seen Eddie Stiles.

The girl, who appears to have a couple of fully inflated footballs stuffed under her jersey, ignores my gaze, which has lingered a little too long (I suspect it's not the first time) and smiles pleasantly at me. "I've seen him all afternoon. You passed him on your way in. He's sitting in the first booth by himself."

"Great!" I say, feeling equally pleasant. I pull out a five and leave it. "I think I'll go join him."

She winks, happy with a three-dollar tip. So Eddie is a white guy, I think stupidly as I saunter back toward the entrance. I had assumed he was black and would look like some kind of dude who specializes in drive-by shootings when his drug deals go sour. Despite my liberal past, my preconceptions, unfailingly wrong, never fail to amaze me.

"Eddie," I say sliding in across from him, "I'm Gideon Page. I'd like to visit with you for a few minutes."

Eddie Stiles is a short, pudgy young man with watery

gray eyes and with a hint of a mustache (or maybe it's just dirt) above his lips. Though the temperature outside is pleasant, he is wearing an expensive dark blue two-pocket chambray workshirt unbuttoned over a muted striped T. I can't see his pants or his shoes, but Eddie apparently doesn't need any help spending his money. "You're Dade's lawyer," he says, eagerly reaching for my hand.

Ridiculously flattered that he knows who I am, I allow him to pump my hand as if I were visiting royalty or a major dope supplier. I realize I was nervous about this encounter, but this kid is hardly an intimidating figure. "Eddie, let me get to the point. I want you to stay away from Dade. I don't want you to talk to him; I don't want him using your house. I don't know what your story is, but the prosecutor says you're one of their favorite topics of conversation."

Eddie, his soft face as innocent as a baby's, whines, "I been stayin' away from him! The cops think I sell drugs, but they're crazy! They'd bust me so fast, man! It's just that I like the Razorbacks. They're great athletes. Dade could go pro right now. Are you gonna negotiate his contract if you beat the rape charge? It'd be worth a bundle."

I look at this guy in amazement. Words tumble from his mouth like a string of firecrackers being shot off. I prefer him on the defensive. "You're violating NCAA rules," I tell him, "by letting players use your house."

Eddie taps his glass against the Formica tabletop like a judge gaveling an unruly lawyer out of order. "No way, man! I let nonathlete students use my house for parties. If I do that, there's no violation."

Eddie, like other criminals I have known, has an answer for everything. "Listen, I can help Dade if you'll let me. I saw Robin coming out of the house that night when Dade was supposed to have raped her. I'd just pulled into the yard and could see her face in the porch light. She wasn't upset at all. She was smiling even."

I believe that like I believe I'm going to grow wings and a halo. I knock back a slug of beer. What do guys like this do when they allegedly grow up? Become lobbyists, I guess. Always wanting to help somebody out. "Somehow, you failed to mention this to the cops."

Eddie has his hands up as soon as I get the words out. "They didn't really ask. Those guys hate my guts. They even think I'm a fag. That's bullshit. Ask Dade. He wouldn't put up with that kind of shit."

What a pathetic little creature. "Sometime soon, when I'm back up here, I'd like Dade to show me inside the house where the rape was supposed to have happened, but you never seem to be at home. You must spend a lot of time at the library."

Eddie smiles at my little joke. "Anytime you say, man. Anytime you say. Anything I can do to help, I will. Just call here and ask for Eddie."

"I'll do that," I say and slide out of the booth and head for my car, figuring it will do no good to stop by Dickson Street and have a chat with the owner of Chuck's Grill. He's not going to admit that he gives free drinks to star athletes. Dade will have to take responsibility for himself. I drive home, wondering if I'm any different from Chuck and Eddie. That little weasel acted as if he had known me forever.

9

"I CONFESS I feared the worst," Amy says, laying her knife and fork on the chipped plastic dish in front of us. "Actually, this was delicious. Here you've cooked me dinner, and you should be preparing for your burned-baby case tomorrow."

"For the money she's paid," I say, "I'm overprepared, believe me." Amy must really have it bad for me. All I've done is burn a steak on the grill, popped two potatoes in the microwave, and thrown together a salad. I pick up the plates and take them to the sink. Dirty dishes make me feel queasy. "The best part of our relationship," I add, "is that you have such low expectations."

Still seated, Amy leans down and pets Woogie, who has stationed himself by her chair. "As long as I can still get a heartbeat," she says, grinning at me, "I'm not gonna complain. You're a low-maintenance kind of guy."

I turn on the hot water and rinse vegetable juice off the faded dishes, wondering if she means I'm cheap. It hasn't occurred to me until tonight that new cutlery wouldn't send me to the poorhouse. It's not as if I'd be outfitting a restaurant chain. "I still can't get over the fact you like

215

'em so old," I say, returning to a subject I know I am worrying to death. Yet, most people don't go prospecting in a
played-out mine if they have other options. As cute as she
is, Amy doesn't even have to dip her pan into the water.
Tonight, her tight jeans are making my heart speed up.
Clothed, her short, compact frame had led me to believe
in the past she was always on the verge of carrying too
much weight. Seeing her at the track cured that miscon-
ception. Unlike most humans, the more flesh Amy re-
veals, the better. Though her waist is short, her stomach,
which is partially revealed beneath a jade shirt that is tied
at the bottom, is as taut as a drawn bowstring. Above the
waist she is delightfully voluptuous, a fact usually con-
cealed by business suits and running bras.

"Let's get this resolved once and for all," she says,
coming over to load my ancient dishwasher, and in the
process patting me on the butt in a proprietary manner. "I
know this isn't very original, but you remind me of my
father."

Damn. And they say men aren't romantic. But if you
don't want spinach, don't ask for it. "I'm flattered," I lie.

"You should be. He was a wonderful man," Amy says
firmly. "Am I getting you for dessert?" She pinches my
right cheek through my favorite pair of old jeans, thread-
bare in the extreme but totally comfortable.

Again, I am reminded of the contrast with Rainey. She
would have cut off her hand before she would have
played grab-ass with me. "You want me to get out the
Cool Whip?"

"I like you plain, Gideon," Amy says seriously before
pressing her full mouth against mine. Though I'm not

crazy about making love on a full stomach, Amy's tongue is delightful. So warm and eager. How nice it is to be wanted by her. If I have a heart attack, it will have been for a good cause.

In the bedroom I turn off the phone. Gina Whitehall has already called me once tonight. I know she is anxious about tomorrow, but surely I deserve to be off the clock a little while. As before, Amy proves to be a delightful, appreciative lover. From her purse she takes a vial of liquid and rubs oil over our vital parts until they smell like vanilla ice cream cones. After we do it twice in the same bed where I made love to Rosa thousands of times, curious, yet a little afraid of the answer, I ask, "So what was your father like?"

Cradled in the crook of my right arm like a child with a fairly fresh sheet almost but not quite covering her breasts, she says, "He felt responsible, the way you do. Like him, you're a worrier. You worry about Sarah. You're always worried about your clients. You're like an old mother hen. I like that. A lot of men my age just worry about their cash flow."

I reach across her and turn the phone back on, feeling her slightly damp hair against my left ear. "You're doing wonders for my masculinity."

"You don't need a bit of help in that department," she says, her voice playful, yet, I hope, respectful, too.

The phone rings immediately as if to protest my audacity in briefly silencing it. She giggles like a child caught playing doctor. Since Sarah has been off at school, I have moved her telephone into my room. Twenty years ago telephones seemed as immovable as

218   Grif Stockley

bathroom fixtures. Now it's like a drug I need on the hour. "Hello," I say, fearing it might be Rainey. She still calls occasionally.

"Dad, are you okay?" Sarah asks. "You sound out of breath."

"I'm fine, babe," I say. "I just came in from running. How's WAR doing? Have y'all taken over any government buildings or seized any university bureaucrats?" I mouth the word "Sarah" to Amy, who puts her hand over her mouth to keep from laughing out loud. The bed, an heirloom from my parents' home in Bear Creek, groans at my insolence. Amy cannot contain her giggles and smothers her face against her pillow. To complicate matters, Woogie, whose sleep underneath the bed has apparently been disturbed, appears from the side and jumps up on the sheets between me and Amy, who now is almost hysterical.

"Who's with you?" Sarah asks, dryly. "She sounds like she's having a good time."

"Woogie's entertaining Amy Gilchrist," I say, at least partially correct.

There is silence. Though Amy and Sarah have never met, Sarah knows our age difference; furthermore, even after all this time she is still loyal to Rainey. I wait her out. "I take it," she says curtly, "that you're not as upset as I thought you'd be."

"Upset at what, babe?" I ask, putting my finger to my mouth to shush Amy. Damn, Sarah will think she is terrible.

"Both the vice-chancellor and the chancellor have upheld the 'J' Board's position! Dade is off the team! We won!"

I look over at the digital clock. "They announced the decision at nine o'clock at night?"

"It got out," she explains. "And they finally confirmed it tonight. I can't believe you didn't know. Are you mad?"

I relay the message to Amy. "Hell yes, I'm mad! What good is this going to do?"

"Because it's right, Dad!" Sarah says, her voice shrill. "It says that women are more than football games; it tells kids that rape is serious; it tells guys that this campus will listen to women instead of football coaches." She sounds indignant all over again.

I'm pissed as hell. "All it tells me is that if a pressure group makes enough noise that it can get its way," I sputter. Amy has withdrawn to her side of the bed and is looking at me with an irritated expression. I don't care. "It's not a question of right or wrong but who's got the upper hand. It's racism, too. Do you think if the chancellor had been a black male, the decision would have been the same? Hell, no. Your group got what it wanted because it screamed the loudest and made some white males feel guilty and so they threw your group a bone. Dade is a victim, pure and simple. He wasn't harming anybody by staying on the team; in fact, he was a contributor to the school and to the entire state, and now WAR has taken that away."

"Daddy!" Sarah yelps. "You sound like some redneck! I can't believe you're saying all this!"

I look up to see Amy getting dressed. I say hastily, "Sarah, I have to get off the phone. I've got to call Dade and his parents. I'll talk to you later. I'm sorry if I sounded mean." Damn it to hell. It's always the messenger who gets shot. After she murmurs something I don't catch, she hangs up, allowing me to say to Amy, "You don't have to go."

Most women would gather up their clothes and go into the bathroom. Not Amy. Standing by the bed in her panties, she fastens her bra and looks right through me. "I wouldn't stay here if you paid me a million dollars. I'm just appalled by the way you talked to Sarah. Have you heard of the First Amendment? If this had come out the way you wanted it to, the administration would have been wise and wonderful. You don't get your way one time and you practically call your daughter a fascist. So Dade Cunningham doesn't play in a few football games—it doesn't mean the world is coming to an end. One of the reasons I liked you is that I thought you had some perspective on things. I don't think you do." All the while she is pulling on her jeans and sweater as fast as she can.

I reach down to the floor for my underwear. I don't have the guts to admit to Amy that I have begun thinking of this case as a potential oil well. "A few minutes ago you were telling me why you liked me," I remind her.

She sits on the bed to put on her running shoes. Woogie, smarter than I am, has gone back under the bed. "Well, I guess I was wrong. I don't mind admitting that."

"Well, I think you're overreacting," I say, pulling my pants up. With no clothes on I feel at a distinct disadvantage.

"And you're not?" she scoffs and turns on her heels and is out the door.

"Amy!" I yell, but I hear the front door slam.

Shit! Am I not allowed to get mad just once without the women in my life going nuts? Poor Dade. I bet he has been trying to call me. Before I can pick up the phone to call him, the phone rings again. It is Clarise Dozier, who tells me she has been trying to get me for an hour. She says that she has already spoken with Dade and insists on reading the chancellor's statement to me. It is about what I expected—full of trite, high-sounding phrases. "The university is a venue where education takes place, and it is in this spirit I make this decision. . . ." Bullshit, I think. The university is a venue where shoving matches take place, and my client just got outshoved. Still, it is not Clarise Dozier's fault, and I calm down enough to keep a civil tongue in my head. I thank her and tell her I need to call Dade, and she graciously hangs up, proving, I guess, that not every female I know ends a conversation with me by hating my guts.

By the time I get through to Dade's parents, I have begun to put a different spin on events entirely. "You need to keep in mind," I tell Roy, who has answered the phone and has complained bitterly about the decision, "that Dade got to play in the most important game in his life and was terrific. The fact that he won't finish the season won't matter that much in the long run if there's an acquittal. In fact, he'll just avoid a career-ending injury. I know he sounded down tonight, but what he has to realize and what you do too, is that people will remember the Alabama game for a long time—especially the pro

scouts. That last catch alone was worth millions to him."
I hope I'm not coming on too strong. Ideally, the idea
will occur to them that I will be the ideal person to negotiate his contract. It can't hurt to plant a few seeds.

"It sounds like they just caved in to a bunch of
women," Roy says, but sounding not quite as aggrieved.

"I agree," I say, on safe ground at last. To Lucy Cunningham, who takes the phone from her husband, I
explain that the case could still be dismissed by the
prosecutor and tell her that Dade's statement went okay.
I'll have plenty of time later to go back and tell her and
Roy the bad parts, but they have enough to deal with
tonight. "The prosecuting attorney said he'd think about
it."

Lucy Cunningham scoffs at the possibility. "Why
should he do that? He gets elected by how many he con-
victs, not how many he lets go. What's another black boy
to him?" Her voice is resigned. Don't try to fool me, her
tone implies. How many games Dade played is history.
The news is that he won't play any more. Roy may be
fooled into thinking the glass is half full, but she isn't.

Yet, for some reason I have a good feeling about
Binkie Cross: maybe it is unjustified, but I have the sense
he likes Dade and would like to have an excuse not to
have to try him. Justice is what every prosecutor is supposed to do, not try people, who are more likely than not,
innocent. "We may be surprised," I say, not having the
nerve to offer up a platitude to her. "What's important is
to explore any opportunity to avoid trial."

"You mean, make a deal?" Lucy asks, way ahead of
her husband.

"One hasn't been offered," I say quickly, but I don't see any harm in preparing the way for something down the road. If Binkie were willing to knock this case down to a misdemeanor, I'd advise Dade to take it. I have no doubt his parents will have a major influence on his decision. "If that opportunity presents itself, it'd be a mistake not to consider it."

Nothing if not pragmatic, Lucy tells me she agrees, and I tell her I will be in touch again soon. There is no doubt in my mind about who runs things in the Cunningham family. His father, Dade told me, got to take off to drive up to the Alabama game, but his mother was the one he called to tell he wasn't being allowed to play anymore.

Ten minutes after I put the phone down, the phone rings again and I am asked if I can get down to Channel 4 for a live interview on the ten o'clock news to give my reaction to the Chancellor's decision. The caller, who identifies himself as an assistant producer, says, barely containing his fury, that I haven't been breathlessly waiting by the phone for his call, that he has been trying to get me all night. Still in my underwear, I look at my watch. It is a quarter to ten, and I need a lot of work. I say I can't make it but will give a statement. In a weary voice, he says go ahead, and I say I am disappointed and reaffirm my belief in Dade's innocence.

On the ten o'clock news I watch as Coma Newby, the station's newest anchor, chops my comment to one word—"disappointed"—and spends a good two minutes on the phone with Chancellor Henry, letting him pontificate about how educational values have been served.

Shit, I should have gone down there naked and demanded equal time.

I wait for the phone to ring after the news, but mercifully it is silent and I go to bed, unable to get out of my mind the words from an old song: "Mama said there'd be days like this, Mama said."

"The problem-solving ability of the average two-and-a-half-year-old child," Steve Huddleston testifies in a booming, authoritative tone, "is not developed to such an extent that it can be assumed that she would know by climbing out of the tub she could avoid the hot water."

The consternation registered on the faces of the guardian ad litem, Joe Heavener, the attorney appointed to represent the child, and the attorney for the Department of Human Services, Cassie McKenzie, is so obvious I have to resist the temptation to laugh. From my past experiences as a caseworker I know there is no time for preparation of these cases, no discovery of witnesses by the attorneys, and consequently no thinking about the cross-examination of experts, who almost never appear in juvenile court on behalf of typically indigent parents.

"Your Honor, I object," Joe whines, pushing his big frame to a standing position. "There's no evidence the child in question is average. The witness admits he's never seen her."

Fighting the urge to lean on the podium in front of me, I turn to Judge Sloan. "Your Honor, Glenetta's doctor at St. Thomas has previously testified she was of average size and weight and seemed normally developed. Dr. Huddleston has been qualified as an expert in child development and can testify about what he knows from the literature."

Joe looks helplessly at Cassie, who shrugs as if to warn him not to make too big a deal over this. If this testimony can't be kept out, the only course of action at the trial level is to make an objection and to act as if it is of no importance. Until this moment the case for the Department of Human Services has been going more or less as planned. The photographs of the burned child have been enough to turn my stomach. After seeing the pictures, I marvel at the fact that the little girl is still breathing. The term "stocking and glove" burns does not adequately describe the discolored, cooked flesh in the photographs. The treating physician at St. Thomas has testified that it was his opinion the burns occurred as a result of the child having been held down in a sitting position in about ten inches of water.

The only real hitch in the case has been the social worker's failure to measure the water that was still standing in the tub when she arrived to investigate. As expected, a detective from the police department has testified that the heat of the water from the faucet coming into the tub is 140 degrees, which links up with the doctor's statement that assuming a water temperature of 140 degrees a child could receive full and partial thickness burns after only five seconds. Steve, decked out in red suspenders and a polka-dotted blue bow tie over a pink shirt and blue suit, is allowed to step down after a few harmless questions from Joe and then Cassie. He plops down in the back of the courtroom to watch the rest of the trial. He may have second thoughts in the morning

about what he has done, but now he seems proud to have
come through unscathed and gives me a nod as if to say
that now I owe him one.

Chastely outfitted in a teal pleated dress that comes
well below her knees, Gina Whitehall makes a tearful
witness on direct examination. The pleats emphasize
rather than hide her already ample hips, but she is not
modeling lingerie. One would never suspect she makes
part of her living as a prostitute. "I realized Glenetta
didn't have a towel and went downstairs to get one after I
turned off the water and left her playing," she says, her
voice tremulous and soft. "I stopped to get myself a glass
of water, and that was when I heard her screaming."
Here, the tears well up in her clear blue eyes. This isn't
quite the version we had rehearsed (she told me Glenetta
didn't have a clean towel, not that she didn't have one at
all), but in juvenile court not every attorney will pick up
on the discrepancy between the story she is telling now
and the statement she made to the police and to the social
worker. If she is charged with a crime, the attorneys in
the prosecuting attorney's office will be swarming all
over her.

I pause in my questioning to let the tears come. Her
credibility here is everything. "What happened then,
Gina?" I ask, putting as much sympathy into my voice as
I know how.

She brushes her eyes with her knuckles and continues
in a low but intense tone. "I ran upstairs and saw she had
managed to turn the tap and I snatched her out of the water and went and called 911."

I glance at Judge Sloan's face. He is one of our

younger judges with kids still in grade school. I am hoping he will remember what it is like to have small children bumping into corners of tables, running shoeless over hot-air vents, pulling pans off stoves. If you turn your head for a second, and all of us do, they have fallen or grabbed a pair of scissors from a table. I will remind him of this during my closing argument, but likely he will have made up his mind long before then. I can't read his expression, but he is listening closely to Gina, and that is all I can ask. He has to be wondering what if he returns the child to her and he's wrong, will this young woman do it again? He knows as well as I do that child abuse isn't usually a one-time event. The next time the child may be DOA. I break the crucial moments down for Gina, so she can give the judge as much detail as possible and then finish with her visits to the hospital.

"They watch me like I'm going to steal her," Gina says bitterly, her voice hostile for the first time. "I don't think the nurses care whether I visit Glenetta or not. They just want to see how I act."

No one from the other table will deny this. If she weren't visiting regularly or showed little interest in Glenetta when she did, someone from St. Thomas would have been called to testify about her behavior and demeanor. Instead, I have subpoenaed the records and have forced a nurse to tell the judge she has come to see her child almost every day and has acted appropriately (talking, holding Glenetta's hand even though the child had been barely conscious in the beginning) during her visits.

"Were you angry at Glenetta the morning this accident happened?" I ask Gina, whose own anger at the nurses at

St. Thomas has given her voice some steel. It is impera-
tive we overcome the testimony by Glenetta's doctor that
child abuse of this type sometimes occurs as a punishment for bedwetting.

Gina shakes her head as if she has never considered
being angry at her child in her life. "Not at all," she says.
"She was in a good mood, laughing and playing like she
always did. Her bath is one of our favorite times because
she's always so happy in the mornings."

I ask if Glenetta is completely potty trained and how
she is punished. Seemingly without a hint of guile, Gina
turns to Judge Sloan and tells him that her child occasionally has an accident in her pants but what two year
old hasn't? As for punishment, you don't hit children. All
it does is teach them to hit back. As a prostitute, a successful one anyway, a woman must be a successful actress, and it crosses my mind that Gina is playing the role
of the good mother no less skillfully than a woman who
convinces a man she is dying to have sex with him. Being
the hopeless creatures of ego we are, men want desperately to believe women, and as I listen to my client's answers, I realize how lucky she is that this case didn't land
in Anne (Queen Anne) Tongin's division. It wouldn't
even be close. I introduce into evidence the photographs
of the bathtub fixtures Gina has taken. A child, they
clearly show, could easily have turned the handle.

During my closing argument, I tell the judge that the
burns, though horrible, were accidental and that a single
negligent act is not child abuse. Harley Sloan, who likes
to brag he has been mistaken for David Letterman, is
courteous and attentive. Instead of displaying impatience

(he has three more cases to hear this afternoon), he follows me closely as if he is still pondering the outcome. As I review the evidence favorable to Gina, I remind him that it is indisputable she called 911 and by so doing saved her child's life. Gina Whitehall's behavior throughout this case simply does not fit the profile of a child abuser. Do I believe my own words? I don't know.

At the end of the hearing, Judge Sloan says he wants a few minutes, and we are in recess. Outside on the grass in brilliant sunshine, Gina, like a condemned prisoner taking her last cigarette, lights up and asks me anxiously, "How'd I do?"

I look across the street at McDonald's, and, having missed lunch, wonder if I have time for a chocolate milkshake. Probably not, and besides, it would be stretching civilized behavior to mention food at a time like this. Even if my client has given the performance of her life, the odds are against her. "You did great," I tell her sincerely. If I were your customer, I'd give you a tip. Did she hold her kid down in a tub of unbearably hot water? Regardless of what Sloan does, I'll never know the answer for certain. There is no doubt in the minds of anyone involved in the presentation of the case by the Department of Human Services. They have all been righteously indignant. The pictures are too horrible not to provoke outrage. Yet, as Gina testified, no one feels worse about what happened than she does (with the exception of Glenetta).

"I don't have any money to pay you yet," Gina says, not quite able to look me in the eye.

I am afraid she is about to suggest again that I take it

out in trade and say hastily, "You don't need to worry about that now."

She gives me an uncertain smile and studies the shrubs in front of the building. "I want to pay you."

I nod, knowing this is her way of expressing gratitude, regardless of the outcome.

The bailiff, an elderly ex-cop named Sonny McDill, whom I've known for years, waves at me through the glass window that the judge has reached a decision. Knowing this haste is not a good sign, I take a deep breath, realizing that I've come to like Gina. "I think they're ready for us," I say, as gently as I can.

In plain view of Sonny she flips the cigarette into the shrubs, and I resist the urge to tell her to pick it up, realizing I think of her as a child and not a woman.

As Judge Sloan enters the courtroom, I search his face for an answer, but he seems preoccupied as if he has already mentally moved onto the next case. "Be seated, please," he says nodding to Sonny to close the door.

These moments in a courtroom before a decision is announced are an eternity and usually the climax of wishful thinking. Somehow, despite the evidence, the jury will acquit, the judge will remember what it was like when he was young, etc. Virginia, not only is there a Santa Claus, but out of all the billions of boys and girls, he remembers your name! We sit down and I turn and catch Steve Huddleston's eye. He looks as if he has been holding his breath since the judge left the room. His almost bug-eyed expression suggests that he couldn't be more impressed than if the United States Supreme Court had chosen to announce its most momentous decision in an obscure

Arkansas courtroom. Yet, for Gina and her daughter, no decision will affect their lives more decisively.

"This is an especially difficult decision," Judge Sloan begins, looking directly at the social worker, Laura Holmes, who filed the petition on behalf of the department, "because of the seriousness of the injuries to the child, but in this particular case I am persuaded by a number of factors that Ms. Whitehall did not injure her child deliberately, and therefore I'm dismissing the petition against her."

Tears spurt from Gina's eyes as she gasps with joy, and I glance at the social worker, who is crying just as hard.

Joe Heavener is outraged. "Your Honor," he says, his voice high with indignation as he struggles to his feet. "There was overwhelming medical evidence in this case!"

"Sit down, Mr. Heavener," Judge Sloan says placidly. "And I'll tell you the reasons for my decision. Just because you bring in a doctor to testify doesn't mean I'm obligated to accept his testimony. What would be the point of having judges to hear these cases? I'm the finder of fact here, and I wasn't persuaded by the evidence that the child was held down. . . ."

Like a schoolboy naming the causes of the Civil War, the judge begins to tick off on his fingers the evidence favorable to Gina. While he does, I think how this decision would have been virtually unthinkable only a few years ago. It has only been since 1987 that the Arkansas Supreme Court has required juvenile proceedings to be truly adversarial. I pat Gina on the back and whisper that after the judge is finished she should go thank Steve Huddleston who now seems a little stunned by his part in the outcome. In his summary Judge Sloan has noted that he found Dr. Huddleston's testimony helpful in understanding why Glenetta simply didn't crawl out of the tub when she began to be burned by the water.

Outside the courtroom I pump Steve's hand and ask him if he would be interested in doing more research for me some other time. His hands in his pockets, he stares at the floor and says sheepishly, "One case like this is enough for me. I'll worry about this kid until she leaves home."

"All you did was give the judge information," I assure him, "he wouldn't have had otherwise."

Apparently relieved to be thought in some manner as a technician, Steve's face brightens visibly. "I guess so."

Outside in the parking lot, Gina, her face shining with joy, gives me a big hug. "You were great!"

Hardly, I think, but she got her money's worth. I'd give what little I'm getting on this case to know if she really burned her kid deliberately. "Was it an accident?" I ask. "You can tell me now."

"Of course it was!" she says indignantly. "I wouldn't hurt my child!"

I say quickly, "I didn't think you did."

Driving back to the office, I muse on what a dumb question I asked her. Nearly every defendant I've ever represented says he or she is innocent. It's the nature of the beast. Did Dade rape Robin? That's an even dumber question.

10

"DADE WOULD HAVE made all the difference in the world against Auburn," Dan says, staring out my window into the street below. Each Monday he comes into my office and dissects the Hogs' performance from the previous Saturday. "They knew we didn't have anybody who could get open long without Dade."

The Razorbacks kept it close (21 to 14), but it was painfully obvious how much they missed Dade. Only five completions in twenty attempts and none more than ten yards. "It serves them right," I say, still angry about the administration's decision to uphold the "J" Board. "If they lose the rest of their games, you might see some heads roll."

Dan lets out his belt a notch, even though it is only nine in the morning. "People have been fired for less."

He was almost absurdly pleased that I got the dependency-neglect petition against Gina dismissed on Friday. I noticed he took off the rest of the day. Surely he isn't still sleeping with her. If he is, he deserves what he gets. "It pisses me that Carter didn't even mention Dade on his TV show Sunday. It's like the Soviet Union when they used to rewrite their history. Dade never existed. I wanted him to be a character witness at Dade's hearing, but he wouldn't do it."

"The pressure on coaches must be enormous," Dan says, taking up for him. "He probably had done all he could do for Dade."

"Shit! If they're winning, they can get away with murder."

My phone rings. Julia tells me it is Binkie Cross, calling from Fayetteville. I give Dan the thumbs-up sign, and pushing the button on the speakerphone, I tell Julia to put him through. This could be good news.

"Binkie Cross, Gideon," Binkie says, wasting no time on pleasantries. "I'd like Dade to take a polygraph. If he passes, I really might be able to see my way to a dismissal."

Polygraph tests aren't admissible in court in Arkansas unless both sides agree. Yet, law enforcement types use them frequently to weed out suspects. Dan nods. What does Dade have to lose? I ask, "Has Robin taken one?"

"Her parents are balking at it," Binkie admits. "They think it's an insult. I understand their feelings, but if your client were to pass with flying colors, and she still won't take it, it'd be a lot easier to justify a dismissal."

Damn right it would, Dan mouths the words. "Let me talk to him," I say, "and get back to you. It might take a couple of days. I'll have to talk to his parents, too."

"No big rush," Binkie says. "Just give me a call, and I'll set it up."

"I'll do it." Before he gets off the phone, he tells me he has subpoenaed the tape of the "J" Board hearing and will provide me a copy of the transcript when it has been typed. I look down at the calendar on my desk. Though it promises to be a gorgeous, mild Indian summer day, we are into the second week of November. Still, the trial is almost two months away. I thank him and hang up, thinking this is about as good an offer as Dade is going to get. "If he dismisses charges, the school might reverse itself and put Dade back on the team," Dan points out. "It'd be worth a shot."

I pick up the phone and call Dade but as usual get his answering machine. I leave a message for him to call me as soon as he gets in. Because he has only been suspended for the rest of the season, he is still being allowed to keep his athletic scholarship and live in the dorm. Actually, the university could have been a lot tougher on him. Before Dan leaves, I ask, "You're not still screwing Gina, are you?"

Standing at my door, he nods like some three-month-old puppy who has been caught standing in his water dish. "It's not really like you think," he says. "She's fun to be around. I'm crazy about her."

How foolish and pathetic we are! "She'll give you AIDS, goddamn it, Dan!" I yell at him. "You may be exposing Brenda, too! Are you crazy?"

Embarrassed, Dan mutters something under his breath and scurries out the door. I shake my head at his back. I don't think he and Gina are spending their time trying to figure out ways to solve the national debt. Yet, if I were married to Brenda, I'd have trouble going home, too.

*   *   *

At noon, as I am about to go downstairs to lunch, I get a coquettish call from Julia telling me I have a visitor. She won't say more, and I go out to the waiting room fully expecting to see Amy. Instead, it is my old girl-friend Rainey McCorkle.

"Gideon, I wouldn't be asking you to help this client," Rainey says, two minutes later, leaning against my desk on her elbows, "if it weren't so terrible where she is re-quired to stay right now. Confederate Gardens is driving her crazy."

Though we haven't seen each other in months, we still talk occasionally. I notice, not without satisfaction, there is more gray in her red hair. She has lost weight, too, and even seems a little gaunt, her skin tight against her jaw. I can't help comparing her to Amy, who usually can't help flirting even if she is discussing the weather. Rainey is far more serious. There is something to be said for youth. "I take it she is crazy," I comment. Confederate Gardens is a big boardinghouse-like facility that provides care for in-dividuals released from the state hospital.

"She's in good shape," Rainey says, sounding like a car salesman. "She's got a fixed delusion that Bill Clin-ton owes her some money, but that's all. She doesn't act on it, and other than that, she's as normal as you are."

That's not saying much. I resist drumming my fingers on my desk. "Wonderful. She's threatened the President of the United States. She's lucky to be out of the state hospital. The Secret Service has a file on her the size of a telephone book."

Rainey, persistent as a bad cold, shakes her head. "The incident happened when he was governor. All she did was show up at the Mansion and try to speak to him." She looks down at some notes in her lap. "She was arrested and found not guilty by reason of insanity and was conditionally released by Judge Blake last November and ordered to live in Confederate Gardens. I just want you to go out there with me, and you'll see why it's so inappropriate for her."

While she talks, it is hard to keep certain memories at bay. Though in all the time that we dated we never made love, we had some delicious make-out sessions on her couch. It seemed as if we had regressed to being teenagers, but the desire I felt I remember more than actual intercourse with other women before her. "So you want me to go to court with her," I ask, "and try to get her conditional release amended to let her move?"

"Not just that. Amended to allow her to try to get a job, too. Her conditional release says she has to go to a day treatment program every day. They sit and stare at each other all day. It's a total waste," Rainey says bitterly.

I smile at this familiar refrain. I first met Rainey when I was with the public defender's office, which had the job of representing patients in involuntary commitment proceedings. She thought the Blackwell County community mental health center was a joke and never hesitated to tell me so. Instead of helping persons with mental illness to find decent places to live and jobs, they wasted millions of dollars pushing paper around. "Does she have a job history?" I ask.

"She was a respiratory therapist at St. Thomas for five years."

I never even saw Rainey nude. The day she found out

she had a lump in her breast she spent the night in my bed, but with me on the couch. How strange our relationship was! I thought she was perfect for me. So did Sarah. "I suppose she had a big pension plan," I say sarcastically.

Rainey says, "I'll pay her fee."

"I'll do it for nothing," I say grudgingly. "You don't have any money." I remember the day Mays & Burton fired me, and she, with her modest state salary and a kid in college, offered to loan me money. Rainey would have done anything for me except make love.

For the first time Rainey smiles. "I'll buy you a yogurt if you get her out of Confederate Gardens."

"Whoopee," I say, and twirl the index finger of my right hand in the air. Rainey was never much of a drinker, and her idea of a hot date was to drive to Turbo's for a kiddie cup of sorbet and white chocolate mousse swirled together.

"Can you go see her now with me?" Rainey asks. She never stops pushing when she wants something. "You can follow me to the hospital and drive us over. It's only a few minutes from there."

I look at my watch. "Sure," I say. Maybe we can go to lunch afterward. I don't have a client coming in until four.

"You don't come out here by yourself?" I ask Rainey, when we pull up front. Confederate Gardens is not going to be featured in the real estate section of the paper featuring choice residential areas anytime soon. An adult video arcade, a liquor store, and an auto parts store make perfect neighbors for a former motel whose occupants now consist entirely of persons with all manner of disabilities, ranging from retardation to mental illness.

"You're such a baby," my old girlfriend says, shrugging. "Nothing will happen," she adds, indicating a parking space in front of the sign that announces this dump as a retirement center.

Rainey seems overdressed for the occasion in a strawberry tunic and skirt set that matches her hair. When I picked her up at the hospital it seemed like old times. Loosening up a bit, she has teased me ever since she got in the Blazer. Rainey has always been able to puncture any illusions I have about my importance and make me laugh at the same time. "This place gives me the creeps," I confess, "and I haven't been here two seconds. What happened to the zoning laws?"

Rainey gives me a familiar smirk as if to say that some smart lawyer thought he knew what he was doing. I have been around persons with mental illness at the state hospital, but it has always been in such a clean, safe environment that I never felt the slightest uneasiness. As we pass one buff-colored brick unit after another, I look around for security but don't see any. Instead, we encounter several men and women some of whom are angrily muttering to themselves. One black guy, who looks as if he might weight three hundred pounds, yells something incomprehensible at me. I smile brightly and nod as if he is welcoming me as the newest resident. "They make sure they take their medication," Rainey whispers, "but otherwise the residents can leave during the day. Of course, they don't have any money to spend. Confederate Gar-

dens is allowed to get all of their disability checks except
fifty dollars a month."

After years of representing patients at involuntary civil
commitment hearings at the Blackwell County public defender's office, I had convinced myself that I had been
doing something noble. Institutionalization by the state
was bad, I thought. Confederate Gardens looks like more
of the same thing, but definitely more seedy. Rainey
stops at number 114 and knocks at the door. I feel relieved to be going inside.

After thirty seconds, the door opens a crack, and Rainey
says gently across the chain, "Delores, it's Rainey. Are you
dressed?"

The door opens, and a pleasant-looking woman in her
mid-thirties emerges into the warm sunlight. "I was taking a nap," she says, looking at me.

She is wearing baggy gray shorts, no shoes, and a rumpled T-shirt that advertises Michael Bolton's Love and
Tenderness Tour. Her shiny black hair could stand to be
combed, but with a little work she could be attractive.
Rainey explains, "This is Gideon Page, the lawyer I was
telling you about. Can we come in for a moment?"

Delores seems a little overwhelmed, but says, "Sure."

As I follow Rainey into the room, I realize Delores has
a roommate. A black woman I would estimate to be at
least seventy lies on top of the bed, fully clothed, watching us. She works her lips but no sound emerges. Rainey
says in her most cheery social worker voice, "How are
you?"

"Don't mind Betty," Delores says, giving me a good

once-over. "I'd send her out for a little bit, but sometimes she gets lost and it's too hot today."

"We can go to that Wendy's on the corner," I say quickly, feeling claustrophobic. It is only a standard-sized motel room with two twin beds. There is a wooden chair at a desk, where Delores motions me to sit.

"This is all right," Delores says. "It's close to lunch. I don't mind if she hears."

The woman, who has long white hair, mutters under her breath and turns on her side facing away from us. I say, "Rainey says you'd like to leave here and try to get a job."

Delores nods eagerly. "I'd like to have a place by my-self."

I can't imagine why. Before judges are allowed to or-der someone to stay in conditions like this, they ought to have to live here themselves. The room is picked up, even neat, but it must be fifty years old and smells of bug spray. "How long have you lived here?" Rainey asks, ap-parently testing her for me.

"Almost a year," Delores answers promptly. "I came here last November." She sits down on her bed beside Rainey.

Thanksgiving, I think, wondering if Delores sees the irony. How can she have managed to stay here for an en-tire year without shooting herself? If I don't get out of here in a minute, I am going to start screaming. "Have you got your conditional release papers signed by the judge?"

Delores hops off the bed and opens a drawer on the

table in front of me. She points at a piece of paper.
"That's it."

I unfold the creased paper and read the boilerplate language. She is ordered to take her medication as directed.
She can't leave Blackwell County. She has to attend a
day treatment program. She is required to live at Confederate Gardens. The order is good for five years. "Do you
mind if we all go sit in my car?" I almost beg. I feel suddenly depressed. If this is the best the law can do, why
bother with it?

"Okay," Delores says. "But I have to go for a med
check in ten minutes."

Before leaving, I glance around the room. The sole
possessions consist of a black-and-white TV that must be
at least twenty years old, a clock radio, and a picture of
Bill Clinton. As I stand up to leave, I ask, "How much
does President Clinton owe you?"

Delores stares at his picture. "Five hundred seventeen
dollars and eighty-five cents."

The recitation of this precise amount is unnerving. I
wish she had picked anyone but Clinton, but I am not surprised. Delusions of grandeur can come with the territory
of schizophrenia. I once represented a man at an involuntary civil commitment hearing who was convinced that
he had written the words to "Blue Eyes Crying in the
Rain" and was owed half a million dollars. I walk out
the door ahead of Rainey and Delores and look across
the street at another row of identical motel rooms. How
can anyone call this place a residential care facility? It
even looks like a warehouse. As we walk toward my

car, I ask, "Delores, how do you figure Clinton owes you money?"

She is wearing a cheap pair of sandals that she has trouble keeping on her feet and she reaches down to adjust a strap. Rainey and I stop to wait for her. She looks up at me. "One day he came jogging into McDonald's downtown and needed a loan. He didn't say why. I figured he was just hungry."

It is hard to resist smiling. With that skimpy little pair of shorts he wears, he couldn't have been carrying a lot of money. But even he couldn't eat five hundred bucks' worth of Big Macs. I ask, "When you tried to collect, did you threaten him or have a gun or anything like that?"

"No!" she says emphatically. "I hate guns. I just wanted my money. I kept going to the Governor's Mansion, and finally they arrested me."

"You don't have any plans to go to Washington to try to collect, do you?" I ask. I have learned from experience it does no good to argue with people who suffer from this form of mental illness.

She looks at me as though I am one who is sick. "It's not worth all the hassle."

"Good idea," I tell her. Her attitude will be important. If the judge is satisfied that she is no threat, we shouldn't have any trouble getting her order amended. We sit in my car for ten minutes talking, until she tells us she has to leave. I am reasonably satisfied that she has no more delusions, and I drive Rainey back to the state hospital, optimistic I can help her. Rainey has declined my offer for lunch, pleading work. She had always been too conscientious for her own good.

As I pull up in front of the administration building, Rainey thanks me profusely and asks me to turn off the motor for a minute because she has something to tell me.

I do, knowing that she wants to start dating again. I have missed her. Amy, as cute as she is, can't hold a candle to her. Rainey is solid gold and is worth whatever effort it costs to get her. "I'm glad to help," I say, wondering if I could get away with kissing her in front of the state hospital. "What's up?"

She pauses for a moment and holds up her left hand. "I'm getting married!"

Finally, I see the ring. What an idiot I am! She practically rubbed my nose in it. My mouth goes dry, and there is no concealing my shock. "You are?" I say, unable to utter anything intelligent.

Her blue eyes round and serious, she nods. "December twenty-sixth."

My mind is racing. I can't seem to focus. Shit, why not make it Christmas Day? Kill two birds with one stone. All these months I have assumed she hasn't been seeing anyone in particular. When years ago we first began to date and had become serious, Rainey broke it off temporarily because an old boyfriend had resurfaced—a big, hairy psychologist at the state hospital by the name of Norris Kelsey. Then, within weeks, she had ditched him and resumed our relationship, until one thing after another seemed to kill it. The hard part is that I didn't even realize she was seeing a guy. I feel utterly devastated. She and I have talked occasionally, but too late I realize that none of the conversations have been about her. Numb, I ask, "Do I know the guy?"

She smiles and reaches over and pats my hand. "I don't think so. Dennis Stanley. He's never heard of you."

About to explode in the heat, I unroll the window and rack my brain in vain for the name. The only Stanley I've ever heard of is the explorer. Dr. Livingston, I presume? "What does he do?"

Rainey twists the ring on her finger. It is huge, now that I look at it. "He's a pediatrician. He's five years younger. Never been married. He doesn't care about having kids."

A doctor who is younger! I could picture her with a guy that much older. This is too weird. It won't last six months. She'll go nuts worrying that she won't be able to hold on to him. "How long have you known him?" I can't bring myself to congratulate her.

"Only for a couple of months," she says, smiling. "But I've never been surer of anything in my life."

This is outrageous! Nothing could be more out of character. Rainey agonizes over things. "Did you meet him at Christian Life?" I ask, knowing I sound childish. Her conversion to fundamentalist Christianity was the final straw as far as I was concerned. I could never understand how she could close her eyes to reality.

"He's a Presbyterian," she says, with just a trace of irony. "He's very tolerant."

"You'll never see each other," I say, knowing I sound like an old curmudgeon.

"Gideon," she commands, "be happy for me!"

I try to get a grip. "It's a little difficult at the moment since until two minutes ago I was thinking that you and I might try to get back together." I know this is not the cool thing to say, but I feel as if I had been kicked in the stomach by a mule.

"I've got to go," she says, and puts her hand on the door.

I summon my best fake smile. I don't want the whole damn staff of the state hospital feeling sorry for me. "I'm real happy for you, Raincy. We'll always be friends."

Whether she believes me or not, she pretends that she does. Her lips come back from her teeth, and she says, "I know we will."

I drive off, and get to the corner before I let myself feel anything. Damn her! On again, off again, on again, off again. She jerked me around like a yo-yo. I wipe my eyes and decide to go home instead of back to the office. I could stand a drink.

At the house, after getting into some shorts and taking Woogie out, I call the office and without any explanation tell Julia to see if she can postpone my four o'clock appointment. I ice down a twelve-pack, and Woogie and I go into the backyard. It is delightfully warm. If I start drinking bourbon, I will be sick tomorrow, and I don't want anyone to think I am bothered by this. I can hear Julia reminding Dan when she hears I've been dumped: "He was a no-show the day after she told him." Fuck all women, I think. I haven't met a decent one since Rosa. What made her so special? Guts. She had guts. Left her mother, learned English, came to Arkansas, passed the state nursing exam, got a job. Rosa was a class act. Instead of putting the empties back in the box, I drop them in the yard by my chair. To hell with what the neighbors think. "Come here, boy," I say to Woogie, who is sitting in the shade staring at me. Reluctantly, he gets up and ambles over toward me. I stroke his warm back. So warm. I take off my shirt. It is wonderful out here today. In the eighties, a record for this time of year. Rosa never would have finked out like Rainey. When things got tough, Rosa didn't run. I know I am getting drunk, but so what? It's easier to remember Rosa when I've had a few. . . .

I wake up and look at my watch. Almost four-thirty. I have been out here almost three hours. My face and chest feel on fire. I look down and see my stomach is pink as the inside of a salmon. Woogie, seeing I am awake, comes over to me and licks my hand. I must be a total idiot. I will look like a lobster tomorrow. I count six empties, glad I have a six-pack left. Inside, I can hear the phone ringing and push myself up out of the cheap nylon webbing and lurch toward the house, Woogie at my heels. Rainey, I think stupidly, calling to say she has changed her mind.

"Hello," I say, grabbing the phone in the kitchen and trying not to sound drunk.

"Dad?" Sarah says. "Are you okay? I tried to get you at your office."

"Rainey's getting married!" I blurt.

"She is?" Sarah asks, her voice sounding far away. "Dad, you must feel terrible. Who is she marrying?"

"Some doctor whose last name is Stanley," I say, unable to keep tears from sliding down my face. "I don't know him."

"Promise me you won't drive anywhere tonight,"

Sarah says. "Get something to eat and go on to bed, okay? It will be all right."

Do I sound that bad? I sigh, "I'm fine."

"Check and see if there is a pizza in the freezer and fix that," Sarah says. "I'll be home in two weeks. Remember, we're going to Bear Creek, okay?"

Why? I think. I can't wake up. "Okay," I say.

"Remember to feed Woogie and make sure he has water before you go to bed."

Bed? It's not even dark. "I will," I say irritably. It seems as if all the women I know treat me like a child. I hang up and look for Woogie's dog food.

At six, after trying to get through a few bites of some stuff that tastes like frozen glue (it doesn't seem cooked enough), I decide to call Amy. I know I shouldn't, but damn it, I want to.

"You sound skunked," Amy says cheerfully. "Does it take that much nerve just to call and say you're wrong?"

I try to choose my words carefully. "You remember saying that you were jealous of Rainey McCorkle?"

There is silence on the other end for a moment. "Yes?" Amy asks, her voice no longer so friendly.

"She's getting married," I say casually, "next month."

"Poor Gideon!" Amy says instantly. "No wonder you're shitfaced. Who's she marrying?"

"I'm not shitfaced," I say shakily. "A doctor who is five years younger. Some guy named Dennis Stanley."

"I know Dennis!" Amy says. "He's a wonderful man and a fantastic doctor. A hunk, too! God, I'm impressed with your old girlfriend. She's getting a real prize. Cheer up. It's not like you lost her to a vacuum cleaner salesman."

"Was he your boyfriend, too?" I ask sourly. If he's so great, why doesn't he have a better name?

Amy laughs. "You sound so pitiful! He was the head resident at St. Thomas and testified in a couple of rape cases when I was at the prosecutor's. He didn't go to medical school until he was in his thirties."

I crumple the empty beer can I am holding. I couldn't have gotten into med school even if I owned it. "A late bloomer," I say, as though this were a terrible indictment.

"Gideon, would you like for me to come over and spend the night?" Amy asks.

"Yes," I say. "That would be very nice."

Amy laughs again. "I'll be there in an hour."

"I'll time you," I say, looking at the clock over the kitchen sink.

"That won't be necessary," Amy giggles. "Why don't you take a shower?"

The idea of anything touching my skin, even if it is cold water, makes me wince. "Do you have some ointment for sunburn?" I ask, bringing my left hand to my chest. It feels like pie crust. "I fell asleep for a little while outside."

Amy's reaction is swift. "Oh, Gideon, you didn't pass out in this sun, did you?"

"Just took a little nap," I whimper. I feel terribly thirsty. "Have you got some juice or something like that? All I've got is beer."

"I can tell," Amy says. "You're probably so dehydrated that you're about to go into shock. Drink as much water as you can. I'll be there as soon as I can."

She hangs up before I can answer her. I ease over to

the sink and rinse out a glass and fill it up with tap water. Good ol' Amy. I haven't been very nice to her lately. I should have called her when I wasn't drunk. Poor women. They're such suckers for us. They deserve to be in a better species. The water tastes good. I wish I had thought of it a couple of hours ago. I look through the kitchen window and see the beer cans scattered around the lawn chair. They look terrible. Get that white guy out of the neighborhood before he turns it into a slum. I laugh at my little joke and look at Woogie, who is lapping up his own water. "Hey, boy, are we having fun or what?"

He won't even look at me and goes off to the couch after he finishes. At least he had enough sense to lie in the shade.

Amy arrives about thirty minutes later with a quart of orange juice and an overnight bag. "Oh, Gideon!" she wails. "You look like you've been electrocuted!"

"Damn, it's November! It shouldn't be this hot." I look down at myself again. My knees look like stoplights. While I take off my clothes, Amy runs the tub full of water and helps me get into it. "This is what it must be like to be old," I complain.

"If you keep this up," she says, taking my arm, "you'll never find out."

The water feels good. It is cool but not freezing. I lie back against the porcelain and sigh. "Maybe we can make love later."

Amy looks down at my shriveled penis which is limply floating in the water. "Unless you can think of a way to detach it," she says, giggling, "I don't think you're going to be terribly interested."

Thirty minutes later Amy turns down the sheet and helps me into bed. Amy has rubbed so much Benadryl cream and Aloe into my skin that I feel like a greased pig. Grateful beyond words, I watch her while she arranges the water and juice on my nightstand. Why is she here? This hasn't exactly been my finest hour. If the situation were reversed, I don't think I would be playing her nursemaid. I sink back onto my pillow. "This Florence Nightingale business is a side I haven't seen before, Gilchrist. I think I like it."

She sits down on the bed beside me and rubs cream into my feet. Even the soles are tender. "I have a masochistic side. Most women do. I think it must be genetic. Here I am doing everything but changing your diapers while you're trying to turn yourself into a brisket because of another woman."

What do I say? She is correct, of course. If I had a decent bone in my body, I would have called anybody except her. "I could have called Dan, but I don't think he would have been of much use."

Amy laughs at the thought. From long acquaintance, she knows Dan is as helpless as I am. "He might have brought you a gun, so you could have done the job right."

I look down at my cooked flesh and wonder if I'm the one who has the masochistic streak. Rainey and I haven't had a real romantic relationship in more than a year. Still, true feeling dies hard. I admit it to myself outright for the first time: I did love her. Yet, we could never make a commitment. To her credit, she has moved on to another man who obviously inspires more confidence. "What bothers me," I admit to Amy, "is that I didn't really even know she was seriously dating somebody. I just kind of figured everything would finally fall into place some day, and we'd end up together."

A melancholy expression comes over Amy's face. "You miss the boat that way. Even the dumbest dog will leave if you won't feed it."

"I know," I say, growing more sober by the moment. I know she is telling me that she isn't going to take care of me indefinitely. I don't even know if I want her to try.

"You don't know shit," she says, putting away the Benadryl. She bends down and searches through her bag and withdraws a pink nightie with poodles on it. "Don't even think about saying a word about this gown. I grabbed the first thing I saw."

I grin. Poodles aren't Amy's style. Yet, how do I know? I haven't given her a chance. For all I know she may sleep with a security blanket and her thumb in her mouth. I seem to be floating through life more and more these days. Why? It is as if when Rosa died, I quit trying. She made everything so simple, or at least it seemed that way. Something tells me that it probably wasn't, and I just don't want to remember how life really was. I watch as Amy pulls her T-shirt over her head. As unselfconscious as a two-year-old child, she slips out of her sandals, shorts, and bra and pulls the gown over her head. I feel a stir between my legs but it flickers and dies. As the old saying goes, tonight, at least, my eyes are bigger than my stomach. She eases into bed beside me, and watches me sleep.

*   *   *

"Good Lord!" Julia exclaims when I walk in the next morning. "Did you fall asleep in your oven?"

"Just got a little too much sun," I say, checking for my messages.

"Shit!" she whistles. "It looks like you laid out drunk all afternoon."

As usual, Julia is revealing more of her own skin than is appropriate in a law office. Behind the counter that separates her from our clients, her lime sherbet colored skirt has crept up almost to her panty line, revealing two nicely tanned legs. I've seen belts wider than her skirt. "I get to take off occasionally," I mutter as I walk down the hall.

In my office I dial Dade's number, waking him up. Instantly I wish I had called his parents first. "I don't want to take a lie detector test," he tells me after I have explained why I called. "I had a friend who took one and flunked it. I know he was telling the truth."

My head still throbbing from yesterday's fiasco, I go ballistic. "This is your chance to get your charges dropped! You might even get back on the team! Damn it, you've got to take it."

"I don't have to do anything!" he says. "A white bitch says that I raped her, a white dude kicks me off the team, and now I'm supposed to let a white cop or lawyer hook me up to a machine and say whether I'm lying or not? Get real, man!"

I back off and lower my voice. This is the first outburst of racism I've seen from Dade, but from his point of view, he makes sense. The only white person who has stood up for him was Carter, and he folded like he was holding a pair of deuces. I explain the test isn't admissible in court and that he has nothing to lose, but it is like trying to convince a child not to be afraid of the dark. It occurs to me that Dade may be lying after all. Maybe he's into drugs, too, or is trying to protect someone. I tell him I want him to think about it some, and that I will be calling him back.

As soon as I get off, I call his parents and get Roy, who doesn't react much better. "Why can't the prosecutor make the girl take the test, and if she flunks, or won't take it, dismiss the charges?"

"Cross doesn't have to do anything," I explain. "But there's no way Dade can lose by taking it."

"Yeah, he can," Roy says. "If he takes it and don't pass, you'll figure he's lying and won't do anything else on his case. Let me hand you over to Lucy."

This pisses me royally. In the last few weeks I might as well have closed my practice and moved to Fayetteville. "What have I done to give you the idea that I'm going to lie down on this case?" I ask, close to losing my temper. I'm getting peanuts, and I've worried about this case until it's about all I think about. I explain to her how important it is for Dade to cooperate with the prosecutor but get only a little further with her.

"Gideon, notice it's always the black person who has to do the accommodating. Robin won't take the test, but Dade has to. It gets old."

"Well"—I state the obvious—"he is the one accused of rape."

"If someone had made her take a test before the charges were filed," Lucy complains, "Dade wouldn't be in this mess."

At least she has conceded that a polygraph test has some validity. "I don't doubt that for a moment," I say, encouraging her, "but we didn't have any control over that. Now we do."

In the background I hear a customer complaining about the price of a jar of Maxwell House coffee, and Roy's voice as he commiserates with her. They must be together twenty-four hours a day. The joys of small business. Finally, Lucy says, "I'll talk to him, but it may take a while. He's got his father's stubbornness."

"This would be far and away the best way to handle it," I assure her. "I don't want to try this case in front of a Washington County jury if we can avoid it."

"I know that," she says.

Convinced she can bring Dade around, I tell her to call me back when she's talked to him but that she doesn't have to rush him. With the passage of a little time, Dade will begin to feel the pressure. Before I get off the phone, I decide to ask her, "Is your grandmother still alive? Sarah and I are thinking of driving over Thanksgiving weekend to Bear Creek, and I thought maybe I'd go by and talk to her if you think that'd be all right."

Lucy resists gloating. "Certainly. I'll call her and tell her you may be coming by. Let me give you her address."

As she talks and waits on a customer at the same time, I wonder what my motives are. I still don't believe there is any family connection. Am I sucking up to Lucy so I can be her son's agent? Or am I doing this just to pacify Sarah? Unlike myself, she seems determined to know the truth. As a criminal defense lawyer, I realize most of the time I'd rather not know.

11

II DEPLOY MOTION   257

"DR. BEEKMAN SAYS neither blacks nor whites used to celebrate the Fourth of July in some parts of the South," my daughter instructs me from behind the wheel of the Blazer. "Whites were reminded of the fall of Vicksburg, and it obviously meant nothing to African-Americans."

Life according to Beekman. Anxious to get to Bear Creek, we have taken I-40 east to Forrest City and then south on Highway 1, arriving on the outskirts of Bear Creek at noon. "Proportionately, the South sent more men to Vietnam than any other region of the country," I say, recalling something I think I read on the subject. A patriotic act or one confirming our stupidity, depending on your point of view. Thanks to a heart murmur, which has never affected me (other than probably to save my life), I was classified 4-F.

We turn off to the right onto Highway 79 and go for a mile before I announce, "Here's where your grandparents are buried."

There is nothing picturesque about Pinewood cemetery. Off the highway a good fifty yards, it is little more than a flat field, and it takes us ten minutes this cool Saturday in November to find my parents' graves. "I haven't been back here since your grandmother died seventeen years ago," I explain to Sarah as we finally come upon their markers. I bend down to pull up some weeds around the stone. "You were too little to remember, but you came, too."

Sarah, dressed in jeans and a bulky tan sweater, studies the simple tombstones. "Were they racists?" she asks, squinting against the sun that has suddenly appeared from the low flying clouds.

"We all were," I say, wondering how I can explain the South without sounding too defensive. "Back then, I don't think we believed that blacks were really human the same way we were. We thought they were so inferior genetically, that it was okay to treat them like we did."

Sarah bends down to snap off a weed growing at a forty-five-degree angle from my father's grave marker. "You make it sound as if you weren't responsible for your own racism."

Surely she has learned in her history classes that a later generation can't judge an earlier one by its standards. "Of course we were, but back when we were in the middle of that era, it wasn't so easy to accept we were wrong. We had a lot invested in it." To my own daughter I can't admit that even today my mind contains an informal hierarchy of ethnic mental superiority: Japanese, Jews, followed by whites of northern European ancestry, and blacks on the bottom. The evidence seems all too apparent. Yet, I dare not voice it, for fear Sarah will again tar and feather me with her own labels.

"But it was worse than that," she insists. "It wasn't just

stigma and forced separation in schools and in public. They were exploited, cheated, even still being lynched in your parents' generation."

"True," I concede, not wanting to argue over the details. As I stand erect, my knees snap, and I feel dizzy. At my age, seeing my parents' names so permanently etched in stone has made me aware of how much of my life I've already lived. "But individual relationships weren't all like that. You can care about somebody even if the relationship is based on paternalism. As soon as my mother got to know your mother, she forgot about her skin and loved her as much as I did. We weren't as bad as it seems today."

Leading me to the car left on the side of the road that runs through the cemetery, Sarah says over her shoulder, "Is that how you justify what your grandfather did?"

I sigh, knowing the situation is impossible. "I don't know what he did," I say, catching up to her. "That's why we're here."

We drive into town, and as usual I am struck by the sad shabbiness of the buildings on Main Street. When I was a child, the town didn't seem so poor. In a rectangular park that centers the town the most prominent structures are a statue of Robert E. Lee and a concrete platform used by politicians and musical groups. Underneath it are four separate bathrooms, an architectural reminder of segregation. Here, almost in this exact spot, I recall seeing Governor Orval Faubus as he waited to be introduced at a campaign rally. It was after he had become famous the world over for stopping nine black children from entering Little Rock's Central High School in 1957 and temporarily defying the federal government. Squatting on his heels with his coat slung over his shoulder, he seemed totally at ease with himself. He maintained he had acted to prevent violence. We are all politically correct, even our rascals.

"Do you want to stop and see anybody else while we're here?" Sarah asks, inspecting my hometown carefully as if she were considering buying some property here.

"No," I say, more abruptly than I intend. "That won't be necessary."

Sarah, stopping at the first of Bear Creek's two lights in the downtown area, says scornfully, "Would that embarrass you?"

She knows it would if I were truthful about the purpose of our visit, but not for the first time I am forced to confront my own cowardice. "I didn't come back to Bear Creek to be gossiped about. And that's what would happen if I told people why we're here, and you know it."

"Why didn't you say so when we were driving over?" she asks.

She is being deliberately disingenuous. "I thought it was understood."

She says archly, "Being partly African myself, I'm not ashamed of what I'll find."

She sounds so superior and sanctimonious I want to gag. "I wish I were worthy to be in your company," I hiss, retreating to my usual weapons of guilt and sarcasm. "But I haven't quite achieved your status as a moral saint."

My scathing comments surprise me and hush her into a

shocked silence. I didn't know I felt so edgy about this visit. I apologize, but my offering is understandably met with a hostile glare. Typically having left at the office the address Lucy gave me, I find a Fina station and a telephone booth and direct Sarah to stop. Sure enough, the name of Mayola Washington is in the tiny Bear Creek phone book at #7 Terrace. I should telephone and warn her we are coming over, but if I'd had that kind of basic courage and decency, I'd have called her from home over four hours ago.

From behind her opaque sunglasses in the Blazer, Sarah protests, "You're going to upset her just dropping in out of the blue this way."

Why am I doing this? I can live without this family reunion. "Her granddaughter called her to say we were coming. If the story is true, our showing up at her door won't surprise her at all."

Accustomed to my intransigence, Sarah shrugs. Others have tried to civilize me and have failed. Why should she be successful? I turn down Utah and notice that at least the streets have been paved in the black neighborhoods. When I was growing up, gravel was the main surface. Separate has never meant equal in much of anything over here.

The Bear Creek housing development for the elderly is actually pleasant. Unlike Needle Park, there is no spilled trash in anyone's yard or junked cars on the streets; I don't see half the apartments boarded up or burned out. Trees and flowers flourish in front of the redbrick apartments, and it is possible to imagine living here. Since these are units for the elderly, there are no children about;

in Needle Park, the children play inside because of the drug dealers and violence outside.

With Sarah at my side nervously tugging at her hair (my anxiety is catching), I knock at the door, and soon a light-skinned elderly black woman opens it.

"Ma'am, I'm Gideon Page and this is my daughter, Sarah," I introduce myself, my voice scratchy with anxiety. "Your granddaughter, Lucy Cunningham, gave me some information I'd like to discuss with you."

At the mention of Lucy's name, the old lady's face softens and she invites us in. "Lucy said you might be callin'." Her voice is high and fragile but not as reedy as some old folks' get. She is wearing a flowery ironed dress, as if she might be expecting company; perhaps her great-grandchildren are coming over later to eat leftover turkey. Sarah and I are invited to sit on a green sofa while our hostess sits down on an uncomfortable-looking rocker across from us. The living room is modestly furnished but has a homey touch supplied by obvious family portraits (I recognize my client and his family in one snapshot) and needlework on the walls, and a weathered Bible on the coffee table in front of us. On a nineteen-inch Sears model TV in a corner grim-faced actors battle through inane dialogue on a videotape of *The Guiding Light*. She offers us something to drink but I wouldn't dream of putting this old lady to trouble and decline for both of us. Sure I wouldn't.

"You're the lawyer for Dade," the old lady says softly. "You think he done what they say?"

"He says he didn't," I hedge. "He seems like a very fine young man to me."

"That's the truth," she replies, chuckling mechanically. She squints at Sarah. "Why, this child looks like one of my nieces!"

Sarah smiles self-consciously while I explain, "Her mother was from South America. They had slaves from Africa brought there, too."

"South America!" she marvels as if I had announced something profound. "Can you imagine?"

Mrs. Washington and I are barely connecting. This old lady is as nervous as I am, I realize. She is an old-fashioned Negro, one to whom the civil rights movement never was very convincing. Never mind all the speeches and legislation; white folks still have the say-so, and it is no use to pretend otherwise. What must she have been like fifty years ago? Though she is too old and wrinkled now to be called pretty, I have little doubt that she was attractive as a girl. Even now, she has a firm chin and healthy skin. She has a Caucasian nose, no work of art itself, but preferable, at least in white eyes, to the broad nostrils characteristic of most African-Americans. Underneath the cotton dress is a bosom that seems to have defied time and logic. She has something of a stomach to go with it, but nothing that explains the mountains above it. Is this what attracted my grandfather? "Did you know my parents?" I ask awkwardly. "My father owned Page Drugs."

Mrs. Washington clears her throat. "Mr. Calvin was a good man, 'fore he took so sick. He sure was."

"Sarah, here, unfortunately never knew either of them," I say. Our mission here is a monumental invasion of her privacy. What happened half a century ago between her and a man whose memory I have little knowledge of or connection with is none of our business. Yet, my curiosity is growing. But if she clams up, I won't pry.

"That's too bad," Mrs. Washington clucks automatically. "It sure is."

I do not think I will get a direct answer from her and ask, "Did you know my grandfather Frank Page? At one time he owned a bunch of property on Cleveland Street."

Mrs. Washington begins to pick at a thread on her couch. "Lucy sent you over here to as't these questions, didn't she?"

"She told me a story or two," I admit. If I had a decent bone in my body, I'd get up and make us leave. This old woman is afraid of us. If this had occurred in the last twenty years, surely her attitude would be different. She could have gotten child support out of him, at least. In fact, today, the state of Arkansas would have demanded she divulge his identity and then brought suit to recoup welfare payments to her.

"You want your child to hear?" she asks, her voice low and trembling.

I glance at Sarah, who, as if I had cued her, says, "It's all right, Mrs. Washington. If you don't want to talk, I understand. But I would like to hear if it won't upset you. I want to know my history. I don't know very much about my mother's family in South America and probably never will. Daddy's family is all I have, and all I know is that my grandfather was mentally ill and hung himself in the state hospital. I don't know what his parents were like. All Daddy tells me is that his grandfather owned several businesses in Bear Creek and didn't get along with his son. I want to know more than that, and I think Daddy does, too."

I nod, but find that I am thinking that Sarah is not quite telling her the truth. Until now, I thought her motive was to try to document a fifty-year-old case of rape in the cause of feminism. Yet, by her questions at the cemetery, she wants to know more than I gave her credit for.

The old lady smooths her dress, avoiding our eyes. "It was such a long time ago."

Sarah slides off the couch and places herself at Mrs. Washington's feet. Her voice almost a whisper, Sarah asks, "Did my great-granddaddy hurt you?"

Mrs. Washington stares over Sarah's head at me and replies in a firm voice, "Why, Mr. Frank, he never jump on me or nothin' like that. He'd come by and say he was checkin' on his property or to get the rent, but I know he was comin' by to see me. Momma be off cleanin' white folks' houses, and I'd be takin' care of my little sister. We didn't have no daddy. Least not one who lived with us."

Sarah asks, "How old were you, ma'am?"

Mrs. Washington looks down at Sarah to gauge her answer. "'Bout sixteen when Mr. Frank started comin' round. I was a pretty girl. Least that what folks said. Mr. Frank, he said so, too."

"Do you know about how old he was?" Sarah prompts.

Mrs. Washington squints at me and answers, "Mr. Frank was a full-grown man. Thirty, maybe."

I nod but do not speak, afraid if I do, she will stop talking. Each time she uses the words, "Mr. Frank," I feel sick. Even as a child, I was called by the man who swept the store for my father "Mr. Gideon." Damn, underneath all that passive behavior, how they must have hated us! I wish this old woman were angry, but either she is masking it well, or time has erased the bitterness it seems she ought to have toward my grandfather. "What was my great-grandfather like?" Sarah asks.

"He was all right. When he started visitin' reg'lar, he'd forget to collect all the rent. Say he'd git it next time. After Calcutta was born, he never as't for nothin'."

"Calcutta was his daughter?" Sarah says. I realize how skillful a questioner she is. She should be the lawyer in the family, not her old man.

"Couldn'ta been another daddy," Mrs. Washington says, a melancholy expression on her weathered face. "My mama be real strict, but white folks kinda do what they want. I liked Mr. Frank. He never meant no harm. Jus' a reg'lar man."

Sarah cuts her eyes at me to make sure I heard that last remark. For good reason my choice of women hasn't always pleased her. I got high marks for Rainey; she will like Amy, too, if she gives her a chance. "Did he ever acknowledge that Calcutta was his daughter?"

Mrs. Washington is silent for a long moment. "After he seen how light Cal was," she says, "he quit comin' 'round to the house. Not even to git the rent money. Mama said he got a li'l shy after that."

Sarah begins to pull at her hair. She asks, "Where was your daughter born?"

"In the house," Mrs. Washington says, her tone matter-of-fact. "Wudn't no hospital in Bear Creek then."

Sarah knows Marty and I were born in the Baptist Hospital in Memphis. "Did you see a doctor before or after your daughter was born?"

"Never did," Mrs. Washington says ruefully. "Mama didn't have no money for that. When I had a bad toothache once that wouldn't quit, Mama took me on the train to a colored dentist over in Memphis. White dentists didn't like the colored even if you had money."

Her cheeks now blazing, Sarah asks, "Do you remember if the house your mother rented from him was in good condition?"

Mrs. Washington has come to terms with her life in a way Sarah will never understand. The philosophy of stoicism is not in my daughter's bones. Patting at the back of her white head, Mrs. Washington says, "It was all right, but it didn't have no toilet. Still had to go out back. It was hot, too."

I wince at the thought of the house. When I was fourteen and received my restricted driver's license, each week I was allowed to drive a basket of laundry to a house in one of the black sections of Bear Creek. Lula Mae (I never knew her last name) did her ironing in the front room of her house, but all I really remember is the stifling heat in the room, the ironing board, and her asthmatic wheezing. I couldn't wait to get out of the house each time the feeling was so oppressive. How could people live in such poverty? At that age I never made any connection between our lives and theirs.

Sarah has fallen silent, a sign that she has begun to brood. I will hear a sermon on the way home. Mrs. Washington volunteers that when Cal was about three, my grandfather sold their house to someone else, and she rarely saw him again. He didn't send her money, see the child, or acknowledge them in any way. Again, she doesn't seem perturbed about the lack of support. After some urging from me, she adds a few details about her own life. She was married when she was eighteen to a mechanic who ran off after she had four children by him. Until five years ago when her arthritis got too bad, she cleaned houses for a living.

Mrs. Washington confirms that Calcutta is Lucy's mother, and I calculate Frank Page became a father more than sixty years ago. Unlike many blacks who left the county to go North to find work, the family has stayed in eastern Arkansas. "They started coming back these last few years. It ain't no better up there now, and it be a little worse." Though it is not warm in the house, she picks up a fan from the table by her chair and stirs the air in front of her face. She seems a little breathless now, and I suspect we have tired her out. She does not object when I announce we have to be going. As we stand to leave, Mrs. Washington, nodding at Sarah, tells me, "She's a pretty girl." It sounds more like a warning than a compliment.

We thank her for talking with us, and Sarah adds, "I hope this wasn't too hard on you."

Mrs. Washington smiles for the first time. Talking, her expression says, hasn't been the difficult part.

In the Blazer, Sarah complains bitterly. "He was a terrible person! First, he rents her family probably a pigsty; then he knocks some off the rent if she'll have sex with him; then after she gets pregnant and has a child, he sells the property and pretends it never happened. That's just simply evil! How could he have done such a thing?"

I direct Sarah to drive back on Highway 79 through Clarendon and Stuttgart to keep us off the interstate. As we drive past the cemetery again, I try to put the matter in some perspective. "You need to remember that they were in the Depression then, so the housing isn't a surprise. And, we still don't know if she felt coerced to have sex with him. He may have genuinely cared for her. If she hated him, I couldn't tell it."

Sarah passes an ancient pickup with two dogs and three black children in the back. "How can you defend him?" she says shrilly. "She was practically a child. He might as well have raped her for all she could do to stop him! It's all true. Whatever white people over here can get away with, they will. I'm so glad we don't live over here!"

"I'm not defending him, but it's not that simple, Sarah," I lecture her. "Geography doesn't have a lot to do with how much we humans rationalize our behavior. Give any of us too much power, and we'll abuse it. There's some wonderful people, black and white, living in Bear Creek. Granted, my grandfather may not have been one of them, but the older you get, the more you re-alize we're pretty much all the same. You just haven't lived long enough yet to find that out."

Predictably, I have infuriated her. "I don't want power," she snaps at me. "That's all I hear about! Whether it's here or up at Fayetteville. Politics, sports, sororities, fraternities, grades, money—it's all about win-ning. Somebody being better than somebody else, having more than somebody else. Why can't Americans learn how to cooperate with each other and quit trying to beat each other's brains out?"

My stubborn, idealistic daughter. I look over at her and hope that, as angry as she is, she doesn't drive us off into a ditch. I am a poor choice to answer this question. Almost twenty-five years ago, when I came back from the Peace Corps with my mixed-blood bride and moved into an integrated neighborhood, I, like my daughter, thought that if the country just tried hard enough, social and economic equality would be achievable. Black and white, rich and poor would vanish. Or, in the words of John Lennon, heaven and hell would disappear and we would all be one. Well, I was wrong. "You're wanting something to happen that's totally foreign to the average person in the United States. Competition to the death is bred into us from the moment we learn that walking is better than crawling. The national bird ought to be a gamecock. The stereotypical American hero is a type A personality who succeeds whatever the cost, and sacrifices everyone else in the process. While we might give lip service to altruism, it's no accident this is a capitalist country."

"And meanwhile most of an entire race of people have been trampled over to get what we want." As Sarah talks, we go slower and slower, settling in behind Ma and Pa Kettle in a twenty-year-old Ford pickup.

"I don't know what the hell has happened to them," I say honestly. "Do you really think that everything bad that transpires in this country is due to racism? Why can't they compete any better? Get them off the playground, and they lose their drive. Look at all the other minorities who have come to this country and succeeded. Why can't they?"

Sarah swerves to avoid hitting a dead skunk. "That's really great. You're back in Bear Creek an hour, and you sound just like the whites. The short answer is that despite all the discrimination there is a growing African-American middle class. Maybe there's not much of one in Bear Creek, which is in one of the poorest counties in the country, but there is in Blackwell County, and you know it because you can see the evidence right on our street. You just don't read about it in the papers."

"That's for sure," I concede, glad to have an area where we can agree. "All I read about is drive-by shootings, the drug deals in Needle Park, gangs controlling the streets, and teenagers having babies. It just seems like things have really gotten out of control."

Sarah begins to respond but merely shakes her head. In her eyes I'm simply one more racist, an obstacle to progress and enlightenment. As we pass over the White River in Clarendon, I look down into the water and realize how little I believe in the possibility of the advancement of humanity, whatever the race. The best evidence available suggests that we are a violent, greedy, and appallingly wasteful species, intent on pulling the plug on ourselves as fast as we can. Capitalism, stripped of its pretensions, is merely the big rats eating the little ones. The Soviet Union, of course, demonstrated the utter ineptness of socialism. The only redeeming fact is that I love my daughter even more now than when the day started. I love her for her capacity to be outraged; her willingness to care. Right now, she doesn't love me, but she will. She always has.

Outside of England, my bladder can't take another mile, and I tell Sarah to stop at a nondenominational gas station to let me pee. Made of sterner stuff, she waits in the Blazer while I relieve myself in an ancient commode so black with bacteria that out of it could emerge a prehistoric monster. Sarah was right to wait. Feeling guilty that we aren't buying gas, I buy some suckers (a trip wouldn't be complete without hard candy) and two Diet Cokes. The clerk, a grizzled white male whose foreign travel may have taken place in the jungles in Vietnam, judging from his Army jacket and insignia, takes my money complacently. His status notwithstanding, he could stand a little competition, too.

Back in the Blazer I divide my goodies and say, "I wonder what your aunt Marty will say when I tell her that our family tree has a few more branches than we thought."

"What can she say?" Sarah says, pulling back onto the highway. She's a worse racist than you are, her expression says. "What do you feel about it?"

"I haven't had time to assimilate it," I say, glad my parents aren't alive to have Sarah rub their noses in this unfortunate chapter of our family history. She would, too.

"It was rape, pure and simple," Sarah pronounces. "She had no choice."

Pure and simple? What is ever pure and simple? I try to keep from clenching my fists and stare out at the bare fields, the rice and bean harvests already completed in this dry and mild fall. Now that we have proof (I can't imagine the old woman was lying, having heard her) of our kinship with Dade and his family, I wonder if Sarah's attitude will eventually soften about his case. Is Dade now a victim in her eyes, too? Or does his maleness transcend race? What a battle for her ideological soul!

On the outskirts of Blackwell County, I ask, "Isn't it odd that neither Dade nor his father have mentioned the fact that we are related?"

The sun disappears entirely, and Sarah takes off her dark glasses. "It's probably their male pride that prevents them. Their women were raped, and they were helpless to stop it. They probably don't like it any better than you do. Women are different. Once the baby was born, all Ms. Washington could do was love it. The baby was innocent."

We drive in silence the rest of the way home. I hope she remembers that someday. Dade didn't ask to be born either. As we turn in our driveway, she asks me, not for the first time, "Do you still think Dade is innocent?"

Though he is still refusing to take the polygraph test (for reasons I don't understand), I say stubbornly, "Yeah, I do. If he's convicted and goes to prison, and you find out later that he was telling the truth, how will you feel? After all, he's sort of a half cousin."

Sarah picks up her purse from the floor and opens the door, refusing my invitation to feel guilty. "What I found out today is that women don't usually lie about what men do to them. All those years you didn't believe that poor woman had been raped by your grandfather. If we hadn't gone over there today, you never would have known the truth."

Sarah has a way of learning her own lessons from events, but I let this pass. Anything I say will be seen as denial. I grunt and pick up candy wrappers strewn on the floor before following her into the house.

"What time will you be home?" I ask from the couch in the den as I watch Sarah study herself in a compact mirror. She is going out to meet some friends from high school. I look at my watch. It is almost eight. Amy was supposed to be here by now to meet her. I pet Woogie, who has jumped up on the couch beside me now that he sees Sarah is deserting us.

"I have no idea," she says vaguely.

"Do you think you'll be back by noon tomorrow?" I ask sarcastically. I didn't think it was such a difficult question.

"Oh, Dad!" Sarah says, picking up her purse.

There is a knock at the door, and it is Amy who breezes in past me. "Did I miss Sarah?"

"Almost," I say, irritated with both of them.

Sarah, dressed in jeans and an old bomber jacket she has found in her closet, is just barely civil. Rainey, her expression says, was an appropriate companion, but this woman is too young.

Indeed, with her hair in a ponytail and wearing white sweats, Amy looks more like a college student than a woman who surely has to be close to thirty. "Have fun!" Amy calls to her as Sarah bounds down the front stoop, keys in hand. My daughter, who has barely said hello to her, nods but doesn't speak.

I had wanted Sarah to sit down and visit, but Amy was

delayed by a phone call. I shut the door and complain, "That was successful, wasn't it?"

Amy reaches down to pet Woogie, saying mischievously, "Well, you should have had me over to dinner. I would have been on time."

I lead her into the den. "Sarah could have waited a few more minutes. It wasn't as if she had to go put out a fire somewhere."

Amy comes up behind me and bumps me with her shoulder. "She's darling. And mad as hell at her old man for blowing it with Rainey, and taking up with a young bimbo, and probably for a million other sins you've committed that I don't know about."

"You're not a bimbo!" I yelp.

Amy sits on the couch, and I plop down beside her. "I've got my work cut out if I want to hang around the Page gang, don't I?" she says merrily, but I can't tell whether she's kidding or not. "The old guy's a lush and still mooning over his former girlfriend who's getting married on him; his daughter is furious because she's nearly the same age as his girlfriend. This is a tough crowd, huh, Woogie?" she says to my dog, who has jumped up beside her.

"I'm not a lush!" I say plaintively.

"It's a bit dog that barks," Amy says cryptically, then reaches up and kisses me.

I don't get this woman and tell her so. "Why do you like me?"

"I can't explain it either," Amy says, a big grin on her face. "I know this will end in disaster for me. But what else is new? How was your day?"

Before I tell her, I get the Arkansas-LSU game on the radio from Baton Rouge. As I expected, the rest of the Hogs' season has been terrible. Without Dade, the offense has shut down completely, and we haven't won another game. While we listen, I explain to Amy for the first time about my grandfather.

"Goodness gracious!" she exclaims when I am finished. "A little Southern gothic soap opera. Why didn't you tell me before?"

I turn off the game. We're hopelessly behind (21 to 0 in the fourth quarter). "Hell, I don't know. I was embarrassed, I guess," I admit. I get up to get a beer. Amy has already refused one.

"*You* didn't do it," she says. "Besides there're a million stories like that all over the South. Some worse, some better."

I come sit back down by her. Things heat up on the couch, and I am all for going back into the bedroom, but am deterred by the possibility that Sarah may return for something. "She's practically heard us," I say, as I put my hand under the top part of her sweats, "she might as well see us."

"I can't imagine a more delightful scene," Amy says, only halfheartedly pushing my hand away. "This is your new mother, Sarah. She's even cuter without any clothes on, isn't she? Stop it!"

The next morning during breakfast I manage only two sips of coffee before asking Sarah, "Well, what did you think of Amy?"

Sarah chews on a piece of buttered toast, swallows,

and then lectures me: "Dad, don't do anything foolish like getting married right now. You'd just be doing it to spite Rainey. You're on the rebound. Don't forget it."

I put down the sports pages, unable to continue reading about the massacre last night. My daughter is a piece of work. "I wasn't sending you a wedding invitation. I just asked, what did you think about Amy?"

"She's all right," Sarah says grudgingly.

More than satisfied, I do not risk a followup question.

An hour later after she drives off to return to school, I pick up the house and realize that Sarah did not make me try to agree again that I would ask the court to let me withdraw as Dade's attorney. Maybe she thinks we should be all one big happy family. The court wouldn't let me withdraw at this late date anyway.

12

"YOUR DAUGHTER IS on the phone," Julia says, appearing in the doorway to my office. "She sounds a little anxious."

I have been ignoring the beeping sound in my ear that indicates another call. Julia does not make a practice of being sensitive to anything involving my welfare, so I dare not ignore her. I check the calendar. December 18. The last time I talked to Sarah was on Pearl Harbor Day. It was a curious conversation. The day before, Dr. Beekman, an unlikely ally if there ever was one, had taken up Dade's cause and argued that Dade might well be innocent. I had to give her a hard time, since the guy parroted every argument I made to her. God knows what else Beekman knows. He probably can trace my family tree now better than I can. "Tell her to hang on," I say. "I'll be off in two seconds. Thanks."

Julia nods. Women have to stick together, her expression says. I am on the phone with Gordon Dyson, who has told me his wife is flying off to New Zealand the day after Christmas. I had completely forgotten about him. He is reminding me to send him a power of attorney for

277

his wife to sign before she departs. He says excitedly, "I can't even get my son to rake the leaves in the front yard!"

I am amazed that he is actually following through with the eviction. Most of my clients ignore my advice and perhaps for good reason. Now, two months later, my suggestion seems a little extreme. "Call me the day after your wife leaves, and I'll draw up the complaint. Don't worry; we'll get him out."

"You've got to," he pleads. "He's driving me crazy."

"It'll be a piece of cake." I feel like a pest exterminator. I remind him of my fee and tell him I have to get off. I pick up Sarah's line, wondering what she wants. She finishes her first-semester exams tomorrow afternoon, and I can't imagine any call that can't wait twenty-four hours. "What's up, babe?" I ask. "Julia says it sounded important."

"Well, it's probably not, and I don't feel good about telling you this, because I don't know how relevant it is, but here goes: there's a rumor that's been going around, and it's only a rumor, that Robin was having an affair with Dr. Hofstra in the history department this summer. Depending on the source, it was still going on this fall when Robin filed rape charges against Dade. That may not be true at all though, because the girl who said Robin was still involved with Dr. Hofstra when she said she was raped is a cheerleader and was her big rival."

I make notes furiously. Ever since Thanksgiving it's been as if Dade's case was on hold. He is still refusing to take the polygraph despite his mother's encouragement. I have been hoping he would begin to feel some pressure of the upcoming trial date and would cooperate. "How long have you known about this?" I ask, marveling at my daughter's ability to keep a secret, a feat, despite my obligations as a lawyer, that I don't always manage.

"I heard it the day before I quit the jayvee cheerleaders," Sarah admits, "but Paula convinced me not to say anything. She said it was gossip and that a statute called the 'rape shield law' made it inadmissible in court. Is that true?"

I try to contain my exasperation. That was back in October! "It's up to the judge. If the court can be convinced that a past sexual relationship has some particular bearing on the case, evidence of it can be admitted, but under most situations, the statute prohibits mention of it," I explain. "Why are you telling me now? Have you been talking to Dr. Beekman again?" I ask, hoping she has had a falling out with WAR.

"Some," she admits, "but I've been thinking about this ever since we got back from Bear Creek, and so I finally called Dade this morning and confronted him. He swears he didn't rape Robin. I think I believe him. He's pretty convincing."

Family ties. Even as distant as these are, Sarah must feel them. How odd! Yet, is it? She must have a hundred questions about her own racial past. Now, she has a connection, however slight, right on campus. "I still believe him, too," I say, encouragingly. "I take it you heard this from another cheerleader." If I can get someone to testify, this case might be back in business.

"Dad," Sarah blurts, "I'm sworn to secrecy! I've violated a confidence telling you this."

"The rest of Dade's life is at stake," I press her. "This may be crucial evidence in the case. It would be horribly unfair to Dade if the case turned on this point and it never got presented to the jury."

"Don't make me do this!" Sarah says, her voice anguished.

"You have to, babe," I scold her. I have no qualms about leaning on my own daughter. She should have told me weeks ago. "I need the names of everybody you've talked to."

Sarah, her voice now choked with tears, says, "I've got to talk to them first."

Her tears always get to me. I know I'm putting her in a bind. Yet, it is wrong for her to sit on this information. "I understand," I say. "Just let me know as soon as possible. I'll be in Fayetteville tomorrow afternoon."

I make her promise to call me back as soon as she can, and then I go in to Dan's office to talk this over with him. For the last month Dan has been disappearing during the day. I know he is still seeing Gina, but today, it appears, he is actually doing some work for a change. He puts down his Dictaphone as soon as I mention I have some juicy gossip about the case. "What would be the possible relevance to Robin's allegation that she was raped by Dade?" I ask, after going through Sarah's story.

As he thinks, Dan's right forefinger wanders up his face but fortunately misses his nose and comes to rest below his eye. "Maybe she was trying to make her professor jealous," he muses, "and she went to the hottest guy she knew."

"With a black athlete on a southern campus?" I ask,

unable to accept this scenario. I sit down across from him. "Maybe this professor knocked her up, and she wanted to get an abortion but needed an excuse, so she claimed Dade raped her."

Dan shakes his head. "Why wouldn't she just get one?" he scoffs. "It's no big deal."

"It is," I say, "if you're raised to think abortion is a sin, and the only thing that justifies it would be rape or saving the mother's life. Robin's parents are big Baptists. She wouldn't be able to admit to them she got pregnant. That's too big a scandal. But if they knew, they'd make her have the baby. So she lets herself get into a situation with Dade and convinces herself that he has raped her, which justifies an abortion."

Dan rocks back and forth in his chair like a child. "You've got a vivid imagination," he says, tacitly admitting I may be onto something. "Do you have any proof?"

"Not a shred," I admit, realizing that up until now Robin has been able to create an image of herself that has been nauseatingly pristine. I still know almost nothing about her. That's going to change. I need to get back up to Fayetteville and start to work on this case again.

I go back to my office and call Dade and, for a change, get him in his room. "I understand Sarah called you today," I begin, not at all sure how he will react. "I didn't know she was going to. She's kind of impulsive sometimes."

"She's all right," Dade says. "At least she told me you went to Bear Creek. Of course, I already knew."

"I figured you did," I say awkwardly. In the two conversations I've had with him since we came back, I never quite knew how to bring it up.

"Mama said she had told you, but you didn't believe her!" he says.

I should have had this conversation with him long before now, but I kept putting it off. "All my life I had been told it wasn't true," I say weakly. "I needed to find out for myself whether it was or not."

"Your daughter says it was her idea to go over there."

I shift uncomfortably in my chair. They had a longer conversation than Sarah led me to believe. "That's true."

"You see why I don't want to take a lie detector test? I can't trust white people."

Who does he think will be on the jury? We have been over this a dozen times. "Then trust the polygraph: it's a machine; it just records changes in your body as you answer questions."

"You've said that it's not what the machine does that's important; it's what the man says the answers mean."

The Man. How do we get past that? I switch subjects and tell him I am coming up tomorrow. "Have you heard anything about Robin in the last few days that you haven't already told me?" I ask, determined not to put words in his mouth. I will save Sarah's story until I've talked to her again. "Anything that could give us a motive as to why she would say you raped her?"

"Not really," Dade says, sounding genuinely perplexed. "I keep asking, but nobody I talked to knows her that good."

Dade and his sources are out of the loop. The only black faces in the Chi Omega House are the ones who clean up after the whites. I tell him to call me at the Ozark tomorrow if he hears anything. His last exam is not until Friday. Sometimes, it is hard to forget these kids are really in school.

My first stop the next afternoon is Jefferson Memorial Hospital. My sophomore year I broke my arm playing touch football one fall and spent a long afternoon in its emergency room. Things are relatively slow this afternoon, and after only a half hour of searching and waiting, I sit down with the nurse who talked with Robin Perry the morning she came in to be examined.

She had been out of town the day of the administrative hearing conducted by the university, and I am eager to check her out. A tall, gangly, dishwater blonde in her early forties, wearing blue hospital scrubs, Joan Chestnut isn't particularly eager to talk to me, but does so after I show her the release on the state crime lab report form that Robin had signed. In the corner of a breakroom shared by two other employees who are watching a daytime soap, I whisper, "Do you remember how Robin Perry seemed to you the morning she came in and reported she had been raped?"

Ms. Chestnut gives me the patient smile of a woman used to dealing with attorneys. "Her reactions were quite consistent for a rape victim," she says, slowly and deliberately as if she already sees herself being cross-examined. "She was very articulate besides being angry. I remember her in particular because even with all that she had been through she was a beautiful girl."

I hand her the section of the nurse's notes. In it she has

noted that the patient was "calm." "Why wouldn't she be upset?"

She flips through the entire document and hands it back to me. "I've done ER over twenty years, and I've seen scores of rape victims. I've seen women numb, in shock, and then some who were relatively composed even minutes after an attack had occurred. It depends entirely on the individual. If she was raped the night before, she'd had time to work through the initial shock."

"So you have no doubt Robin Perry was coerced into having sex?" I ask, over a commercial for breath mints.

"That's not something you can ever know with any certainty, but just because she wasn't hysterical doesn't mean anything," Ms. Chestnut responds, remaining unruffled. "The girl said she had been crying the entire night, and I believed her. I could look at her and tell she hadn't had any sleep."

Even though she isn't saying anything particularly damaging, this woman, unlike the Rape Crisis counselor, is going to be helpful to the prosecution. She radiates such competence that a jury is going to believe anything that comes out of her mouth.

"Didn't her roommate come in with her?" I ask, curious about Shannon Kennsit's reaction. If her roommate was at all suspicious of her story, I might begin to get some hints now.

Looking at her watch, Joan Chestnut says, "I didn't remember until now that that girl was her roommate. She was very supportive, I know that. From what I recall, I think she felt in some way responsible. Like if she hadn't been going out that night, Robin wouldn't have gone out there by herself, and it wouldn't have happened."

Ms. Chestnut has told me that she is supposed to be checking on a patient, but I say, "One more question. Was Robin worried about being pregnant?"

"Of course she was!" she says, looking at me as if I were slightly insane.

I spread my hands in a dismissive gesture. "She could have gotten an abortion if that had been the case."

Ms. Chestnut puckers her mouth as if she has been forced to swallow something unpleasant. "That's a terrible burden to place on a young woman, Mr. Page. I know lots of people who would only allow abortion if the mother's life were in danger."

Despite what this nurse thinks, I'm not out to make an enemy of her. I need her a lot more than she will ever need me. "Thanks for your time, ma'am," I say politely. "I'm glad women have someone like you to support them."

She stands up, ready to make her getaway. "If you saw what we do," she says, "you'd react the same way."

"I have no doubt," I say scrambling to my feet. "One very last question. I know the lab report says she wasn't pregnant at the time of the incident. Would she have found that out before she left the hospital?"

Ms. Chestnut looks puzzled. "She would have known she wasn't pregnant."

"But if she thought she had been," I persist, "she would have known that she wasn't by the time the hospital got through with her, is that right?"

As usual, one last question has become two or three. "She would have known," Ms. Chestnut agrees.

"Do you know how she reacted to the information," I ask, "that she wasn't pregnant at the time of the alleged rape?"

Ms. Chestnut gives me a blank stare. "She didn't react to that news at all," she says, clearly nonplussed by my question. "It was the trauma of being raped she was reacting to."

Shit. So much for my theory that she thought she was pregnant by her professor and had concocted a rape story so she could justify getting an abortion. "If you think of something you didn't tell me," I say sincerely, "I'd appreciate it if you'd call me collect."

Now that I am leaving, she smiles and lights up the entire room. "I'll be happy to," she says, dropping my card into a pocket on her thigh. "Am I going to be subpoenaed?"

I won't hold my breath waiting for her call. "Not by me." I walk out the automatic double doors of the emergency room realizing I'm not going to be able to do anything with this woman at the trial except pretend she's boring the jury to death.

Like an old drunk who can't remember anything except where he lives, I check into my room at the Ozark, which seems to be having a heating problem. It must be fifty degrees in here. I'd move, but I'm too damn lazy. After complaining to the manager, I call Sarah. Reluctantly, she gives me the telephone number of a girl named Lauren Denney at the Tri-Delt House. "She's the one who's the cheerleader," Sarah says irritably. "She's too eager, Dad. She wants to talk to you. Her last exam was this morning, but she said she could see you before she leaves town tonight."

"What's she like?" I ask.

"Two-faced," Sarah warns me. "She's got more ex-friends than anybody I know."

"She sounds charming," I comment. Defense witnesses, like clients, don't come with a Good Housekeeping Seal of Approval stamped on them. When they appear sincere and competent like Joan Chestnut, they are usually on the other side.

"Actually, she is," Sarah says, "for the first twenty minutes or so you're around her. But she can be a bitch!"

I rarely hear Sarah attack another girl, but I know she isn't all sugar and spice either. There's got to be some of me in her somewhere. "Any other names?"

"Jenny Taylor," Sarah says. "I got her as she was just leaving to go home. She lives in Heber Springs, and she said she'd probably talk to you after Christmas if you went up there to see her. She wanted to talk to her parents first. She doesn't want to be involved and is mad at me for telling you."

She'll get over it, I think but don't say. "What's her number in Heber Springs?"

Sarah gives it to me, and I hang up and dial Lauren Denney's number. She may be a terrible person, but she has a nice voice, unusually low but distinct, and she agrees at once to meet me at Danny's, my diner that plays the golden oldies. I started to suggest the Ozark, but one rumor floating around is enough in this case.

When Lauren strolls into the restaurant twenty minutes

later, I get a good look. She is wearing tight jeans and a tobacco-colored sweater that blends nicely with her long, honey-colored hair. If I were a Razorback, I wouldn't have any trouble being inspired. We are escorted to a booth in the rear by a boy in a ponytail. I ask her what she would like to eat, but she says she just wants coffee, and I order some for both of us. She looks tired and admits it. "Exams," she explains needlessly. "I haven't slept for two days."

I feel self-conscious, but she could easily pass for my daughter. "I won't keep you long," I say, deciding to get to the point. If Sarah is correct, this girl doesn't need any priming. I explain briefly what Sarah has told me and that I believe Dade has been set up, but that I can't explain the motive. "Why would she pretend she was raped?"

As if on cue, Lauren narrows her eyes. "To keep Dr. Hofstra seeing her for as long as she could. He was trying to break it off, and she thought she could get his sympathy by claiming she had been raped."

I put down my spoon. "How do you know this?" I ask, dumbfounded.

Lauren doesn't miss a beat. She tries her coffee first and then says, "She told me."

"Told you when?" This girl has a way of dramatizing everything she does. I see what Sarah means. She is charming, but I don't trust her and I've only been with her five minutes. The jukebox plays "Runaround Sue" by Dion. There must be five guys my age in here by themselves. It suddenly occurs to me that Danny's is a gay hangout. Boy, I'm dumb. I thought they just liked the music.

"See, Robin and I used to be good friends. We were in school together up here this past summer, and we shared an apartment. She took a history course, and like an idiot, he showed up one day in our living room. I wasn't supposed to be there that weekend, and I walked in on them. They were just sitting there, but after he left, it was so obvious they were sleeping together that I made her admit it."

All this comes out in a voice that drops even lower as she continues to talk. The lack of sleep has turned her into a junior Lauren Bacall. I ask, "Did he say anything?"

She stretches, straining her breasts against the wool until I think they are going to pop through. I don't know whether this is for my benefit or she thinks I'm so harmless that I don't even notice. "He muttered something ridiculous about her exam, turned red as a beet, and got out of there. You see, Robin is supposed to be so sweet and demure, but she attracts guys like you wouldn't believe. When I heard she spoke at the WAR rally, I nearly died laughing. She's no more a feminist than I am. What a hoot!"

It sounds as if Lauren is the jealous one, but I can't imagine why. Even exhausted, she looks great. "How do you know she was still having an affair with him when she accused Dade of raping her?"

"Just the week before she told me she was!" Lauren says, wide-eyed and innocent as a lamb. "We had just finished practice, and were walking across campus, and I asked her if she was still seeing him. She didn't say anything, but she nodded her head like this." Lauren moves her head quickly up and down, and then stares into my face to see what kind of effect she has made. "She said he was trying to break it off, but she had gotten in so deep that she'd do anything to keep him."

Do anything, huh? It sounds plausible, but because of Sarah's skepticism, I find I am doubting her. Why? If people were disqualified from testifying in court because of character flaws, there would be no judicial system. "What did you say?"

"I told her that she'd just end up getting him and her both in all kinds of trouble."

St. Lauren. It's a bit of a stretch. "Why did y'all have a falling out?" I ask.

"Because she's a hypocrite!" Lauren exclaims. "I was sympathetic until she started acting like such a martyr. Robin knows exactly what kind of impression she makes when she walks into a room. Lots of guys love an ice queen like her. They want to be the one to melt her. I can't prove this, but I think she had liked Dade back in the spring. She never would admit it, and gave out all that crap about helping him in communications. I could understand her liking him, but he's black and that's just not worth it up here."

The jukebox starts up with "The Great Pretender" by The Platters, but she doesn't seem to be holding much back. "Who else did she tell about the affair with her teacher?"

"I have no idea," Lauren says breezily. "I haven't told but a couple of girls about it."

A couple of dozen probably. Honesty mixed in with lies is an irresistible combination, but her story is for the jury to decide. "Would you be willing to testify at the trial and at a hearing before then if I need you?" If I'm going to be able to get this information into evidence, according to the rape shield statute, I'll have to file a motion with the court and ask for a hearing.

Lauren stares at the bright red lipstick she has left on the lip of her cinnamon-colored coffee cup. "Do I have to?" she asks. "I'd hate to hurt Robin."

Yeah, right. I resist the temptation to laugh in this girl's face. Lauren would run over her with a truck if she had the opportunity. "I'll have subpoenas issued for you, and that way you won't have any choice about coming. You'll have to come back early from Christmas vacation. Is that okay?"

"Cool," she says, the fingers of her right hand beginning to tap out the beat of the song though I can't imagine she has ever heard it.

I take out my card and slide it across the Formica top. "What's the worst thing Robin knows about you?" I ask, wondering what ax is being grinded here.

"That I can be a real bitch sometimes," Lauren says, smiling sweetly at me.

I just barely resist saying that I have heard that. We talk for a few more minutes, and then she leaves, but not before I get an address and phone number at her home in El Dorado. I watch her walk out. The other guys don't even look up. With friends like Lauren, who needs enemies?

At ten o'clock the next morning I watch as a student comes out of Dr. Joseph Hofstra's office and heads for his door. I want to surprise the guy and watch his immediate reaction. My guess is that he might like to avoid Dade's trial almost as much as Dade. If Robin is still involved emotionally with him, she might not want to go forward with the trial if he is going to be dragged into it.

The door to his office is open, and I introduce myself to a dark-haired man who looks around the eyes like a young Warren Beatty. He is around thirty, dressed in blue denim pants and a blue workshirt. I can see how the co-eds could keep his office hours busy. He squints as if he ought to know who I am but can't place me. He puts down a book whose title I can't make out, and asks, his voice droll, "Are you one of my students?"

He probably thinks I'm a book salesman. From the hundreds lining the walls I'd say he doesn't need any more. I say bluntly, "I represent Dade Cunningham in the rape trial that is coming up in a couple of weeks. I understand Robin was one of your students last summer."

I have to give the guy credit. For an instant only I think I see him react, but, in fact, I can't be sure. He pushes his chair back from his desk and says blandly, "Yes, I had Robin in summer school. I was shocked to hear she had been assaulted, but I don't see the relevance to my class."

I look behind his head and see he was awarded his Ph.D. from the University of Michigan only three years ago. He must feel he has come down in the world, but a guy has to start somewhere. "Let me get to the point. I just talked to a friend of Robin's who said you had a sexual relationship with Robin this summer. Do you deny it?"

With as much dignity as he can muster under the circumstances, Hofstra stands up, and in a hoarse voice says, "I think you better leave my office immediately."

I pretend he hasn't moved a muscle. "Dr. Hofstra, if you will answer a couple of questions right now, it will be a lot easier on you than if I have to embarrass you at the trial. I'd appreciate it if you'd talk to me."

"Whatever you've heard is purely gossip," he blurts. "Now, leave my office before I call security."

"If you get a lawyer," I say, dropping my card on his desk, "ask him to call me, please."

His brown eyes beginning to bulge, he loses his composure. "Get out!" he screams, his voice betraying his panic.

On his desk I can see a picture of what must be his family. Two girls. His wife is pretty, a blonde just like Robin. I stand and walk out, not feeling so good. How much nicer it would be to be a book salesman.

After checking out of the Ozark and stopping by Barton's office (only to find that he is in Colorado skiing), I head the Blazer east for home, wondering how this latest turn of events will play out. Hofstra may be my best weapon to keep this case from going to trial. Right about now, I imagine he's calling his lawyer or is on the phone to Robin. Outside of Fayetteville, the solitude gets to me, and I turn on the radio. "The Little Drummer Boy." In less than a week it will be Christmas. Not a favorite holiday since Rosa's death. I nudge the heater up a bit. It is cold up here in the mountains. This morning there was so much frost on the grass in front of the motel it looked as if it had snowed. Though it has been the mildest fall I can remember in central Arkansas, it will be a frigid January for some people up here. I will file a motion for a hearing, and then in two or three days, after they've had a chance to stew, I will drive south to Texarkana to visit Robin and her parents. With a chance that it will turn messy beyond their wildest dreams, they may not want to see this case go to court after all.

13

DECEMBER 21 — THE shortest day of the year, I realize, looking at the calendar behind Judge Blake's head. He doesn't look sympathetic. For Rainey's sake, I hope it isn't the year's shortest hearing. "Ms. McCorkle," I say, "would you tell the court about Ms. Alvarez's ability to live more independently?"

Rainey smiles at Delores, who is sitting next to me and proceeds to testify about my client's management of routine household skills. It is nothing short of bizarre to be calling as a witness the woman I would have married, but Rainey acts as though we have perfected a dog and pony show that we've been taking on the road for years. She turns to Judge Blake and tells him that Delores is a better shopper than she is. "Your Honor, I went to Megamarket with Ms. Alvarez, and she not only picked out the food but did comparison shopping by using a pocket calculator and then cooked a full dinner on my stove. I have no doubt she can live very well independently."

Judge Blake massages the temple of his large, bald head as if he is hearing a complicated tax case involving millions of dollars instead of a two-page petition to modify a mental patient's conditional release. He interrupts, "How can I be certain she will take her medication each day?"

Prepared for the question, Rainey barely lets him finish. "She takes a Prolixin injection at the Community Mental Health Center every two weeks. If she doesn't come in, the case manager can call her to find out what happened, and if she's not satisfied with her answer, she can ask the court for an emergency pickup order."

Judge Blake comes dangerously close to picking his nose in front of us. "Now what is so wrong with where Ms. Alvarez is right now?"

Rainey launches into a passionate denunciation of the Confederate Gardens. After describing physical conditions that make even the judge wince, she says, "It's especially inappropriate for a woman who can manage as well as Ms. Alvarez, Your Honor. The Blackwell County Community Mental Health Center is supposed to be acting as an advocate to help people like Ms. Alvarez live in the community as independently as possible. In this woman's case it means helping her find an apartment and a job. Instead, the case managers do the easiest thing possible—find them a place like Confederate Gardens, which lumps all persons with mental illness together in what amounts to a hellhole and takes their Social Security Disability checks. With just a little help from BCCMHC Ms. Alvarez can be a productive, taxpaying citizen . . ."

As I listen to Rainey sing a song whose verses are all the same (she has sung it to me more than once), I realize again how much I will be missing. Her spunk alone is worth the price of admission. As a social worker at the state hospital, she is deliberately courting criticism by daring to attack publicly a community mental health center for not doing its job. The rule in the mental health bureaucracy is: Don't break my rice bowl and I won't break yours. The beautiful thing about Rainey is that she doesn't give a shit. I realize belatedly how much she is like Rosa, who never thought twice about telling a doctor to his face that he needed to call in a specialist.

Judge Blake finally cuts Rainey off. "I understand your point, Ms. McCorkle, but my concern with Ms. Alvarez is that she has threatened the life of the President of the United States. I'm surprised to hear that she has as much freedom as she does."

The old fraud, I think. He ordered her placed there himself. He's either stupid or dishonest. Rainey speaks to him as if they were the only ones in the courtroom. "She didn't threaten him, Your Honor. She just went to the Mansion to try to collect money she thought she was owed."

"She went three times until she was arrested," the judge says, his tone becoming frosty. "As I'm sure you know, just a month or so ago, a mental patient killed an innocent person here in Blackwell County. We need more confinement, not less."

"You're not listening, Your Honor," Rainey says, near tears. "This woman is not dangerous to anybody!"

Judge Blake is not the type of jurist who likes to be told he is nothing short of perfect. A vein bulging in his forehead, he says to me, "Call your next witness!"

The attorney from the prosecution coordinator's office,

Diana Bateman, giggles, "No questions, Your Honor."
She is too chickenshit to point out that she isn't being allowed to cross-examine Rainey. Of course, she doesn't
need to. Since the community mental health psychiatrist,
the case manager, and Ms. Alvarez have already testified,
I have no choice but to rest my case, and the judge rules
before Rainey has even gotten back to her seat that he is
refusing to modify the order requiring Ms. Alvarez to live
at the Confederate Gardens. As a sop to me, he grants my
motion to review her case in six months.

Once we are outside in the hall, Rainey begins to cry.
"You tried as hard as you could," Ms. Alvarez says, patting Rainey's shoulder as if she were the social worker
trying to ease the pain of a dejected client. "That judge
wouldn't have let Hillary Clinton out today. He was
scared."

I marvel at the accuracy of the remark. As the old saying goes, Ms. Alvarez may be crazy, but she isn't stupid.
"We'll try again in six months," I volunteer, relieved I
haven't wasted more than a couple of hours. "If there
hasn't been any recent negative publicity, Blake might
change his mind."

"Can't we appeal?" Rainey asks, biting her lip.

"The state doesn't pay for an appeal on this kind of
case," I say quickly to discourage her. "It's better just to
come back." I am not willing to pay for a transcript out of
my own pocket and then waste my time by writing a
brief. The court of appeals is elected, too. "We're better
off waiting until the headlines shrink a little."

"It just makes me so angry!" Rainey says, wiping her

eyes. "They're all so lazy, and the judge is such a coward."

I look around uneasily, hoping there is nobody to repeat this comment. Rainey is in enough trouble as it is. Why should I care, I think irritably. In a few days, she'll never have to work again. "I've got to go," I tell Rainey. "Sorry it didn't go better."

Preoccupied, she nods perfunctorily. "Thanks, Gideon."

She'll be married the next time I see her. Resisting the temptation to hug her, I say, "Sure."

As I turn to go, she reaches in her purse and pulls out a small box wrapped in Christmas paper. How odd that she should get me a present. "This is for Sarah," she says, before I can make a fool of myself.

"How nice!" I reply, trying to smile. Amy is coming over on Christmas Day. For the last three years it has been Rainey who has come by.

Before I know it, Rainey reaches up and kisses me on the cheek. "I won't see you again before I'm married," she whispers. "Be good!"

I nod, and turn away, not trusting myself to speak. I drive back downtown to get back to a case that has begun to seem more promising.

From my office I call Lucy and Roy Cunningham to let them know that I will be driving down to Texarkana late this afternoon to drop in on the parents of Robin Perry. If this case is dismissed, I want them to realize who is responsible.

It is Roy who answers the phone, and as I explain to him what is going on, he becomes more communicative

than he has been since this case began. "I figured she was
setting him up!" he says in a loud voice.

I tell him that yesterday I filed a motion with the court
that is a prerequisite to introducing evidence at the trial
of Robin's sex life. The judge has scheduled the hearing
to take place January 3, four days before the trial begins.
"If Robin tells the prosecutor that she doesn't want to go
through with the trial, he'll ask the judge to dismiss it."

Roy listens quietly. "Why wouldn't she wait to make a
decision until the hearing is over to see what the judge
does?" he asks, his voice booming. I can't hear any noise
in the background. It must be a slow day.

"She might," I concede, "but her family surely knows
by now that this is a boat that is beginning to spring some
real bad leaks. The less people know, the better. Despite
the fact that this will be a closed hearing, they can assume correctly that word will get out, and it'll be all over
Fayetteville and the university in no time. This is the kind
of scandal that people like to head off as much as possible. All I want to do is emphasize to them how much better it would be for everyone concerned if Robin drops the
case right now."

"Do you want to speak to Dade? He's home. I can have
him call you," Roy says, a tone of respect coming into his
voice for the first time since the night I took the case in
his brother's living room.

I look at my watch and tell him that I'll call tomorrow
with a report. I'm ready to get on the road. I ask him to
keep this within their family and hang up, thinking Roy
may yet end up wanting me for his son's agent.

As I am getting up to head out the door, Dan comes in,

his double chin nearly to the floor. He looks like a child who has had his toys ripped away from him by another kid. "Heading south, huh?" he says without enthusiasm. I have told him everything that has been going on.

"Yep," I say, reaching for my briefcase. I shouldn't need anything, but I want to look the part. He looks so pitiful that I can't avoid asking, "Did you just get run over by a truck?"

Dan sighs and leans back against my door, prohibiting me from leaving. "Gina wants me to leave Brenda and move in with her. She's in love with me."

God, the holidays! They make everybody weird. "That would give the legal community a juicy little nut for their Christmas stockings," I say, not taking him seriously.

"I love her, Gideon," Dan says miserably. "She makes me happier than I've ever been in my life."

What a screwball Dan's become! "She's a hooker, for God's sake!" I say for what must be the tenth time.

"You don't understand," Dan answers softly, looking down at the argyle socks in which he pads around the office more and more. "Gina's a good person. She's crazy about her little girl. She makes me feel alive in a way that I haven't for years! It isn't just the sex; the truth is, I'm so scared of getting AIDS from her I don't even enjoy it. We just have fun together. Brenda hasn't cracked a smile since I choked and nearly died on a piece of her meatloaf nearly two years ago."

I shake my head as I visualize the dismal little duplex Gina calls home. "Have you thought about going to marriage counseling?"

Dan wipes his eyes. "The last one we went to admitted

she had been divorced three times. Brenda said she wouldn't pay someone to watch us fight. We can do that for free."

I laugh despite myself. "You can't really be thinking about moving in with her."

"I won't," Dan sighs. "I don't have the guts. I'm too middle class. As pathetic a human being as I am, I'm still enough of a snob to care about what other people think. There goes fat Dan. He lives with a whore dog who nearly cooked her baby. Nah, I couldn't handle that."

Poor guy. He seems about to cry. "I couldn't either," I say sympathetically. "Just hang on until January. Things will seem better then."

With a blank expression on his face, Dan turns and wanders down the hall, and I follow him out, realizing I have a grudging admiration for him. The difference between me and Dan is that I wouldn't have the integrity to admit that I had fallen in love with a whore. Dan is pitiful, but at least he is honest about it. I ride the elevator down to the street thinking that the evolution of the species may be more of a short-term proposition than scientists think.

I point the Blazer south on I-30 to Texarkana, and two and a half hours later, after stopping for gas in Arkadelphia, I exit at a service station just before crossing the Texas line to ask for directions. I walk into the office hugging myself and wishing I had brought my overcoat. A cold front has moved across the state. An attendant wearing a New York Yankees baseball cap points east on a city map, and five minutes later I am shivering in front of Robin's parents' ranch-style home, which occupies two lots, and trying to recall what I know about this family. All I remember is that the husband gives or gave a shitload of money to the Razorback scholarship fund and is a conservative Baptist, a profile that could fit any number of Arkansans.

Though I've never seen her, I'd know Mrs. Perry anywhere. An older, more voluptuous version of the daughter, she comes to the door wearing a red knit outfit that suggests they may have dinner plans. It is almost six o'clock, and two cars, a Buick sedan and a Cherokee, sit in the driveway. If they brush me off, there will be nothing I can do except to head back in the other direction.

"Mrs. Perry, I'm Gideon Page, Dade Cunningham's lawyer," I begin, as gently as I can. "I'd like to visit just a very few minutes with you and your husband. I'm sorry to be disturbing you, but it's important that we talk before the hearing."

There is no effort to conceal the shock that is apparent on her carefully made-up face. It is as if Dade himself had appeared on their doorstep. I look past her to see if I can get a glimpse of Robin, but she is nowhere to be seen. I do not want her to be present for this conversation, if it takes place. They will feel too protective of her if she is sitting there. "Just a moment," Mrs. Perry says frostily through the screen door in an accent even more Southern than her daughter's. She turns and is gone. I feel as though I am a representative of the Mormons, a long way from Utah. At least she didn't slam the door in my face.

A full three minutes later a tall, athletic-looking man in his early forties opens the door and the screen and says, "Come in." He does not offer to shake hands, and not

wanting to wear out my welcome in the first five seconds,
I don't extend mine. Gerald Perry leads me into a living
room, which even to my unobservant eye comes together
in an elegant, understated way. Whoever decorated it had
a flair for color. Royal blues, golds, and muted reds give
the room a regal holiday look. Holly, mistletoe, and a
crèche crowd together on a mantle above a hearth in
which a fire is roaring. A twelve-foot Christmas tree
winking with lights, colored balls, and ribbons and surrounded by presents stands in a far corner. Gerald Perry
points to the least comfortable-looking chair in the room.
As if I were a child whose baseball had crashed into his
picture window, I perch on the edge and wait for him to
give me a lecture about dropping in without calling beforehand. Less formally dressed than his wife, he is
wearing a white shirt, no tie, and pleated slacks. This
may be about as relaxed as they ever get. "What do you
want?" he asks, sitting down by his wife on an enormous
beige sofa.

I look into their faces and realize they must despise
me. If I am to succeed here, I must somehow humanize
the cause I represent. "I have a daughter Robin's age at
Fayetteville. Whether you can imagine it or not, I am
truly sorry for what I'm putting you through."

I tell myself I see the flicker of a response in the father's eyes, but it is Mrs. Perry who answers. "If our feelings made any difference to you," she says, "you
wouldn't have taken the case."

Though her words come out soft as honeysuckle, her
expression is eerie in its sudden ferocity. "My job is to
represent Dade Cunningham, but the last thing I want to

do in this case is embarrass you or your daughter," I say, hoping sincerity counts for something with this couple.

Goaded by his wife's anger, Mr. Perry says, in a wounded tone, "How can you possibly even imply that Robin isn't telling the truth? You have no idea what it is costing her to go through this."

The male is the one I have to approach. He seems more hurt than actively hostile. On the other hand, his wife seems, in her home at least, like a time bomb. I say, "As presumptuous as this may sound, I think I do. Whatever happens, she will bear scars that will never heal, and so will you, and so will Dade Cunningham."

"I hope your client rots in hell after he dies in prison," Mrs. Perry says quietly, her feet flat on the carpet as her blue eyes bore into me.

Her fury is making me nervous. I know I must not anger this woman any more than necessary, or she will explode. "I don't think I could put my own daughter," I say, feeling the weight of my words, "through a trial like this one is going to be, Mrs. Perry."

She answers as I have hoped. "She's done it once!" she says, her jaw firm with determination. "The second time won't be any worse."

"It's going to be much worse," I reply quickly. "I don't have any choice but to try to bring out in court the relationship with her history professor. Right now, it's just a rumor among a few sorority girls in Fayetteville. If this goes any further, it will be discussed in every house in the state."

Mrs. Perry's face flushes crimson. "He seduced her. I grant you that he isn't any higher on the human scale than your client. But let me tell you something about my daughter, Mr. Page. She's not afraid of anything."

"People underestimate Robin," Gerald Perry adds, feeling he needs to support his wife. "They assume that because she's beautiful she doesn't have a backbone. They find out real quick they're wrong."

The only way to endure this chair is to sit up straight, and I'm not capable of it. I lean forward with my hands on my knees. "I know she'll make an excellent witness," I say, focusing on Gerald Perry. "I heard her testify at the university disciplinary hearing. But Joe Hofstra will be fighting for his job. You can bet that he's going to tell an entirely different story than Robin does about their relationship."

For the first time Mrs. Perry seems uneasy. Her eyes begin to flutter. "Robin has told us everything," she counters.

"You can imagine what kind of picture he will paint of your daughter, Mrs. Perry," I say, deciding I have to meet her head on. "He'll say that Robin started showing up in his office, and though he tried to keep it on a professor-student basis, she wouldn't leave him alone. You can bet the farm that he'll say and do whatever is necessary to keep it from appearing that he sexually harassed her. Has he contacted you or your daughter?"

"That's none of your business," she says, her face reddening.

Mr. Perry is listening. He begins to press the bridge of his broad nose as if what I am saying is finally getting through. He may not be smarter than his wife, but he isn't slobbering like an attack dog either. If Robin had inherited his looks, we probably wouldn't be here now. "The press would write about this anyway if Robin doesn't go through with it," he says, but his voice is tentative.

"Reporters won't know the reason unless Robin tells them," I say, my eyes on Mrs. Perry's face. "Hofstra certainly isn't going to respond to questions, and they won't report any gossip for fear of a libel suit." Blanche Perry seems about to burst, and I speak as fast as I can. I want her husband to hear me even if she doesn't. "Assume this goes to trial, and the judge allows evidence of your daughter's affair with her professor. If we were in a more liberal state, perhaps the prosecutor could get away with characterizing both Dade and Hofstra as rapists who differ only in degree, but even in a best-case scenario for you, what people will remember here twenty years later is your daughter was carrying on with her professor, and somehow got raped by a black football player as a consequence. I know how cruel and unfair that is, but you have to think about the future."

Gerald Perry is so quiet that I know he has to be thinking about what I have said, but as soon as I have finished, Blanche Perry explodes. "Get out of my house!" she shouts. "What gall you have coming here and telling us what people will think in twenty years. I wouldn't let my daughter give in to somebody like you in a million years. That nigger you represent is scum, and you're even worse. My daughter has held up her head, and she's not about to start hiding now. Now get out!"

Her face is terrible, her features twisted by hatred and rage. I scramble to my feet and head for the door, afraid she might actually try to attack me. I manage to keep my mouth shut, conscious that Gerald is not echoing his wife's sentiments. I resent the hell out of his wife's behavior, but it won't do any good to say anything now. As I reach the foyer, I see Robin, who has appeared, obviously in response to her mother's outburst. Dressed to go out in dark slacks and a white frilly blouse, she has a frightened look on her face. I have no idea whether or not she has been listening the entire time. If her mother can lose it this badly, perhaps on cross-examination Robin will, too. I go through the two doors as quickly as possible, hoping to avoid any further confrontation, and don't look back until I reach the Blazer. From the door Gerald holds up my briefcase and trots out to the curb with it. Wordlessly, he hands it to me, but for a fleeting second, I detect the slightest sign of an apology as his eyes meet mine in recognition. Though I have incensed his wife, he does not hate me for what I have done.

I take the briefcase and through the window murmur, "Thanks," knowing his wife and daughter are at the door watching this final moment of what has turned into a humiliating debacle. He nods, and I pull away slowly, hoping to retain some of my dignity. I begin to settle down by the time I get on the interstate. I am soaked in sweat. I must have been out of my mind to think that I could talk them out of going to court. I can imagine the stories that will make their way back to Fayetteville. Page was in Texarkana trying to intimidate the family and they kicked his ass out. I wonder if I have done anything unethical. The last thing I need to do is lose my license over this. I get off the interstate in Arkadelphia and order a chocolate milkshake from the drive-through at McDonald's. I'm glad Sarah wasn't along. She would have been appalled by what happened. The girl who hands me my change can't be more than sixteen. She smiles as if she doesn't have a care in the world. I wish I could trade places with her.

I get back home around eight-thirty to find Woogie hiding in Sarah's old room and discover he has pissed on the rug in the living room. Poor guy. He couldn't hold it. This is the third time in the last month. His bladder is in no better shape than his master's. He can't stand being cooped up in the backyard, howling day and night. I have spoiled him beyond belief and now I'm paying for it. I let him outside, and he doesn't make it out of the yard before he is squatting. He trots back in, thoroughly hacked at me. "My fault, boy," I tell him as he watches from the door that leads into the kitchen as I clean up. My eyes water and I start to gag. If I get disbarred, I don't think I'll become a nurse.

Christmas morning I receive a call from Gordon Dyson, who tells me that he will put his wife on a plane for New Zealand in two days. Flabbergasted that a client would call me at my home on Christmas, I rack my brain, and it finally comes to me that Dyson is the ex-cop who wants to evict his son. Irritated, I ask, "Couldn't this have waited until tomorrow?"

Dyson whispers into the phone, "I'm sorry, but this is the only present I'm getting that I've ever wanted, and it didn't seem real unless I called you."

Good God in heaven! What people will do to make themselves happy on Christmas. "It's okay," I say, managing to remember our plan. "I'll prepare a power of attorney for your wife to sign tomorrow morning. You can drop by and pick it up from my secretary and then bring it back after she leaves. We'll file an unlawful detainer action immediately."

"If this works," he says fervently, "I'll install a security system in your house for free in addition to paying your fee."

I look around the living room. Most of the furniture is so ratty I couldn't pay a thief to carry anything off. "That'd be great."

After giving me his wife's name (Dora Lou), Dyson begins to tell me about how his son set a new personal record by sleeping until two in the afternoon on Christmas Eve. Fortunately, we are interrupted by the doorbell, and even though Sarah could get it, I take this opportunity to tell Mr. Dyson good-bye.

"Ho! Ho! Ho!" Amy says merrily as I let her in the door the same time as Woogie scampers past me into the yard. "Merry Christmas!" I take her coat and escort her over to the tree to speak to Sarah who hasn't mentioned Amy's name once since she's been home. She had wanted to miss this visit, but I have insisted that she stick around for a while before she goes off this afternoon to visit her friends.

Dressed comfortably in pleated jeans and a bulky white sweater, Amy has a large package for me and an envelope for Sarah who looks at me as if to say, what is this? She's hardly met her. I watch my daughter's face as she rips open the paper to find a subscription to *Ms.* magazine. She scans the enclosed brochure and smiles. "You shouldn't have gotten me anything," she says, but I can tell by her expression she is pleased. The way to her heart these days is to take her as seriously as a brain tumor.

"I don't read every article, but it helps me keep up," Amy says, as I hand my present to her. It is in a small box that I had gift-wrapped at Dillard's. She winks at Sarah and says, "My adoption papers at last!"

Totally disarmed by Amy's outrageousness, Sarah laughs and says candidly, "I was afraid it was a ring."

"No, no," Amy says, tearing open the paper. "He's too cheap for that. If I wanted a ring, I'd have to go get one myself."

Sarah grins, but looks at me to see how I am taking it. I laugh gamely. Presents, in my opinion, are a waste of money. "If I could find one that would go through your nose . . ." I say to Amy, not bothering to finish.

"They're sweet!" Amy says holding up a pair of silver earrings. She stands on her toes and kisses me on the cheek. "Thank you!"

"You're welcome," I say, giving her a hug. I already gave her my real present two nights ago, a red teddy I got for her at Victoria's Secret. She modeled it for me fifteen minutes later in her bedroom. It wasn't the kind of gift that I felt comfortable presenting in front of Sarah.

"Dad's so original," Sarah says, pointing to her own ears. The earrings I got for her are turquoise.

"Well, they were having this two-for-one sale at Sterling's," I say, winking.

Amy rolls her eyes. "I thought these looked familiar."

It is my turn to open Amy's present. I can tell by the box it must be clothes, but I have no idea what. Amy has been ridiculously secretive, not even giving me a hint. I open the box and find a dark blue pinstriped suit in a box from Bachrach's, a men's clothing store in the mall. I've been by it a dozen times, but the clothes always cost an arm and a leg. "Good Lord, Amy, this is expensive!"

"It's for his trial," Amy says to Sarah. "I'm tired of him looking so tacky. He's been wearing the same suits since law school." To me, she says, "Don't worry—I waited until it got marked down twice."

I try on the coat and find it is my size, a 40 regular. She must have looked through my closet. "You still spent too much," I chide her gently. "It's beautiful."

"You've got time to get the pants altered," she says, getting in a slight dig at my waistline.

I hug her anyway. "Thanks a lot," I say. Damn, I feel cheap. Sarah has given me a new briefcase, which probably cost twice as much as her earrings. Her mother always went overboard on presents, too. As I go back into the kitchen to pour me and Amy a cup of coffee, I promise myself I won't be so tight if this case works out and I get Dade signed to a pro contract. I have already called this morning to wish him and his family a Merry Christmas. But even with the commotion and excitement of four other children opening presents, Lucy sounded depressed. She knows that this time next year she may be loading up the car to go visit their oldest child at the state prison in Grady. Though I tried to minimize it in my call the day after I returned, she could tell I was shaken by the reaction of Blanche Perry to my suggestion that the case be dropped. I've had a fantasy that this case wouldn't go to trial. As January 7 approaches, it is fading fast.

Sarah serves the coffee cake we made earlier today. Amy, who isn't much of a cook herself, pronounces it excellent, prompting Sarah to tell her about the time we went through three boxes of Jiffy cake mix before we gave up and went out for doughnuts. "First we undercooked it; then we burned it; then the last time it looked like we had made a pan of cornbread."

Amy has a way of drawing my daughter out and gets Sarah to talk about WAR. I learn that WAR is planning to hold demonstrations outside the courthouse during Dade's trial. The difficulty is that students won't be back on campus until the next week.

"It sounds like the judge outsmarted you," Amy says to Sarah, her voice sympathetic.

I swallow a mouthful of cake and shake my head. "The trial was set long before WAR was even more than a gleam in Paula Crawford's eye. The trial date comes, not so coincidentally, after all the bowl games are played."

"But Dade was suspended from playing," Amy says, missing the point.

"The judge didn't know the university would take any action. At the time he was just doing what he could to cooperate."

"So he's biased!" Sarah exclaims. She is seated on the couch beside Amy. As usual, I am being ganged up against by the women in my life.

"Not at all," I explain. "He's just a true Hog fan. He probably assumed that the university wouldn't do anything to Dade during the season. That's usually what happens. This was a bigger victory for WAR than you realized."

My daughter puts down her fork, protesting, "That's so cynical! They just would have used Dade and then put him on trial."

"That's one way to look at it," I concede. Another way is that Dade would be using the university to show how good he was.

We are interrupted by a knock at the front door, and I open it, realizing that Woogie has not returned. I should have taken him out and walked him.

"Your dog just ate one of our newborn kittens," Fred Mosely, who lives across the street and four doors down toward the school tells me, "and if I find him, I'm going to kill him."

Shocked into silence by this totally bizarre allegation, I try to look around Fred, who easily weighs three hundred pounds, to see if Woogie is hiding somewhere across the street. Fred, one of the few remaining whites on the street, is not the most stable guy in the neighborhood. Chronically out of work, alcoholic, and abusive toward his wife, he is more than capable of doing what he says. Still, this is so ridiculous I'm tempted to make a joke out of it and tell Fred that after twelve years of dog food, Woogie probably thought it was time for a little variety in his diet, but Fred doesn't seem in the mood. "Are you sure?" I say weakly. "Maybe the mother ate it."

"You're damn right I'm sure!" Fred thunders. "My wife saw him do it! You get rid of that dog, or I'll do it for you!"

Candice, Fred's wife, isn't nearly as loony as her husband, but still I can't believe it. Woogie has his faults, but eating kittens has never been one of them. I catch a strong whiff of Christmas cheer on Fred's breath and decide that he might not appreciate any cross-examination right now. What does he want me to say—that I'll have a talk with Woogie? I can hear that conversation. Woogie, I know cats are a dime a dozen, but you've got to quit eating them. Sarah comes up behind me and asks, "What's wrong, Dad?"

I say hastily to Fred, "I'll do what's necessary. Thanks for letting me know." I shut the door before Sarah can find out what is going on. She would want to argue Woogie's case to the Supreme Court, but this isn't the time to do it.

I tell her and Amy that Woogie may be lost, and we need to go search for him. Before we can get our coats on, however, there is a familiar scratching at the door, and Sarah lets him in. The little murderer prances in as if he didn't have a care in the world. As we watch Woogie lap water at his bowl in the kitchen, I tell Sarah and Amy about my conversation with Fred.

"That's crazy, Dad!" Sarah exclaims. "Woogie wouldn't eat a kitten!"

I am not so sure. We need to keep in mind that Woogie is not Sarah's ugly little brother who couldn't find any sugar cookies lying around and went outside looking for a snack. "He is a dog," I say, bending down to check him for signs of cat hair.

Woogie coughs suspiciously as Sarah strokes his head. Amy, who has followed us into the kitchen, giggles. "Move over, Sherlock. Gideon Page is on the case."

Annoyed, I say, "I'll call Candice tonight. She wouldn't make something like this up."

"Dad!" Sarah shrieks. "You can't just take her word for it."

"Well, for God's sake! What are we supposed to do?" I ask. "Look for hair balls? We can't cut his stomach open."

Woogie yawns as if he had just finished a big meal and ambles over to his favorite corner in the living room and closes his eyes. The phone rings, and I pick it up, fearful that we have a serial cat killer asleep on our rug. It is my sister Marty, calling to wish us a Merry Christmas. I haven't talked to her since I went out to her house almost two months ago. "Marty," I say, without preliminaries, "how's Olaf these days? I didn't see him around when I was out there last time." Olaf was a big-chested boxer whose only trick was to pretend to devour your hand.

"Olaf?" my sister says, accustomed to my rudeness. "Since he's been dead for three months, I'd have to say he's been pretty quiet."

Have I got a dog for you, sister. "I'm sorry to hear that," I say politely. "Listen, we may need to find Woogie a new home. . . ."

The next morning, after drawing up a power of attorney for Gordon Dyson's wife, I drive north on Highway 5 to Heber Springs, passing through towns with such wonderful names as Romance and Rose Bud, on my way to interview Jenny Taylor, Sarah's other source of information about Robin's affair with her professor. I feel depressed and edgy, knowing today is Rainey's wedding day. How can she be marrying someone else?

Tonight will be sad, too. Sarah and I are taking Woogie

to live with Marty. His dark deed has been confirmed by Fred's wife, and Woogie will be the newest canine resident of Hutto, the dog capital of the western hemisphere, according to my sister. Last night after the arrangements were made I could hear Sarah talking to Woogie in her room, next to mine. Woogie has been her only brother for twelve years, but it is for the best, I told her. With his bladder going the way of all flesh, Woogie needs open spaces. Fred, when he is boozed up, is fully capable of killing him, too.

Without Amy, the day would have been a complete disaster. Usually, part of each Christmas Day has been spent with Rainey for the past three years. Amy filled in nicely. Nothing stays the same forever, I told my daughter, before we went to bed, whether we want change or not. With that truism out of the way, I went to sleep and dreamed about the day Rosa, Sarah, and I got Woogie as a puppy from the animal shelter. It served me right for trying to be so stoical.

In little more than an hour I am standing on the wraparound porch of Jenny Taylor's home, a three-story red-brick structure only two blocks from the Cleburne County Court House. I rap hard on the door, hoping Jenny is home by herself, but it is her mother who opens it. Mrs. Taylor, who looks remarkably like my own mother with her prematurely gray hair and straight Roman nose, invites me in and calls her daughter from upstairs. "She should never have gone to the university," Mrs. Taylor says, leading me into her living room. "I shouldn't let her go back next semester. That school is

nothing but trouble." She points to a chair and sits on a
sofa across from me.

I sit down and look around the living room and notice
a water stain on the ceiling. Though the house is large, it
is not in good condition and could stand a paint job. The
Christmas tree, in the process of being taken down, is a
small and scraggly spruce. There may be another reason
why Jenny should transfer. By the time you pay for all
the extras at the University of Arkansas, the family budget has been depleted. "Ma'am, I've got a daughter up
there, too," I say, trying to ingratiate myself. "I know exactly what you mean. All I'm trying to do is find out what
your daughter knows about Robin's relationship with her
professor. If my client is guilty of rape, he'll be punished.
But if he isn't, that should come out."

"Of course, he's guilty!" Mrs. Taylor shouts. "What
girl is going to lie about being raped? It's not worth the
hassle. What upsets me is that if the damn state didn't
care so much about sports, there wouldn't be any blacks
up there in the first place. They're not up there to get an
education, and don't you try to tell me any different. My
husband and I moved from Forrest City to get away from
them, but there's only so much you can do."

Eastern Arkansas. I can't seem to get away from it either. If this is the kind of racism that Dade is going to
face from his jury, God help him. I wonder if Jenny is sitting on the stairs listening. "Ma'am, the more I know
now about what happened, the better I can advise my
client. If I find out he doesn't have a chance, I might advise him to plead guilty in the hope he'll get a lighter sentence."

Mrs. Taylor gives her head a vigorous shake. "They damn well better have a trial. I know how you lawyers do. You want to sweep this under the rug like everything else that happens up there. A jury ought to string that boy up by his you-know-what."

At this moment Jenny Taylor comes down the stairs and pleads, "Mom, please." Jenny Taylor looks so much like her parent that I have the feeling I am looking at my own mother as a college girl. She must have been pretty. Jenny is a brunette with big gray eyes and a full mouth. I introduce myself, and she smiles. Sarah must have been kind. She sits down by her mother on the sofa and says tentatively, "I don't know much about this at all."

"I'm sure you don't," I say, wishing her mother would go clean the bathroom or something. "I just need to hear what you know about Robin's relationship with Dr. Hofstra. I understand you're in the same sorority house with her."

"Not much," Jenny says, nervously running her hands up and down her jeans. "Robin told me during the summer that she was having an affair with him, but she broke it off before she came back this fall. I asked her about it after she had been raped, and she said he didn't even call. That's all I know."

Damn. This is what I was afraid would happen. "What if I told you," I say, before Mrs. Taylor can get in her two cents, "one of the cheerleaders said that Robin was still having an affair with him as recently as a week before the incident with Dade."

"Who was it?" Jenny asks, her gray eyes narrowing.

"Lauren Denney," I answer, thinking it must not be easy to be a girl.

Her young face becomes hard. "Lauren's the biggest liar at the university. She hates Robin and every girl up there who is as pretty as she is. Robin wouldn't tell her that anyway. She couldn't stand Lauren after this summer. I'd be surprised if she said two words to her this fall. Lauren was lying if she said that."

I try not to sigh. Her mother gives me a look that makes me feel as if I were out scouting for guests to be on Geraldo Rivera. Sorority girls who lie. We talk a few more minutes, but I get nothing I can use. I tell her that I won't be needing her as a witness and leave.

To keep the trip from being a total waste of time I drive across Greers Ferry Dam and get out of the Blazer at the overlook to stare at the massive structure and think about the hearing next week. If Binkie Cross knows about Jenny Taylor, I'll have no chance. As it stands now, I have no idea what the judge will do. If he doesn't let Lauren testify, Dade is going to have an uphill battle. If it comes down to a question of nothing more than whom the jury believes—Dade or Robin—I can't imagine an acquittal. If I couldn't believe that my grandfather had sex with a black girl from my hometown, how can I expect twelve men and women to believe Dade Cunningham when he tells them that he didn't rape a white girl? Why didn't I believe Lucy that day when she told me?

A few yards from the overlook I come upon a bronze plaque bearing a likeness of John F. Kennedy, who I learn dedicated the dam on October 3, 1963. It is sobering to realize that this man, who was such a hero of mine, had stood in this same spot, and was murdered only a little over a month later. By joining the Peace Corps and working in the rural areas of the northern coast of Colombia, where most people had a mixed racial background, I thought I had overcome my racial prejudices, but maybe I didn't. Why did I join? For years I have told myself it was some form of youthful idealism, a manifestation of the hubris that came with being American during our golden age of seemingly unlimited power before Vietnam so rudely interrupted our global fantasies. I remember seeing an American propaganda film ostensibly about Kennedy's South American foreign policy, the Alliance for Progress, that was shown before the regular feature in the outdoor theater in the town where I worked on the Magdalena River. Actually, the film had been a testament to Jack Kennedy. God, how the Colombians had loved him. Only the Pope inspired more adoration. "Ask not what your country can do for you," his words had implored my generation of college students, "but what you can do for your country." I remember tears coming to my eyes as he thundered, over Spanish subtitles, *"Ich bin ein Berliner!"*

Bear Creek was, in relative terms, as poor as Plato, Magdalena. If I was so hell-bent on saving the world, why didn't I start at home in the thirteenth-poorest county in the United States? Perhaps the truth was that by joining the Peace Corps I was staging a mini-rebellion against the status quo. But if I had wanted to stand on my two feet and tell my mother and Bear Creek, Arkansas, to go to hell, why didn't I have the guts to do so directly instead of trying to organize in my hideously accented

Spanish unbelievably poor communities to build out-houses, schools, and health centers?

I stop to have lunch in a diner on the outskirts of Heber Springs and stare at the middle-aged waitress, a delightfully saucy confection of a woman with dyed blond hair and big breasts under a T-shirt that advertises her employer's business: Leo's Eats. Lewdly, I think of the message as a profoundly self-satisfied sexual communication. The feeling that I have been telling lies to myself for a long time is as inescapable as my own libido. I didn't have the guts to stay in Bear Creek and say what I thought. I smile at the woman who, paid to please, or at least to bring the food out, grins as if she knows exactly what I'm thinking.

What did I think back then? Nothing remarkable for a twenty-one year old. That God was probably dead or at least sleeping and that east Arkansas was a pretty crappy place for treating blacks so badly. Yet, if I didn't have the emotional wherewithal to come back to Bear Creek with my mixed-blood wife from Colombia and preach this unoriginal coming-of-age sermon to my mother and her friends, what else have I been kidding myself about? Obviously, my psyche and I have some unfinished business. As I contemplate myself as a newly married ex-Peace Corps volunteer, I've always realized that Sarah is much more direct and assertive than I am, even though I'm almost fifty. She was the one who insisted that we return to Bear Creek to confront my past. She is like her mother not only physically but emotionally. Rosa was the realist in our family of three: she confronted her own breast cancer and mortality and insisted that I face it. My good intentions, I've always thought until now, were enough. I sip at the glass of weak tea in front of me and watch my waitress banter with the regulars. Enough for what? To call what I do living, I suppose. The women in my life have been grittier than I have and consequently have often dominated me. Should that come as a shock? Oddly, it does. Thinking I should be in control, I have tried to bully them with guilt, the coward's ultimate weapon. Rosa, when I brought her to Arkansas, accepted my decision not to move back to Bear Creek as my unquestioned right to decide where we should live. Later, when I offered the explanation that I had not returned home out of consideration for how she would have been treated, she wouldn't buy it. "You didn't want to go! I did. She was *tu madre*, no?" Leaving her own mother, Rosa expected to find another one. Not able to screw up my courage, I pretended I couldn't have found a job and moved us to the center of the state.

I pay the check and point the Blazer south toward Blackwell County, thinking I'd go out to eat more often if all the help flirted with me like the waitress at Leo's just did. As I settle in behind a Dodge Caravan on the winding road, almost obsessively my thoughts return to my mother and Bear Creek. Guilt and sarcasm. She was a master of both. She was stronger, too. "Are you trying to kill me, son?" she asked when I had said I wanted to come home to live with my new bride. "First, you leave me and go to South America, then you marry a nigra, and now you want to bring her home to live next to me. Was I that terrible as a mother? With your father sick all the time, maybe I was." Weak. That's what I was. Buying into all that. I should have told her that, by God, this is my wife and you'll accept her and love her. Instead, for a quarter of a century from a safe distance of a hundred miles, I told myself that mother did learn to love her, but we just didn't have the opportunity to visit much. Bullshit!

I stop in Rose Bud to get gas and see on the wall in the service station a six-month-old notice of a parade and a barbecue sponsored by the Rose Bud volunteer fire department and ladies' auxiliary. A parade of a single fire truck? Bear Creek was too small. We were better off not going home. After all these years, it is the reason I can't abide. As I drive on, I wonder why has it taken so long to come to terms with my past? No wonder I am so afraid of a jury in this case.

"You can come see Woogie anytime you want to," Marty tells Sarah as we say good-bye. We have been invited for dinner, and though the reason for our coming is a sad one, we have had a good visit. With some trepidation I told Marty about our visit to eastern Arkansas over Thanksgiving, but instead of lecturing me again, Marty listened for a change and said little in response. She is not interested in the past, her demeanor says. If I am nutty enough to put myself through that meat grinder, it's my problem.

Woogie, knowing something is up, won't leave Sarah long enough for us to slip out the door. Sarah wipes away her tears and gently nuzzles his battle-scarred ears. "Be good, Woogie!" she whispers and kisses him on his graying muzzle.

Marty's husband, Sweetness, holds out a dog biscuit in the shape of a bone. "Come here, boy," he coaxes. "You'll like it here."

I like Sweetness better all the time. He can't help hating Bill Clinton any more than I could help liking the looks of that waitress in Heber Springs this afternoon. If he loves my sister and likes dogs, he can't be all bad. A sucker for food, Woogie trots over to Sweetness, who grabs his collar and gives him the biscuit to distract him.

I wave at my sister and brother-in-law, and nudge Sarah, and we go out into the cold night air. "We'll never see him again!" Sarah wails as we get into the Blazer. "We never come out here."

"We will, more and more," I say, grinding the Blazer's starter in the darkness. "As Nazis go, Sweetness isn't so terrible."

"He was a good dog!" she pronounces, as if we had carried Woogie to his grave.

"A wonderful dog," I concur, no longer feeling the need to play the strong, silent type. I will miss him more than Sarah will. I'm the one who will be alone.

14

WEDNESDAY AFTERNOON, BEFORE I leave for Fayetteville
for the hearing on my motion to introduce evidence of
Robin's past sexual conduct, I have an inspiration and
call Amy to ask her to sit at the counsel table with me for
the trial on the seventh, still five days away. We have
been inseparable since her successful Christmas Day
visit. With Sarah invited by a friend from school to a
party New Year's Eve in Memphis, I spent the entire
night at Amy's, where we conducted our own private celebration to welcome in the new year.

When she finally picks up the phone in her office, I
ask, "Would you be interested in coming up to Fayetteville for the trial next week? You could examine a couple
of the witnesses. I'll have plenty of time before then to
prepare you."

Amy is too smart not to guess my motive. "You want a
female lawyer to try to add credibility to Dade's defense,
don't you?"

"What would be so wrong with that?" I ask, trying to
conceal my irritation with her tone. She knows what
lawyers do.

"I don't think you'll want me," Amy says abruptly. "I feel sorry for the girl. She's been through hell."

Standing in my kitchen, I watch the faucet drip in the sink. This room could stand some major work if I'm going to remain in the house. Lately, I've been thinking it's time I ought to move. "Bullshit!" I say emphatically. "The National Weather Service, or whoever names storms, ought to name a tornado after her. If you get in Robin Perry's way, you're history. . . ."

Amy interrupts, "First, she gets seduced by a professor, then probably raped by a student, and now she's going to be publicly humiliated at a trial. She's just a kid. What if this had happened to Sarah? Then you'd see Robin Perry a lot differently."

Why did I call Amy? Bad idea. "You should have stayed a prosecutor, Gilchrist," I say, unwilling to start a fight, but wanting to have the last word. Yet, I know I'm not being fair. We both know she loved the prosecutor's office.

"Men say they understand, but you don't," Amy lectures me. "The emotional pain and frustration women go through in a rape case is absolutely sickening. Men can't even imagine it."

Amy's beginning to sound like Paula Crawford. I look at my watch. It's four o'clock. I'll be driving in darkness over the mountain. "I need to get on the road," I tell her, and hang up a moment later, after trying to smooth things over between us. I should have known better than to call her. I need her right now a lot more than she needs me.

* * *

Thursday morning, as Dade and I enter the Washington County courthouse for the hearing, I wince at the irony of the mural's written script, OUR HOPE LIES IN HEROIC MEN. My hope is in a man who is hardly heroic. Joe Hofstra, according to Barton, who has had his feelers out for gossip, is suicidal because of having to appear at this hearing. The hearing is closed to the public, and with no students in town and the actual trial not to begin until Monday, we have attracted no media attention. Unless I miss my guess, however, word will get around that something big is going on in Judge Franklin's court, and we'll have a handful of reporters interested in talking to us when we come out.

In his chambers Judge Franklin studies my Motion to Introduce Evidence of Past Sexual Conduct as if he is seeing it for the first time. He has asked us to leave our witnesses in the courtroom. I pick a piece of lint from my new suit. It fits great, unlike my old standby gray pinstripe, which was so tight that if I didn't wear my coat, the inside of my front pockets were exposed.

Seated across the table from me, Binkie Cross gives me a pained look, as if what I am doing is somehow unethical. We have barely talked since he suggested that Dade take a lie detector test. Glowering at me over dime-store reading glasses identical to my own, he seems his usual rumpled, world-weary self. Doubtless, before this morning is over, we will be at each other's throats. He seems to be taking this rather routine defense tactic a little too personally; yet, by the time this hearing is over, the case may be changed from a relatively straightforward swearing match to a situation that has implications beyond the Razorback athletic program. If Judge Franklin grants my motion, this case will turn much uglier than it is already. The University of Arkansas looms over everything up here.

I glance at Judge Franklin's stenographer. A handsome woman, in her early sixties, I would guess, she, too, seems to be irritated at me. Hasn't your client caused trouble enough? How dare you accuse a professor? I warn myself against the typical paranoia of the outsider and busy myself with the display on Judge Franklin's walls. A hunter, he has pictures of himself surrounded by dead animals and dogs. Yet, even in this masculine corner of the world, he may be offending somebody. He asks me to summarize my position, and as precisely as I can, I take him through my argument. I conclude by saying, "The bottom line, Your Honor, is that Robin Perry's past sexual conduct is part and parcel of this case. There was no rape, or if there was, it was purely in the mind of Robin Perry, who couldn't stand the thought that she was about to lose the attention of Dr. Hofstra, and my evidence is going to show that this morning."

Judge Franklin grunts and asks abruptly, "Does the prosecution want to respond?"

"Indeed, I do, Your Honor," Binkie says, his voice already harsh and combative. "This case is no different from any other situation in which the defense tries to put a rape victim on trial. Following Mr. Page's reasoning, evidence of prior sexual conduct by any rape victim can be introduced to show some supposed motive to lie. To allow this type of evidence would be to circumvent the rape shield law in its entirety. The probative value of any evidence of a prior sexual relationship in this case is outweighed by its prejudicial and inflammatory nature, which this court has the discretion, fixed by statute, to prohibit. Mr. Page wants to put the University of Arkansas on trial, Your Honor, instead of his client."

This is weak. Binkie is down to his last bullet. The judge looks at me, and says, his voice slightly ironic, "Is that what you're trying to do, Mr. Page?"

Binkie is already anticipating my closing statement to the jury Monday, but I'm damned if I'm going to admit it. "The last thing I want to do in this case is take on the university, Judge. What this case has been about since day one is credibility. If Robin Perry had any motive to lie about what she says occurred to her as a result of my client's actions, the jury is entitled to hear it."

Binkie tosses his pen on the table, a gesture ordinarily reserved for a jury and not a hearing back in chambers. "He wants to turn the case into a circus, Judge," he complains.

Poor Binkie. This case is unraveling right in front of him. Judge Franklin leans back in his padded chair and puts his hand over his eyes as if to shield the prosecutor from his sight. Finally, he says, "Well, let's go out to the courtroom and hear some testimony."

I feel in control of things for the first time. If this hearing goes as I intend, we could conceivably get a dismissal by Binkie this afternoon. This case will be a black eye for too many people. I come out to the counsel table and smile at Dade, who has been waiting in the courtroom with the other witnesses, who include Lauren, Robin, Joe Hofstra, and Robin's roommate, Shannon Kennsit. Following my advice, Dade is wearing the same too-tight suit he wore at the administrative hearing. If I have my way, he'll wear the same clothes throughout the trial, if there is one. The last thing I want him looking like is some slick black pro athlete. As he sits down by me, I tell him that things are going fine. All he will have to do today is watch. I "invoke the rule" so that the witnesses will not be present in the courtroom. As Judge Franklin instructs each witness not to discuss his or her testimony with any other, I glance back and forth between the faces of Robin and Joe Hofstra. They are about as far from each other in the courtroom as two people can get. As Lauren leaves the courtroom for the witness room, I nod at her, trying to get her to smile. She looks more scared than I would like. Yet, testifying can be an unnerving experience if you haven't done it before. I forget how young these kids are.

Before Robin can make her exit, I tell the judge I will call her as my first witness. I want to hear what Robin and Joe Hofstra say first, so I can try to keep Lauren from getting sandbagged. Robin looks at the judge, who tells her to remain in the courtroom and directs her to the witness box. For this hearing she is wearing black heels, a red and green jumper, and a white blouse. She looks stunning. Her blond hair is soft and silky and has grown out since I last saw her. Since the only issue is her past sexual conduct, the judge cautions me to ask only the most basic preliminary questions, and in less than a minute I get to the point. "Ms. Perry, have you at any time had a sexual relationship with Dr. Joe Hofstra?"

Though I expected to have to pull the story from her,

Robin answers without any hesitation, "Yes, I did. It occurred last summer. I was in his history class the first
term of summer school and began seeing him in June. I
stopped seeing him at the end of the summer session in
August. I haven't been alone with him or talked to him
since then."

Binkie has her well prepared, and though I didn't expect her to admit that she was sleeping with Hofstra at
the time she was raped, I am impressed at how poised she
is concerning a subject that has to be a source of embarrassment to her. I can't imagine it will last too long.
There is too much pressure on her. "Did you tell anyone
you were having sexual relations with Dr. Hofstra?"

"I told Lauren Denney, who was my roommate last
summer."

"Did you tell Lauren Denney this fall approximately a
week before you say you were raped by my client that
you were still sleeping with Dr. Hofstra?"

Robin's face flushes. "No! I never told Lauren any
such thing!"

I press her. "You don't recall having a conversation
with her to that effect one day after cheerleading practice
as you were walking across campus?"

"I didn't tell her that!" Robin says, losing her composure. "I hated Lauren by that time!"

She begins to cry. I ask, "You don't recall telling Lauren that afternoon you'd do anything to keep the relation
going with Dr. Hofstra, or words to that effect?"

"No! No! No!" Robin yells, wiping at her eyes. "I
didn't ever, ever tell her any such thing."

"Isn't it a fact that you hated Lauren, in part at least,

because you were afraid she would tell others that you had been sleeping with your professor?"

"She's a liar!" Robin blurts. "I knew I couldn't trust her not to tell, even though she said she wouldn't."

"But you told somebody, didn't you?" I ask, knowing I have an easy guess. "Didn't you tell your roommate this fall, Shannon Kennsit?"

Binkie gets to his feet and objects, "Your Honor, who she told is irrelevant."

Judge Franklin shakes his head, not even requiring me to respond. "I don't think so. Answer the question."

Robin, still wiping her eyes, answers, "I can trust Shannon. I did tell her."

"Isn't it a fact that you trusted Lauren enough to share an apartment for three months last summer?"

"I didn't know her very well," Robin says, sniffing.

"You had been a cheerleader with her the entire past year, hadn't you?" I scoff, and wait for her answer.

Robin mumbles, "But I still didn't know her."

This is a good stopping place, but I need to get her to admit how intimate she and Hofstra became. "How often did you see Dr. Hofstra last summer?"

Binkie pops out of his chair. "Objection, Your Honor! The issue is whether Ms. Perry was raped by Dade Cunningham in October, not what was happening in the summer."

On my feet, I respond, "The issue is her credibility, Your Honor. If this was a casual, one-time thing, it might be a lot easier to believe her testimony that she broke it off."

"Answer the question," Judge Franklin says, looking at Robin.

Binkie is furious, but he can't do a thing except sit down. Robin blushes deeply. "I would go up to his office after class two or three times a week to talk to him."

"How many times did you have intercourse?" I press.

Binkie again objects. "Your Honor, that question is irrelevant," he says. "It doesn't prove one thing in this case."

"I would hope it tends to show, Your Honor," I say, "how deeply involved they were." I look at Franklin, willing him to agree. The more specifics I can get out of her, the more likely Hofstra is to contradict her.

"You have to answer," Franklin instructs her.

Robin closes her eyes as if she has begun to pray. If Sarah could have known what Robin would go through, I doubt she would have given me any information. "I think," she says through her tears, "six separate occasions."

I draw out the moment, pretending I am making notes. "Where did these six separate acts of intercourse take place?"

"I met him every time at the Ozark Motel."

The Ozark! I almost laugh out loud. I haven't even watched a dirty movie there. "Who paid for the room?"

Binkie objects, and Judge Franklin tells me to move on. "That's not what is at issue here," he says, giving me a hard look.

I could make an argument, but not wanting to piss him off, I don't. "Why did you end the relationship in August?"

Robin's eyes are as red as the material of her dress. "I felt guilty," she says, her voice now thin and reedy like an old woman's. "I met his wife and children at his office. Before I went home that weekend, I told him we had to stop. He knew it, too, and agreed we shouldn't see each other again."

Until she came back for the fall semester, I think, certain my cynicism is justified. "So either you or Lauren is lying about whether you said you were still involved with your professor in October, is that correct?"

"I'm telling the truth!" Robin insists.

"Tell me, Ms. Perry," I say, unconcerned what her answer will be, "did you care about the truth of the statements that were being told to Professor Hofstra's wife on the six occasions you slept with him?"

Binkie is on his feet objecting. "Your Honor, there is no evidence of any statements. Counsel is assuming facts not in evidence. I doubt if he was going home and telling his wife, 'Honey, I had some really great sex with a student today.' "

"Sustained," Judge Franklin rules, smirking at me.

Though I violate the law school rule that a lawyer is supposed to end cross-examination with some kind of admission, if possible, I pass the witness to Binkie. I have made my point. If you're having an illicit affair, it is a little hard to stand up and brag about what an honest person you are, whether you've told any outright lies or not.

Walking even slower than usual, Binkie comes over to the podium and has Robin reinforce her testimony that she broke off the relationship with Hofstra during the summer, but he stays away from the details of the affair except its time frame. "Did you go home or remain at the university the end of the second semester summer school in August?"

Robin, who is no longer crying, says, "My algebra exam was over August eleventh, and I didn't return to school until almost two weeks later for the fall term."

Binkie, slouching against the podium, asks, "Did you have any contact with Dr. Hofstra during this period?"

"None at all," Robin responds.

"Did you have any contact of any kind with Dr. Hofstra after you returned to school for the fall term?"

"No, I didn't!" Robin says even more vehemently.

I let her step down, certain she hasn't killed us. Beside me, Dade is wide-eyed at Robin's testimony. It is clear she didn't give a speech in communications class about what she had done during summer vacation. "I call Joe Hofstra," I say, feeling my stomach tighten with anticipation.

Sporting a beard he didn't have when I went to his office almost two weeks ago, and wearing a black suit and black wingtip shoes, he looks as if he has dressed for his own funeral. I don't waste any time trying to bury him. "How many times did you have intercourse with Robin Perry?"

He looks helplessly at Binkie, and puts his hand to his mouth. For a moment I think he will be sick right on the witness stand. "Six, six, I think," he stammers.

"Who, Dr. Hofstra, in your opinion, initiated the relationship between you and Robin?" I ask, realizing I will enjoy making this guy sweat.

Hofstra hesitates, knowing this is an important question. His career as well as a sexual harassment suit may hang in the balance. "She began dropping by my office a couple of times a week," he says carefully. "She was smart and an excellent student, and I enjoyed talking to her. After my class ended the first semester of summer school, I called her. She agreed to see me, and I began getting a room for us at the Ozark Motel."

"Did you ever go to her apartment that summer?"

Hofstra looks pained but says, "I went there three or four times."

This is news to me, but it shouldn't come as a surprise that Lauren didn't know everything. If Hofstra weren't such a sleaze, I might feel sorry for him. In addition to his miserable expression, his voice exudes the right tone of contrition, the perfect note of guilt. He is letter perfect in his role as erring husband and teacher. I realize his wife will probably forgive him and nothing will happen to him. For all I know, some of his male colleagues may be secretly envious when this case is all over. "While you were there, did you ever see Robin's roommate Lauren Denney?"

"She came in once while I was at the apartment," Hofstra admits. "I think Robin thought she was gone for the weekend. I got up and left."

Grudgingly, I realize that Binkie has done a great job of woodshedding this guy. It couldn't have been easy. "Who ended the affair, in your opinion?"

Hofstra tugs at his collar. "It was a mutual decision."

This is a departure from the party line, but if he wants to save his marriage, he had to say it. "Do you recall what was said by each of you to end your relationship?"

Hofstra winces. "We both acknowledged we felt guilty because of my family. We agreed that we would think about it over the break after summer school. That was the last time we spoke. I haven't seen or talked to her until today."

This last comment seems false. Either she is protecting him, or he is protecting her. Even if he is telling the truth, one of them would have wanted more closure than that. I glance over at Judge Franklin to see how much of this he is buying. His expression, detached but alert, tells me nothing. "You're asking the court to believe," I say, pretending incredulity, "that neither of you said a word to the other after you agreed to go home and think about it for almost two weeks?"

He shifts uncomfortably in the witness chair. "There was nothing left to say."

I make a show of wrinkling my nose at this answer but decide to let it go. Franklin surely has gotten the point by now that I think his answer stinks. "Dr. Hofstra, did Robin tell you at any time during the summer that she was in love with you or that she loved you or words to that effect?"

Hofstra swallows hard. "Yes."

"And you, sir, did you tell Robin that you loved her or words to that effect?"

Hofstra studies his hands but says in an audible voice, "Yes."

I stand by the lectern, feigning more amazement. I know what I'd be saying on closing argument to a jury: Ladies and gentlemen, can you really believe that after a gloriously exciting summer of twice a week office visits, sneaking off to a motel on six separate occasions and a mutual declaration of love, these two just ended it and never even said another word to each other? "Your witness," I tell Binkie.

Binkie, to my surprise, declines to question Hofstra, who sighs audibly as he leaves the witness box. I say more dramatically than I intend, "I call Lauren Denney."

Lauren, who practically swaggered out of the restaurant when I met her less than two weeks ago, seems considerably less sure of herself today and walks almost on tiptoe to the witness box. Rehearsing her story earlier this morning at Barton's office, I had sensed she was nervous, but now she won't even look me in the eye. Judge Franklin tells her twice to speak up, and I have a terrible premonition she is going to change her story. Wearing a red skirt that comes down to her ankles, and her hair in a French braid down her back, Lauren looks about twelve. Where is the sexy vixen who seemed so eager to testify? As a Razorback cheerleader she has pranced around in front of a national TV audience; today she looks like Little Orphan Annie. I have no choice but to act as though I don't have a care in the world as I take her back through the summer. "Did you ever have an occasion to meet Dr. Joe Hofstra?" I ask after I have gotten through some preliminary questions.

Her voice tight, she says, "I met him last summer once in our apartment, but he left almost immediately."

Lauren timidly recites her story more or less as we have rehearsed it twice now, and finally, about to burst, I ask her, "Did you have a conversation with Robin after the football season began about Dr. Hofstra?"

Lauren stares right past me. "No."

No? Damn it to hell! I want to walk up to this girl and grab her by the throat. Judge Franklin is practically falling out of his chair to hear her. "Didn't you tell me again just two hours ago that Robin Perry had admitted in October that she was still having intercourse with Joe Hofstra?"

"Yes, but that's not right. She never told me that," Lauren says, her voice trembling.

I feel like the biggest idiot on the face of the earth. "It's not right?" I repeat stupidly. "Wasn't that the second time in less than two weeks you told me about Robin Perry and Joe Hofstra?"

"I don't know," she says in a little girl's voice, looking directly at Binkie. "All I know is Robin didn't tell me she was still having an affair with him after summer school ended."

Somebody has been applying the screws to Lauren. "Have you been talking to somebody to make you change your story?" I ask, barely able to keep my voice under control. I have begun to sweat profusely. I take a wadded up tissue from my pants pocket and wipe my face. I've never had a case blow up this badly. I look back at Dade, who has a confused look on his face. Join the club, I think, as I wait for this girl's answer.

"No," Lauren replies, breathing hard now. "I just realized how wrong it would have been to say that. I took an oath to tell the truth, and that's what I'm doing."

If this girl has had some kind of attack of scruples, then I'm Billy Graham. I grip the lectern to keep my hands from shaking. "So your testimony is that absolutely no one has approached you about your appearance here today?"

"I talked to Mr. Cross on the telephone after Christmas," Lauren says. "He just told me to tell the truth, and that's what I'm doing." Lauren has begun to recover her composure.

"What else did he tell you?" I ask.

"Nothing," she says. "He just wanted to know what I was going to say today. I told him I couldn't talk to him right then, but that I'd call him back, but I never did."

"Has anyone in this case offered you something," I ask, searching her face fruitlessly for clues, "or threatened you in regard to your testimony?"

"No."

"Do you realize you could go to jail for perjury," I say, my voice harsh, "if you're not telling me the truth?"

Binkie is on his feet, objecting. "Your Honor, Ms. Denney is Mr. Page's witness, not mine. He can't try to impeach her testimony."

Disgusted, I say, "No more questions," and sit down. Something stinks, and I don't need to go to Denmark to find it out. What makes this a no-win situation is that Lauren, I realize, may now be telling the truth. What the hell happened? Unless she admits she was bribed or coerced, there is nothing I can do.

I barely listen as Binkie makes clear through his questioning of Lauren that in no way did he act improperly. I have no proof that he did, but damn, do I feel snookered! As soon as Binkie finishes with Lauren, I ask the court if we can take a recess and confer about this case in chambers. Without batting an eye, he says formally to the empty courtroom that we'll be in recess for five minutes.

"Something is going on," I tell the judge once we're all seated in his office, "that I don't know about. Somebody is leaning on Lauren Denney, Your Honor. That much is clear as day. We shouldn't have the trial until I've had an opportunity to get to the bottom of this." The judge has picked up a three-inch model of a Labrador retriever from his desk and is examining it. I can't tell whether he is paying any attention to me or not.

Binkie, seated on my right, crosses his long legs. "Judge, all this says to me is that some people take the oath more seriously than others. This girl just happens to be one of them."

Judge Franklin looks at me unsympathetically. "I take it that you're out of witnesses."

I admit that I am. Franklin stands up and says coldly, "You certainly can request a continuance, but I suggest you make it on the record, because I'll tell you right now that I'm going to deny it and deny your motion today. I think this Denney girl is telling the truth, and I just hope you didn't have anything to do with the fact that she apparently was about to lie to the court. The only thing we're going to do right now is go back into the courtroom and say this for my court reporter."

In five minutes the hearing is over. Things have happened so fast that I feel as if I'd been hit on the head by a sledgehammer. As Dade and I begin to walk out of the courtroom, Binkie calls me over and asks if I can come by his office in fifteen minutes. Thinking he will give me a clue as to what has happened here today, I say that I'll be over after I've visited with my client. He nods, and Dade and I go outside, only to be accosted by a couple of reporters who have gotten wind that something was going on in the case. "It was a closed hearing," I say, telling them what they already know. "We have no comment."

A young bearded guy taps a pocket-sized notebook against the palm of his hand. "We just looked at the pleadings filed with the court and know this hearing concerned the rape shield law. Is it safe to assume," he asks without sarcasm, "that you must have lost?"

I must look as if I'm about to cry. What happened in there? I put my game face back on and say, "It's best not to make any assumptions in this case."

In the parking lot next to his ten-year-old Pontiac, I tell Dade not to worry. Panic won't do either of us any good. He nods, without changing his expression. There is no point in his staying up here for the next three days. "You might as well drive back home," I add, sounding like a doctor who advises his patient to start getting his affairs in order. "There is nothing you can do here."

"I'm going to go to jail, aren't I?" he says, wrenching open the rusty door that has been through at least two paint jobs and is now a strange salmon color.

I turn up my overcoat collar. According to the radio, there is a thirty percent chance of snow. It is not supposed to get above twenty-five degrees up here today. "Not necessarily," I say uncertainly. "It depends on how good a witness you make."

"They'll believe her," Dade says, bitterness creeping into his voice. "When it comes right down to it, people stick together. I saw how that works today."

I look out into the street. There isn't a single car going by. Despite its prosperity, without the students, this place, like all college towns, is dead. "I'm not so sure she didn't tell the truth, Dade," I say, and recount my trip to Heber Springs to talk to Jenny Taylor.

He gets in the car. "White folks stick together," he mutters again.

I don't have the energy to argue with him right now, but I have the feeling that Lauren's about-face wasn't related to Dade's skin color. "I want you to let me ask the prosecutor if you can still take the polygraph." It is probably too late now.

"Huh," he says stubbornly, "after what I saw today, I don't trust anybody."

Including his lawyer, obviously. I bite my lower lip to keep from blowing up at him. I grab the door handle, and before pushing it shut against him, I tell him I'll see him and his parents at the Ozark Motel Sunday afternoon. It's in the Cunninghams' price range, too.

I watch him drive off and then walk in the cold on College two blocks to the prosecutor's office, thinking how I've been spinning my wheels in this case. I can imagine how a doctor feels treating a patient with a terminal illness. No matter what I do, I can't escape a sense of doom.

Five minutes later, Binkie follows me into the reception area of the Washington County prosecuting attorney's office. He motions me to accompany him back to his office, and, after taking off my overcoat, I take a seat across from his desk. "Want some coffee?" he asks as if we were now old friends instead of combatants. He points at a tray beside him containing a full glass pot, a sugar bowl, and a jar of nondairy creamer.

I nod, eager to take the chill out of my bones. "I'll take a little whitener in it," I say, watching him fuss with the spoons and cups. His hands, I notice for the first time, are arthritic and swollen. He keeps them in his pockets when he is in court. "Do you know what made Lauren Denney change her mind?" I ask, impatient to get this conversation going. Binkie, however, doesn't seem the type to rub it in.

Binkie hands me a cup decorated with Razorback insignia. The red lettering below a picture of a pig dribbling a basketball reads "National Champions 1993–94." "I have no idea," he say offhandedly. "But that's not why I wanted to talk to you. What I'd like is for Dade to plead guilty to a charge of carnal abuse and take a six-year sentence. You know under the new sentencing statutes if he kept his nose clean he could conceivably be eligible for parole after only one-sixth of that. He could be home in a year."

Astounded by his offer, I sip at the coffee. It tastes amazingly good. Given the circumstances, it is an incredibly generous offer. "Would the Perrys go for that?" I ask, my mind racing. Dade is already on his way back to St. Francis County. I'll have to call his parents.

Binkie lifts his cup to his mouth and swallows. "Regardless of what they've said, they don't want a trial even though now I'll be able to keep out any mention of Robin's relationship with Dr. Hofstra. I got them to agree before the hearing this morning that I'd make this offer to you regardless of how it turned out."

I feel an enormous sense of relief. Dade could easily get twenty years or even more. His football career is probably over, but so what? "I'll talk to his family as soon as I can. Dade's already on the road back to Hughes, but I should be able to get back to you late this afternoon or the first thing in the morning."

For a response, Binkie writes a number on the back of his card. "This is my home phone number," he says, handing it to me. "You can reach me there or here."

Why is the guy doing this? As far as I am concerned, he's in the driver's seat. Yet, maybe he believes that Dade will be giving up enough. I stand up, eager to get out of here and get on the phone. I offer him my hand. "The judge won't have any trouble with six years?"

Binkie stands and despite the condition of his hands crushes my fingers with a grip I couldn't come close to if I worked out for the next decade. "I don't think so. It's not as if he hurt her, too."

"I should be able to sell his parents," I say, reasonably optimistic. Once they hear about this morning's results, they'll have to be realistic about the chances of going to trial.

"I hope so," he says, his face suddenly gloomy. "Maybe we ought to be caning criminals like they do in Singapore. Locking kids up and throwing away the key isn't the answer. Something the hell's wrong with this country. It didn't use to be like this."

The least I can do is agree. "I guess not," I say. "We've been going downhill for years. When you're right in the middle of it, you don't notice it though."

Binkie shrugs and picks up his cup again. He didn't

ask for my philosophy of life. "Get him to take this deal," he says. "Though I haven't tried a rape case involving a black before," he adds, his voice dry, "I doubt if a jury in these parts will be defense oriented in a case like this."

I doubt it, too. "How many blacks am I likely to have?"

Binkie reaches into his desk and pulls out some papers. "This is the jury list. It'll save you a trip to the Clerk's office if you haven't already been," he says handing me papers with some jury data information on them. "You might have a couple."

That's two more than I thought. "Thanks, I appreciate it."

I leave Binkie's office, wondering if he is just fundamentally decent or whether, for some reason I don't know about, he is scared to try this case, too.

15

I REACH ROY Cunningham at his grocery from Barton's office. In a weary voice, Roy explains that he has no help. Lucy has taken their youngest child, Lashondra, to a doctor in Memphis because of an ear infection. Though I know this is an inappropriate time to talk, I insist on telling him what happened at the hearing this morning. Already the court's decision to prevent me from introducing evidence of Robin Perry's affair with her professor seems far in the past, but it is a necessary part of the story if I am to prepare Roy and Lucy to accept a six-year prison sentence for their son. He listens without comment, as if I were explaining a minor technicality instead of what I fear is the turning point in the case.

"But just a few minutes ago," I say over a customer's voice in the background, "the prosecutor offered us a deal. He'll let Dade plead guilty to a charge of carnal abuse and a six-year prison term. On this kind of charge that could mean with maximum credit for good behavior he could be out in just a year. My opinion is that it's something we need to think about. By the way, Dade's on the road headed for home. He doesn't know about the prosecutor's offer yet."

"He's not guilty!" Roy Cunningham yells into the phone. I wish Lucy were there. She is the realist in the family and will understand what we're up against. Before I can respond, Roy orders, "Just a second!"

I hear the cash register ring, and my brain slips into idle while Roy again talks to a customer. I should have waited for Lucy to return from Memphis, but I want Roy especially to have as much time as possible to get used to the idea of a plea bargain before he sees his son. If I have learned anything about Dade, it is that like most kids his age, he has had too many things going his way the last few years to believe the worst can and will happen. "Go on!" Roy says finally.

"It doesn't matter," I say brutally, "whether he's guilty or not. What matters is what the jury will do. After all is said and done, what this case comes down to is whether the jury, which will be mostly white, will believe Robin or Dade. And now we're in the position of having to go into the trial without a plausible explanation of why she would make this story up."

"She could have had a dozen reasons!" Roy sputters.

"And they'll all be speculation," I say. "We don't have any hard evidence."

There is silence on the other end for a moment. "He'll probably never play pro ball," Roy says. "Even if he got a tryout, he'd be at a terrible disadvantage."

"That's true," I say, wishing I could sugarcoat the message but knowing I can't. "But if they want to make an example of him, they can give him life."

I hear the jangle of multiple voices in the background, and Roy says, his voice now heavy with resentment, "I'll talk to Lucy and we'll call you back."

"Call me at home or my office," I instruct him. "I'd like to drive over and talk to you."

"We'll call you later today," Roy says curtly, dismissing me.

I hang up, wondering if I'm botching this. I should have driven over there and talked to Lucy and not even bothered with Roy. The men in the family have too much pride to act in their own best interest.

Fearful of being caught in a snowstorm in the mountains, I don't stick around to visit with Barton, who has a client in with him, and drive east with a heavy foot, replaying over and over the events of this morning. I should have known I wouldn't be able to trust Lauren Denney. I knew that from the moment she walked into Danny's that afternoon. Turning south off Highway 16 onto the Pig Trail, I see a band of snow-swollen clouds that appears almost to touch the roof of the Blazer. All I need is a slick road on these turns. Lauren. Sex oozed from her that day. Maybe I have it wrong. Maybe sex was oozing from me and she never was as confident as she seemed. This morning she was a nervous, apologetic schoolgirl. Still, what choice did I have but to try to use her? What bothers me is that if I truly thought about it, I would have admitted to myself that she was probably lying even before I talked to Jenny Taylor. Down deep, do I know that Dade is lying, too?

The snow holds off, and I breathe a sigh of relief when I see the sign for Interstate 40. The sky is lighter in the east. One year is not a lifetime, though it will seem that way to Dade and to Roy, who can close his eyes and see Dade being named all-pro wide receiver. I can, too, damn it. Part of me wants me to say to them that we should stiff Binkie's offer and go for it. As I slow down behind a Buick Skylark, I hit a patch of ice and almost shimmy off the pavement down a steep embankment, but the Blazer straightens out at the last moment. I slow down to thirty. Fear. It does wonders for your judgment.

At home there is no one to greet me. I have just missed Sarah, who begins work at five during the holidays at her old video store, and, of course, Woogie now makes his home in Hutto. I check the thermostat, which Sarah has turned up to seventy-five, and rotate the switch to sixty-eight. If Sarah had her way, we could have a greenhouse in here. When she starts paying for her own utilities, she won't think I keep the house so cold. I walk into the kitchen before I realize I don't need to check Woogie's bowl to make sure he has water. I miss the old kitten eater. Marty called New Year's Day to say that he was doing great. He goes anywhere he wants. Dogs, she reminds me, practically run the town.

As I am checking the mail (a Christmas card from my old friend Skip, still in Atlanta and gay, fat, and happy, he says. He didn't use to be fat), the phone rings. It is Lucy, who asks if I would mind driving over tomorrow morning to help them decide if Dade should take the prosecutor's offer. Her voice holds no clue as to how she feels. Dade, who is about an hour ahead of me, has called a few minutes ago from a service station on Interstate 40 near Brinkley and should be home in an hour or so. I have nothing on my schedule tomorrow morning, but have to be back for Gordon Dyson's unlawful detainer hearing in the afternoon. Lucy gives me directions to the store, which she tells me is easier to find than their house, and I ask about Lashondra's ears.

"They'll be all right," she says, her voice flat and lifeless. "At least it won't take a year to fix them."

"Why don't we talk about it tomorrow?" I suggest. She sounds wrung out. I don't want her to lock into a position I can't change.

"That's why you're coming," she says without sarcasm.

I can hear a child crying in the background. Bad ears are no fun. We had to put tubes in Sarah's. "Did you tell Dade?"

"No," she says. "We'll wait until you get here."

"That's fine," I respond. I do not push her. I tell her I'll be at the store at eight tomorrow morning and hang up. I am hungry (I missed lunch again), but all I find in the pantry are five cans of Campbell's soup. I pick up the phone to call Amy and see if she wants to go out to eat but realize she is visiting her mother in Pine Bluff for a couple of days. Well, soup it is. This case is good for losing some weight, at least. I call Sarah and tell her I won't be waiting up for her. Tomorrow will be another long day.

Cunningham's Grocery is on the right-hand side of Highway 79 on the road to Memphis outside the small town of Hughes. A small, green wooden structure (perhaps only twelve hundred square feet), it is badly in need of a paint job. With the economy in the Delta so bad and the store this tiny, I wonder how Lucy and Roy survive. I push the door open and set a bell to tinkling and become immediately claustrophobic. The shelves in the store look jam-packed with everything from razor blades to cigarette papers. It reminds me of the Chinese stores in Bear Creek when I was a boy. If you had to, you probably could live out of here for the next fifty years, but at first glance it is visually oppressive because of the cramped space, dinginess, and sheer mass of goods.

On my way to the back of the store, I nearly trip over Lashondra, whom I've never met. It has to be Lashondra because she is cradling her tiny ears with both hands. Standing in the middle of the center aisle, she raises her head and says distinctly, "Hurt."

Since she barely comes past my knees, I squat down on my heels to make conversation easier. Her dark chocolate skin would make her a mirror of her father but for her straight nose and thin lips. Without a doubt, except for her complexion she looks like Dade. Her huge black eyes and grave manner suggest that she will break some hearts before she is done. "I'm sorry," I say sympathetically. I point to my ears. "Do they make you cry? Mine hurt too, sometimes."

Perhaps reminded that she isn't supposed to be worrying them, Lashondra slides her hands down the sides of a white, long-sleeved cotton sweater decorated with pictures of five-flavored Life Savers and into the pockets of her bright red slacks. Her tea-party expression, so brave until now, collapses following my unexpected empathy.

Her eyes filling, miserably, she nods, "Mama said not to pick at 'em."

"It's hard, isn't it?" I commiserate. I wonder if she understands anything about what is happening to her brother. How many other brothers and sisters does she have? Two, I think. I have shielded myself from knowing anything about Lucy and her family as if ignorance would lessen my bond to them. This child is making it hard to do. I hear Roy's voice in the back and say to Lashondra, "I hope you feel better."

Lashondra stands on her toes and plucks a can of black-eyed peas from the shelf to her right and examines it like a smoker trying to find anything to take her mind off her habit. "Mama says I will if I don't pick at them."

If only life were that easy, I think, and stand up, my knees snapping with the effort. I stand and see Roy in the back next to a refrigerated bin containing milk products. I walk to the front on cold concrete and find a Borden's milk salesman on his knees beside Roy, stocking his product. Roy pushes up the sleeves of a blue cotton pullover sweater and tells me to go on around the counter and through the door in the back where I will find Dade and Lucy. "I can't close the store because this is when a lot of the salesmen come in," he explains, counting milk cartons. "I'll come back and stand at the door when I get through here." He glances past me, apparently looking for his daughter.

"Lashondra's a doll," I say, wondering if it is too late to reach this guy. Even if he lived next door to me for ten years, Roy wouldn't be my best friend, but we can do better than this.

"I'll be there in a minute," he says, his eyes on the salesman, who is switching out milk cartons so fast I feel I'm watching one of those guys who cheats you at card games on the streets of New York.

In the back is a combination small office and storeroom. Dade and his mother are seated at a rickety card table, pouring themselves cups of coffee from a brown thermos, and not for the first time I am struck by the resemblance between mother and son: even their facial expressions are the same. Both look up and scowl at me at the same time, making the same crease in their broad foreheads. She has just told him, I realize. As the messenger of bad news, I should have expected their disapproval. Again, I realize I know too little about them. The chasm that separates us can't be overcome by telling them my ears sometimes hurt, too.

"Would you like some coffee?" Lucy asks politely, her words at variance with her expression. "I told Dade," she says, unnecessarily. Like her son and husband she is wearing jeans; a red bandanna covers her hair, reminding me of some angry black militant from the sixties and seventies.

"I'll take a little," I say, needing to take a leak, but too embarrassed to ask. If there is a bathroom, it is hidden from me among the scores of boxes stacked all around us. I study Lucy's face, looking for cues, knowing intuitively that she is the key to Dade's decision.

She takes out a mug from a cloth bag by her chair and pours. "Go ahead, Dade," she says, her voice low and intense. "Tell him how you feel."

Dade, who has barely looked at me, studies his cup. "I

can't go to jail for a whole year!" he says fiercely. "That's twelve months of my life!"

Though they haven't invited me to, I ease into the third folding chair and warm my lips with the coffee. It is chilly back here despite the presence of a glowing space heater four feet away from my feet. I'm afraid if I argue with him, all he'll do is dig his heels in. "Okay, then, what evidence do we put on in court?" I ask.

"She waited until the next morning to go to the hospital," Dade replies.

I glance up to see Roy filling the entrance that divides the back room from the grocery. His expression is so melancholy that for a moment I think he has been crying. I notice the gray in his hair and the beginning of a gut. Dade is his dream, his escape from the store. "She'll say she couldn't make up her mind," I point out, "whether to report it."

"She admits she wasn't hurt," Dade responds, glowering at me.

If he looks this angry in court, we won't have a chance. "She'll testify you threatened her and it would have been dangerous for her to resist."

Hands on his hips, Roy mutters, "Whose side are you on?"

To keep from launching into a sermon, I place my palms flat down on the table, and my fingers almost stick to the surface. This table must serve as the family dining table for Roy and Lucy more often than not. "My job right now is to give you the best advice I can. If I thought Dade could beat this charge, I'd be the first to say so."

"You're selling my boy out!" Roy cries, his face anguished.

I feel certain he would like to fire me, but at this late date the judge wouldn't permit Dade to get another lawyer. The bell on the front door jingles loudly, and Roy stalks off to the front, followed by Dade, who is furious with me. Somehow, I have to make Lucy trust my judgment. I wait until Dade clears the doorway and then I whisper, "The reason I took this case was that I hoped I could get it dismissed and you'd hire me as Dade's agent when he turned professional. I know that wasn't the most noble reason on earth for undertaking to defend him on his rape charge, but you need to understand that it was in my interest to try this case. The truth is, the closer the trial gets, the less likely it is that Dade will escape serving some significant time. I can't in good conscience tell him to go to trial. The only way to avoid that risk is to accept the prosecutor's offer and concentrate on getting this behind him as soon as possible."

Lucy shakes her head in apparent disbelief. "So that was your motivation?" she asks, her eyes suddenly bright with tears. "You were out to exploit him from the beginning?"

"For God's sake, Lucy!" I cry, feeling my face burning. "I'm no different from any other lawyer in this state. If I can make a buck, I'll do it. If there's something wrong with that, you're going to have to put most of this country out of its misery. All I'm trying to say is that Dade should take this offer and then get on with his life. The prisons are filled with people who either entered into a plea bargain or wish they had. If you're looking for a hero, I nominate the man who's prosecuting Dade. After this morning, I wouldn't have given a plugged nickel for our chances to knock this case down to carnal abuse and a six-year sentence, but the prosecutor made this offer because he said Robin's parents have finally been convinced not to put their child through a trial if they can get this deal."

These sentiments have come straight from my gut, and I am out of breath when I finish. Lucy makes a small fist with her right hand but shows no other emotion. "I thought you'd be different."

"Well, I'm not," I say hoarsely. "I can't change history. By the way, I'm sorry about your grandmother. My daughter thinks that under the circumstances she was raped. I guess she was. I can't do anything about that, just as I can't really do anything about the kind of person who will serve on Dade's jury. All I can do is tell you what's likely to happen to Dade if he goes to trial."

She unclenches her hand. "You're putting your racism on that jury," she says fiercely. "That's what's making you afraid."

Is that what I'm doing? "I know what people are like," I say, breaking it down as simply as I can. "And so do you."

Her jaw flexing in anger and her dark eyes flashing, she leans across the table to shake a long black finger in my face. "I don't want my son in prison, you hear me!" Pushing up from the table with both hands, she walks past me and through the door. I am already tired, and it is not even nine o'clock. I close my eyes, wishing I had kept my mouth shut about what has motivated me in this case. In the other room, I hear all three talking at once, Lucy's voice the loudest. I strain to hear but can't distinguish more than a few words. I hear Lucy saying, "If you didn't do it . . ." and then her voice is drowned out by Roy and Dade.

Just moments later, all three are back, surrounding the table. Dade glares at me as if I were a prisoner who had been charged with some heinous crime. "I want to go to trial," he announces. "I'm innocent."

I judge by the expression on Lucy's face that she is fully supportive of this decision. "That's fine with me," I say automatically. "I'll do the best job I can."

"See that you do," Roy adds, in a menacing tone.

I don't like to be bullied by anyone, especially a client who isn't paying me a third of what a case is worth, but Roy, I have the feeling, is out of the loop here. This is between Dade and his mother, I surmise, without any hard evidence to support my intuition. I have the distinct feeling he has chosen to do what he thinks will maintain her image of him. To save his pride, Roy has been given his say, but it is his mother whom Dade wants to please. As I am leaving, ten minutes later, only Lashondra, who is rearranging toilet paper on the shelf next to bar soap, waves good-bye. If she were the client, I'd feel a lot better.

Furious, I gun the Blazer hard westward through the desolate flatness of the Arkansas Delta, already feeling the pressure imposed by Dade's decision. I know who will be the fall guy in this scenario. Yet, damn it, would he really be risking a trial if he weren't innocent? Dade and Lucy will drive to Fayetteville Sunday morning so we can work on his testimony. Roy will stay in Hughes to keep the grocery open. Damn. He can't even take off to see his son's trial.

I call Binkie from my office and give him the bad news. "I think he's making a mistake, Gideon," Binkie says, sounding disappointed.

"I do, too," I confess, as I pull Dade's file from my briefcase. I had hoped when I walked into my office there would be a phone call from Lucy. There is nothing else to say and I hang up with a sick feeling in my stomach.

Gordon Dyson is waiting for me outside Judge Butler's chambers with an embarrassed grin on his face. This shouldn't take long even if "Gucci" shows up. I shake hands with Dyson, who hands me an envelope, presumably my fee. "How is your son taking this?"

Dyson smiles. "He's pissed as hell. He called his mother, but I talked to her and it's okay. I don't think he's even gonna show."

I take off my overcoat in the poorly ventilated building. The Blackwell County courthouse is undergoing extensive repairs, and the building the county is using has all the charm of a bus station in a third world country.

We enter the judge's outside office, and his secretary tells us to go right on back. The judge will take Mr. Dyson's testimony in his chambers.

Sonny Butler is an ex-prosecutor and likes cops. He greets my client like an old friend, and I relax, knowing this will be a piece of cake. Across Sonny's massive desk they chat, each bragging about how well he is doing. Why the hell not? Cop to businessman, prosecutor to judge. They both have prospered as a result of crime.

Butler is not a bad judge for a man who claimed during his recent campaign that any person who didn't believe in the death penalty would change his mind if his wife were raped and killed in front of him. His opponent, my old boss at the public defender's office, Greta Darby, cracked that it was hard to tell whether Sonny was running for judge or executioner. To know Greta is to hate her, and I voted for Sonny, despite his ranting during the campaign. Sonny kids Gordon about evicting his son and needles him gently about his failure to prosecute him under Arkansas's criminal eviction statute, the only one left in the country, according to Dan.

"His mother would have killed me," Gordon says sheepishly, which makes me realize he had considered it.

At this moment a woman charges into the room, followed by a college-age kid who has to be "Gucci." My client's face, now ashen, tells me it is his wife. "Dora Lou, what are you doing back here?"

"I couldn't let you throw our son out on the street!" she cries dramatically. It is obvious she has had no sleep for some time. She must have come straight from the airport. Her bright orange jumpsuit, the color county prisoners wear, is badly wrinkled. Beneath her reddened eyes are plum-colored pouches that emphasize the rest of her underbaked pie crust of a face. In contrast, Dyson's son is wearing an immaculate blue pinstriped three-piece suit.

"Your Honor, can we take a minute?" I ask plaintively.

Judge Butler nods and motions us outside. Lawyers are the first line of defense against unruly litigants.

"What is he going to do?" Mrs. Dyson shrieks once we

are outside in the hall. She gestures at "Gucci," who is staring pitifully at his father.

"Go to work full-time like most other Americans?" the ex-policeman asks, his voice trembling as it rises to a new level.

"You hate him!" his wife rages. "You hate him because he looks like me!"

This insight is fraught with danger, and I intervene, pulling my client to one side and whispering, "Can't you bribe him to leave? Give him a new car, a thousand for a couple of months' rent, and we'll go back to my office and sign a contract that if he moves home again he agrees to sign over the title to you."

Gordon Dyson contemplates his family and nods. "A contract won't mean anything, but maybe he'll have a wreck and kill himself."

Fortunately, "Gucci," perhaps fearing that he might die unexpectedly in his sleep if he remains home, agrees. An hour later after mother and son have departed my office, I escort Gordon to the elevators and offer to return half my fee. "We didn't actually go to court."

"We were close enough," Dyson mutters as the door opens. "Hell, I'd rather give it to you than to him."

I thank him, and go back inside to work on Dade's case. What is this world coming to?

Monday morning the Fayetteville media circus begins early. Dade is not even out of the Blazer when a college-age kid with three cameras around his neck spots us and begins snapping pictures. Out on the sidewalk in front of the courthouse there is a small contingent of demonstra-

tors carrying signs: STOP THE VIOLENCE, JUSTICE FOR
WOMEN, and of course, WOMEN AGAINST RAPE. It must be
twenty degrees, but there are five or six girls bundled up
in brightly colored ski jackets, knit caps, mittens, and
earmuffs and looking miserable. I recognize Paula Crawford and wonder how Sarah will feel when she shows up.
Paula and I never had our lunch. Since the dorms aren't
open, Sarah has spent the night with a friend from Fayetteville and will be arriving later. Two reporters shove
microphones in Lucy's face, but as I have instructed, we
smile and keep walking. "Is it true that Dade turned down
a deal?" the beautiful green-eyed reporter from Channel
5 asks. Like a zombie, I give her a frozen grin, not even
bothering with "no comment."

Inside the second-floor courtroom, I shake hands with
Binkie, who squints hard at Dade as if to say that he has
had his chance at mercy. Without a word, he turns his
back and sits down next to his assistant Mike Cash, who,
I suspect, will be seen but not heard today. I notice that
Binkie is wearing a new suit, too. Though it can't make
him look handsome (his rawboned face precludes anyone
but his mother from regarding him that charitably), the
nice fit of the light blue herringbone worsted wool,
padded in the shoulders, fills him out and gives him less
of an angular, hillbilly look. Like myself, someone has
taken a look at Binkie's courtroom apparel and said it
was time to dial 911 and ask for an emergency department store run. Judging by his demeanor, I have the feeling that by not forcing my client to take the deal he
offered, I have lost some respect in his eyes. Yet, there is
nothing I can do about it now.

After I have seated Dade and organized my files
around me on the table (I have revised my opening statement five times in the last two days and have it outlined
in a yellow legal pad on top of the stack to my right), I
watch spectators being admitted into the courtroom and
try to rein in what I hope is a temporary panic attack. The
glittering, expectant expressions on the faces of some of
the doddering old men suggest they are hoping for a
bloodbath. Yet, these are probably the regulars who have
seen every trial for the last twenty years. I smile uneasily
at Dade, who seems to be holding his breath. He is looking at his mother. Lucy, to my dismay, has dressed in
black as if she were attending Dade's funeral. Her dress,
plain and unadorned by jewelry, emphasizes her light
skin. Is she thinking about what it will be like to visit her
son in the hellhole that is Cummins prison? Last night at
the restaurant at the Holiday Inn (Dade's choice), she
was unusually quiet, as if she had already resigned herself to a bad outcome. From the defense viewpoint, a
criminal trial is like surgery on a high-risk patient. Denial
becomes difficult when the patient has been prepped and
the cutting is about to begin.

At the door I see the Perrys, who are clutching hands
like three children lost in the woods. Despite Blanche
Perry's bravura performance at their home in Texarkana,
they don't want to be in a Fayetteville courtroom any
more than we do. This morning Blanche Perry is nothing
but a frightened parent, just as I would be if the situation
were reversed. Her eyes flutter rapidly as her husband
whispers in her ear. In the name of justice, her daughter is
about to undergo one of the most wrenching experiences

humanity has devised. If the jury finds Dade innocent, Robin faces a lifetime of humiliation. I marvel at my willingness to add to it. I was itching to call Joe Hofstra at this trial. Not for the first time in my career, I realize the job of defense attorney is too much of a game for me. I'll walk away from this courtroom thinking I've won or lost. The Perrys may leave here feeling their daughter has been stripped of all her dignity. No wonder they were willing to capitulate and settle for something far less than they think justice demands. Maybe they know something I don't. I wonder if even now it is not too late to accept Binkie's offer. If their expressions are any guide, the Perrys would go for it. Robin, who will be leaving the courtroom after the witnesses are sworn in, has an ethereal Alice-in-Wonderland quality about her. Her breasts have been made to disappear under a simple white wool dress that extends from her throat to the floor, and her blond hair is in bangs. The word "virginal" doesn't do her justice. This girl, I must remember, takes communication seriously, and she will be telling the jury she couldn't act sexually aggressive if she were given lessons every day for a year. Not one word will be spoken about this past summer's torrid affair. Ladies and gentlemen, this young woman is not what she seems. Just ask her professor. If only I could. Yet, even as I think of it, the sleaziness of such a tactic finally hits me. Sarah could have been seduced by Beekman. If she were, would that automatically make her less credible if she got raped later by another man? Obviously not. Though it makes my job more difficult, I finally admit to myself that it was only justice that

I lost the motion to introduce into evidence Robin's past sexual conduct.

Before we begin the process of selecting the men and women who will decide this case, I look over my proposed instructions, which the judge will read to the jury before closing arguments. Arkansas rape law, from my research, seems to be typical of other jurisdictions. "Penetration, however slight . . ." is sufficient to show the act occurred; proof of a threat to the victim satisfies the statutory definition of "forcible compulsion." This case, like almost every criminal case I've ever tried, will turn on the facts, not legal arguments.

A jury is seated quickly, probably too quickly, since Binkie knows the jury panel and I don't. We end up with only one African-American, the wife of an assistant professor in the music department. Marla Chastain, age thirty, with two children who are at home during the Christmas vacation with her husband, appears intelligent and thoroughly delighted to get out of the house. The rest of the panel is a mixed bag that includes three retirees, two people who own their own businesses, one professor from the university, a claims adjuster, two schoolteachers, a civil engineer, and an unemployed waitress. By Blackwell County standards this is a well-educated jury, but I'd prefer them to be more shrewd than smart. Curiously, only one, a retired executive who worked for Tyson's, has admitted to being a hardcore fanatic Razorback supporter (though in answer to my question, four of the six men and three of the women raised their hands to signify they knew the last time the Hogs had played in a bowl game). Binkie used most of his peremptory strikes to exclude any male under thirty; I systematically knocked off women who seemed a little too knowledgeable about WAR and the women's movement. Naturally, none of them would admit she couldn't be fair to an individual accused of rape, thus denying me the opportunity to exclude them for cause.

By eleven o'clock we are ready for opening statements. As fast as this case is going, we could be through tonight. In four long strides Binkie places himself in front of the jury rail and slowly scans the twelve men and women who will decide Dade's fate. He folds his arms across his chest and studies the floor as he begins modestly, "Ladies and gentlemen, I've never sat on a jury, and frankly I've always wondered how I would discharge this truly awesome responsibility, because in this kind of case, there has got to be a temptation to come to the conclusion that it's just too hard to decide who to believe. I hope as we listen to each witness, you'll all fight against that. In this part, the opening statement, I'm bound by the rules not to argue that Robin Perry was raped by Dade Cunningham, and so is Mr. Page when he has his turn. All we can say right now is what we expect each witness will say. Later, Judge Franklin will, in his formal jury instructions, tell you the elements of rape, but in the end you twelve women and men will have to decide who is telling the truth and who isn't. . . ."

I watch helplessly as some of the jury already begin to nod in agreement. From our questions to them in voir dire, some of them surely have already guessed from Binkie's questions that there is no physical evidence in the case, and now he is stealing the lines I had planned to deliver. But what else can either of us say? All he can do is ask them to place their faith in the word of a twenty-year-old girl, and as he takes them through the expected testimony of his witnesses, ending with Robin's, I try in vain to think of how to use Binkie's words about belief to my advantage.

When my turn comes, I leave my notes on top of the table, forcing myself to rely on my memory. I have a bad habit of fumbling around and reading too much if I don't. I walk to a spot a foot in front of the lectern so I won't be tempted to hang onto it while I speak. Dan has told me that on occasion I look more like a lizard hanging on a rock than an advocate for a client while I'm addressing the jury. I take a deep breath to still the bad case of nerves I developed during Binkie's straightforward recitation of what he expected Robin to say. Beside me, Dade remained motionless for the most part but began to blink rapidly during Binkie's description of the actual moment of intercourse. Too many moments like that and we can start worrying about the length of the sentence. "Mr. Cross began his opening statement by rather eloquently imploring you to do your duty in this case and come to a conclusion, witness by witness, whether that person was telling the truth. Ladies and gentlemen, I think it is within the rules that I can tell you Judge Franklin will instruct you, in fancier words, that you weren't expected to check your brains at the door. Nor is anybody asking you to have a religious experience and decide this case on faith. Dade Cunningham will swear to you he didn't force Robin Perry to have sex that October night, and Robin Perry will swear that he did, but in many respects their testimony will be identical. As I go through what I expect the witnesses to tell you, ask yourselves whose version of the events makes the most sense before you bite the bullet and decide who's telling the truth and who's not. . . ."

I talk for thirteen minutes and don't screw up anybody's name or forget any major detail. When I come back to the table, the expression on Dade's face tells me I made a decent impression on him, anyway. Too bad he can't vote.

16

BINKIE CALLS AS his first witness Robin's roommate, Shannon Kennsit. It is a good choice. She is a slightly awkward-looking girl with a manner so engaging that you do not even notice she is as chunky as a jar of peanut butter. Shannon captivates the jury with her admitted weakness for the Razorbacks. Describing the time she first met Dade at the party on Happy Hollow Road, she can't keep a smile off her round face. "Robin threatened to give me a tranquilizer to calm me down! I can't remember being more excited except for the night the Hogs beat Duke for the national championship. It was like going to meet somebody you knew you'd see playing in the pro bowl someday."

Anticipating the direction I'd like to take this case on cross-examination, Binkie asks about Robin's feelings for Dade. Shannon unselfconsciously tugs at the side of her mauve sweater to adjust her bra. This girl couldn't be more relaxed than if we were seated in her room at the Chi Omega House. "She said she liked him. I asked her once if she meant did she like him as a boyfriend, and she said just as a friend. She said he really tried in class, and she admired that. Lots of players don't care about school, but she said Dade did, and she was glad to help him."

As the most important witness (besides Robin) Binkie will call, Shannon is utterly believable, and she describes the moment that Robin's crying woke her up with such genuine feeling that it is impossible not to be moved. "She was already in bed when I came in about twelve and didn't say anything, but about four I heard her crying. She couldn't stop, and I turned on the light. She looked awful! She was just crying and crying. I kept asking her what was wrong, and finally she said that Dade had raped her. I thought, Oh my God, how terrible! She's got to go to the police or the hospital or someplace! But when I said this, she just shook her head."

I close my eyes, realizing I have been affected by what I've just heard. There is no doubt in my mind (nor can there be in the jury's) that Shannon is telling the truth. Robin's suffering was profound, at least to this girl. She has finally made her roommate and best friend real to me in a way that Robin herself has not. Why? All this time I've been able to think of Robin as an actress. What if she's not? I glance at Dade. He is hunched over the table with his right hand over his eyes. I nudge him and he lowers the hand to his lap and sits up straighter, but it doesn't matter. Nobody is watching him. From behind the podium, Binkie asks, "Why didn't you wake up your housemother or call her parents?"

"She wouldn't let me!" Shannon says, her voice anguished. "I wanted to, but she kept saying that nobody would believe that she had met him off campus just to study together. She said she was afraid that her parents would think she had been dating him. They're real conservative."

I glance quickly at the Perrys, who appear slightly dazed. What if I were Gerald Perry? I'd want to kill Dade. "What happened then?" Binkie asks, like some second banana prompting a talk-show host.

"I continued to try to convince her that she had to go to the hospital. She kept saying he didn't hurt her, but I told her it didn't matter. She had to go tell somebody! Finally, about five-thirty she said okay, and I drove her to the hospital."

"Did you see her that evening before she went over to the house on Happy Hollow Road?" Binkie asks.

Shannon presses her hands together under her chin as if this were a difficult question. "I sat next to her at dinner that night and she told me later in the room she was going out to that same little house we went to in the spring so she could help Dade get ready for a speech in communications the next day. I wish I had said something or gone with her. Then it wouldn't have happened." Tears well up in her eyes. From the right sleeve of her sweater, she pulls out a tissue and dabs at her eyes.

I scan the transcript of the "J" Board hearing and her statement but find nothing inconsistent. Binkie asks her if she knows whether Robin had any alcohol before she left the sorority house.

"Not that I was aware of," Shannon says, "and we were together from about five until she left around eight that night."

"She smelled like wine!" Dade whispers fiercely in my ear.

I nod, not sure I believe him, since he has already lied to me on this subject.

Binkie asks if Robin described what Dade had done to her, but Shannon wrinkles her nose in distaste. "I didn't ask her. It seemed too personal. If she had wanted to tell me, I would have listened, but she was too upset to make her talk about something like that. I knew she'd have to go over it a million times anyway."

Binkie keeps her on the stand for another ten minutes going on about the details of the time before she took Robin to the hospital, but according to Shannon she did most of the talking. Abruptly, Binkie announces, "Your witness."

I take my time getting to the podium, wondering how honest this girl will be under cross-examination. I start off focusing on the party she attended in the spring. "Did you talk to Dade the entire time?" I ask after a couple of preliminary questions.

"No, I talked to Harris and Tyrone and some to the two girls who were there. Tyrone actually wasn't very nice," Shannon sniffs.

So far I haven't met anyone who is a member of Tyrone's fan club. "Do you remember if you were in the same room all the time with Dade?" I ask.

"No, he was in the kitchen part of the time talking to Robin," Shannon says. This was a big event in her life. She remembers it all.

I return to the table and pick up the "J" Board transcript. "Do you recall saying in answer to a question at Dade's disciplinary hearing in November that Robin was, and I'm quoting here, 'kind of a private person'?"

"Yes, but we always talked about everything," Shannon insists.

"She never told you the details of what happened between her and Dade the night she said she was raped by him, did she?" I ask.

"Not really," Shannon says, her voice defensive. "Just that he raped her."

Suddenly, it hits me that Shannon probably is the type of person who didn't want to know the details. She may not have ever really asked Robin, and this was why Binkie never got specific with her in his questioning. I tell the judge I have no more questions and sit down beside Dade.

Binkie confirms my suspicion by having no more questions for Shannon. He introduces Robin's medical records through Joan Chestnut, the nurse from Memorial who saw Robin. Binkie and I have agreed that since Dr. Cowling had no time that day to do more than a physical examination, his nurse will read into evidence his brief entries that he observed no trauma and will be allowed to explain that the doctor was called to an emergency in Springdale before he had finished talking to her.

As I have feared, Joan Chestnut bristles with competence. She explains that in her long experience there is no typical rape victim. "How a woman reacts after having been raped depends on many factors," she says in a strong, careful voice that needs no amplification.

My only consolation is that today she does not look like a nurse. Apparently unable to resist the possibility she might be photographed or filmed, she has piled her blond hair on top of her head and is wearing a fancy sequined black dress that would be more appropriate for a cocktail party than a court appearance. Binkie must have died when she showed up at the courthouse not wearing her scrubs. She repeats substantially what she told me earlier, yet, here again is an absence of specifics, which Joan Chestnut shrugs off as normal. She tells Binkie that having to repeat the step-by-step actions of the perpetrator simply forces the victim to relive the horror of the event and is beyond some women's power to do so soon afterward. "It's all some women can do to say something like, 'He forced me to have sex with him,' " she says didactically. "I might have been suspicious if she had come up with some elaborate story which took her thirty minutes to tell."

"As a nurse giving care to a patient, you weren't immediately concerned with investigating whether Robin Perry might have been making up this story, I presume?" I ask on cross-examination.

Joan Chestnut crosses her long, not unattractive legs and swings her left shoe, which has a four-inch heel. Maybe she has a date after she is through testifying. "If a person is making up symptoms, for whatever reason, and it happens occasionally," she says, her tone now droll, "it's just as important that we be alert to misinformation as opposed to real symptoms. As you are surely aware, these days a hospital's resources are severely restricted."

Though she has mentioned a subject most people don't have much sympathy for, I beat back an urge to spar with her. She has admitted that some people who go to a hospital lie, and I'm satisfied with any little bone thrown my way. People like nurses, even if this one looks like an aspiring Junior Leaguer.

During an hour's recess for lunch I review the "J" Board transcript. Binkie's next witness, Mary Purvis, the student volunteer from the Rape Crisis Center, seems even younger than she did at the "J" Board hearing and readily admits her inexperience. Brushing long, unruly strands of brown hair from her eyes as she speaks, the young woman adds little, if anything, to what the nurse has already said. She admits on cross-examination that Robin had little to say to her.

Without further ado, Binkie calls Robin Perry, and the jury, which had been about to doze off, snaps to attention.

As if she were interrupting grownups to come in and say good-night, Robin shyly enters the courtroom. I realize how much window dressing other witnesses are in a case like this. You believe either the victim or the accused.

Binkie starts Robin off slowly, letting her talk about herself to give the jury a sense of who she is. Though she is trying to maintain the poise that has carried her to this moment, today she seems fragile as a glass mirror. Doubtless Binkie is hoping she will become more comfortable the longer she talks. Gone is the confident actress of past performances. This is a girl, not a woman. In a trembling voice she tells the jury that her father had originally served in the Navy and that her family had moved around from base to base until she was ten. I let this go for a moment and then get to my feet. "Your Honor, this is a rape trial. The jury can decide this case without knowing the name of the family dog. Can't we at least start with the witness in college?"

A couple of the jurors chuckle, and Judge Franklin responds, "Let's get this going faster, Mr. Cross."

Unruffled, Binkie asks, "What year are you in at the university, Ms. Perry?" He would have gone on for an hour if I had let him. The one advantage I have is that the jury think they already know Dade. They've seen him on TV, read about him. Yet, they thought they knew O.J. Simpson, too.

Robin answers and, more quickly than Binkie appears to like, begins to talk about Dade. As she tells about the class last spring, I notice that beside me Dade has begun to hold his breath and then release it. What if he is lying and every word she utters about what happened is true?

As she talks, despite my efforts to concentrate, a memory of an event when I was a senior begins to form at the back of my brain. I was dating a Tri-Delt sophomore named Bonnie Edwards, and one Friday night when we were both drunk I took her to my room in the Sigma Nu House. Within minutes we were naked in my bed, but just as I was beginning to enter her, she told me to stop. Drunk, I didn't. Did I rape her? Of course I did! Then, like a freight train bearing down on me, another long-ago moment, this one an impression more than a fully remembered event, appears at the edge of my consciousness: late one night after returning from a party where we both had drunk too much, I had insisted on sex with Rosa, who was too helpless to resist, though she made her reluctance known. She had vomited a few hours later, or perhaps it was the next day. I raped my own wife. I have begun to sweat profusely. For the first time since I took this case, I cannot avoid the feeling that whoever is telling the truth, Robin was, at some point that night, completely vulnerable. Yet, whatever he has done, I am no better than the boy sitting beside me.

"Dade tried so hard," Robin is saying. "But sometimes in class he'd get real nervous, and it was hard to understand him. When we'd practice, I'd get him to slow down. . . ."

Robin has a way of making everything she does seem innocent, and the little party on Happy Hollow Road last spring becomes, in her words, purely a favor to Shannon. There is no mention of an attempted kiss by Dade, and I realize that Binkie does not know about it, for surely he would deal with it now, instead of letting me bring it out when I cross-examine Robin.

"Why did you choose the house on Happy Hollow Road to practice the speech?" Binkie asks, a few minutes later, his voice tightening a bit and betraying the importance of this answer.

It will be the hardest question Robin has to answer. Why, indeed, with so many other choices? "Now it seems the stupidest thing I ever did," Robin says. "But I trusted Dade. He really cared about his classes. He never horsed around at all when it came to studying. He wanted to make a good grade. I didn't really want to go over to Darby Hall because of all that's happened there, and boys aren't allowed upstairs in our rooms at my sorority house, and the classrooms are usually locked."

Binkie has to decide whether to ask her to clarify what she means about Darby Hall. It won't help him, but it can't do Dade any good either. Binkie uncharacteristically takes his hands from his pockets and grips the side of the podium. "Why didn't you get a conference room in the library?"

Robin cocks her head, embarrassed by the question. "I had forgotten you could. I didn't even think about it. Dade just suggested we go to his friend's house, and I said okay."

"Did you drive together?" Binkie asks, knowing she still has some explaining to do.

I steal a look at the jury. They are interested. If she is so pure and good, why not meet in public where she can get some Brownie points? Robin sighs audibly. "No, I told him I'd meet him there. I know it doesn't make sense, but my father has told me over and over never to let myself get in a situation I can't get out of. I just figured that if Dade tried to get fresh, I'd leave. It never occurred to me that he would rape me." Her voice becomes tiny here, though she doesn't cry.

Despite the welter of emotions building in me, I rock my chair and roll my eyes, communicating to the jury that this explanation is garbage. *Fresh?* Nobody uses that word. The fact is, Robin could have seduced her professor, fucked him happily on a weekly basis in my motel, and now she's worried about Dade being "fresh." The lawyer part of me wants to get up and scream at the jury that Alice is disappearing through the looking-glass, and what remains is a first-class liar. Do I believe this? I don't know what I believe.

Binkie ignores me and tells Robin to continue. "What happened next?"

"Well, I got there sometime around eight, and he was already in the house. For the first few minutes he acted okay, but then he came over to the chair where I was sitting and grabbed me by the arm. I just froze. He said he wanted to take a shower with me. I remember asking him if he were crazy. Then, I smelled beer on his breath and knew he had been drinking. I said, 'I have to leave,' but he said, 'Don't make me have to hurt you.' He pulled me up and took me into the bathroom and told me to take off my clothes. I started crying and told him to let me go home. He just shook his head. I could tell he would hurt me if I didn't do what he said."

Robin stops and begins to cry, her first tears of the day. As her roommate has done, she reaches inside the sleeve of her sweater and pulls out a tissue and wipes her eyes. Sighing heavily, she begins again, this time looking down at her lap but making sure her voice is loud enough for the jury to hear. "I took off my clothes and did what he said. He did the same and got in with me and made me wash him. Afterward, he took a towel and dried me off and then made me get on the bed in his room. He put his penis inside my vagina and made me have sex with him. I was scared not to. He had this horrible look on his face."

"Did he ejaculate inside of you?" Binkie asks.

"Yes."

"Was he wearing a condom?"

"No."

"How long did this take?" Binkie asks, his hands twisting inside his suit pockets.

"About thirty minutes from the time he made me take

off my clothes and get in the shower with him to the time when he rolled off of me and let me go."

I watch the faces of the jurors, who are paying close attention. Unfortunately, Marla Chastain, the one black juror, seems more engrossed than anyone. I've got to give Robin credit: fearful or not, she can captivate an audience.

"Did he hurt you?" Binkie asks.

"No," Robin says, looking up at him. "I did what he wanted."

"Did he say anything or did you say anything in those thirty minutes?"

"I was crying," Robin says, sniffing. "I think he said some other things but I don't remember."

"What did you do after he was finished?" Binkie says, his voice stoical. He doesn't like rape cases, his manner suggests.

"I put on my clothes. He watched me and said that if I told anybody, nobody would believe me, and he'd spread it all over campus that I was a slut."

"Did you say anything?"

Robin dabs at her eyes. "I was too afraid."

"What happened next?"

Robin sighs as if she knows she has finished the hardest part and says, "I drove straight back to the sorority house and went up and took a shower and got in bed."

"Did anyone see you?" Binkie asks. "Did you speak to anyone?"

"I don't think so. I didn't want to see or talk to anybody. I just wanted to be alone."

Robin's voice is tense with anxiety. Beside me, Dade is

shaking his head. He whispers urgently in my ear, "She's lying and she knows it! She wanted to get in the shower. I didn't tell her no such thing about hurting her or her being a slut or anything!"

Watching the jury, I nod, realizing he didn't deny he raped her. Binkie leads Robin through the reasons why she didn't go to the police or hospital immediately. She says nothing that is not in her statement or in the transcript of the "J" Board hearing. "I just couldn't face going through it then," she concludes tearfully. "If it hadn't been for Shannon, I might not have gone. I knew it would be horrible, and it has been."

Binkie turns to me and says sternly, "Your witness."

I take my time getting up. One of the reasons I'm convinced that Robin didn't tell anybody for nine hours is that she was worried that her escapade the past summer would come out, but if I ask about it the judge will declare a mistrial and probably would throw me in jail and bury the key. From beside the podium, I ask, "Where is the house you went to that night, Ms. Perry?"

Robin runs the fingers of her right hand through her hair. "About two miles east of campus."

"Is it in the city limits?"

Robin hunches her shoulders. "I don't know."

"Do you recall if it has a well beside it?"

"I remember seeing a well, but I think it's boarded up."

"Does it have a house across from it?"

"No."

"Immediately on either side?"

"No."

"In fact, the house you went to that night is at the end of the road there. You can't go any further, can you?"

"No."

"Would you agree that some people might consider the house somewhat isolated?"

"Yes."

"What are you majoring in, Ms. Perry?"

"Communications," she answers, her hands beginning to twist a bit in her lap.

"You get almost straight A's, don't you?"

"Yes," she says, undoubtedly schooled by Binkie to make her answers as short as possible.

"Are you planning a career in the theater?" I ask, as snidely as I can, not caring how she answers.

Binkie objects, however, and I withdraw the question, knowing I've made my point on the jury. "Had you ever dated an African-American before Dade?"

Too sharp for her own good, she answers vehemently, "I didn't date Dade."

I take my time and return to the table and pull out a copy of the local paper and bring it back to the podium. "Let me read you a quote attributed to you from the *Northwest Arkansas Times* from October twenty-third. This was at a rally on campus where you addressed several hundred students and others. 'I want to thank everybody for their support. I can't tell you how many other girls have told me that they have been a victim of date rape since this has occurred. It is a crime that most girls still do not talk about, but it happens much more frequently than we are aware. Thank you for being here.' Do you deny saying those words?"

"No, but that's not what I meant," Robin contends. "We never had a date."

I fold the paper and take it back to the table and hand it to Dade. When I return to the podium, I ask, "That's an important distinction to you, isn't it, Ms. Perry?"

"I don't understand," she says, feigning ignorance or hoping I'm talking about something else.

"It's important to you that no one think you dated Dade, isn't that correct?" I ask.

"I've already explained that my parents are very conservative," she says. "They asked me not to date anybody who wasn't white and wasn't from the South."

"So you won't deny that during your first visit last spring to the house on Happy Hollow Road with your roommate at one point you and Dade were back in the kitchen alone and he tried to kiss you, but you wouldn't let him."

For an instant Robin's face reflects the unmistakable ambivalence that all witnesses experience when they don't want to answer a question they suspect might help them. She purses her lips, then bites down on her lower one before finally answering, "Dade didn't try to kiss me last spring."

I let her words hang for a moment. "Now you wouldn't just be answering this question the way you did to please your parents, would you?"

"No!" she says, her face flushed.

I am certain she is lying, but the jury has no real reason to believe she is. I move on to other areas of her testimony but don't come close again to breaking her composure. She is no longer crying and is quite believable in her insistence that she was afraid that Dade would hurt her. "He didn't leave a mark on you, did he, Ms. Perry?"

"He didn't have to," Robin says. "I was scared to death."

"We just have your word on that, don't we, Ms. Perry?" I ask.

"Yes, you have my word."

I return to my seat, knowing the rest is up to Dade.

Binkie says that the state rests, and after the judge denies my routine motion for a dismissal of the charges, I tell the bailiff that I call Harris Warford to the witness stand.

Nothing Harris could do would disguise his size (he will be a big black man until the day he dies), but even slightly nervous, he has a slow, patient smile that signals he is, off the football field at least, a gentle, nonaggressive man. He says that he and Dade have been good friends since they went through that terrible freshman season when the team won only three games. Hoping to give him some credibility, I draw from him that he is on track to graduate next spring with a degree in accounting. He repeats almost word for word his testimony from the "J" Board hearing: that he had talked to Dade in his room at Darby Hall about an hour after the rape was supposed to have occurred. Dade had seemed normal. "He said she wanted sex but that after it was over, she got out of there. That's all he told me about it."

I exhale, glad that I have gotten no surprises and that Harris has avoided saying that Dade said he "did" Robin. I ask him about the party, and try to anticipate Binkie by asking if Dade had ever said that he liked Robin.

Harris smooths down a lapel on his midnight blue wool blazer and wrinkles his face. "You asked me that at that hearing at the school, and I said then he never said nothing about her except she was helping him. Dade had lots of girls. Me and Tyrone ragged him some after she and her roommate came to the house that day, but, see, you don't know Dade. If he don't want to talk, nothing can make him. He talks when he's ready."

Well, I hope he's ready, I think to myself. He's got some explaining to do. "How did he act the night he said he had sex with Robin?"

As if I were a slow student he is duty bound to try to help, Harris leans forward, resting his forearms on his colossal thighs. "He didn't act any different than usual. He was listening to his stereo when I went by his room. I asked him what he had been doing. That's when he said what I just told you."

"Are you certain Dade didn't give you any details then or later about what had occurred that night?" I ask, stealing a look at the jury to see what kind of impression Harris is making on them. I notice in particular the face of the unemployed waitress, who is sitting in the front row of the jury box and is the closest to Harris. She is plainly skeptical. All humans gossip, her expression says. This would have been the normal time for Dade to have bragged about it. Robin was beautiful, a cheerleader, and, not least, a white girl.

"No," Harris says finally, rubbing his hands along the tops of his thighs. "He didn't talk."

I pass the witness.

Binkie approaches the podium with the demeanor of

someone who doesn't believe what he is hearing. "Mr. Warford," he says, now bringing his gnarled hands out of his pockets and draping them over the lectern as if he wants the jury to inspect them, "weren't you a little curious about the way Robin Perry had supposedly acted that night?"

"Yeah," Harris says, "I was."

Binkie drums his thumbs against wood. "Did you ask him what Robin had been like?"

"I asked, but like I told you, when Dade don't want to talk, nobody's gonna make him."

"What about the time when Robin and her roommate came out to the house on Happy Hollow Road—did Dade act as if he was attracted to Robin?"

"I don't know," Harris answers. "I was so busy answering questions her roommate was asking, I hardly noticed her."

"So if Dade tried to kiss Robin back in the kitchen that afternoon, you didn't see it?" Binkie asks, his voice beginning to boom like shots from a cannon.

"Naw," Harris says, looking genuinely puzzled. "He didn't tell me he tried to kiss her."

Binkie has surely interviewed the others who were there that afternoon and found nothing useful. "So as far as you know from all you saw or heard, there was nothing in either the behavior or actual words of either Dade or Robin to suggest they were more than friends who worked together in class?"

"Not that I could tell," Harris says calmly.

"No more questions, Your Honor."

I lean over and tell Dade he is next. "Just take your time and remember to think about your answers."

I stand up and tell the judge, "I call Dade Cunningham."

Dade turns to look at Lucy, whose forced smile can't be fooling him. Everyone in the courtroom seems to have drawn to the edge of their seats. He knows it has all come down to him.

Harris's nervousness has infected Dade, and judging from his answers to some easy biographical questions, it will take a while to settle him down. His voice is tight and raspy as I repeatedly have to ask him to speak up. He momentarily forgets whether the family store is in the city limits of Hughes, and I have to correct him.

Wooden-faced, he sits pinned against the witness chair straining to give the most basic information. Finally, I decide to change my approach and simply ask him, "Dade, did you rape Robin Perry?"

At this direct question, his face becomes expressive and alive as he yells back at me, "No! I didn't! She wanted it! I was just there to practice on my speech for class!"

This emotional outburst has dynamited an internal logjam, and I wish I had made this my first question. "Just tell the jury what happened that night."

Dade repeats the story that I have heard half a dozen times, but now there is passion in his face, and for the first time since he told me that afternoon in the motel I find he is believable. Robin was the aggressor. It was her idea to get in the shower; she washed him and told him to wash her. "I didn't even bring protection," he volunteers. "We were just friends up until that night."

"Why did you think you were just friends, Dade?" I ask, willing him to answer.

For a moment he looks directly at his mother and then drops his eyes. His voice low, he says, "I had tried to kiss her in the kitchen that time she and her roommate came over to Eddie's house last spring. She's lying when she said I didn't. She stopped me and said she was gonna leave if I tried to do that again. After that, we didn't say much until all of a sudden she got friendly again in the fall. After about a month she started talking to me, and we began working together again like we had before. But I wouldn't have touched her if she hadn't wanted it."

Delighted that he has not mumbled his way through an answer, I ask, "Had you been drinking that night?"

Dade grimaces but answers, "I stopped at a bar and had a couple of beers before I got there."

"Had she been drinking?" I ask.

"I thought I smelled wine," Dade says, "but I'm not sure."

"How many times did you have intercourse with her?"

"Just once. She got up and left real quick."

"Did you threaten her in any way?"

"No!" Dade says defiantly.

"Did you hurt her in any way?"

"She acted like she liked it okay," Dade says. "Naw, I didn't hurt her."

"Then why did she leave so quickly?" I ask, knowing Binkie will hit hard here.

"She didn't say," Dade says, his voice sullen for the first time.

"What did you do afterward?" I ask.

In an assertive, almost strident voice he tells the jury that he drove back to Darby Hall and went to his room. When Harris came by later, he told him that he'd had sex with Robin but didn't give him any details and went on to bed that night around midnight after he finished studying. I get him to go back and fill in some details, but I got what I wanted with that one impassioned denial. He will have to hold up on cross-examination. There will be little I can do to protect him.

Binkie goes after him hard. Standing beside the podium with his feet planted apart, Binkie asks, his voice dripping with sarcasm, "Now, correct me if I am wrong, but the story you're asking this jury to believe is that after this voluntary sex act Robin Perry was so eager to have was over, both of you became deaf mutes and didn't say a word, is that right?"

Dade's tone, as I had feared, immediately becomes defensive. "She said she had to go."

"What did you say when she told you she was leaving?"

"Nothing much, I guess," Dade says.

"How long was she out there from start to finish?" Binkie asks.

Dade won't look Binkie in the eye as I had instructed. Instead, he seems to be staring at his belt buckle. "About an hour, I guess," he says, hesitating.

"Well, if this was her idea of a big fling, she had gone to a lot of trouble for just an hour, hadn't she?" Binkie says, swinging his hands together as if he were about to challenge Dade to a fight.

To Dade's credit, he answers, "I don't know what her idea was. I just know what she did."

"So your testimony is that you were sitting there together in the room working on the speech and she just up and attacked you, got what she wanted and left without a word, huh?"

Behind me a couple of people snicker. With some dignity, Dade says, "She didn't attack me. I could just tell by the way she came over and sat by me she wanted me to kiss her."

"Do more than kiss her," Binkie says, smirking at him. "She wanted you to ravish her, didn't she?"

Dade says grimly, "She wanted sex."

Deadpan, Binkie goads him, "She didn't tear your clothes off, did she?"

Dade looks over at me as if he is wondering whether he has to answer, and I nod. He sighs and says, "No."

"Did she leave any passion marks on you?" Binkie asks, now folding his arms in front of him but exposing his big ugly knuckles.

"No."

Binkie's plan is obviously to ridicule Dade, and he keeps him on the witness stand a solid hour, asking his questions in the most scathing tone he can muster. "So she didn't say anything after you were finished," he finally concludes, "about what kind of a lover you were?"

Throughout, Dade has looked increasingly hostile, glaring at Binkie between questions as the prosecutor has postured in front of him. My warnings to Dade that

Binkie would try to make him angry have been all but forgotten. "I've said five times she didn't say anything!"

Binkie shrugs and abruptly turns his back as Dade answers. "Your witness."

I wish desperately I could call a time-out and confer with Dade, but, of course, I am not permitted to do so. Dade may be too pissed to answer my questions on redirect honestly, but I will have to risk that he understands that it is in his interest to convey to the jury that Robin was more to him than a football groupie. Suddenly, I realize I have sold him short by not forcing him to admit that he did feel something other than lust for Robin those few minutes that night. The jury badly needs to see another side of Dade. I wait until the prosecutor sits down and ask Dade in a serious tone, "Had you liked Robin before the night she said you raped her?"

For the first time since I've known him, Dade looks glad to see me. "She had really been nice to me, helping me so much," he says earnestly.

I could hug him. He is smarter than I thought. "Did you think she was pretty?"

"Uh-huh," Dade responds. Long gone is the attitude that she was too skinny for his tastes.

"Had you ever before had a romantic or sexual relationship with a white girl?" I ask.

His face becomes stiff. "No."

"Why not?"

"I was told not to."

Binkie is on his feet objecting. "We're getting into hearsay, Your Honor."

I respond, "He can say what motivated him, Judge."

"He just did, Mr. Page," Judge Franklin says.

I'm happy to leave things as they are. Maybe the jury will think the chancellor of the university has a talk with all the incoming black freshmen. I sit down, happy in this instance to let the judge have the last word.

Having chosen to go down this road, Binkie has to stay with it. He strides to the lectern and rubs his hands together. "So you were in love with Robin Perry," he says, making the word sound as hokey as it does on daytime soap operas.

In control of himself, Dade answers softly, "I liked Robin a lot."

"Did you like her so much you couldn't stop from raping her?" Binkie yells.

"I didn't rape her," Dade says softly.

With as much contempt as he can muster, Binkie shakes his head at Dade and returns to his table and sits down. For once, I don't feel a need to rehabilitate Dade. He has done as well as he can do.

"Your Honor," I say quietly, "I'd like to recall Shannon Kennsit." I can only hope that Shannon and Robin have obeyed the instruction not to discuss their testimony.

Wide-eyed as a small child, Shannon returns to the witness stand. Her eyes narrow into slits as I remind her that she is under oath. "Robin has told you, has she not," I ask abruptly, "that at the party you and she went to on Happy Hollow Road last spring Dade had tried to kiss her while they were in the kitchen?"

"Yes," Shannon admits in a soft voice, but there is no mistaking what she has said. "But she said she didn't let him."

"No more questions," I say, having rolled the dice and won. Maybe it is small-time craps, but if this case is about telling the truth, it will be something to argue to the jury.   .

Binkie shrugs as if I had stopped the trial to pick a piece of lint off my jacket. "No questions, Your Honor."

At precisely four-thirty Judge Franklin instructs the jury that for them to find Dade guilty of rape, the state must prove beyond a reasonable doubt that he engaged in sexual intercourse with Robin and that he did so by forcible compulsion. Putting on a pair of reading glasses for the first time all day, Franklin reads, "Forcible compulsion means physical force, or a threat, express or implied, of death or serious physical injury to, or kidnapping of, any person. . . ."

When he finishes, Judge Franklin looks down from the bench and says formally, "Mr. Cross, you may give the first part of your closing argument to the jury."

As Binkie gets up and slowly walks to the jury rail, for the first time since noon I look at Sarah, who is sitting with Lucy. I wonder what kind of bond has been forged between them. So far as I know they have not talked until today. Is it race that they have in common or the fact that they are women? More probably, it is simply the two imperfect men in their lives sitting at the defense table. Sarah tugs anxiously at her hair and glances up at me with a wan, scared look on her face. Are things that bad? Probably. I can't read this jury at all. I look at the sole black juror. Her dark, brooding face is a study in concentration as Binkie, jamming his hands in his pants pockets for the time being, begins.

"Ladies and gentlemen, when we began this morning, I said you'd be tempted to throw up your hands and say it was too hard to decide whom to believe in a case like this," Binkie says, positioning himself at the middle of the jury rail. He has stopped in front of the oldest retiree and wags his head from side to side. "But after hearing the testimony, I don't think it is really all that hard if you use your common sense. Why would Robin Perry, a varsity cheerleader, an outstanding student, a girl who is from a deeply conservative family, tell a story this humiliating and embarrassing to herself if it wasn't true? For the sake of argument, let's assume for a minute that she consented to the sexual act. Why claim she was raped, when all she had to do was keep quiet? If Dade started talking about it, she merely had to deny it. Nobody was there to see. It was her word against Dade's. Common sense tells you that if she denied it vigorously enough, most people would have chalked it up to sexual posturing on a young man's part, assuming Dade would even have talked about it. After all, by both accounts she left as soon as it was over. There wasn't much to brag about. What we tend to forget in our concern with the judicial system and justice and due process for the accused is the victim. It is excruciating to go through this. The fear, and shame, and emotional pain are terrible. Some of you may be thinking that Robin Perry can't be believed because it appears she didn't tell the truth to you about an attempted kiss that she resisted by the accused. I ask you to consider what realistic alternative she had if she hoped to convince you she was telling the truth about what happened the second time she went to the house on Happy

Hollow Road. If she admitted the man who later raped her had tried to kiss her even months earlier, you would think she couldn't have possibly driven out to that house alone unless she had changed her mind about him. So, like many of us, she told you a lie when she would have been better served by an embarrassing admission that, in fact, shows she was pathetically naive and trusting. She thought she and Dade were friends. She thought she could trust this boy that she was helping. This kind of faith in human nature is so old-fashioned, Robin herself knew it would make you doubt that a girl can actually be this naive in this day and age. Well, you heard her tell you. Her parents are so conservative they didn't want her even dating someone who wasn't from the South. A different race was out of the question. Robin went along with it, but that didn't mean she couldn't help somebody who needed it. Mr. Page told you that you didn't have to check your brains at the door, and I couldn't agree with him more. . . ."

As Binkie talks, my heart sinks. At least two of the damn jurors are nodding, and all are listening as if he is saying the most obvious thing in the world. Sweet, innocent Robin lied to make the truth believable. I helplessly watch faces as Binkie grinds his argument into their gullible brains. Unfortunately, I find myself believing him, too. What could be worth the hassle of saying you were raped unless you were? Binkie tells the jury that all his witnesses' testimony pointed to rape. "Not one person who saw her afterward, whether it was her friend and roommate Shannon Kennsit, or three strangers, including an experienced nurse and physician, had any doubt that

Robin had been forced against her will to have sex. We haven't heard one word from a single witness today that anyone questioned her story except the accused. . . ."

Dade has begun to sink inside his suit coat and I wonder what I can say to counter Binkie. He can think on his feet better than I can.

When Binkie finally is done, I begin my argument standing by Dade. "Ladies and gentlemen, you've heard the old saying 'Necessity is the mother of invention.' Well, the prosecutor desperately needs to explain away Robin Perry's lie, and he has come up with as good a rationalization of it as you're going to hear."

I walk over to the jury rail. "The trouble with lying is that one leads to another and we all know it, because at one time or another everybody has told a lie about something. Granted, it is not outside the realm of possibility that Robin Perry could be lying about one thing and telling the truth about another, but what her lie tells me is how conflicted she was about Dade Cunningham. He was the forbidden fruit, and Robin had been warned away from it. What I think probably happened that night is that Robin told herself another lie, and one that was perfectly understandable. She and Dade were going to work on a speech, but what she was really going out there for that night was to do something she had wanted to do back in the spring and that was to kiss Dade Cunningham."

I stop and catch the eye of the unemployed waitress, who has begun looking sympathetic. "What happened next was that these two very attractive young people ended up making love, but when it was over, the guilt Robin Perry felt was intolerable to her. She left immediately, and finally after nine sleepless hours decided that the only way she could handle her feelings was to tell another lie and that was to say she had been raped."

I stop and walk back to the podium to give them a moment to absorb what I am saying. I've got everyone's attention, but a couple of the retirees on the jury are frowning. Hell, this argument is not everyone's cup of tea, but I don't need them all. I'll take a hung jury at this point. I pick out the professor and start again: "When it comes to sex, none of us, at a given moment, likes to admit what we're really thinking, even to ourselves, probably because we've been told much of our lives our feelings are bad and wrong, and so we lie. It's human nature. Part of the problem is there's so much freedom these days, and it's hard to accept the consequences of it. We get mad at our kids and say they're all going to hell in a handbasket when maybe it's our fault for allowing them to do practically anything they want. The plain fact is, I don't know for sure what happened that night on Happy Hollow Road and neither does Mr. Cross. The only people who know are telling totally opposite stories when it comes to the most important part—whether there was consent or not. Based on the evidence, I can't swear to you that Dade Cunningham did or didn't rape Robin Perry and neither can the prosecuting attorney. None of the other witnesses for either the prosecution or the defense can really help us, because there is no physical evidence in the case. All any of them can do is speculate about what happened, whether it was a nurse, counselor, or her roommate Shannon who, by the way, admitted that Robin is kind of a private person. Let's face it, folks, this girl is close to being a professional actress. If she wanted to lie, she was fully capable of it. Despite what Mr. Cross told you or will tell you when he gets up on rebuttal, I don't think there is a naive bone in Robin Perry's body. She was a Razorback cheerleader; she got up and spoke in front of several hundred people at a women's rally; she is a communications major and an excellent student, so she is fully capable of pushing whatever buttons she needs to push. It comes down to one thing: there is reasonable doubt in this case. . . ."

By the time I am finished and sit down again by Dade, I feel okay, but, as usual, since the prosecutor has the last word, it doesn't last. Binkie storms up and down in front of the jury box like a preacher at a tent meeting. "Folks," he exhorts them, "you weren't born yesterday! Mr. Page wants you to ignore what you saw and what you heard Robin Perry say and psychoanalyze her motives like she was some patient in a mental hospital. He doesn't want you to do the one thing that will put away his client: decide who is telling the truth about whether there was consent or not—Robin Perry or Dade Cunningham. I didn't believe Dade Cunningham when he said he didn't threaten her; I didn't believe him when he said Robin wanted sex. What Mr. Page wants you to forget is that both the accused and the victim testified they were meeting on Happy Hollow Road to work on a speech. If Robin had decided for some reason she was attracted to Dade Cunningham, do you think for a minute she would have needed to pretend in her own mind she was meeting him to study? That's nonsense. Dade Cunningham would have been telling you a totally different story. He would have been saying they simply agreed to meet at the house on Happy Hollow Road. Folks, you don't have to be Sigmund Freud to decide this case. You just have to remember to use your common sense in deciding whom to believe and whom not to believe. . . ."

Finally, Binkie is done, and the court lets the jury file out and goes into recess. As Judge Franklin disappears into his chambers, Dade turns to me and asks hopefully, "What do you think they'll do?"

I watch his mother whisper something to Sarah as the spectators begin to stand and talk in normal tones. "It's hard to say," I hedge. Again, I am reminded that there is so much that the jury wasn't allowed to hear. "I don't know," I say honestly. "It could go either way."

Sarah and Lucy pass through the gate that separates the spectators from the trial area. My daughter hugs me. "You did good, Daddy."

A warm feeling rushes through me. I will myself not to begin thinking of the mistakes I have made today. There will be time for that soon enough. "Thanks, babe," I say into her curly ebony hair. For years she has been too shy to hug me in public. Maybe one of us is finally growing up.

After embracing her son, Lucy extends her hand and says formally, "Thank you, Gideon."

I let my eyes linger on her face as I shake her hand. She looks even sadder than usual, which gives me a premonition that Dade will be convicted. Better to thank me now. She may not feel very thankful in a few hours. "It went okay, I think," I say, unwilling to give her hope I don't feel.

She nods, but it is more of a shrug. She doesn't expect an acquittal. Spectators, even if they aren't objective, can sometimes pick up vibes from the jurors that the lawyers can't. Defense lawyers always hope for miracles. The job would be too depressing if we didn't. A couple of print reporters stand like vultures, but I wave them off, saying that we will have no comment until after the jury comes back. After I send Sarah off to McDonald's with a twenty to get us something to eat, I leave Dade and Lucy at the counsel table and go sit down in the back with Barton, whom I didn't see come in. "Have you been here all afternoon?" I ask, resentfully noting that Barton's brown overcoat, which is draped neatly over a chair beside me, looks like it cost twice as much as my new suit. If he had been trying this case, he couldn't have gotten two words out without throwing up all over his two-hundred-dollar shoes.

"Man, that Binkie can talk," he says admiringly. "He looks so damn country that you don't think he's got it in him, but he's hell on wheels once he gets going!"

Thanks for the encouraging words, I think. Yet, Barton, once he quits babbling, will tell it to me straight. "You think he'll be acquitted?"

"Well," Barton hedges, "I didn't hear all of it." Noting my expression, he blurts, "Actually, I heard a couple of people saying as they left that they thought Dade was lying through his teeth. One of them did say he thought the jury would be out a long time."

That's a wonderful consolation. Hell, I just think I want to know the truth. Sarah returns with our food, but, too nervous to sample more than a couple of fries, I give.

mine to Barton, who scarfs down my McDLT so fast that
I am reminded of Dan, who has been my sidekick in
some of my big cases. No two people could be less alike.
I can't imagine Barton getting involved with a woman
like Gina. I take Barton over to meet Dade and Lucy and
am amazed that he is reduced to jelly at the prospect.
"He's already the greatest wide receiver I ever saw, and
that includes Lance Alworth!"

People never cease to amaze me. Instead of seeing a
kid from the poorest region of the state who any minute
may be pronounced a convicted rapist and about to spend
the best part of his life in prison, Barton would be delighted to get his autograph. "This is the man who gave
me free office space," I say by way of introduction. Now
I know why he did. He wanted to meet Dade. It turned
out that he was always with a client or on the phone when
Dade came by and never met him. Barton begins to gush
so much about Dade's career that it is embarrassing, but
Dade and even Lucy seem to be relieved to have something to talk about other than what the jury is doing.
Why not? Good ol' denial. Life would be unbearable
without it.

At this moment the bailiff rushes in and tells us the
jury is returning. I look down at my watch and try not to
grimace. They've barely been out an hour. How embarrassing.

People begin to stream back into the courtroom, and I
catch sight of all three Perrys, who understandably seem
elated by this quick decision. I watch the faces of the jurors as they troop back in. I've never seen twelve people
look so solemn. The lone black juror won't even look at

me. She studies her feet as if she'd never seen them before.

Judge Franklin, who seems equally ready to get home, asks the bailiff to take the verdict form from the foreman, who turns out to be the oldest person on the jury.

Franklin fumbles with the piece of paper and then, frowning, reads in a loud voice, "We, the jury, find Dade Cunningham not guilty of the charge of rape."

I catch the expression on Lucy's face as the courtroom erupts in the back when two of the WAR protestors (one of them Paula Crawford) who have smuggled in signs under their coats, begin to shout, "No justice for women! No justice for women!" For one brief instant Lucy's eyes gleam with unmistakable joy as Judge Franklin begins banging his gavel and orders the courtroom cleared. Dade turns to me and offers his hand, and says, smiling, "I thought I was gone."

"I did, too," I admit. "I did, too."

"Look at her, Dad!" Sarah exclaims. "She looks so sweet."

I bend down to the bottom cage and peer in at the greyhound staring back at me. These dogs are bigger than I expected. "What a weird color," I say to the attendant standing beside us. Black mixed in with tan. White socks on her feet and a white stripe running down her chest.

"Brindle," the girl says enthusiastically. "Want to see her?" She is about Sarah's age and clearly a greyhound lover. She has been smiling and talking to these strange, skinny, big-faced, little-eared creatures nonstop. I look around the room at the other cages. For the number of

dogs in here, there is very little noise. It is as if these retirees from the racetrack sense adoption is their last hope
before they are sent to the glue factory or wherever it is
doomed greyhounds go to die, and are on their best behavior.

Sarah answers for us, "Yeah!"

The girl, whose name is Barbara, opens the cage and
slips a choke collar around the dog. "Mindy Marie," she
coos, "come on out, girl."

Mindy Marie heads straight for Sarah and presses her
huge muzzle into my daughter's waiting hands. "She's
wonderful!" Sarah exclaims. "She's so gentle."

Though it has been only a month since Woogie went to
live with Marty, I need a dog in the house. Not a horse.
"Do people ever change their names?" I ask. Mindy
Marie is too dainty for this animal.

"Sure," the girl says. "Just use her first name with the
name you choose for a couple of weeks and then gradu-
ally drop her old name. She'll learn."

"Feel her face. She's so silky!" Sarah instructs me,
rubbing her face against Mindy Marie's muzzle.

I squat down on my heels and bring my face close.
"Hi, girl." She licks my ear.

"She likes you, Dad!" Sarah giggles delightedly. "Can
we take her outside?"

I suspect Mindy Marie would like Saddam Hussein if
he took the trouble to pet her. Barbara, as smooth as a car
salesman, hands Sarah the leash. "When you get out the
door, you can take her off this. It's all fenced in."

Sarah's eyes shine with excitement. "She looks more

like a 'Jessie' to me," she says as we step outside into a cold, gray drizzle.

Mindy Marie scampers away from us to the corner of the enclosure and deposits an impressive pile of shit near the fence. Shades of Woogie. The sight of her squatting on long, powerful haunches is comical. "Jessie suits her," I agree. "She's too solemn to be a Mindy Marie."

Mindy Jessie, her business done for now, trots back over to us, and Sarah hugs her. "She'll be easy to housebreak."

This is a done deal. I have already applied to be an "adoptive" parent; my references (Dan and Amy) have checked out. I had seen an article in the *Democrat-Gazette* about the greyhound adoption program in West Memphis and got the paperwork done before even telling Sarah. "I hope so. I'll be the one cleaning it up." According to the literature, greyhounds shouldn't live outside—too delicate. "So you think I should get her?"

"You know you want her," Sarah says. "She'll be wonderful."

She will be. She'll probably tear up the house the first time my back is turned. But that'll be okay. I can fix the house. It's the rest of life that is beyond control. While I was making love to Amy this past weekend, I thought of Rainey, whose naked body I never saw. Dan, who scores a perfect ten on the domestic misery index, told me yesterday that he has dreamed of Gina for the past three nights. "Let's go inside, Mindy Jessie, and sign your papers," I pretend to grumble.

* * *

In the Blazer going home Sarah chatters about her first-semester exams and turns in her seat to reassure Mindy Jessie, who seems to be wondering what she is getting into. As we cross the line into Blackwell County, she becomes quiet, and I ask her what she is thinking about. She leans back against the window and begins to finger a patch of curls above her right ear. "I heard some gossip about what really happened between Dade and Robin," she says.

"You have?" I say, instantly alert, but reluctant to sound too interested lest she decide to clam up. I had not counted on Dade's being acquitted and consequently had not prepared him for the media, and he shot off his mouth more than he should have to a TV reporter about the university's lack of support for him, a fact particularly galling to Coach Carter. I read in the *Democrat-Gazette* only last week that Dade may make himself available for the National Football League draft and not return for his senior year. Since I spilled the beans on myself, I know I have no chance to be his agent.

My daughter shifts uncomfortably in her seat. "This may not be true, but it's what I heard. About a week after the trial, Robin supposedly told Shannon that she and Dade both had lied, but that he had raped her."

The word "rape" hangs in the air between us like a poisonous cloud. It is too ugly a sound to pretend it doesn't affect me. "So what did they lie about?" I ask, staring straight down Interstate 40.

"Supposedly, Robin admitted that she had gone out to that house on Happy Hollow Road not really caring whether they worked on Dade's speech or not. They had started to make love, but she changed her mind and told him she didn't want to. He made her anyway."

Poor Robin. My heart feels as if it is about to stop. I cut my eyes over to Sarah. I can't tell her that I have been guilty of the same behavior. It feels uncomfortably hot in the Blazer, and I crack the window on my side. "Do you believe that's what happened?"

Sarah nods. "Shannon's her best friend, and she doesn't have a reputation for making stuff up."

"Who'd she tell?" I ask.

Sarah presses her lips together, then mutters, "I can't say."

I understand. She probably has told me too much, certainly more than she ever wanted to. "Given Robin's promiscuity and the fact that she lied," I ask, "do you think Dade should have been punished?"

Sarah says angrily, "He still raped her, Dad! Of course he should go to jail."

I check the rearview mirror and stare into the soulful eyes of Mindy Jessie, whose main virtue is that she isn't interested in this conversation. "But under the circumstances, which I doubt if Shannon knew, it probably wasn't all that easy for Dade to restrain himself."

"Come on, Dad," Sarah scoffs. "When a girl says 'Stop!' anything else is without her consent."

To shut her up, I nod, "You're right." I don't have the appetite to argue the point. If her father had been dealt with the way she wishes Dade had been, she wouldn't have been born. I'm not up to it. I want my daughter to love me, not judge me. Prison. Not a great start for a college kid. If I had gone to Cummins for a year, my life would have been totally different. No Peace Corps, no Rosa, no Sarah, no law degree. It seems like a good argument to me, but one I'll forgo for the time being.

As the traffic on the interstate begins to build, Sarah asks, "Do you think we'll see the Cunninghams again?"

"I don't know," I say, slowing down behind a truck hauling lawn fertilizer.

"I liked his mother," Sarah says, "and I liked Dade until I heard this. I had really felt a bond after we went over to Bear Creek."

Unless Lucy told her at the trial, Sarah doesn't know that I took Dade's case because I wanted to be his pro agent. "One wrong act in a person's life shouldn't condemn a person for life, should it?" I ask.

"It depends on what it is," Sarah says stubbornly.

I go on around the truck. "Mindy Jessie," I say, determined to change the subject. "She's gonna be a fine pet."

Don't miss any of the cases of
Arkansas public defender
Gideon Page—
in the novels by
GRIF STOCKLEY

"Sheer reading pleasure."
—*Publishers Weekly*

EXPERT TESTIMONY

A prominent Arkansas state senator is murdered, and the man accused of the crime has an ironclad insanity plea. Everyone, including Gideon Page, the public defender, thinks this case is nailed shut. But Gideon discovers that sex and betrayal severely reduce the odds of finding the truth.

PROBABLE CAUSE

Psychologist Andrew Chapman is charged with manslaughter when a seriously retarded girl dies in his care during a risky procedure. But when Gideon Page takes the case, he discovers that everything is far from cut-and-dried.

RELIGIOUS CONVICTION

Leigh Wallace, the knockout daughter of a big-time minister, is accused of murdering her wealthy husband—and Gideon Page is invited to assist the county's legendary trial lawyer on the case. But thoughts of victory quickly fade as hidden truths about the serpentine case begin to emerge.

**Published by Ivy Books.
Available at your local bookstore.**